MAGIC RIFT

THE LAST MAGE SERIES

by C.C.S. Jones

Map of Aetherealm

Hardcover ISBN 979-8-9934513-3-6
Dust Jacket ISBN 979-8993451305
Paperback ISBN 979-8-9934513-2-9

A Radiant Quill Publishing imprint.

To those who live with the ache of their own dark thoughts but refuse to let it define them—you are stronger than what haunts you.

CHAPTER 1

The Price of Power

The ocean stretched endlessly, a mirror of silver under a bruised, restless sky. Waves curled against Izier's shore, their whispers carrying a melody of mermaids that rose and fell with a brittle kind of beauty. The notes were glass-like, cutting through the hollow ache in Lusa's chest, a heart long bled dry of tears. She stood barefoot on the wet sand, the cold brine licking her toes, her Izerian gown fluttering against the wind's insistence while the salt-laden air burned her lungs.

The Temple of Mages had once reached for the heavens, its spires a testament to hope and knowledge. Now, in her mind, they were jagged shadows, crumbled into ash, drifting in the winds of memory. Its halls echoed with voices—students calling to one another, the sharp intonations of Master Aron, and the hushed chattering of her pupils—but all of it had been devoured by fire and darkness.

Her mother's face rose, unbidden, behind her closed eyes. Twisted by the Magics, consumed, now lifeless by Lusa's very own hand. The memory played on an unending loop, dragging her heart deeper with every repeat, each fragment of that moment etched into her soul with cruel precision. Her nails bit into her arms as she gripped herself tighter, welcoming the pain. It felt deserved.

Peace was for others… those who had not watched the world burn and lit the match themselves. Those who had not turned the blade on their own blood, who had not let darkness crawl into their veins and take root. The curse that had bound her memories in fog had lifted, leaving her adrift in a sea of recollection she hadn't asked for. Each face, each voice, came back clearer than the horizon before her, and with them, a tidal wave of grief she couldn't fight.

The shoreline had become her retreat, though it offered no comfort. Day after day, she wandered its edge, searching for… something. Reality had slowed, leaving her with the gift, and burden, of time. Time to breathe. Time to hurt. Time to wait. The rehabilitation of Izier had brought peace to Aetherealm, but peace had not found her.

The crisp sea breeze snapped against her gown, thin and impractical for the stinging winds of the coast. The Empress's endless generosity had provided an array of elegant but useless dresses, each one making Lusa feel more like a stranger in her own skin.

She sighed, closing her eyes as the wind tugged at her hair, a constant reminder of what it felt like to mourn a life that no longer fit. It wasn't just grief. It was the weight of an empire's expectations, the chains of memories she couldn't escape, and the hollow truth of saving a world she no longer knew how to live in. But grief wasn't the only thing knotting her insides now.

The council meeting was tonight, no longer a distant obligation she could push to the back of her mind. It loomed ahead, a shadow she couldn't ignore, stealing the space she'd hoped to use to gather herself. To appear whole. The summons had come with no explanation, but Lusa didn't need one. She'd seen the way the nobles avoided her, their eyes darting away too quickly, their hushed whispers filling the silences she left behind. A mage who had saved them but was still unpredictable. Still dangerous. They whispered about the last mage as though the title itself were a curse. She wished she knew why it belonged to her.

Her mind churned with possibilities, each one darker than the last. What did they want from her? To praise her? To control her? To decide what to do with a weapon they feared but couldn't discard? Every careful breath she took felt like a fragile step on a breaking bridge, and the silence of her Dark Magics only made the cracks feel bigger. She couldn't shake the thought that the peace she'd fought for wasn't hers at all—it was theirs, and tonight, they would decide if she had a place in it.

The crunch of sand broke the steady rhythm of the waves, pulling Lusa's gaze to Kaden's approaching figure. His silhouette blurred against the glare of the sun, his face slightly out of focus as he came closer. Wind tugged at his brown hair, tousling it into a wilder mess—but the rugged look worked for him more than she cared to admit.

"Startin' ta' think I need ta' build you a hut out here," he said with a smirk, shrugging off his cloak.

Without waiting for her reply, he draped it over her shoulders, the worn fabric heavy with his warmth. Fingers curled into the edges of the cloak, pulling it tighter as the chill of the wind faded.

"Thanks," she murmured, voice barely audible over the crash of the waves.

"'Course."

His reply was casual, but his hand lingered on her shoulders before sliding around her, pressing lightly into her side… a gentle squeeze that carried more meaning than he'd ever say out loud.

Without thinking, Lusa leaned into him, her head settling against his shoulder as if it had always belonged there.

"Sorry I'm like this," she whispered, frustration obvious.

Staring out at the horizon, she recalled the first time she met him—bounty hunter, mercenary, enemy. He was still all of those things, sharp-edged when the world demanded it. Yet somehow, through blood and betrayals, he was the one she trusted most now.

The smirk vanished from his face. He turned her toward him, hands steadying her by the arms, almond-brown eyes intent and searching.

"This ain't all y'er burden, Lusa. Stop tryin' ta' carry it all by yourself."

Her mouth opened to snap back, to tell him he didn't understand, but he pulled her into his chest before a word could form. Normally, she would've shoved him away, pride bruised and temper flaring. But now? She couldn't summon the energy, the fight inside her a faint echo.

So, she closed her eyes and let herself feel the rise and fall of his chest, the steady rhythm of his heartbeat. His warmth surrounded her, a quiet reminder that not everything was broken.

The moment ended too soon, his hand tilting her chin, forcing her to meet his gaze.

"Hey," he said. "What's goin' on in that heada' y'ers?"

"Processing," she muttered.

Kaden studied her for a beat longer, then let out a deep breath. Without another word, he draped his arm over her shoulder and pulled her close again, his gaze turning toward the ocean. She appreciated how he didn't push, how he always seemed to know when she needed space and when she needed this: him, solid and supportive, without expectations.

Kaden's muscles tensed and she knew the question before it left his lips. "They haven't returned?"

It had become a daily question, one that grated on her nerves despite the kindness behind it. He meant well, she was sure, but it was a constant reminder of the narrow bridge she walked. The entire Imperial Court seemed to be holding its breath, waiting for her Dark Magics to resurface. Waiting for the inevitable. Waiting for the unknown.

Weeks of silence in her head was the only peace she'd claimed since destroying Lazorious. The Aether, source of every spell she'd ever cast, had yet to recover from what she'd done. Neither had she. The amulet had lent her strength enough to finish the sorcerer, splitting its power between her and Kaden before choosing her outright.

That victory came with a cost: emptiness. She'd burned through the Magics, and until They returned, silence was its own kind of torment—a consequence born of pushing her core too far.

Ever since Lazorious's fall, there were nights when the wind would shift and she'd feel a pull inside her weakened core. Arcturius said it could be a fracture in the Weave.

She remembered that lesson from the Temple of Mages: the Aether was the current, and the Weave was the pattern that held it together—the pulse and the vessel, neither whole without the other. Disrupt a single thread, Master Aron used to warn, and the whole flow would start to unravel.

But was it really a fracture in the Weave... or her Magics, too stubborn to recalibrate? They were still there, slowly rebuilding what she'd burned through. Each night she meditated through recalibration. The word sounded clinical for something that felt like waiting to drown. The longer Their silence stretched, the tighter anxiety coiled in her chest.

Silence left too much room for thought. For questions she didn't want to answer. Was this all she was without Them? She didn't know anymore. The cold, distant woman who longed for peace but could never reach it, or the volatile mage who only felt alive when the world was burning. Both felt foreign, but what unsettled her most wasn't the difference—it was not knowing which version of herself would return when Their voices finally came back.

She pulled Kaden's cloak tighter around her shoulders, the fabric rough against her fingertips.

"You'll be the first to know," she finally said, forcing a playful smile that didn't reach her eyes.

Turning toward the shoreline, she let her bare feet sink into the cool sand as another unshakeable thought surfaced. She hesitated, then decided it was now or never.

"If They ever win, don't let me become Them."

He managed a small, humorless smile, maybe to cover the shock of her blunt statement. "Just keep winning. I believe in you."

But the way his hand tightened at his side betrayed his confidence. He tactfully redirected the conversation.

"Y'er comin' tonight, right? The Empress's ladies already delivered a gown."

Of course he'd pivot. It would've annoyed her if it weren't so heartbreakingly kind. And truth be told, she'd rather deflect the conversation anyway.

"Do I really have a choice?"

"Always." His smirk widened. "But ya'd never hear the end of it if ya didn't."

Her laugh came easier than expected, startling her with how foreign it sounded. "True."

Kaden nudged her shoulder. "It'll be fun. Ya've never been to one in the Imperial capital. It's somethin' else, I promise."

But his smile faltered slightly, his gaze drifting toward the horizon. The lightness in his tone dimmed, replaced with something heavier.

"Truth is, that ain't why I came ta' fetch ya."

Her stomach tightened, the knot growing larger.

"What is it?"

"The council moved the meeting up," he said, rubbing the back of his neck—a sure sign he wasn't thrilled about it. "The Aeonian Envoy arrived earlier than expected, and they decided it'd be better ta' get this outta the way before the festival."

Lusa's mind churned, cycling through a hundred worst-case scenarios. She glanced down at her gown, damp and clinging from the salty breeze, and her bare feet still dusted with sand. She wasn't even presentable, let alone emotionally or mentally prepared.

She moved to her shoes, shaking the sand out of them with more force than necessary. "Do you know what it's about?"

"Not a clue. But the Empress was already meetin' with 'em by the time I left. That's why we gotta go."

"I'm not ready for this," she mumbled under her breath, but apparently not soft enough.

Kaden stepped closer. "Lus… you'll be fine."

She sighed sharply, slipping her shoes on.

"Easy for you to say. They're not wondering about what to do with *you.*" The bitterness in her voice hung in the air, but she didn't have the energy to take it back.

Kaden didn't argue. Instead, he whistled and Brogan's answering whinny echoed from the grove of beach trees. The stallion trotted toward them, his dark brown coat gleaming in the midday sun as sand churned under his hooves.

"I'll take ya back," Kaden said, swinging onto Brogan's back with effortless grace.

Lusa almost arched a brow, wondering if he knew how good he looked doing it. He patted the horse's neck and held out a hand to her.

"He's missed ya."

She snorted. "He tolerates me."

Brogan snorted back, as if to confirm her point, though he stood still enough as she let Kaden haul her up behind him. As if sensing the tension that wound tighter inside her, Kaden offered a distraction.

"Try not ta' think about it. Think about the festival instead."

Twenty seasons of Lady Fira. That's how many she'd seen. Her hands settled at his waist as they began their journey back to the palace.

Back in Myttica, the celebrations had been her favorite time of year—a vibrant gathering of food, music, and laughter. It had always felt like a promise that brighter days lay ahead, even as the frost shimmered at the edges of the fields.

"Fira's different here, yeah? In Anora?" Kaden asked over the steady rhythm of Brogan's hooves. They both ducked under a low-hanging branch.

She nodded absently, her thoughts far away. The grandeur of Izier's Lady Fira celebrations dwarfed Myttica's modest festivities, but it didn't matter. The joy of celebrating the arrival of the hot season, the kind she used to cherish, felt unreachable now.

Excitement belonged to a life she could no longer touch. Once, she might have celebrated among other mages. Now she was the only one left to carry a legacy she didn't understand.

Lusa sighed, resting her cheek against Kaden's back. This wasn't Myttica. And she wasn't the girl who had once laughed and danced under lantern-lit skies. That life was a distant dream; one she knew she'd never wake up to again.

The rest of the ride passed in anticipatory silence, Kaden giving her the space to prepare herself. The crash of waves was far behind them now, replaced by the steady clop of Brogan's hooves on stone as they approached the palace gates.

They opened with mechanical efficiency, the guards rigid and formal as always. The sprawling grounds were pristine, almost boastful in their grandeur, a beauty that left Lusa feeling small.

By the time they stabled Brogan and reached the exterior lifts, the knot in Lusa's stomach had doubled. The council meeting loomed like a sentence waiting to be read. Lusa warily eyed the swaying platform suspended by ropes as Kaden stopped in front of it.

"Couldn't we take the stairs?" she asked dryly.

"Unless ya wanna climb a dozen flights in that gown, I'd say this is the better option. Besides, it's perfectly safe." Kaden smirked. "Mostly."

She shot a glare at him, which only made him smile, and stepped onto the platform, gripping the flimsy railing that barely reached her hips.

The men operating the pulley system shouted orders, their practiced movements doing little to calm her nerves. With a jolt, the lift began its ascent, the ropes groaning as they tightened.

The platform swayed, and Lusa's grip tightened until her knuckles turned white. She fixed her eyes on the floors as they passed, determined to ignore the dizzying open space below. The breeze didn't help, blowing her hair into her face and catching at the edges of her gown. She sighed in frustration, trying to smooth her hair with one hand while holding onto the railing with the other.

"Ya doin' alright there?" Kaden asked, his tone annoyingly casual as he leaned against the railing.

"I'm fine," she said through clenched teeth.

The wind whipped at her again, and she growled under her breath, brushing a strand of hair out of her mouth.

"Enjoying my torment?"

Kaden chuckled. "Maybe a little."

She tugged his cloak off her shoulders, holding it out to him. "Here."

Kaden waved her off with a grin.

"Nah, ya keep it. Covers up the, uh… morning-at-the-beach look ya got goin' on."

Her eyes narrowed. "Morning-at-the-beach look?"

He gestured vaguely at her windblown hair and the wet sand stubbornly clinging to the hem of her gown. "Wild. Untamed. Very you."

Lusa's lips pressed into a thin line as she glanced down at herself, her heartbeat pulsing a little faster. She probably did look wild, disheveled and unkempt after pacing the shoreline like some restless ghost. The thought only amplified her anxiety.

If she looked like this now, what impression would she leave? Would they see her as unbalanced, unpredictable, everything they already feared? She jabbed the cloak back into Kaden's chest.

"I'll manage."

He only laughed, ignoring her stubborn protest and draping it over her shoulders again. "Seriously, Lus. Keep it."

She grabbed at the edges of the cloak despite herself, pulling it tighter. It didn't ease the anxiety eating away at her, but it helped hold the pieces together… just enough to keep going.

As soon as the platform swayed to a stop at the fifth floor, Lusa stepped off quickly, running her fingers through her tangled hair. The lump of unease in her throat grew heavier with every step. She'd never been comfortable around large groups, especially when everyone present held some kind of importance… and judgment.

"You'll be fine, love," Kaden said, giving her shoulder a gentle squeeze before striding ahead toward the council chamber.

She tried to draw strength from his words. At the far end of the hallway, the heavy oak doors waited, flanked by two royal guards. Her gaze landed on the taller one. Glon. His familiar grin softened the tension in her chest, even as his posture remained professional.

"Captain," Kaden greeted, nodding at him.

Glon's dark eyes flicked to her, a glimmer of warmth in his tone. "Miss Lusa. Always a pleasure."

"Captain Glon," she replied, managing a faint smile.

The other guard stepped forward to open the doors, but Lusa hesitated. Glon caught her gaze and nodded. "You got this, Lus," he whispered.

Neither empire nor elves wanted mages alive. Izier would cage her. Lazorious would've bled her. The elves, she suspected, only tolerated her because they feared what she might become. Taking a steadying breath, she turned to Kaden, who waited beyond the threshold, his hand extended toward her.

"Ready?"

She wasn't. But she nodded anyway and stepped inside as the heavy doors groaned shut behind her. Her Dark Magics had been silent for weeks, but she knew better than to trust Their absence. Perhaps the council had already decided: a Dark Mage, even one who saved them, was too dangerous to let live.

CHAPTER 2

What Unity Demands

The chamber was a fortress where sound and silence waged an uneasy battle. High-arched ceilings disappeared into shadow, while the polished table at the center gleamed like black glass beneath flickering sconces.

Lusa's gaze darted to the head of the table, where Empress Nolanna sat draped in dark blue and gold. The candlelit chandelier above cast a warm glow, illuminating the embellishments of her gown and making her long golden ringlets shimmer. The Empress's eyes flicked over her briefly, their intensity leaving Lusa feeling exposed. She could almost sense the disappointment in her appearance, but could she really blame her? The meeting had been abruptly moved up by hours, with no notice.

Beside the Empress, General Vallas stood as still as a sword at rest, all discipline and control. Seeing him reminded her of Tryston… memories she had no desire to confront here. She moved her focus to the next familiar individual. Arcturius, now known to her as the Grand Vizier, exuded his usual calm, though the lines on his face hinted at unseen burdens. When his eyes met hers, he offered the faintest smile—a gesture probably meant to comfort her, but it only weighed her down more.

The rest of the people sitting at the table were strangers to Lusa, figures brimming with power and purpose, their murmured conversations humming like an undercurrent. One figure caught Lusa's attention: an elf. Moonlit hair flowed over her intricately woven robes, each thread shimmering faintly with magic. Her lavender gaze was razor-sharp, dissecting every detail of the room as if it were all beneath her.

Kaden leaned toward her. "Envoy of the Aeonian Throne," he whispered.

She barely had time to process his words before Arcturius rose, his voice carrying a gravity that silenced the room. "Miss Lusa. Master Kaden. Please have a seat. We have much to discuss."

Lusa's fingers brushed the back of the chair as she took her seat, a mask for the unease winding through her.

"Disturbances have been reported near Anadine," Arcturius began, letting the name hang in the air. "Strange weather patterns. Crops failing. Forests darkening."

Lusa's pulse quickened, mind snagging on the list. Weather that turned on its own. Fields dying. She wasn't a scholar—not like the mages who used to lecture endlessly about theory and balance—but she knew enough to recognize when something was off. Magic didn't twist nature like that unless something deeper was stirring. Something old.

Had something disturbed the balance in the Weave? Balance, Arcturius warned during one of their talks, was all that kept the Aeon asleep. The word still unsettled her.

Aeon. The living current said to pulse beneath all magic, older than the gods, older than Aetherealm itself.

The elf inclined her head. "Not disturbances. Decay." She spat out the last word. "It spreads through our lands like a shadow. If left unchecked, it will consume Aeonia. And your empire will not escape it."

Murmurs rippled across the table, but Lusa's thoughts spiraled inward. Decay? Weather? Magic? The possibilities swirled, unformed and chaotic, but she held her tongue. Her voice meant nothing among those with real authority.

Empress Nolanna cut through the noise. "This is why this council was convened, Envoy Caelithia. Izier and Aeonia must act as one to confront this threat."

The elf's expression tightened, her icy demeanor cracking. "With respect, Empress, unity is difficult to envision when you send... him." Caelithia's piercing gaze landed on Kaden, disdain threading her tone.

Lusa doubted it was only about Kaden. She'd seen that look before in courts, corridors… battlefields. The quiet conviction of the righteous. Prejudice wasn't born of ignorance; it was forged, shaped, and taught until it became law.

Beside her, Kaden stiffened, his easy confidence slipping for the first time. Before he could respond, the Empress spoke again, her voice like tempered steel. "He is my choice."

The weight of those words settled over the room, but Lusa's chest tightened. *Her choice.* A part of her bristled at how easily the Empress claimed him, even knowing the words weren't meant in that way. Kaden wasn't hers to claim. Not Lusa's, not the Empress's, not anyone's.

She stole a glance at him, catching the tension in his jaw, the way his hands had curled into fists under the table. It was rare to see him unsettled, and it pulled at her in ways she didn't have time to untangle.

The Empress continued, "Kaden represents Izier. He has earned his place through courage and loyalty, not the blood that runs in his veins."

Lusa blinked, her thoughts snagging on the word. *Blood?* She glanced at Kaden, waiting for him to correct her, to laugh it off. He didn't. A spark of anger flared, fanned by the thought that Kaden hadn't been as open with her as she'd believed. But here wasn't the place to push for answers.

Arcturius cleared his throat. "There is more. Whispers... rumors. Something, or someone, is using magic near the Citadels."

Lusa's gaze snapped to Arcturius. "Another mage?"

The Grand Vizier nodded. "If true, your role grows more critical. The Mage Citadels must be reclaimed. You must take steps toward becoming what this world needs: an interim Sorceress."

Her breath caught in her throat. *Interim Sorceress.* The words settled over her like a shroud. She thought of the Citadels… now in ruins, echoes of what they once were. The idea of returning there filled her with a rising unease she couldn't ignore.

"Reestablishing the Mage Order isn't just about reclaiming the Citadels. It's about stability—for magic, for this empire, and for Aetherealm. Without it, the decay in Anadine will spread unchecked, and if rumors of another mage are true, their power could turn against us all."

Suddenly, all her anxiety pooled together to transform into defensiveness and the heat of anger crept its way into her veins. "And if I say no?"

The silence that followed was deafening, broken only by the faint crackle of the chandelier's flames.

The Empress leaned forward, her gaze unwavering. "You won't."

Lusa clenched her fists, the fight still burning in her chest, but her words stuck in her throat. Not because she agreed, but because she knew the Empress was right. She hated it. She hated them for deciding her future. Hated herself more for knowing they were right—that she couldn't walk away. Not when the last mage still didn't know why she was the last.

"If I do," she started, the edge of her defiance yielding to cold calculation. "If I reclaim the Citadels, if I find this other mage, then what? Will magic finally have a place in this empire, or is this another means to an end?"

Arcturius answered first. "That depends on what you find and how you proceed, Miss Lusa. Stability is the goal, but how we achieve it will be shaped by your actions."

"Stability," Lusa repeated, the word sour in her mouth. "You keep saying that word as if it means something. But we both know stability has always meant control to you."

The elf envoy, Caelithia, jumped in, her pale face riddled with impatience. "Enough of this. Your suspicions don't change the task ahead. If you refuse to act, you'll only delay what must be done."

Lusa had a mind to spit some nasty words at this Caelithia as she met her gaze with a cold intensity of her own.

General Vallas cleared his throat. "If Lusa is to journey to the Citadels, she'll need… protection. The roads to Myttica remain unstable."

"I don't need—"

"You'll need it," he interrupted firmly. "Whether you think so or not."

Arcturius's pale blue eyes caught the candlelight, glinting faintly green as they settled on her. "The General is correct. These are dangerous times, Lusa. And you are more than a mage now. You are a symbol."

A symbol of survival, they meant. But survival felt like a crime. At the Temple, it had come at the cost of others. And everywhere else, she didn't even know why no one remained. Unless the reason was her, somehow—her presence, her curse. Either way, Izier didn't see her… only what they wanted her to represent. The thought suffocated her, but she swallowed her anger, forcing it to simmer beneath the surface instead of boiling over.

"Then who's going with her?" Kaden finally broke his silence, arms crossed as he leaned back in his chair.

Lusa's gaze flicked to him, her emotions a whirlwind of gratitude and frustration. She didn't want to be handled, but the thought of facing the Citadels alone wasn't exactly ideal, either.

"I'll go," General Vallas answered, his tone clipped and authoritative. Despite everything they'd endured together—even her saving him from the martyaxwar—the General's distrust clung to him like armor. Perhaps gratitude was beyond him, too deeply buried beneath his rigid adherence to rank and the belief that tradition outweighed merit.

Mistrust from others wasn't a new problem for Lusa. Tryston's distrust when they first met had cut the same way. But Tryston had come around in the end, his belief in her hard-won but genuine. Losing him in the crystal chambers had left a scar, one that still hadn't fully healed. Vallas, on the other hand, seemed content to remain unmoved. The thought twisted like a splinter in her mind.

The Empress looked at Kaden. "You will not accompany her."

"What?" Lusa sat up a little straighter.

Arcturius answered, "Kaden has been appointed ambassador to Anadine. He will aid in negotiations and investigate the disturbances."

Kaden started, "Y'er Majesty, with respect, I can't—"

"You can," Empress Nolanna interrupted. "And you will. The time has come to serve Izier as your blood demands."

Lusa turned to Kaden, her confusion morphing into disbelief. "What is she talking about?"

Kaden hesitated, a vein in his neck suddenly becoming more prominent. "I'm… her cousin," he muttered under his breath.

The words landed, shifting her perception in an instant. *Cousin. Royalty.* Lusa stared, too in shock to respond. Kaden, the bounty hunter who had walked the edges of light and shadow with effortless ease, now stood as someone bound by titles and bloodlines. A moment ago, she'd trusted him as an equal. Someone she was almost certain she loved. But with a few simple words, he'd become as unknown as the rest of the people sitting in the chamber. She took a few measured breaths.

Caelithia scoffed. "A half-blood ambassador? This appointment is... unconventional at best."

"And yet you will accept it," the Empress said, her tone frosty. "Or risk our alliance."

Lusa's fingers tightened around the edges of the chair. Empress Nolanna's conviction rang clear, but the fractures in their alliance were glaring. The elf's disdain mirrored the scorn Lusa had endured on her journey. Tryston's prejudice, the palace whispers, Vallas's cold detachment—all of it had been a reminder of how little faith anyone had in her, despite all she'd done. This was the same rot festering between nations and races, a slow corrosion eating away at any chance of unity. Prejudice was a poison, seeping into their world and infecting everything it touched.

Caelithia's slanted eyes narrowed, but she said nothing more. Lusa's mind spun as the council's conversation moved on without her. Her eyes remained fixed on the polished table for the rest of the meeting, her mind spiraling as she replayed the revelations. *Kaden, the Empress, the Mage Order… another mage.* Each link of anger and disbelief forged a chain that bound her tighter.

The room blurred at the edges. She heard voices—figures she hadn't bothered to learn titles or names for—discussing logistics, protection, and alliances. Their words became noise. She didn't lift her gaze, didn't acknowledge the side glances or whispers she could feel crawling over her like static.

Finally, the Empress rose, her commanding presence silencing the room. "Miss Lusa, you'll leave for Myttica in five days. Prepare yourself accordingly. General Vallas will oversee your arrangements. Master Kaden," she continued, her tone softening ever so slightly, "your departure to Anadine with the Aeonian Envoy will be in three. See to your preparations."

Lusa pushed back her chair, her lips pressed into a thin line, and her face betraying nothing. "Five days. Understood." The words were clipped, formal, as she inclined her head toward the Empress and stepped away from the table.

Weaving around other council members who barely moved aside, Lusa ignored their judging glances and whispered exchanges. The sand-stained hem of her ivory gown brushed against polished boots and embroidered robes, but she didn't care. She lifted the fabric to avoid tripping over herself, her focus fixed on the doors ahead.

She didn't say goodbye to Glon, didn't spare him more than a flicker of acknowledgment as she pushed past the heavy doors into the corridor. Her chest tightened with the effort it took to keep her composure, but her steps were steady, quickening only when she turned down a quieter hallway, away from prying eyes and ears.

The soft echo of boots behind her told her Kaden had followed.

"Lusa, wait," he pleaded.

She stopped, turning to face him with such abruptness it made him hesitate. Her expression was a carefully controlled storm. She tugged his cloak off her shoulders and shoved it into his hands.

"Take it," she said coldly.

Kaden reluctantly grabbed it. "Let me explain."

"There's nothing to explain," she snapped. "You're her cousin. You knew this, kept this from me. After everything. After you promised to be honest with me. So forgive me if I don't feel like hearing your excuses right now."

Kaden gripped the cloak tighter and for a second, she thought he might argue. But instead, he took a step closer. "Ye're right. I should've told you. Should've told you a lot of things, but this… " He gestured vaguely, frustration flickering across his face. "This wasn't somethin' I wanted to hide. It's somethin' I wanted to forget. Bein' a bounty hunter, walkin' in the shadows… that's who I've been for decades. Not this. Not her cousin."

Lusa stared at him, her anger still simmering but dissolving the slightest when she took in his sincere expression.

"You're mad. You've got every right ta' be," he continued. "But don't let this ruin what we've built. I kept this from you because I didn't want it to change things. I didn't want it to change us."

"Us?"

Kaden sighed, raking a hand through his hair. "Yes, us. Whatever we are… whatever we're becomin'." His gaze softened, holding hers. "Don't let this be the thing that breaks it."

The fire in her dimmed enough for the tightness in her chest to ease. She sighed.

"I'm still angry." she said thinly.

"I can live with that," Kaden replied with a faint smirk. "At least it means ye're still talkin' to me."

She almost rolled her eyes but instead glanced toward the staircase at the end of the corridor. "I need space. Time to think."

He nodded, stepping back. "Take all the time ya need. Just… meet me later? For Lady Fira?"

Lusa hesitated, the fire threatening to rekindle, but she extinguished it with another sigh. "Fine. I'll meet you."

The faint smile that crossed his face was genuine, softening the edges of her frustration. She turned without another word, her steps measured as she made way for the stairs. As she moved further from Kaden, her ire thinned, swallowed by the darker thoughts she'd been circling for days. Was she the last mage because she'd survived… or because her Magics had wiped out everyone else?

CHAPTER 3

The Lady Fira Festival

The bone corset was a menace, a weapon in disguise, and Lusa was convinced its sole purpose was to remind women of their mortality. Every breath was a battle against its death grip, and Nem was far too pleased with herself as she tightened the bindings.

"You're trying to kill me, aren't you?" Lusa wheezed, gripping the bedpost.

Nem smirked. "If I wanted you dead, Miss Lusa, I'd choose a quicker method. This is fashion."

"Fashion should allow breathing," Lusa growled, earning a snicker from Tyssa, who twirled a gold ribbon between her fingers as she worked on Lusa's hair.

"What's beauty without a little sacrifice?" Tyssa teased, winding the ribbon through one of Lusa's braids.

The banter was a faint distraction, but Lusa's thoughts swirled relentlessly: the Mage Citadels, rumors of another mage, Kaden's revelation. It all circled like vultures over a battlefield, a storm pressing harder with each tug of the corset. Even the warm water of the bathhouse, faintly scented with solivine petals, hadn't washed away the weight of the council meeting. The effort to scrub her worries clean had been in vain, though her skin now glowed, and her hair shone like polished ebony in the flickering light of the room.

"Five days," she murmured, barely audible, her grip tightening on the bedpost.

"What's that?" Tyssa paused mid-braid, her hands hovering near Lusa's temple.

"Nothing," Lusa replied quickly.

Five days to leave, five days to prepare for a journey she didn't want for an empire that barely tolerated her.

Nem retrieved the crimson gown, its fabric shimmering like liquid fire. The intricate gold and black embroidery licked across the sleeves like ancient flames, and the high collar framed her neck with sharp elegance. Wearing it felt less like dressing for a festival and more like preparing for a coronation.

Tyssa wove the final ribbon through Lusa's hair, stepping back with a look of satisfaction. Thick braids framed her face and twisted into a crown at the back of her head, the remaining lengths cascading down her back in glossy waves.

When the maids finally stepped back, Tyssa clapped her hands. "Fit for Lady Fira herself."

Nem raised a brow. "Let's hope she just survives the festival."

Lusa glanced at her reflection. The woman staring back looked regal, even poised, but the storm behind her eyes betrayed her. She couldn't think about the Citadels now, or her impending separation from Kaden. Tonight, she'd play her part.

A knock pulled her from her thoughts. Tyssa hurried to open the door, revealing Kaden. His presence stirred the air like a gust of wind, his smirk faltering for a moment as his eyes swept over her. He quickly recovered, leaning casually against the doorframe. "Well, don't you clean up nice."

"Don't start," Lusa muttered, crossing her arms, though his gaze had already unraveled her carefully maintained composure. He kept staring at her, making his way closer.

"What?"

"Nothin'," he said, brushing a stray strand of hair from her face. His finger grazed her jawline and made her breath catch. "Just didn't think you could look better than you already do."

She cleared her throat to regain some sense of control. She hated how easily he managed to disarm her.

"Don't let Nem hear you say that," she said, trying to keep her tone light. "She'll take all the credit."

Nem giggled somewhere behind her.

Kaden chuckled and stepped back to offer his arm. "Come on. We've got blossomfire toffee to catch before it sells out."

Lusa hesitated, then took his arm, the warmth of his presence calming the storm swirling inside her.

The cool night air greeted them as they exited the palace, a welcome reprieve from its stifling grandeur. At the foot of the marble steps stood Glon, arms crossed and grinning as if the night were his to conquer. His leather uniform gleamed under the streetlamps, the midnight-blue sash of his captaincy draped neatly over one shoulder, its gold embellishments catching the light like starlight.

"If you'd entered the Lady Fira pageant like I suggested, you'd have won," Glon teased with a bow. "Dressed to charm all of Anora, I see."

Lusa rolled her eyes, her hand slipping from Kaden's arm as she descended the steps. "You look rather handsome yourself, Captain."

"Handsome?" Kaden's voice broke in, heavy with mock incredulity. "You're handing out compliments already, and I don't even get an honorable mention?"

Lusa glanced over her shoulder, taking in the dark elegance of his attire. Gone were the practical leathers and well-worn cloak she was used to seeing him in. Instead, he wore a tailored black tunic embroidered with subtle crimson patterns along the edges, cinched with a decorative silk red belt. The high collar framed his neck perfectly, and the layered fabric fell slightly above his boots, resembling something befitting a nobleman rather than a bounty hunter. It wasn't just the clothes—though they certainly didn't hurt—but the way he wore them, the quiet confidence in his stance, that sent her heart stumbling over itself.

Kaden smirked, catching her lingering stare. "What? Speechless?"

She collected herself and cleared her throat, feigning indifference. "You look... different," she said finally, making sure her voice betrayed none of the admiration she knew he was fishing for.

"Different," he repeated. "Glon gets 'handsome,' and I get 'different'? Startin' to think I should'a worn my leathers."

Glon chuckled. "Can't win them all, Kaden."

"Oh, don't worry about me," Kaden said, his smirk returning in full force. "I know I clean up well." He adjusted the cuff of his tunic with a flick of his fingers, as if entirely unbothered.

Lusa groaned, brushing past them both as she mumbled, "You're both insufferable."

"Only when we're around you, love," Kaden called after her, falling into step beside her once more.

Glon caught up on her other side and she eyed him playfully. "Shouldn't you be guarding something? Or someone?"

He shrugged. "Royal guards get festival privileges too, you know. We take shifts. Mine starts after the second bell of the evening."

The three of them passed through the palace gates, leaving behind its grand yet stifling air for the lively chaos of Anora's streets. The capital pulsed with energy, a maze of vibrant colors and sound. Silk banners fluttered from rooftops; their edges embroidered with the golden sigil of Lady Fira: a radiant sun cradled by a wreath of ivy. Lanterns hung from every possible perch, their soft glow painting the cobblestones in warm hues of amber and crimson. The air brimmed with roasted chestnuts, spiced meats, and blossomfire toffee.

Lusa found herself drawn to the rhythm of it all: the hum of conversations, the laughter of children darting through the crowd, the melodic notes of a lyre drifting from a nearby corner. Anora seemed to have transformed for the festival, its usual refinement replaced by something freer, more vibrant.

"You know," Glon started, "you'd blend in just fine if you weren't dressed like you belonged in a noble's parade."

"I didn't ask for this," she countered, her fingers brushing the high collar of her gown. "Nem would've stuffed me into this thing even if I'd threatened to set it on fire."

"Remind me to thank her," Kaden said with a wink.

Lusa huffed, but the banter eased the tension that had lived in her chest since the council meeting. For all their teasing, Glon and Kaden had a way of keeping her present, their companionship a comfort she rarely acknowledged. Her heart twisted, that restless knot tightening beneath the laughter. Five days. Then it was over. No more Glon's easy jabs, no more of Kaden's infuriating smirks. No more distractions from the fact that she was sinking under the pressure of expectations she never asked for.

The ache pressed harder with each step, until something vivid and unexpected broke through her spiral. A crimson stick, glossy and dusted with golden sugar crystals, hovered in front of her face. The scent of warm honey and a hint of spice curled into her senses, pulling her from her brooding. She halted mid-step, glancing at Kaden and wondering when he'd had the time to pick up a treat.

"Here," he said, his grin infuriatingly smug. "Figured you could use a little sweetness."

Lusa blinked at the offering, then took it cautiously. "What is it?"

"Try it and see," Glon called from her other side, already crunching into one of his own. The sharp crack of the candy echoed through the festival din, releasing a swirl of spiced fragrance into the warm night air.

With a wary glance between the two, Lusa nibbled the edge. The initial sweetness melted into a fiery burst that tingled on her tongue, the heat requiring a sip of water but the sweetness enough to make her take another bite.

"What is this?" she asked, licking the sticky sweetness from her fingers.

"Blossomfire toffee," Kaden said, clearly pleased with her reaction. "Perfect for someone who's got a little fire of her own."

Ahead, the festival's heart unfolded in the central plaza, its towering willow trees illuminated by glowing lanterns that swayed like fireflies caught in a dance. The sight was mesmerizing, even if it was different from the traditions Lusa had grown up with in Myttica, where lanterns painted with wishes rose into the night sky, carried by magic. Here, the lanterns stayed close to the earth, floating across basins at the base of each tree.

She paused near one of the basins, watching as a child crouched to release a fragile lantern he must have built himself. Its somewhat lopsided structure of delicate wood and dyed paper bobbed on the shimmering water, its flame flickering faintly. The lantern drifted forward, catching the gentle current, but Lusa couldn't help but frown in confusion.

"Why don't they float them into the sky?"

Kaden placed his hand on the small of her back and watched with her. "Different lands, different customs. Here, they float them on water."

Glon gestured toward the carved wooden gate at the far end of the basin. "The goal is to make it past the gate. The creek takes over after that, carrying the lantern all the way to the ocean."

"And if it reaches the ocean?"

"Lady Fira grants y'er wish," Kaden explained, his tone softening. He leaned closer, his lips brushing the edge of her ear as he added, "But only if the flame survives the whole journey."

She ignored the flutter in her chest at the warmth of his breath, forcing her attention back to the creek as it wound through the plaza and disappeared beyond the city gates.

"That seems... unlikely."

"That's the point," Glon replied with a knowing chuckle. "A wish isn't worth much if it doesn't have to fight for it."

Lusa's gaze returned to the boy's lantern as it struggled against the ripples, dipping dangerously close to the waterline. "And if it doesn't make it?"

"It goes out, like mosta' them do," Kaden said with a slight shrug. "But the ones that survive? They don't just carry the wish… they prove they're strong enough to endure the journey."

The boy's lantern wobbled but passed through the gate, earning a small, triumphant cheer from him and his family. Lusa looked away, her thoughts drifting to Myttica. She could still imagine painted lanterns rising into the night sky, carried by the spells of mages. Each one was a fragment of hope sent soaring to the stars.

Anora's tradition felt different. Here, wishes weren't carried upward but surrendered to the current, left to find their way downstream. It reminded her of something Master Aron once said—that magic moved like water through the Weave, always seeking its own path, reshaping what tried to contain it. She hadn't really understood it then and wasn't sure she did now. But lately, she was beginning to think she might. When its course was forced, it would carve new ones, no matter the cost.

"It's not so different from Myttica," she thought out loud. "We painted our lanterns and sent them into the sky. Our spells carried them upward."

Kaden tilted his head; his eyes shaded with curiosity. "Upward, huh? Sounds like they didn't have ta' fight the current."

"They didn't," Lusa admitted, watching another lantern as it dipped sideways and sank into the basin with a soft hiss. "But they weren't indestructible. The wind could snuff them out, or the spell could falter. Fragile, just like these."

"Fragile doesn't mean weak," Kaden said after a moment, his voice quieter, and his palm pressed a little firmer into her back. "Sometimes the ones that seem the most delicate are the ones holding on the hardest."

Lusa glanced at him, surprised by the sincerity in his tone, but he had already turned his attention back to the basin. The stream of lanterns flickered like stars in the water, their soft light dancing against the ripples. Hope wasn't about guarantees. It was about holding on, even when everything seemed poised to extinguish you.

She watched the stream of lanterns, their flickering lights carried forward by the current, the whispers of wishes and unspoken hopes drifting with them. Her thoughts, tangled and restless, were interrupted by Glon's voice.

"Well, standing here staring at the water won't get you crowned Lady Fira," Glon teased, nudging her shoulder lightly. "Let's see if you're as good at haggling as you are at glaring."

She blinked, wondering if that merited a punch to his arm, and followed his gaze toward the vibrant sprawl of vendor stalls ahead.

The plaza stretched out before them, alive with color and motion. Stalls lined the pathways like a kaleidoscope of possibilities. Vendors called out with practiced enthusiasm, their voices rising over the symphony of laughter, chatter, and music.

Kaden kept his hand on her waist, as if unwilling to let any distance come between them. She couldn't tell if it was because Glon was with them or if he shared the same quiet dread of their impending separation.

The labyrinth of stalls within the plaza each brimmed with wares that dazzled the eye and tempted the senses. Jewelry sparkled, and delicate chains adorned with shimmering stones seemed to hold starlight inside them. Vendors called out over the hum of the crowd, offering rolls of silk, jars of spiced honey, and carvings of mythic beasts.

Lusa paused at a stall nestled beneath the sweeping canopy of a solivine tree, its white blossoms edged in crimson like the first blush of dawn. The solivine, she'd noticed, had become Lady Fira's emblem in Izier, adorning countless banners and gowns throughout the festival. The stall's display gleamed with intricate hairpins, each crafted with remarkable care. Some were modest, featuring polished wood or smooth beads, while others were miniature works of art, their designs resembling delicate sculptures. Her gaze caught on one in particular: a silver pin shaped like a cluster of gypsophila blooms, its petals encrusted with marcasite that sparkled like dew beneath the lantern light.

Her fingers hovered over it, captivated by the intricate detail and the way the petals seemed to come alive with every shift of the light. She never saw herself as a woman who cared for fancy jewels or trinkets, but she had to admit this piece was beautiful.

Kaden took in the inventory, noticing her discovery. "That one suits you."

"Suits me? How so?"

The look he gave her nearly unraveled her again. "Delicate but strong," he murmured, holding her gaze. "Like you."

Flustered, she scoffed. "It's hair jewelry, Kaden. Not a weapon."

"Then buy it," he said, motioning to the nearby stall where she'd paused. When she shook her head, he added, "Need isn't the point, it's about what makes you happy."

Before she could respond, Glon's voice interrupted, his arms overflowing with dozens of lantern materials. "Hope you're ready to craft, Lus! I've got enough here to light up the whole creek."

Lusa chuckled, her worries momentarily lifting as she reached to help him. "You're a disaster waiting to happen. Here, let me help." She stepped forward, flicking her gown sleeves out of the way as she grabbed some of the materials from him.

She turned toward Kaden, wondering why he hadn't already offered to help, only to find him standing stock-still, his expression that of an imp paralyzed by one of her spells. His sheepish grin and the faint flicker of mischief in his eyes only deepened her curiosity.

Lusa arched a brow, her suspicion flaring. "What are you doing?"

"Nothin'," Kaden said, too quickly, his grin widening as he pulled a hand from inside his tunic, clearly trying to look nonchalant.

"Right," she said, her tone dripping with disbelief. Without missing a beat, she shoved a stack of Glon's materials into his arms, cutting off any chance for him to object. "You can explain your 'nothin' later."

Glon snorted with laughter, clearly entertained.

As they wandered deeper into the market, Lusa noticed a group of nobles standing near one of the basins. They were immaculately dressed, their lanterns works of art crafted from materials that glittered even in the dim light. One noblewoman handed a small bag of coins to a vendor, while her attendant distributed simple paper lanterns to a cluster of children.

Kaden followed her gaze. "Charitable offerings," he explained. "Makes them look good while keeping their own lanterns pristine for the palace ceremony."

"Convenient," Lusa murmured, though her words lacked venom. She watched as one child, clutching their new lantern, eagerly hurried to the basin to release it. "At least the kids get something out of it."

The hum of the crowd swelled to a pulsing rhythm of voices and music that wrapped around Lusa as they pressed forward. Heat licked at her skin before she even saw the source, the scent of burning oil thick in the air. Flashes of gold and orange flared ahead. Flames spun through the darkness, twisting in controlled arcs as fire dancers commanded the space at the heart of the street.

Lusa slowed, drawn in despite herself. The dancers moved like the flames were an extension of their bodies, sweeping torches in wide circles, sending embers scattering like dying stars. A female performer clad in crimson silk arched her back, balancing a ring of fire along her arms before tossing it high. Gasps rippled through the crowd as the ring spun, a halo of light against the night sky, before she caught it effortlessly and let it roll down her body in a flickering spiral.

Applause erupted into a wave of cheers. Lusa barely heard it. Her eyes remained fixed on the fire, mesmerized by the way it lived and breathed in the dancers' hands. Controlled but wild. Dangerous but beautiful. A force that could consume, or illuminate, depending on whose hands wielded it.

Kaden leaned in. "You're staring."

She blinked, dragging herself back to the present. "It's impressive," she admitted.

"Remind me never to hand you a torch," Glon quipped, nudging her arm. "I'd rather not be roasted alive."

Lusa smirked, but something about the comment settled oddly in her chest. He said it as a joke, but unlike Kaden, Glon had never actually seen her magic in action. He hadn't been there when she'd set an entire forest ablaze, when flames had leapt to her call like living creatures, eager to devour.

She rolled her shoulders, brushing away the thought. "Relax, Captain. You're not flammable."

Glon chuckled. "I'll take your word for it."

Kaden, however, glanced at her, his expression unreadable. He knew better.

As they moved on, the scent of oil and heat faded, replaced by something else: wax, ink, and the faint, comforting spice of old parchment. A group of people had gathered around a nearby booth; their voices hushed in anticipation. On the long wooden tables, rows of lanterns stood proudly on display, each one a masterpiece of careful craftsmanship. Some were shaped like animals, others like celestial bodies, and a few had elaborate filigree designs, their edges gilded with delicate gold leaf.

Lusa brushed her fingers against the edge of the table, her gaze drifting over the lanterns. These weren't the hastily folded paper ones drifting through the basin. These were works of art.

A judge in ceremonial robes moved between them, studying each lantern with an air of solemnity. He traced a fingertip along the painted surface of one, murmuring something to the vendor beside him. The crowd watched with bated breath, awaiting his verdict.

The bells of the evening rang out then, their low chimes rolling across the city, a signal that the final stages of the festival were beginning. The energy of the square shifted, people turning instinctively toward the palace.

Lusa lifted her gaze. The towering spires loomed over the city, bathed in lantern light, their reflections shimmering in the waters below. The sheer presence of the palace had always been imposing, but tonight, with the golden glow of the festival casting long shadows against its walls, it felt like the eye of the empire was watching.

A hush fell over the crowd as a herald emerged onto the grand balcony high above the gates. He raised his hands, his voice cutting through the night with practiced authority.

"Citizens of Izier," he called. "Her Majesty, Empress Nolanna, extends her blessings on this Lady Fira Festival.

May the season ahead bring warmth, renewal, and prosperity to all."

From the shadows of the balcony, the Empress stepped forward. Her golden gown gleamed like sunlight on water, every inch of her presence composed and commanding. The crowd responded in kind, murmurs of awe rippling outward like a wave. She lifted her arms, palms open in a gesture of benediction, and the plaza erupted in cheers.

Lusa stood at the edge of it all, watching, but not cheering.

Kaden shifted beside her. "She knows how to hold a room."

There was something in his tone that struck her sour.

She narrowed her eyes. "You sound like you're close."

His expression didn't change, but she noticed the slight twitch of his jaw muscle, as if she'd struck too close to something.

"Maybe more than I let on," he admitted.

Before she could press further, Glon clapped his hands together, breaking the moment. "Right, let's get back to the palace before this lot crushes us in the rush."

The crowd was starting to veer toward the palace gates, drawn by the pull of the final ceremony. Lusa cast one last glance over her shoulder at the fire dancers, the lanterns, the people whose only concern tonight was making wishes and enjoying the festival. She turned back toward the palace, toward duty, toward whatever awaited her in five days' time and wished she could stay.

The palace's stream shimmered under the glow of lanterns strung above, its gentle current winding toward the ocean, flanked by flowering solivine bushes. Unlike the revelry of Anora's main square, the nobles' gathering was more of a performance—elegant, restrained, polished to the point of suffocation.

Silk-clad women glided in hypnotic circles to the soft strains of lyres, their movements fluid but practiced. Servants moved swiftly between tables, carrying trays of jeweled fruits and spiced wine, their presence ignored except when needed. Small gatherings of nobles murmured among themselves, their laughter hushed, their words laced with veiled intentions. Even the lanterns set afloat bore the same stiff uniformity—crafted to perfection, inscribed with carefully curated wishes that spoke more of status than sincerity.

"Not exactly the festive spirit of Anora," Kaden whispered, his hazel eyes flicking over the scene.

Glon snorted, adjusting his grip on the bundles of lantern supplies. "What did you expect? Nobles don't like to get their hands dirty, even for tradition."

Lusa watched a servant lowering an ostentatious lantern into the water—gilded, encrusted with jewels, its inscription an intricate flourish of empty words. A wish more expensive than meaningful.

Their arrival turned more than a few heads. Fans fluttered, voices dipped, but not low enough. One noblewoman leaned toward her companion, her words carrying across the lantern-lit hush, "The last mage, paraded like a festival relic. Dangerous things should not be dressed in silk."

Her companion's reply was quieter, but Lusa's ears caught it all the same. "And they send a half-blood as ambassador. Izier must be desperate indeed."

Heat flared in Lusa's chest, but before she could summon a retort, Glon strode forward oblivious, dropping their supplies onto a table with a solid thud that earned its own set of disapproving glances.

"Let's show this lot what real lanterns look like," he said, grinning.

Lusa smirked, the kind that kept her from saying what she really wanted. If they thought their petty barbs could wound her, they weren't worth the effort of a reply.

They sifted through the materials, choosing colors and frames. Kaden selected deep green paper, his folds precise, efficient and unexpectedly meticulous. Glon, predictably, went for bold crimson and gold, his construction haphazard but enthusiastic.

Lusa ran her fingers over the selection before settling on a soft silver-blue, a shade reminiscent of moonlight on water. Unlike the extravagant lanterns drifting down the stream, hers would be simple. Unassuming but real.

She had barely begun when a figure approached their table. The woman was as rigid as a drawn blade, her steps measured, her posture unwavering. She stopped precisely at Glon's side, giving the barest nod of acknowledgment before speaking. "Captain Glon."

The tall woman was clad in the marked leather of the royal guard. Her dark skin contrasted against the silver threads woven subtly into her uniform, her coiled hair cropped close to her head. She carried herself with quiet authority.

Glon looked up at the sound of his name, his posture shifting, shoulders squaring to mark the subtle change from friend to captain.

"Noreena," he greeted, his tone measured but still light enough for festival grounds. "Didn't expect you to come find me."

Noreena inclined her head, expression unreadable, her crisp movements reflecting the discipline of someone who had spent years following orders. "I thought it best to deliver this in person."

She handed him a sealed scroll. Glon took it, breaking the wax seal with a flick of his thumb. As his eyes skimmed the contents, his mouth tightened slightly before he rolled the parchment shut with an air of finality.

"Well," he said, slipping back into something looser, but not quite his casual self. "Looks like my recommendations were approved. You'll be in Miss Lusa's envoy with me, along with Jarion and Dak. Inform them."

Noreena absorbed the information without visible reaction. "Understood, Captain."

Lusa straightened, her fingers stilling on the lantern paper. She studied Noreena, searching for some indication of the kind of soldier who'd been assigned to follow her into the unknown. She hadn't known who would be joining her aside from General Vallas. There was no sign of hesitation in Noreena's reaction, no sign of preference, only efficiency.

Noreena met her gaze, a moment of silent acknowledgment before she nodded once. "I'll prepare accordingly."

Glon nodded. "Dismissed."

With nothing more to add, Noreena turned and strode off, disappearing into the shifting glow of festival lanterns. A quiet stretched between them, thin and uneasy, the revelry of the festival now distant. The weight of the next five days pressed between them, breaking the brief escape from reality.

Lusa traced the corner of her lantern paper, suddenly restless. The news should have brought relief. Knowing Glon oversaw her envoy did, but the moment also cemented reality. Her time here was running out.

Glon, perhaps sensing the shift, abruptly pushed himself up. "Well, I'm getting mine in the water." He picked up his lantern and threw Lusa a lopsided grin. "Try not to make yours too pretty, Lus, or you'll make me look bad."

She gave a half-hearted smirk, but the heaviness in her chest remained.

As Glon moved away, Kaden exhaled, rolling his shoulders before finally speaking. "Meet me in the training grounds tomorrow. Before dawn."

Lusa arched a brow. "Why?"

His focus stayed on the lantern in his hands, the flickering light catching the sharp angles of his face. "Figured there were a few things we should go over before I leave."

His voice was even, almost indifferent, but something about it made her hesitate. Lusa studied him a little longer, waiting for him to elaborate. He didn't.

"Alright," she said finally. "Before dawn."

Kaden gave a single nod, still not looking at her, his fingers idly smoothing the paper of his lantern. The conversation, it seemed, was already over.

CHAPTER 4

Steel, Sweat, and Somethin' Else

Before dawn, the training grounds were quiet, save for the faint echo of Kaden's footsteps as he paced the worn dirt. The sky still carried the hush of night, a deep indigo fraying at the edges with threads of approaching light. The torches lining the perimeter burned low, their glow flickering against the wooden posts and racks of training weapons.

Kaden rolled his shoulders, trying to shake the restlessness sitting too deep in his chest. He told himself it was the coming days weighing on him. The mission, the separation. But he knew better.

It was her.

It was always her.

Soft footsteps—not boots, not leather—something lighter. Slippers against stone. His pulse betrayed him before his head even turned.

Lusa stepped onto the grounds, and Evenlore help him—he was not prepared.

She'd probably chosen the simplest gown she had, but it didn't matter. The fabric shifted as she walked, catching on the faintest breeze, the torchlight playing off the deep blue folds in a way that made it impossible to ignore. It clung in all the wrong places, draping over curves that had no business being on a training field.

Kaden crossed his arms, smirking to mask the way his body reacted to her presence. "Not exactly battle-ready, are we?"

Lusa huffed, tugging at the sleeves as if sheer willpower might make them more practical. "Glon's sister isn't finished with my tunic yet. This is the best I could do."

He let his gaze flick over her again, too long, before he forced himself to look away. "At least there ain't a corset."

"Be grateful," she muttered, smoothing the fabric at her waist. "Or I'd bind you in one and see how well you fight."

That nearly pulled a laugh from him. Nearly.

Instead, he stepped forward to grab a training sword, expecting her to move. She didn't.

She wasn't even paying attention, too preoccupied with her sleeves, twisting the fabric like she might wrestle them into submission.

Kaden reached past her, his fingers closing around the hilt of a wooden sword—except his focus had already unraveled.

Sweet Solivine and something uniquely her curled in his senses, weaving into his thoughts before he could push it away. His grip tightened. Distance. He needed distance. But when he looked down, she was already glancing up.

Realization flickered across her face.

For a split second, neither of them moved.

Warmth unfurled in his chest, slow and treacherous, pulling him into the way her breath shallowed, the way her throat worked as she swallowed, the way—

She cleared her throat.

Kaden jerked back, too fast, like he'd been cut. He tossed the weapon her way, forcing the words steady. "Alright. Let's see what you've got."

Lusa caught the weapon with both hands, adjusting her grip, testing the weight with a quick roll of her wrist. A skeptical glance flicked his way, brow arching. "You really think I'll need this?"

Kaden rolled his own weapon in his palm, feeling its balance. "I think magic can be unreliable." He let the words settle before adding, "And I think you don't trust y'er own hands enough."

A spark of challenge flared in her eyes. Chin lifting, she squared her shoulders. "I trust my hands just fine."

Kaden bit back a smirk. There it was. He knew exactly how to get under her skin.

"Fine," she said, stepping back into a loose stance. "Show me."

She barely had the words out before he moved. A swift swing, cutting low to force her into reaction. She barely caught the strike, the force of it knocking her back a step.

His smirk deepened. "Too slow."

Lusa's eyes narrowed.

Good. She always fought better when she was angry. It sharpened her, stripped away hesitation, made her react on instinct instead of overthinking. She had the skill, the raw talent. She just needed to trust it.

He struck again, harder this time, angling toward her ribs. She blocked more firmly, her footing more sure beneath her, but she still wasn't committing.

Kaden exhaled, stepping in. Close enough to see the storm-gray flecks in her blue eyes, to hear the shift in her breath as she braced for his next move. "Y'er hesitatin'."

"I'm thinking."

"That's y'er problem."

Before she could adjust, he shifted, hooking his foot behind her ankle. A quick pull, and down she went. She barely had time to register it before he caught her—one arm tight around her waist, the other still gripping his sword.

Heat licked at the edges of his restraint. Not from exertion or from the fight, but from her. Her breath was quick against his jaw, warm, uneven. His own pulse pounded in his ears, his grip flexing before his mind caught up with his body.

Step back. Let go.

But he felt her. Everywhere. The warmth of her bleeding through the fabric between them, the shape of her pressed into him, igniting something dangerously unguarded.

She wasn't moving. Wasn't speaking.

And he wasn't looking away.

Her lips parted slightly, the barest shift of breath. Heat pooled low, his body teetering on an edge he had no business standing on. Reckless.

Kaden forced his fingers to release the small of her back, willed his body to move. He stepped back like distance alone could sever whatever had wrapped its claws around him.

Lusa's gaze was unreadable, steady beneath the dark strands whispering against her skin, framing her face like ink on parchment.

Bouncing his sword from hand to hand, he cleared his throat, dragging his focus back where it belonged. Training. Discipline.

"Again." His voice was steady, a mask over everything simmering beneath the surface.

Time unraveled between them, slipping from meaning. Hours. Minutes. They ceased to matter. The sky shifted, deep blue bleeding into hazy orange, then bright blue. The torches were all but snuffed out, the sun high in the sky, and still, they fought. No teasing or remarks. Just breath, movement, and the clash of wood on wood.

Lusa was improving—and fast. She read him now, adjusted before he could exploit an opening. He saw it in the way her body flowed with the rhythm of the fight, the way confidence settled in her limbs. Where once there had been hesitation, now there was certainty.

Still, he pushed her harder.

She pivoted, her gown whispering against the packed dirt, catching the light as she moved. His next strike came swift, but she met it head-on, bracing her arms, feet planted. The force of it should have sent her back. It almost did. But she held firm, her determination carved into every tense line of her body, her flushed face a portrait of defiance.

Kaden countered, knocking her off balance just enough to test her reflexes. She adjusted almost instantly, her blade meeting his, the impact ringing up his arm. The fight had melted into something else. It had become more than training. It was the only chance they had to spend time together before he was gone.

And who knew when they'd see each other again? If they'd see each other again…

The thought rooted itself deep, spreading like cracks through stone, slowing his breath, intensifying every second. It was there between them, unsaid but unyielding, woven into each strike and parry. She caught his second of distraction and used it against him.

A shift. A quick, fluid twist of her hips.

Before Kaden could correct his balance, she hooked her foot behind his ankle and yanked. The world tilted. His back hit the ground hard, air slamming from his lungs.

And Lusa followed him down.

Her weight sank into him, heat searing through the layers of fabric like a brand against his skin. Her thighs pressed tight against his hips, caging him. His own sword was at his throat. But that wasn't what had him struggling to breathe.

It was the press of every curve where there should have been distance. Her breath—hot, uneven—ghosting over his skin. Loosened hair spilled forward, framing them in a dark curtain, shutting out the world beyond the space they occupied.

Kaden's fingers twitched at his sides, curled into fists, sheer discipline keeping them there. One shift—one mistake—and he'd reach for her, drag her closer, erase the sliver of space that still remained. A breath and he could taste the salt of her sweat, the faint trace of whatever oil she'd used in her hair. If he barely turned his head, his lips would graze the curve of her jaw.

He shouldn't.

Lusa's gaze flickered to his mouth.

His heart kicked hard in his chest. The weight of her. The warmth. The way her pulse thrummed against him in perfect tandem. It was too much. His restraint hung by a thread, unraveling in slow, steady pulls. The blade at his throat pressed in a fraction deeper. Not enough to hurt but enough to remind him who had the upper hand.

Kaden swallowed. He could flip her in a heartbeat. Could have her beneath him, could—

A sharp clearing of someone's throat broke the moment, reality snapping back into place. Kaden clenched his jaw, staring at the sky for a half-breath before forcing himself upright, shoving down the ache, the heat, the want.

Lusa scrambled off him, brushing dirt from her skirts like it might erase what just happened. They turned in sync to see a figure in muted Imperial garb, standing at attention like he'd rather be anywhere else.

"Ya got timing," Kaden muttered under his breath.

The messenger remained impassive, gaze locked on some very interesting point in the distance and extended a sealed parchment toward Lusa. "A summons," he said simply.

She hesitated before taking it, breaking the seal and unfolding the parchment. Something in the air shifted. The moment had unraveled, but its threads still wove between them, caught in the spaces left behind.

Kaden pushed to his feet, dusting himself off, watching. Lusa's fingers tightened ever so slightly on the parchment as her eyes moved over the words. Kaden's focus narrowed. He forced his pulse back to a decent rhythm, calm, indifferent.

Her lips parted, hesitation flickering again before she finally spoke. "The Grand Vizier wants to see me."

The words settled between them, roping reality back.

"Right," Kaden sighed. "Best not keep 'em waitin'."

Their eyes met, the moment stretching just long enough to make him certain of what she wasn't saying. She turned to the messenger, smoothing her sleeves with feigned ease, expression composed.

"I'll need time to make myself presentable," she said, like this was about formality, not about buying time. "Tell the Vizier I'll be there shortly."

The messenger gave a curt nod. "As you wish." He turned a bit too rigidly and marched himself awkwardly out of the arena.

Kaden huffed a breath, shaking his head as he stepped toward the weapons rack. He slid the training sword back into place, the wood settling against the others with a dull clack. He knew her. Knew exactly what she was doing. Sure enough, when he turned back, she was already watching him with that expectant look of hers, like she still had the upper hand in a fight that had already ended.

He let out a slow breath, raking a hand through his hair. The strands were damp from exertion, sticking at the edges where the heat of the fight still clung to him. He should've been annoyed. Maybe find some way to wipe that look off her face, a smirk, a remark, something to remind her that he wasn't so easily bested.

But he wasn't annoyed.

Because he knew what that look meant.

Lusa wasn't in a hurry to leave. She might've been the one summoned, but she was stretching the moment, their time together, the same way he was. Maybe it shouldn't have made something shift inside him. But it did.

CHAPTER 5

Somethin' to Remember Me

Kaden followed Lusa through the palace's quiet halls, his steps unhurried, as if he could stretch the minutes between now and goodbye.

She walked beside him, her fingers toying with the parchment from the Grand Vizier's summons, but he could tell she wasn't really thinking about it. And if he was being honest, neither was he.

He should've left already. Should've been making his own preparations, tending to the reality waiting for him beyond these walls. But two days. That was all he had left. And right now, there wasn't anywhere he wanted to be more than here.

Lusa glanced at him, blue eyes skimming over his face in that way that always made him feel seen.

"So," she said finally, voice soft, as if the air around them might steal the words before they could land. "You and the Empress. How exactly are you her cousin?"

Kaden sighed, adjusting the cuff of his sleeve. "My mother was her grandfather's sister."

Taking a few understandable seconds to piece that together, Lusa tilted her head. "So… distant cousins."

They reached the grand staircase leading to the second level. She gathered the thin layers of her gown, lifting them enough to keep from stepping on the fabric. He tried not to smirk. He knew how much she hated wearing the damn things. But if he was being honest, she could've shown up in rags and she still would've been the most striking thing in the palace.

"Right," he said, watching her out of the corner of his eye. "My mother was the second princess of the Imperial Court."

Lusa frowned slightly, still working through the family tree. "Then… your father?"

His thumb worked over a knuckle. "Aeonian noble. One'a the high families in Anadine, but not royalty." The words tasted bitter. It had been decades. He should've moved on, but saying it aloud still cut. "Didn't matter though. To the elves, he was still too good for a human."

Elves guarded their Resonance like griffins guard their young—talons out, ready to shred anything that tried to touch it. That Resonance was their lifeblood, the current that tied them to the Aeon, and they didn't share it lightly.

She shot him a sharp glance at the injustice of it. They reached the next set of stairs. "They didn't approve."

Kaden let out a dry chuckle. "Understatement. Their bloodlines are sacred. Even the nobles see themselves above mixin' with humans. Wouldn't wanna taint all that perfect Resonance, right? So, when my father fell for my mother, it was a disgrace. A scandal."

Absorbing that in silence, they continued up the stairs. He could practically feel the gears turning in her mind. The hunted mage, now a symbol of power. A world that didn't want her but was learning it needed her. She of all people would understand him most.

"They married anyway," he continued, rubbing the back of his neck. "My mother gave up her title ta' be with him. Left the court. She chose him over everythin' else."

They reached the next landing, and Lusa slowed, taking a few breaths. Kaden arched a brow, smirk forming before he could stop it. "You alright there, love?"

She shot him a glare, straightening immediately. "Fine."

"Could've taken the lift."

"Shut it."

He chuckled, watching as she collected herself before pushing forward. She let the silence stretch between them for a few steps, then continued feeding her curiosity to know his life story. If it had been anyone else, he would've minded.

"And your father?"

"Left."

Lusa's brows furrowed, but she didn't press him. Just waited. Gave him space to speak. If he were being honest with himself, he was ready to end the conversation. Normally, he would've derailed it with ease—toss in a jest, redirect smoothly, shut it down altogether. He'd done it a thousand times before. But when he glanced at her, about to do just that, something stopped him.

Sunlight spilled through one of the arched windows, catching in her hair, warming the smooth lines of her face. And for a fleeting moment, she looked like she belonged among the imperial portraits lining the grand corridor—something untouchable.

Then her eyes met his and in them, no expectation, only earnest curiosity.

She wanted to know him.

Not his title. Not his reputation. Not the tangled mess of stories whispered in the halls of Izier.

Him.

And for the first time in his life, Kaden felt like someone was worthy of knowing.

"At first, he stayed. My mother raised me in the outskirts of Anadine, but we visited Izier when she was allowed. For a while, it seemed like they could live with the choice they made." His voice dropped. "But the court never let 'em forget."

Lusa nodded and paused on the next landing, taking a few more measured breaths. He shook his head, biting back another chuckle. The sparring had taken its toll, but Evenlore help her, she was stubborn. She loathed the lifts—despised them, really—and despite the clear exhaustion dragging at her, she had still chosen four flights of stairs over the easy route.

The moment she caught him watching, she straightened, cleared her throat like she wasn't winded at all, and pushed forward, chin high, determined to conquer the last set of steps before reaching her floor.

Typical Lusa. Defiant to the last step. And damn if he didn't admire her for it.

"But he left?" she asked, gathering more fabric in her hands, bracing for the final stretch of stairs with a slight sway.

Kaden thrust out a hand, convinced she was about to trip. She cast him a side-eye, and he casually folded his arms behind him like he hadn't just expected her to go sprawling across the stone.

"He stayed long enough ta' be called a fool," Kaden answered. "But the nobles saw him as weak for stayin' with her. Eventually, he started ta' believe it. So, he left to try and regain his standin'." He let out a slow breath, his lips twisting into something humorless. "Didn't work. The Aeonian court still saw him as the fool who sullied his bloodline."

Something flickered over Lusa's face. Quick. Sharp. Anger, maybe. He almost wondered if the Magics stirred in her veins. But as fast as it came, she mastered it, smoothing her expression back to neutrality. "And your mother?"

Kaden swallowed, following some dust specks as they floated in the air, lit by the warm sunlight. "She died."

The word caught in his throat like it had teeth.

Lusa went quiet, only the soft pat of footsteps on the stairs filling the silence, before she said, "And so you became a bounty hunter."

It wasn't a question. He admired her intelligence, her ability to put things together and have the confidence to follow through.

"Yeah." He glanced at her. "That was thirty years ago."

Lusa's lips parted slightly, but the reaction wasn't only sympathy or understanding. A hint of something else… something hesitant. A grimace. Barely there, but he caught it. She recovered quickly, but he knew better. He knew exactly what thought had flashed through her mind.

Thirty years.

To her, that probably sounded like an entire lifetime. Because it was. Kaden didn't look thirty years older than her, but he was over eighty, his elven blood keeping him frozen somewhere between youth and eternity. And in that moment, he saw the briefest flicker of uncertainty in her gaze. It wasn't about who he was, or even what they were—only what they could never be. The thought clawed at something inside him, an ache he didn't know what to do with.

They reached her floor, and her expression softened again. Understanding. Clarity. She knew what it was like to be caught between worlds, never fully belonging to either. She'd also lost everything and been left to figure out what the hell to do with herself. Kaden looked at her… really looked at her, and the weight of it all pressed down at once.

How do you say goodbye to someone who became your world before you realized it?

They had fought together. Bled together. Survived a wicked sorcerer hell-bent on destroying them. For nearly a year, they had moved through this world as a unit. A balance. And in two days, that would be gone.

The thought wound its way beneath his ribs, impossible to ignore. His boots scuffed lightly against the stone as they neared her chamber, and from the corner of his eye he caught movement. A palace servant rounded the corridor, arms full of linens, disappearing through an open doorway and out of sight. No one else. The halls were empty.

Kaden's pulse quickened. Two days left. He should walk away. Say something easy, casual, forgettable.

But that was the problem. He didn't want to be forgotten.

Not as a shadow at her side. Not as the half-elf who fought next to her. He wanted to be remembered—etched into her like a scar, something that stayed. His breath left slow and tight as he rubbed the back of his neck, restraint fraying with every heartbeat. He met her gaze. Her lips parted, like she might speak. That was all it took. The fight died there.

"Ta' hell with it."

He grabbed her wrist and pulled her in. Lusa gasped, but the sound barely left her lips before his mouth was on hers. Soft. Warm. Everything.

Her whole body went still in a moment of uncertainty. But then her fingers curled against his chest, and she gave in, melting into his body.

It nearly undid him.

He angled his head, deepening the kiss, drinking her in like she was something rare, something precious, something he would never get enough of.

This wasn't just a kiss. It was a way to leave something of himself with her. A way to memorize her shape without ever touching her the way he truly wanted. Kaden slid his fingers along the curve of her jaw, his thumb tracing the soft plane of her cheek.

He wanted to remember everything—how she felt beneath his hands, the way her breath hitched when he pulled her closer, the slight tremor in her fingers as they fisted in his tunic. Every part of him screamed to take more, to claim what had never been his to begin with. Stopping was suddenly the hardest thing he'd ever done. She wasn't his to keep.

The thought pierced through the fog of his desires and his grip slackened, lips slowing against hers. He tried drawing out the moment like he could somehow make it last longer before reality crept in, forcing him to breathe through the fire in his chest and do what he should… let go.

He barely pulled away, his forehead against hers. Their breaths tangled, shallow and unsteady in the silence. Lusa's eyes were still closed, lips parted like she wasn't ready to let go either. Kaden brushed his thumb across her cheek, one last stolen touch before finally stepping back.

"Somethin' ta' remember me by," he murmured.

Slowly, Lusa's lashes lifted. She blinked up at him, dazed, breathless. Beautiful.

It took all he had not to close in again and let himself forget everything except the way she felt in his arms, how she looked at him like she saw past every wall he'd ever built. He could easily give in to the reckless, selfish part of him that wanted to keep her here, in this moment, where the rest of the world didn't exist.

But he didn't. He had to walk away. Now. Before he found himself lost in her again, with no way out. The decision should have been simple. It wasn't.

Duty had to come first and whatever lay ahead would demand everything he had left to give. Besides, giving in now would only make it harder if one of them didn't make it back. Lusa had already lost too much. He wouldn't be the reason she lost more.

He hesitated long enough for the moment to become something more, something unfinished, then turned and walked away.

Whether or not he'd made the right decision, he knew this much—no distance, no war, no god of the Aether would keep him from finding her again.

CHAPTER 6

Marked by Passion, Claimed by Power

Lusa barely heard the door click behind her as she pressed her back against it, breath uneven, heart pounding so hard it drummed in her ears. Her palms flattened against the wood, and she let out a slow breath. For half a minute, all she could do was stand there, replaying whatever had just happened between them. The warmth of his hands, the press of his lips, a ghost of a touch lingering in a way that made her stomach flip.

Her fingers drifted to her mouth, tracing the path he'd left behind. Not their first kiss… but if the first had been a spark, this was the full force of a wildfire. She'd already fallen for him, had known it for longer than she wanted to admit, but survival had always come first. Love had no place in wreckage. And yet, in that moment, he'd kissed her like she was more than fate's cruel joke. Like she was his.

Lusa squeezed her eyes shut, trying to carve the memory into herself so she could call it back whenever she wanted: the way Kaden had looked at her like he was memorizing her, his fingers tracing the curve of her jaw, gentle but certain.

Her pulse stuttered at the thought. A pang of something too vast tightened inside her chest. She exhaled and forced herself to move. Arcturius was waiting, and she wasn't even sure why. Was it about the mission? Her magic? Something else? She didn't have the patience to dwell on the possibilities.

Pushing away from the door, she strode toward the basin in the corner, dipping a cloth into the cool water and pressing it against the back of her neck. The contrast of chilled water against overheated skin sent a shiver through her. She pressed it to her collarbone, trying to will away the residual heat.

There was no time for Nem and Tessa to help her dress, and she wasn't about to call them. Whatever she wore had to be something she could manage alone. Her gaze swept over the wardrobe, lips pressing into a thin line.

She barely had the strength to lift her arms, let alone wrestle with buttons or laces. Damn Kaden and his training. Every inch of her ached, a dull reminder of how hard he'd pushed her. As if Recalibration wasn't brutal enough on its own. It always left her body heavy, her magic sluggish. The instructors at the Temple used to say a mage's core simply needed rest. If that were true, hers had clearly missed the lesson.

With a sigh, she reached for the simplest gown she owned: charcoal-blue, fitted at the bodice and loose at the hem. Practical enough, and more importantly, something she could fasten herself.

By the time she'd switched into a less damp, more fresh attire, her mind was still trailing in places it shouldn't. She should be focusing on the meeting ahead, the mission, the weight of everything waiting for her beyond this door. Instead, all she could think about was Kaden and the way he'd kissed her like he was leaving a claim.

She swallowed hard, shoving the thought away.

Their relationship had been anything but simple. A tumultuous, awkward beginning tangled in mistrust and necessity. But despite everything, she'd come to trust him. More than that… he had become the one constant in a world that had stripped her of everything. For nearly a year, he had been at her side. Every day. Every night. Always there. She didn't know what going through a day without him would feel like. But she had a pretty good idea.

Desolation, deep and dark in the pit of her stomach. The one she'd been slowly crawling out of since the dust of survival had settled into something resembling normalcy. Since she'd let herself believe, even for a moment, that she wasn't completely alone.

Lusa strode toward the door, forcing her mind back to where it needed to be… preparing for whatever awaited her with Arcturius. She reached for the knob, wrapped her fingers around the handle—

Pain struck like a blade through her skull, white-hot and merciless. Her vision fractured. Knees buckled. A breath caught halfway to a scream, devoured by the Magics rushing in to claim her as she fell.

Her body convulsed, nerves firing until she lost track of where the pain began. The Magics roared, a chorus of hunger and scorn, tearing through her mind with a ferocity that nearly broke her. She clutched her chest as her core reignited with a rush of raw energy, forcing its way through every vein. Recalibration had never been agony. Not like this. The Magics twisted it, sure, but something else burned beneath—something new.

The agony and voices ebbed with a slow, clawing drag, as if They were reluctant to let go. Each breath came ragged, hard-won. Her limbs trembled as the world slowly began to stitch itself back together.

When she came back to herself, she was on her side, cheek pressed against the cool stone. The world was sluggish, slow to take shape. Lusa braced for the next wave, but the Magics didn't surge again. In Their pause, she felt something else.

She narrowed her eyes at the door inches from her face and pressed a hand to her chest again. Fingers twitched at the strange sensation beneath her ribs. A knot of heaviness, swirling there, like she'd eaten one too many blossomfire toffees. Two currents moved there now, twisting in opposition.

Lusa wiped the taste of blood from her mouth and growled under her breath. No time for questions. If the Magics were holding, she'd take the reprieve no matter how temporary it felt.

CHAPTER 7

Treatise of the Dual Flame

Lusa stood at the threshold of the Grand Vizier's study, her shadow stretching long across the intricate rug. The guards flanking the heavy doors barely acknowledged her, before returning their attention to the dimly lit corridor. The scent of burning tallow and old parchment clung to the air, but not as thick as the silence that filled the space between them.

With a steadying breath, she stepped forward. Her limbs still trembled faintly from the morning's long training. She squared her shoulders and took in this new space.

The study was vast; its walls lined with towering shelves groaning under centuries of knowledge. Scrolls and tomes, bound in cracked leather and gold-stamped vellum, filled every inch of shelf space. A grand desk of dark oak stood at its heart, adorned with ledgers, maps, and an astrolabe that gleamed in the candlelight.

Arcturius stood by the arched window, hands clasped behind his back, his gaze on the city sprawled below. Now that her Magics had returned, Lusa could feel the Weave. Somewhere beyond those walls, the ley network hummed. The Citadels had called it the Aeon's breath, the invisible rhythm that fed every spell. She remembered studying the patterns at the Temple when she was younger, before the massacre had made survival the only lesson that mattered.

The dying light of day cast long shadows across the room, gilding the edges of his robes. "You're late." He didn't turn.

The Magics hissed, curling in the corners of her mind. Irritation needled beneath her skin. "I was—"

"It does not matter."

Only then did he face her. His pale gaze flicked over her, pausing ever so briefly at her eyes. She figured, based on that look, he knew They'd returned. Or at least, he suspected.

"Sit." He gestured to the chair opposite his desk.

Though her limbs dragged and her thoughts felt smeared thin, she followed his request. Something in Their presence had altered… subtle, unnamable. And not knowing what had changed disturbed her more than the change itself.

Arcturius lowered himself into his chair, tapping a single finger against the polished wood before pulling open a drawer. He withdrew a crystal suspended in delicate filigree, its facets catching the flickering candlelight, scattering shards of gold across the table.

The amulet.

"Take it."

Lusa's body jolted instinctively. Fingers twitched. Even drained, she could feel its pull like an artery connecting straight to the Aeon's heart. The amulet wasn't just power; it was memory, probably forged when the Capstones were first raised to anchor the world's magical flow.

Her breath caught in her throat as her hand rose against her will. She bit the insides of her cheeks, in an effort to stop the Magics and Their relentless hunger for power.

They seared her thoughts with commands, chaining her mind in iron will. Her trembling fingers stretched toward the crystal against her better judgement.

Take it. It's yours. The words were a hiss, a chorus, a crown of fire pressing against her thoughts. The Magics did not plead. They promised.

Her vision blurred. The world around her—the desk, the candlelight, even Arcturius—faded into shadow. And in that darkened space, she saw herself. Not as she was, but as They wanted her to be. A great dark sorceress, cloaked in black flame and crowned in starlight. Her presence warped the air itself. Her voice broke realms. Armies bent the knee not out of loyalty, but fear. Her hand rose, and the skies obeyed. Magic bled from her in molten rivers. Boundless. Terrible. Exquisite.

And in the heart of that illusion… she felt something dangerous stir. A part of her, deep and hidden, wanted it. To be more than hunted. To be worshipped. To never be powerless again. It was intoxicating, that glimpse of grandeur. Of becoming untouchable. Of never feeling the ache of loss, or the sting of betrayal, or the weight of helplessness ever again.

The Magics pushed harder. Her hand inched closer. Her breath came shallow and fast, heart thundering beneath her ribs. She was unraveling. Slipping. Almost gone.

But somewhere beneath Their roar, something stirred. It didn't feel like strength she'd summoned. More like something slipped inside her—a presence not Theirs, but not hers either. It rose from her sternum, where her core lived, a thread of stillness woven through the madness. It wasn't loud enough to silence the Magics, but it was strong enough to push back.

The vision faded. The shadows around her crumbled. Her hand froze mid-reach, twitching as if caught between two worlds: the one They offered, and the one she had fought to survive. The Magics shrieked in her mind, thrashing against this new resistance, but They couldn't break it. That strange sensation keeping Them back held firm in her chest.

Her hand fell to her lap. The Magics recoiled, spitting and howling in fury. Denied. Lusa took several beats to collect herself before meeting the Grand Vizier's gaze.

This had to be a trap. A test. A game.

She stared at the old man, waiting for the catch, the moment his mask would slip. But there was no smugness, no challenge. Only patience.

Lusa inhaled, slow and careful, making sure she had the Magics in check before she spoke. "Why?"

The amulet hung between them, this tempting thing of power, and he didn't answer right away. Even if the Magics hadn't been with her, she'd be infuriated.

"I gave that back after the ceremony."

"Yes," he said, setting it on the center of his desk.

Her hands curled in her lap. "I don't trust myself with it." The words grated like sand against her throat, but she forced them out. "And now you're offering it to me?"

"I am."

"But why?"

"Because it is yours."

She shook her head. "No. It belonged to the Eye of Plymus. It was part of the scepter. And the scepter—" She stopped.

The scepter had vanished after the Glorious Ones had been summoned. Yet the amulet had remained. Somehow, through the chaos of their transport to the citadels, it had returned to Kaden. She still wasn't sure how. And then she had taken it. Done what was necessary to rid Aetherealm of Lazorious… and Atraun.

The mere thought of that name was enough to tear open what little she'd managed to stitch shut. Atraun—the hollowed husk that had been her mother once known as

Izabel, twisted and devoured by the Magics until nothing remained. Lusa had been the one to end it. The one to strike her down. A raw ache rose, but the Magics swallowed it whole, stripping it of its weight.

Arcturius leaned back, steepling his fingers, his gaze keen. "Something has changed in you."

Lusa swallowed hard and studied this man who wore wisdom like armor, who seemed to hold the knowledge of centuries behind his pale, knowing eyes. She'd wanted to trust him after he pulled her from the dungeons and offered her a future: hero or executioner's noose. But some part of her kept listening for the condition tucked between his words.

Lusa scanned his features, seeking some sign of his true age. But that was as fruitless as trying to guess how long Glon had been guarding a door.

"I don't know," she finally answered his question.

"You feel different," Arcturius mused, watching her closely. "Describe it to me."

Lusa hesitated, chewing at her lower lip. How could she explain something she didn't understand? The Magics had tried to take her. They tried to hollow her out again, the way They had before… but something had pushed back. Not with fury or more darkness but with… stillness?

"It wasn't like before," she said slowly. "They wanted the amulet. I saw what They wanted me to become." Her jaw clenched, shame and awe warring. "And I almost wanted it, too."

She dragged in a breath. "But something stopped Them. It wasn't me. At least, I don't think it was." Her gaze flicked to Arcturius, uncertain. "There was... something else. Like a thread pulling me back. Just enough to remember who I am."

She looked down at her hands. "I don't know what it was. But it didn't belong to Them."

Arcturius studied her longer than felt comfortable. With measured movements, he pulled a leather-bound book from a stack beside him, flipping through its pages.

"I read your debriefing." His voice was steady, calm, as his eyes searched the text. "Yours and Kaden's."

Lusa's pulse jumped, though she kept her expression neutral. After recovering, her, Kaden, and Vallas were instructed to write everything they could remember that had taken place during their quest. While part of it felt therapeutic, most of it was like ripping open an old wound and pouring salt over it.

"You wrote of the battle at the Citadels," Arcturius continued, finding the page he sought. "You and Kaden activated the Eye of Plymus together. But that wasn't the only time you wielded the amulet, was it?" He looked up at her.

Lusa looked away, her mind racing back to the Citadels. The memories pressed in with pristine clarity of Kaden, cold and lifeless, on the floor. The world had fallen away in that moment; her screams ripped from her throat as hatred for the Magics surged through her. Remembering it still felt like reliving it. She pressed her eyes shut and let out a slow breath, hoping the ache in her chest might ease with it.

The amulet had done something in that second of despair. An unfamiliar, overwhelming warmth had bloomed inside her. She hadn't spoken a spell. A light as bright as the sun had simply rushed from her, into him, pulling him back from death before she'd collapsed beside him.

Arcturius watched her closely. "You wielded something outside of Dark Magic that day."

Lusa's head was shaking before she could get the words out. "It was the amulet. It was a Source. I had to use it."

After a thoughtful pause, Arcturius turned to the shelf behind him. He ran a finger along the spines, then pulled out another worn leather-bound volume and placed it before her. He flipped it to a ribbon-marked page and turned it to her. Faded ink scrolled the top: 'Treatise of the Dual Flame'. Without a word, he tapped a passage halfway down the page.

When Light and Dark as one align,
The path shall wake the wrath divine.
If balance rests in one alone,
The chain shall crack, the seed be sown.
From rift and ruin, all shall break—
Until the Aeon's heart awakes.

She wanted to scoff, to call it superstition, but the lines carried a foreboding that sank deep into her sternum. Something in her core responded there, faint as breath, but she had no idea what any of it meant.

"A Dark Mage bearing Light magic has not been heard of in… any recorded history," Arcturius said.

Lusa stared at the words, willing them to mean something else. She couldn't stop shaking her head. It had to have been the amulet. The Source was powerful. More powerful than anything she had ever wielded. It had saved Kaden. It had shielded them through the storm. That's all it could've been. One was either a Light Mage or a Dark Mage, determined at birth. It was impossible to be both.

But the feeling inside her told her otherwise.

She shoved the book back toward him. "You don't know anything for certain."

A ghost of a smile crossed his face. "No," he admitted. "I don't."

"Then why lead me in riddles?"

"Because you are the only one who can answer this question." He gestured at the amulet on the desk. "That crystal has had few wielders throughout history. It has amplified power, aided battles, and chosen those it deemed worthy. But never has it done what it did with you."

"And what exactly do you think it did with me?"

Arcturius leaned back in his chair. "I think you need to decide for yourself what you believe."

Her gaze flicked back to the Source. Had it accepted her? The Magics stirred instantly, flowing like poison through her veins. Her fingers hovered above the crystal, and They pressed forward. *Ours. Take it.*

Tentatively, she allowed her fingers to brush the crystal. No burn. No rejection. It was cool against her skin, deceptively light for something so powerful. But more than that, something pulsed beneath its surface like a whisper of recognition.

"You must learn to wield Light Magic properly."

Lusa froze. The words didn't make sense. They sounded absurd. "I was trained—"

"Not in what you are now." He leaned forward; his tone edged with conviction. "You were raised in secret. A Dark Mage pretending to be Light. Taught to hide. But the Citadels do not need a hidden mage, Lusa. They need a master."

She glanced down at the amulet, fingers tightening around it. "I don't even know if the Magi still exist."

She didn't have to explain the distinction. Everyone knew it… or had at one point. Mages like her were only wielders, scattered and hunted. But the Magi… they were something older, closer to the Aeon's design. The highest order of their kind.

Arcturius tilted his head. "Then you will find out."

Something in the finality of his voice chilled her.

"Do you still have your *Book of Magics*?"

"Of course."

"Good." His tone softened the slightest. "You will spend the next few days studying it. Your Light spells must be as strong as your Dark. It is the only way to master what has changed within you."

She shifted in her seat. "You sound certain that I'll need them."

"I am."

The fire in the hearth crackled, embers flaring in a brief golden burst before settling. Its warmth failed to penetrate the cold dread seeping into her bones. "Even if the Magi are gone, what does that mean for the Citadels? For me?"

"If you are truly the last, then you are more than a relic of a lost order. You are its future."

She scoffed. "A future of what? Hiding? Running? Being hunted?"

"No." He stood from his chair and moved back to look out at Anora. "A future of rebuilding."

Lusa ran her tongue over her teeth, slightly opening her fingers to study the amulet's imperfect surface, its once-white crystal now dulled with sand-colored edges. It felt different now. Not just a tool or a pretty adornment. It had accepted her without pain… without resistance.

"You truly believe there are others?"

"I believe in magic," Arcturius said. "And I believe power is never lost. Only transformed."

"This shouldn't be possible," she murmured.

"And yet, it is."

Her grip tightened. "Why?"

"Perhaps the better question, Lusa, is not why, but how."

"Stop answering me in riddles," she snapped, rising frustration thick in her voice. Her temples throbbed as the Dark Magics tittered at the sidelines, eager for a crack in her restraint.

He didn't flinch at her defiance. In fact, he seemed to be waiting for it. "You are not merely a Dark Mage trying to balance Light," he said. "You are something else entirely."

Lusa dragged a hand over her face, the weight of everything pressing against her like too much armor.

"You'll leave for the Citadels soon," he continued. "But until then, you will train. Prepare yourself for what is to come."

"And what exactly is coming?"

"The Citadels were never meant to be abandoned. Mages were never meant to fade into myth. The Aether always seeks equilibrium; the Aeon only dreams of being whole again. That dream is stirring, and the world will follow its pull—with or without you. And when it does, Lusa, it will not ask permission before taking what it wants."

CHAPTER 8

Tidebound

New clothes at last.

Lusa ran her palms down the front of the dark, near-black tunic, and sighed content. After everything she'd survived, leave it to a change of wardrobe—one that didn't involve silk or lace—to lift her mood past brooding.

Glon's sister had finally delivered it. The fabric was sturdy, fitted, made for movement. No more pretending. She rolled her shoulders, flexed her fingers, and let the grounding simplicity settle over her. She hadn't seen Kaden except for the occasional glance in the corridors or a brief nod in the council chamber.

Stepping back from the mirror, she gathered herself, aware of how much had changed since the Citadel. She'd pulled her hair into a single braid, a few stubborn strands slipping free to frame her face. Good. Let the court see her not as some delicate ornament swathed in silk, but as the mage who had faced down Lazorious and survived. Let them see the scars, the steel. This was who she was now… wasn't it?

She wasn't sure if the sour edge in her chest came from sheer exhaustion from training, from too many days pretending to be something she wasn't, or if the Magics, with

Their sneering disdain for courtly games, were starting to shape her more than she dared admit.

The amulet sat on her end table, its sand-colored crystal dulled, but no less potent. She reached for it and looped the chain over her head. It settled against her chest, comforting. She glanced toward the door. It was time.

She hated goodbyes. The drawn-out kind. The silent kind. The ones that stole your chance to speak. At least this time, she would get to say something. That was more than she'd had with her mother… gone one day without a trace, and when reunited, she was no longer herself. Just a puppet, eyes blackened, voice no longer her own but Theirs.

Lusa stepped into the corridor and moved quickly, unwilling to let herself dwell. Her boots struck the stone in steady rhythm as she approached the stairs leading to the departure hall. Whatever grand name the court had given it, it didn't matter. Soon, he would be gone.

She reached the landing and paused, drawing in a breath as the nearest lift groaned to life with a mechanical hiss. Lusa glanced over her shoulder as the lift doors opened and out stepped Kaden.

The platform wobbled as he stepped off and made way towards her, all shadow and silhouette. He looked like the bounty hunter she'd first met in the swamplands of Nardonia—lean muscle and sharp lines, cloak slung over one shoulder, twin blades crossed at his back. His tunic sleeves were rolled to the elbow, faint scars along his forearms catching in the sunlight from the windows.

"I was already coming down." The words came out short and clipped before she caught herself. She winced internally. It wasn't fair, not to him. But it was already done. And it wasn't anything he hadn't dealt with before.

Kaden didn't flinch, but his smirk faded, and he dipped his gaze to the amulet. "They're back."

The amulet had never been meant for her. Empress Nolanna had pressed it into Kaden's hands, but when Lusa wore it, the relic had split its power between them—unnatural, impossible. In the end, it had chosen her outright. Its weight now pressed against her chest like a verdict, no less potent for the way it had defied its intended bearer.

The Magics churned behind her eyes, restless and bitter. She could feel Them watching, waiting, Their contempt bleeding into every thought. She was too tired to mask it. Too worn down to care if he saw.

His gaze locked onto hers, and she couldn't look away. Not for the color—she knew every fleck of amber and brown—but for the intensity behind it. A quiet ache. An unspoken goodbye. And in her own eyes, she knew the same thing burned back at him… only now, it was laced with something darker.

"Figured I'd catch ya before ya got down there. Need to give ya somethin'."

She raised a skeptical brow, glad he chose not to linger on the subject of the Magics, though her stomach betrayed her with a flutter. Her cheeks warmed as the memory of their last kiss sparked.

She cleared her throat. "What is it?"

He reached into the inside of his cloak, pulling out a small bundle wrapped in dark cloth. She didn't realize she'd stopped breathing until he unfolded it.

A silver shimmer appeared in his hands, delicate gypsophila blossoms shaped into a hairpin, each petal touched with marcasite that caught the torchlight like morning dew.

The pin from the festival.

"You—" she started, breathless.

"I saw the way you looked at it," he said quietly.

Caught between disbelief, affection, and the sudden warmth behind her eyes she refused to let fall, she blinked.

"Kaden… it's beautiful."

But the moment her fingers reached toward it, the Magics went frantic… instinctive, volatile, recoiling. A jolt of pain knifed through her temples. Her hand flinched away before she could stop it. The hairpin hadn't touched her, but the Magics had already screamed in protest.

"It's more than a hairpin now," he said, stepping closer. "I've imbued it with a ward."

The Magics hissed in her head. Kaden brushed a few loose strands from her temple. "No one's gonna touch ye'r mind again. Not while I'm breathin'."

He didn't explain further. Her breath turned shallow as her mind raced back to the Citadels. Lazorious pressing inside her skull, twisting her will, using her like a puppet. The way it had felt like drowning in her own power, being helpless, no control over anything she was doing.

She stood still beneath Kaden's touch, watching his face and the way his eyes softened as he searched for the right spot to place it. His fingers worked carefully, adjusting her braid and fastening the pin in place.

The shift was immediate.

The Magics fell silent, as though several walls had slammed into place between Them and her thoughts. She could still sense Them—restless, unsettled—but Their voices no longer screamed. They barely whispered. The sudden quiet rang louder than Their fury.

Her body slackened before she realized it, shoulders easing from a tension she hadn't noticed she was holding.

Kaden's knuckles grazed the scar on her cheek, intentional or not, and her pulse thudded beneath the surface. The closeness unraveled something in her, just like it always did, no matter how many times she tried to build a wall against it. She could feel his breath, the pull of him strong and sure as gravity. She wanted to close the distance. To feel his mouth on hers. To drown in it once more before the world demanded its due.

She tilted almost imperceptibly closer, breath caught, waiting for the inevitable. But instead of claiming her mouth, Kaden bent and pressed a kiss to her forehead… gentle, reverent, maddening in its restraint.

He stepped back, and Lusa held his gaze. Something in her chest clenched, hollow and full all at once, and she understood. A kiss like the one she wanted would only make the leaving worse.

She followed him without a word, her footsteps falling in line with his as they made their way toward the lift. She hated the thing—the enclosed space, the slow descent, the creak of ropes and gears—but she stepped inside with him anyway.

The silence between them settled heavy, but not uncomfortable. There was nothing left to say that would make any of this easier. The platform jerked as the ropes engaged, and on instinct, her hand snatched his, fingers entwining tight.

Kaden didn't look at her or speak. He simply closed his fingers around hers and held on. They remained like that for the entire descent. It wasn't a goodbye, but a pause. Or maybe that was the lie she needed to survive it.

When the lift settled at the base level with a soft clunk, Lusa reluctantly let go. The pulley crew stood nearby, their eyes respectfully averted, but the moment was broken all the same. She stepped off the platform, adjusting her sleeves to give her hands something to do.

When they emerged into the palace courtyard, the wind had picked up, tugging at the hem of Lusa's tunic and slapping loose strands of her braid across her face. The sky was a clear, brilliant blue, but gusts howled through the open arches. The day felt too bright for goodbyes.

The convoy had already begun to assemble at the gates. Elven riders in pale silver armor stood beside their sleek, horned steeds, their expressions hidden beneath helms. Near the center of the formation stood Caelithia, envoy of the Aeonian Throne, her moonlit hair catching the sunlight like a frost-woven banner. She spoke to two of her guards in crisp, fluid Elvish, her posture precise and her attention fixed on her own kind. She didn't even spare a glance toward the humans.

Arcturius stood a short distance from the steps, speaking quietly with Empress Nolanna, their silhouettes motionless against the gleaming marble. And just beyond them, standing alone, was General Vallas. His arms were folded behind his back; his calculating gaze fixed on the elven column. The wind pressed against his cloak, revealing the rigid set of his shoulders.

Kaden moved toward the convoy without a word, and Lusa didn't stop him. They both knew anything spoken now would only make it harder, so she remained at the edge of the courtyard, hands curled into fists at her sides, watching as he checked the straps of his pack on Brogan.

The elven riders mounted in unison, their formation tightening like a drawn bow. Kaden spoke to one of the Aeonian soldiers, his brow furrowed, his gestures controlled. Every motion was purposeful. Efficient. Professional.

It made her want to scream.

The wind lifted again, tugging at her braid and biting at her cheeks as she continued watching from the shadows of the palace archway, her chest a knot of hollow ache and smoldering resentment.

Fine. That's what she'd tell herself. That it was duty. Purpose. Not abandonment. But none of that stopped the sting or the heat burning behind her eyes.

A sudden, familiar slap on her shoulder made her jolt.

"On to the next chapter," Glon said, his voice too light to be casual and too kind to be careless. "At least you still got me, Lus."

She didn't respond and Glon didn't press. He stood beside her, a good foot taller, arms crossed as if daring the wind to try something.

She stayed a little longer until the pain in her chest hardened. The Magics stirred, and despite the hairpin's dulling presence, anger spiked. She didn't want to watch him ride away. She didn't want to stand there like some wounded girl carved in silence while everyone else moved forward.

With a sharp breath, Lusa turned, moving toward the far corner of the courtyard where a stableboy held the reins of a saddled horse. She reached for them without pause.

"Hey—!" he started, but she was already swinging into the saddle.

The horse reared slightly, then bolted forward under her command, and she didn't look back. Lusa urged the horse faster, wind tearing past her as she pushed north, back to the ocean. Back to her one place of silence, where no one could see her fall apart.

The ride blurred. Trees. Stone. Wind. All of it streaked past in a whirl of motion and cold. Lusa pushed the horse harder with every mile, her jaw clenched so tight it throbbed. The sting of thin branches slapped across her arms and cheeks, but she didn't flinch. Didn't slow. Her vision tunneled into a single point ahead: open sky, open water, away from goodbyes.

By the time the forest thinned, and the northern shoreline opened before her, her pulse was a hammer beat behind her ribs, breath ragged. She flung herself from the saddle before the horse's hooves hit sand. The animal reared, startled by her sudden dismount, but she didn't care. She didn't even look. Her boots struck the damp shore, sinking slightly, and she screamed, releasing the rage consuming her.

It tore from the pit of her stomach, up through her lungs, scraping her throat as it escaped. Grief twisted into fury, and fury had nowhere to go but out. Her hands flew upward with no thought, no control. Desperate release.

Lightning burst from her palms with the force of a sky splitting open.

It struck the ocean with a violent crack, sending spray and steam hissing into the air. The horse shrieked and bolted, vanishing into the grove without a backward glance.

Lusa sank to her knees, chest heaving, hands shaking, smoke curling from her fingertips.

She stared at the ocean where the lightning had kissed the waves, leaving no lasting scar. Rage still simmered low in her belly, but her arms sagged. Her breath came in uneven pulls, and to her shame, she realized her cheeks were wet.

She swiped at the tears with the heel of her hand and dragged in a rough breath, pulling air thick with salt into her nose, trying to calm herself. She wiped at her nose before clenching a fistful of sand and tilted her face skyward.

The second scream came raw, hoarse, barely more than breath and broken sound. It hollowed her out.

Everything had been taken from her.

The Temple. The truth. The Magics her mother had sworn were meant to protect, twisted into chains. The Academy had raised her to be one thing—bright, hopeful, Light—and in secret, her mother had trained her to be something else.

Then came the massacre. Blood and fire. Her hands. Her sentient magic. She'd been manipulated, controlled, and was just as responsible for the deaths. Everyone she'd ever known was either dead or had betrayed her. The rest of the world hated her, had hunted her for what she was. And even now, those who stood by her barely trusted her.

Except for Kaden.

And Glon, maybe.

But Kaden was gone. She was so tired of pretending this path was one she'd chosen. Lowering her head again with her eyes closed, she felt the wind push against her face. The Magics stirred at the edges of her mind, and even though the hairpin muffled Their voices, They didn't speak. Maybe They were satisfied. Maybe They pitied her. Maybe They were simply waiting.

Whatever it was, it didn't matter. She was alone again. And she didn't know what to do with it.

She didn't know how long she sat there, fists buried in the sand, eyes locked on the place where lightning had struck the sea. But eventually, the fire in her veins dulled, replaced by a quiet emptiness that made her feel too heavy to move.

The waves lapped against the shore in rhythmic hushes, pulling and pressing with ancient patience. Slowly, Lusa pulled off her boots, shoving them aside, and let her toes sink into the cool grit of wet sand. The ground was soft here, uneven with tide-worn shells and strands of kelp.

She walked until she reached a shallow pool hemmed in by dark rocks. The tide had left it behind like an offering. A quiet place. A stillness she could breathe in.

Lusa sank onto one of the flatter rocks, feet submerged in the pool. The water was cold and clean, curling around her ankles. There, she let herself be nothing but a mage with sore limbs and a storm slowly dissolving away within her.

Then the sound came.

A splash like a fin slapping water and a soft, warbling trill that didn't belong to wind or tide.

Lusa straightened.

Movement stirred beneath the surface of the water. A form rose through the shifting blue. At first, she thought it was seaweed, until the shape resolved: a small, lithe body, mottled in shifting hues of green, brown, and pale coral. Fins flared from its elbows like translucent leaves, and long strands of kelp-colored hair floated like a veil over a narrow face. Large, slanted eyes of liquid gold met hers.

Lusa held her breath. She'd always wanted to see a real mermaid. It was no bigger than a child, but her presence radiated something older. Wilder. And she was injured.

Iridescent blood drifted in the water near her side, staining the tide pool. A faint flicker of pain warped her brow. One fin lay limp, torn along the edge. Had she hurt it with her outburst? She glanced past the creature to the open sea, wondering what other things might've been injured beneath the waves due to her carelessness.

The creature made no sound, but Lusa felt it trying to communicate like a song pressing against her mind. Not words. Not thought. But a feeling.

You can help me.

She'd never been able to understand creatures before like Kaden had been able to talk with the griffin, Delova, in mindspeak. Something about it was exciting and terrifying at the same time. That foreign weight returned in her chest, pulsing awake, and despite her apprehension of acknowledging what it truly was, she tuned into it. The Magics stirred at the same time, recoiling from the mermaid like flame moths from rune-glass.

Lusa hesitated, the ache in her limbs nothing compared to the one tightening in her chest. Guilt replaced every other emotion, and she swallowed.

"I didn't mean to hurt you," she whispered.

The mermaid's golden eyes held hers. Her webbed fingers spread across the water's surface, and the melody deepened, quivering with fragile trust and fear laced between the notes.

Lusa inched forward, slipping her hands into the pool. The water brightened the moment her fingers met the silken fin. A soft, golden glow rippled from her palms, illuminating the cuts along the creature's side. She didn't know what she was doing. No spell rose to her lips. It was like when she'd been in the citadel with Kaden, the amulet growing in warmth as she concentrated.

The Light flowed out of her in waves, gathering around the wound and weaving through torn flesh. The pool shimmered with golden brilliance, threads of radiance stitching the mermaid's wound shut. Lusa's breath caught. This wasn't the amulet. This wasn't Them. This was her. Light, rising from a place she'd been denying existed. Her fury and grief dissolved.

The glow faded, the wound healed, and the mermaid gave a final ripple of song, *Thank you*, before slipping beneath the surface. Her tail flashed once, then vanished, swallowed by the sea.

In those golden eyes, Lusa had glimpsed something she thought she'd lost: recognition. Not of what she was… but of who she could still become.

Her gaze dropped to her palms, as if they no longer belonged to her. And in that stillness, the prophecy pressed hard against her chest:

If balance rests in one alone, the chain shall crack, the seed be sown.

The words sounded heavy and cryptic. She didn't want to believe them, didn't even fully understand them.

She grasped the amulet at her chest, warm now from the healing she'd done with a simple thought. Her thumb traced the ancient symbols etched into the filigree, wondering where it had been, what it had seen, and who it had chosen before her.

The stark realization settled in, quiet and undeniable. Her power had changed. She felt it. Feared it. And now, she had no choice but to face what came next.

CHAPTER 9

The Uneven Six

The sun baked the canyon walls, wind dragging grit across Lusa's cheek. Nearly half a moon since the beach—since the lightning, the scream, the mermaid. The days had blurred into hoofbeats and dust, the silence stretching longer with every mile. For Lusa, it wasn't only the silence of her companions. The Magics pressed against her from within, clawing for space beneath her skin. Keeping Them leashed left her muscles tight and her head aching with a constant, dull throb.

Six riders moved in a steady plod across the wilds, each lost in their own thoughts. They had cut southwest through tall grasses and sloping plains, the ocean long behind them, until the prairie thinned and the earth split into rust-colored stone. Breezy warmth shifted into a scorching, breathless heat that offered no reprieve and plenty of sweat.

Lusa didn't mind the change. After weeks of palace stone and stifling decorum, the raw openness of the world felt like breathing again. She filled the silence with sword drills and study, even though the texts Arcturius had given her were infuriatingly vague.

General Vallas led with the stiff-backed rigidity of someone who thought silence was a virtue. His orders were clipped, his glances colder than the desert nights. If he'd agreed to lead this mission, it was only to keep an eye on her. It used to make her angry. Now, she didn't care enough to waste energy on it anymore. Only enough to stuff the amulet beneath her tunic. She was tired of his wandering, judgmental gaze.

Glon, at least, was a steadiness she'd come to appreciate. He didn't speak much, but when he did, it was usually to ease tension or keep spirits from sinking too low. A dry comment here, an upbeat reassurance there. He kept pace beside her when the canyon narrowed, and shifted slightly closer on the ridges, like he was always making sure someone had her back.

Dak, by contrast, hadn't shut up for more than an hour at a time. Young and eager, with too much bravado for his own good, he cracked jokes that often made Glon chuckle. He'd fought the Izierian war against Lazorious, his first battle, and spoke of it like someone trying to prove they'd earned the scars they didn't quite have yet.

Jarion, the rookie, was all hunched shoulders and darting eyes. He'd barely spoken since leaving the palace. He was a boy wearing soldier's gear that didn't fit right. The kind who flinched at canyon echoes and gripped his reins with all the evidence of past trauma.

And then there was Noreena. She only spoke when necessary, direct and tactical. Lusa hadn't seen her fight, but the way she moved, the way she watched, said enough. She kept to the rear, never fully at ease, always scanning. Like she didn't know how to turn it off.

Together, they were a patchwork band of duty, mistrust, and buried tension headed toward a village none of them knew much about, where people had started disappearing without a trace. And somehow that translated to *definitely a mage,* as if they came in only one flavor: disastrous.

The canyon narrowed as twilight deepened, the last rays of sun catching on the stone walls carved over centuries by wind. They made camp at the mouth of a narrow gulch, tucked just enough beneath the ridge to shield them from the evening winds.

Noreena claimed a flat slab of stone near their soon-to-be fire pit, legs crossed, blade in hand. She sharpened it in slow strokes, her gaze fixed on the steel. Jarion fumbled with his bedroll while Dak cracked some half-joke to Glon that Lusa didn't catch. Lusa unsaddled her horse in silence, feeling the pull of fatigue in her limbs and something restless in the air. Even the horses were twitchy with flicking ears and wide eyes.

A glint of movement caught her eye. Pale glimmers drifted through the dark—barely brighter than candlelight, but unmistakably alive. It took her a second to register what she was seeing. Moths, larger than any she'd seen in the cities, with wings like translucent silk, dappled in moonlight. Some glowed with a faint, pulsing blue; others, a warm orange, like they'd been spun from either starlight or embers.

"Flame moths," Glon muttered beside her. "Haven't seen them in years." He unwrapped a packet of dried meat and tossed a strip to Dak, who caught it one-handed and took a large bite.

They were said to drift along the Aeon's breath, drawn to the raw pulse of the Weave where it broke through the surface. Seeing them here meant the ley currents ran close to the skin of the world. She'd only read about them, never traveling far enough to see them in person as a child. They drifted in, drawn to the hushed magic that clung to Lusa. She could feel the gentle tug of her power, the way the moths pulsed brighter when they neared her. One landed on her shoulder, warm and impossibly light.

Dak crouched by the fire pit, his cropped blond hair catching the moonlight, jerky hanging from his mouth. His blue eyes narrowed with concentration before striking the flint against the kindling. The spark landed, then fizzled out. He groaned and tried again. Nothing.

"Here, let me help," Lusa said, stepping closer and lifting a hand.

"You'll do no such thing," Vallas snapped.

"It's just a spark."

"We don't use magic in the field. We rely on discipline. Not shortcuts."

She raised an eyebrow, unimpressed. "It's a campfire, General. Not a siege line."

"She's trying to help," Glon added, tossing the last of the damp wood into the pit. "Might be quicker this way."

Vallas squared his shoulders. "My orders stand."

The scrape of stone against metal didn't pause. Noreena's blade hissed along the whetstone. The Dark Magics stirred at the sound, eager to strike, to cut. Lusa forced Them down.

Her hand hovered over the fire pit, magic already prickling at her fingertips. She didn't need his permission. "I'm not one of your soldiers."

Then, for effect, she lifted her chin to say the spell aloud, even though she no longer had to. "Fira Telum."

Sharp pain pinched behind her eyes, the Magics resenting being bridled into something so small. They wanted more… always more. But she pressed Them down until the ache dulled to a simmer.

A low heat shimmered through the air as flame leapt to life in the pit, clean and contained. The fire cracked. Orange light ate away at the low shadows on the canyon walls. The wind whistled, filling the awkward silence.

Lusa lowered her hand. "No shortcuts. Just results."

"You were given an order."

She turned toward Vallas slowly. "And you are not my general."

"You're part of this unit. You follow the chain of command."

The firelight carved hard lines across Vallas's face, but the set of his shoulders betrayed a crack in his composure. Not fury. Fear. He stepped forward like he meant to close the gap.

"If you disobey again—"

"What'll you do?" she quipped. "Lecture me louder?"

He paused, then straightened. "Command relies on order. If you undermine that, people die."

"If you silence magic, people die," Lusa countered.

His eyes narrowed. "Only when it's wielded by someone who knows where the edge is."

She didn't press it. There was more she could add—about edges and those who forced others to the brink—but it wasn't worth handing him her temper. Not tonight. Not with so many eyes watching, waiting to see if she'd become the thing he feared.

Lusa turned away, eyes drifting across the group. Glon stood still by the horses, hands resting loosely on a saddle strap. Noreena had paused mid-stroke with her blade, eyes half-lidded, unreadable. Dak sat frozen with the strip of jerky in one hand, and Jarion looked like he might shrink into his cloak.

Lusa exhaled and crouched by the fire, letting the heat soak into her palms.

"I didn't do it to provoke anyone," she stated. "Or scare anyone."

She looked up at the others, deliberately ignoring Vallas, who now loomed behind her. "Not all magic is meant to harm. Sometimes it's just… efficient. And sometimes, it's the reason any of us are still here."

She didn't glance back to see the look on the General's face, but the crunch of sand beneath retreating boots told her enough. She'd won this round.

Dak cleared his throat, loud and awkwardly. "So, uh… maybe magic's not such a bad shortcut after all?"

From her rock, Noreena finally spoke. "Or maybe you don't know how to hold a flint."

"I do too," Dak grumbled. "It's just temperamental."

"Mmhm," Noreena drawled. "So is your aim. Doesn't mean we blame the arrows."

Glon chuckled, bending to rearrange his bedroll. "Don't worry, soldier. You'll earn your fire-starting mark eventually," his voice edged lightly on mocking.

Dak sighed, all theatrics again. "I liked it better when we were marching. At least then no one noticed my failures."

"Trust me," Noreena said dryly, finally lifting her eyes, "we noticed."

Dak clutched his chest with exaggerated offense. "You wound me."

"Not yet. But the night's still young."

Even Lusa cracked a smile at that, the tension easing a fraction. Jarion sat a little apart from the group, pale green eyes flicking from face to face like he was waiting for something to go wrong.

The flame moths drifted closer again, their soft radiance swirling lazily through the air above the fire pit. They hung like tiny stars in the dusk, dancing around Lusa's shoulders, trailing after her when she moved. One landed near her fingers as she unrolled her blanket. She blinked at it, then brushed her fingers against the hairpin tucked along her braid, muffling Their anger and resentment. They were still there, a bruise hiding beneath the surface. But the pin and the amulet worked in tandem: one kept the Dark from crowding her, the other gave the Light a clear channel to move. It was as if the longer she wore it, the stronger the barrier grew.

Lusa tugged her satchel closer and slipped out the leather-bound treatise. By firelight she found the same passage she had already read a dozen times: *If balance rests in one alone, the chain shall crack, the seed be sown.*

The words seemed to blur as the moths glow beat in rhythm with her heartbeat. She snapped the book shut before anyone could notice, unsettled by how the prophecy shadowed her even here. She traded the eerie words for knowledge, pulling out her *Book of Magics.*

Its pages smelled of dust and smoke, Master Aron's lessons half-remembered after the memory-erasing spell of her mother had finally cleared. Back before the world went sideways, she hadn't cared for theory, only the thrill of casting. Now, she read every word as if it might save her life.

> *All magic draws from the Weave, the living fabric that binds Aetherealm. The Aether is its breath, the current through which the Weave stirs and answers. Mages touch the Aether to shape the Weave, and the Weave answers in kind.*

Her thumb traced the faded ink. She could almost hear Master Aron's voice from one of his lessons: "The Weave is the world's framework, Lusa. The Aether is how you move through it."

It was easy to drift into the what-ifs.

What if she hadn't gone searching for the truth? Would the Empire have ever known she existed, or would they still have found her, shaped her into their weapon? And what if the Dark Magics had never awakened and learned to hunger on their own? Would she still have burned down the Temple, destroying her own kind, or would she have found a way to save them? What if the Temple still stood, its halls alive with laughter and lessons instead of silence and ash? Would she still be there complaining about lectures, sneaking out between studies, pretending not to care while secretly loving every moment of being seen, of belonging?

Maybe the tragedy had never been her actions, but the fate that allowed her to survive while stealing every chance to truly live.

Regardless of all she'd uncovered, she stood here still—the last of her kind, a living reminder of everything the world tried to erase. Forever battling the demons within while the world waged against her. The ley lines always found their capstones, no matter how they twisted. Fate is a fixed thing.

Perhaps that was the point. That fate wasn't cruel or kind. It simply balanced the scales, demanding that every gift be met with its equal weight in loss.

The Magics writhed in the back of her thoughts, bristling at the thought of her fate belonging to anyone but Them. A bitter truth took shape then… one she'd been running from all along. Every act of light cast a shadow. Every act of creation left a scar. Balance wasn't peace, but Light and Dark coursing through her as they coursed through Aetherealm, their tension the only thing keeping the world from tearing—indifferent to the fact that doing so was breaking her.

Beneath her ribs, that uneven pulse stirred. Two rhythms struggling to settle into one. She pressed a hand to her sternum, unsure whether the ache was hers or something else. She wasn't apart from that balance at all; she was woven into it, a fragile thread pulled tight in a weave that held the world steady even as she feared it would stretch her past her limits.

Maybe balance didn't care at all. Maybe it simply used whatever threads it needed, and she just happened to be the one caught in the pull.

She exhaled softly and looked across the circle of faces by the fire, each one flickering between light and shadow. A different life might have kept her far from this canyon, far from them. But it also might have kept her from ever learning who she truly was.

She closed the book, tracing the worn leather. Too much time in her head. The only benefit now being the heavy drowsiness settling in. Stuffing her book back in the bag, she caught Glon's friendly smile across the fire. She returned a tired one of her own before sliding her gaze to the youngest of the group. Something about him told her he carried just as much trauma within him.

They'd all learned a little more about each other over the past two weeks. Shared canteens and saddle sores had a way of wearing down walls. But Jarion remained the quietest of them all. He never volunteered much, never interrupted, and always seemed to be in his own world. Something in him tugged at an old ache. Not just the bow, or the pale hair tied back the way Tryston once had, but the way he held himself. Cautious, always glancing away before eyes could meet.

It was like seeing Tryston again and the recognition twisted in her chest, guilt pressing in. The Magics stirred with it, feeding on the fissure, whispering how easily loss could be turned to rage if she would only let Them.

The pin dulled Their voices, and she sat on her bedroll, folded her legs, and leaned back on her palms. "Jarion, right?"

He stiffened slightly. "Yes, ma'am."

"Just Lusa."

He nodded, a little too quickly.

"First assignment?"

He hesitated. "Yes."

Dak nudged a stick into the fire. "He barely said two words the whole ride. Thought maybe he'd fallen asleep with his eyes open."

"I just don't talk much."

"That's all right," Glon said, tossing him a casual smile while settling next to Lusa. "More room for the rest of us to run our mouths."

Vallas, who had been standing with arms crossed and eyes scanning the ridge, turned back toward them. "Finish your meals. Briefing follows."

A blue flame moth landed on his cloak. He flicked it off like it was filth.

Dak arched a brow. "You know, in some cultures, those are considered good luck."

Deciding not to respond, Vallas moved to the far edge of camp and knelt to open his rations with the same precision he did everything else, as if he believed even rations could be broken into obedience.

Lusa pulled a bundle of figs and roasted grain from her satchel, muttering under her breath, "Careful what cultures you bring up around him. Pretty sure Vallas only recognizes one."

Brows slightly raised, Jarion glanced at her.

She leaned in, voice lower. "His own."

Glon cleared his throat, cutting her a look that said to tread lightly. She rolled her eyes, but let it go, shifting her attention to the growing cluster of flame moths floating around her. She noticed Jarion hadn't touched much, only picked at his jerky a little.

"You need to eat." She offered a fig.

He blinked, startled by the attention, then gave a quick nod and took the fig. "I know. Just… doesn't sit well before sleep."

Lusa gave a slow nod. She understood. Too many nights haunted by what waited behind closed eyes.

Dak tore into his meat with theatrical misery. "No one said rations were gonna be gourmet, but I swear this one tastes like it was scraped off a stable floor."

"Don't insult the stables," Noreena murmured, staring off in what looked like boredom. Hard to tell.

That earned a laugh from Glon and a choked noise from Jarion that might've been the start of one.

"I don't know, Dak," Glon said, nudging the fire with his boot. "You complain about those strips every night. Might be time we try flame moth."

Dak looked up, aghast. "They glow, Captain. That's practically sacred. Or poisonous. Or both."

"And?" Glon shot, chewing around a smirk.

Dak held up his hands. "Too pretty. I'm not eating anything prettier than me."

"You eat everything," Noreena jabbed.

Lusa smirked, then looked toward the flame moths again. One dipped low, hovered near her hand, then darted up to join the swirling mass above.

Jarion watched them, mesmerized. "They really seem to like you."

Lusa sighed, brushing a thumb across her wrist. "They're just attracted to my magic—"

"Enough chatter." Vallas cut in.

He stood up, silhouetted against the ridge with arms crossed. That was enough to keep most of them focused on their meals for a while.

Lusa chewed in silence, the figs gone too quickly, her stomach still rumbling. Almost without thinking, her hand drifted to the pouch at her belt. She loosened the drawstring and pinched out a sprig of dried juniper and a dusting of pearl grit. They shimmered faintly before dulling to powder again. Enough, if paired with the right words, to conjure a loaf of bread. The thought made her stomach cramp.

Glon's gaze lingered on the silver and blue embroidered thread stitched with the Izerian crest on the pouch. "Those from the Vizier?"

Lusa didn't answer right away. She shook the remnants off her fingers, back into the pouch, before tugging the drawstring shut. Finally, she gave a short nod. "Yeah. He gave me a pouch of reagents before we left."

"What do they do?" Dak asked, leaning forward with open curiosity.

"Conjures food, usually. Depends on the spell." Her tone stayed flat, but unease needled her. Arcturius had carried these himself—a human, not a mage. Unusual. She pushed it down. Too many puzzles stacked on each other, and her skull felt ready to split.

"Huh. Handy."

"I wouldn't get used to it," Vallas said. "Magic like that always comes with a cost."

Lusa's fingers tightened around the pouch, the brittle juniper and pearl grit pressing against her fingers.

"You all seem quick to trust a mage with power she barely controls," Vallas went on, sweeping a cold look over the group. "That's not strategy. That's desperation."

Her jaw twitched as she ground her teeth. "I wasn't planning on using them, I—"

She stopped. No need to explain herself to him.

Glon redirected the conversation. "Maybe the real concern should be the village of Merravale. I mean… we still don't know what we're walking into."

Noreena looked up, her voice coming out like she was reading a battle plan. "People are missing. No signs of a skirmish. No blood. Gone. That's all we know."

Dak added, "Could be bandits. Slavers. Or—"

"Or magic," Vallas said flatly.

"Or not," Glon shot back. "Not every bad thing's got a spell behind it."

Vallas's glare didn't waver, but he offered nothing more. Lusa let her gaze sink into the fire, the silence thickening until only the pops of the flames and the chirping of insects consumed the night. Tomorrow they would reach Merravale. The Magics stirred, threading whispers through her skull, Their tones almost gleeful. Beneath Them, quieter but heavier, the Weave itself seemed to hum in her bones, and the words of the prophecy rolled around in her head:

> *When Light and Dark as one align, the path shall wake the wrath divine.*

CHAPTER 10

Unwelcome Company

Morning crept into the canyon, soft gold peeling down the high stone walls like paint on parchment. The fire was little more than a bed of glowing ash, and the desert air clung with an early chill that hadn't yet burned off.

Lusa stretched, joints stiff, brushing sleep from her eyes. She'd barely dozed. Every time she drifted, her power stirred with those two uneasy rhythms in her chest, never quite agreeing. So, she read by moth light.

The others stirred slowly. Dak muttered something incoherent and rolled over. Jarion sat up with bloodshot eyes, like he hadn't slept at all either. They packed in silence: bedrolls cinched, fire buried, gear checked, horses saddled with sleepy grunts and groans. The cañyon narrowed as they rode, sky tightening overhead. Wind funneled through the stone in low, ghostly whistles.

Dak rode near the back, feet out of the stirrups, already playing his bone-carved flute. The lilting tune echoed between the canyon walls—surprisingly soft, almost wistful.

"Really?" Noreena quipped behind her scarf. "We're trying to stay alert, not summon the local wildlife."

Dak grinned without looking back. "Mornings are better with music, Nori."

Lusa glanced back in time to catch Noreena's glare.

"Call me that again and I'll lodge that flute somewhere hard to retrieve."

"Promises, promises."

The tune carried on.

Lusa didn't mind it. The music wasn't flawless, but it smoothed the edges of her nerves. Her shoulders relaxed, jaw eased. With the rhythm of hooves and the golden hush of morning light, it almost felt peaceful.

Almost.

The tune Dak played dipped low, trailed high, lingered too long on a note that made something ache behind her ribs. She didn't recognize the melody, but it reminded her of a tune Kaden used to hum when he thought she wasn't listening—quiet, unfocused, the kind of sound born more from muscle memory than meaning.

Her gaze dropped to the trail ahead, where shadows shifted beneath the horses' hooves. The canyon narrowed more here, walls stretching higher, sun crawling slow across the rock. It would be hot soon. The air was beginning to thicken with that dry, weightless heat that made sweat feel useless. She rubbed the back of her neck and glanced at the others.

Glon rode a few paces ahead, massive and steady in the saddle. He didn't talk much in the mornings, and honestly, he didn't need to. His presence filled the space like a second sky… broad, grounded, always watching. His stallion had dust caked along its flanks, but the reins were loose in his hand, his posture easy. He looked like he belonged in the canyon.

Jarion, meanwhile, looked like he belonged anywhere else. He rode stiff-backed, eyes flicking toward every curve of the stone. His bow was slung awkwardly across his back, and the strap kept sliding down his shoulder. At one point he caught her looking and flushed, pulling it up with a muttered apology. She offered a half smile but didn't say anything.

They were all tired. Dust-coated. Sun-creased. Still wearing the weight of yesterday.

Ahead, Vallas rode like he was preparing for a war no one had declared. His spine rigid, eyes forward, one hand on the pommel of his sword like it might be needed any moment. He hadn't spoken a word since they'd left camp.

Noreena, for her part, rode to the outer edge of the group to watch the ridgelines. Her expression unreadable behind the scarf pulled up to her nose, tight curls tucked beneath her hood. Lusa had to admit—there was something comforting about Noreena's constant vigilance. She didn't miss much.

Lusa squinted up at the ridges and found herself wondering what creatures made their homes in a place like this—ones that knew how to blend with the dust and disappear between stone.

Her fingers brushed the amulet through her tunic, feeling its faint warmth. Every time she thought about it, a strange sensation swirled in her core like hot and cold water fighting for the same space. Lusa tugged at the strap across her chest, trying to loosen it, the leather sticking in the rising heat. Stone skittered from a ledge above and she jerked her head up.

"Did anyone else—" A prickle danced up Lusa's spine. Movement. High on the ridge. Dust spilled in fine trails. She couldn't see what caused it, only the tremble of loose rock. Instinctively, she reached out into the Aether, searching for power. There was definitely a presence, but it didn't seem magical.

Dak shoved the flute into his satchel and reached for his sword. Jarion twisted in his saddle, fumbled his quiver, and spilled half his arrows. He practically fell off his horse scrambling to gather them.

"Form up!" Vallas barked.

Something massive peeled from the ledge.

It hit the canyon floor like a boulder from the gods. Bone-colored scales unfurled in a wave of dust and sand. Wings snapped wide. Talons gouged stone. Its body unfurled, sinuous and dry as sun-bleached leather.

Two glassy eyes locked on them, bright and faceted like cracked gemstones. The canyon seemed too narrow to hold it. Its wings scraped stone, dust raining down, every beat of air like a battering ram against their chests.

Noreena already had her spear and shield raised. Jarion had miraculously notched an arrow. The others followed suit. The creature shrieked. The sound hit Lusa's chest before it reached her ears.

Glon stepped into her periphery, raising his shield. "Sand wyvern," he said, eyes casting a sideways glance to Dak. "Guess it didn't like your song."

"That's not a real thing," Dak stammered.

"Tell *it* that."

Noreena wrapped the reins tight around one forearm. "Orders, General?"

The wyvern's chest expanded.

Lusa felt it first. The air thickened with pressure before a blast of sand shot out. A concentrated whip of wind and glass tore across the canyon. The men raised their shields, but that was pointless. Dak went flying, his head narrowly missing a jagged outcrop. Vallas and Glon staggered, footing lost. Someone screamed. The sand hissed where it landed, sizzling off the glimmer of a shield her magic had instinctively formed.

Rock faces pitted under the force, edges sheared clean as if struck by blades. Flesh would not have fared better.

Lusa's gut twisted. If they faced it head-on, they were already dead.

She dismounted fast, the Magics tingling along her arms. She'd never seen a sand wyvern before… didn't even know they were real. But it didn't feel mindless. Dangerous, yes. But not wild. Not without reason.

Her boots hit gravel. The Magics surged behind her shielded mind, pressing in. The hairpin dulled Their voices, but her heartbeat only fed Them. *Strike. Kill. Finish it.*

Another pull stirred beneath Their noise. It didn't urge her to strike. It urged her to spare. She didn't understand it. Since when did mercy get louder than fury?

"How do we fight it?" Noreena shouted, trotting up beside Vallas, spear raised.

An arrow zipped past overhead—Jarion's. It pinged off the wyvern's thick scales, barely making a mark.

"Great," Dak muttered, scrambling to his feet. "It has armor."

"Don't kill it!" she shouted. She didn't know if it was her conscience or the Light Magic whispering through her bones, but she trusted it.

She rifled through her memory. New spells from the *Book of Magics*. Subduing flares. Disorienting bursts. A starburst of searing light…

Vallas turned, blood streaking down his temple. "It's attacking us!"

"It's defending its territory!"

Another blast of sand tore across the trail. Jarion dove behind a boulder, but he still fired. A clean shot to the flank. It barely lodged between the scales, but the wyvern roared in fury.

"I can blind it!" Lusa called. "When I signal—run!"

"What's the signal?!" Dak yelled.

"You'll know!"

Lusa gathered the power swirling in her core, feeling the pressure build. She lifted her hands and mentally summoned the spell.

Aelara ignis.

The flare exploded from her palms—a star, white-gold and blinding. Heat surged through her arms as the light tore across the canyon. The wyvern shrieked, stumbling, its wings flailing into stone.

"Now!"

They moved as one. Dak vaulted onto his horse, sword held out ready to strike at oncoming talons and tore past the disoriented creature. Noreena yanked the reins of Jarion's horse and kicked her own into a gallop, pulling his mount after her.

Vallas kicked his mount forward, reached Jarion, and pulled him up behind him. They veered hard, hugging the canyon wall to pass the creature while it staggered.

The wyvern shrieked again, rearing high, nearly touching the top of the canyon. Another sandblast burst from its maw. Lusa ducked. The sand whipped overhead, a few particles pinging off the bubble of shield that surrounded her. She wasn't sure how it worked, but there wasn't time to question it now. Her horse reared, nearly throwing her off.

"Woah!" She held firm, pulled forward, and kicked it into a gallop.

Up ahead, through the dirt, behind the beast, she could see the others make it through.

Except one.

Lusa scoured the rock-streaked canyon.

There—

A lone figure. Glon. Running full tilt, straight past the frenzied beast. One arm clutched his ribs. Dust streaked his face. The wyvern reared high beside him, thrashing in its blindness. Its wings beat the air in wide, furious sweeps, tail carving deep gouges into the canyon wall. It towered above them, ready to slam back down in the next breath.

"Glon!" There wasn't time to think. Only to see Glon's shape too close to the beast, and the part of her that refused to lose him. She steered her horse straight toward them both, yanked the reins hard, and cut a sharp arc across the canyon floor. Dust and wind tore at her eyes as she veered beneath the creature's shadow.

"Get on!"

He grabbed the saddle and hauled himself up right as the creature's front talons slammed into the ground behind them, a breath too late. The impact cracked stone, rattling her spine.

"Owe you one." Glon's voice was tight with pain as his arm locked around her waist. His other arm hung awkwardly, shoulder twisted at a wrong angle. She didn't need a spell to see the joint was gone. Popped, or worse.

She drove her heels into the horse's sides, and they bolted down the canyon, the wyvern's roar chasing them like a wave.

When the canyon finally fell away, the others had already regrouped. Lusa's body felt raw, every nerve still thrumming from adrenaline. She dismounted stiffly. Glon slid down behind her, face tight, one arm clutched to his side. He said nothing but his grunt as his boots hit the ground said enough.

Jarion sat hunched on a boulder, blood soaking through one sleeve. Noreena crouched beside him, her tight-cropped curls streaked with dust and grit. Her dark hands moved quickly over the wound, efficient and calm despite the tension in the air.

Dak slumped against a nearby rock, hacking out the remnants of the canyon from his lungs, while the general paced, sword still in hand. Dust and blood streaked his face;

one temple crusted with blood-stained sand clumps. His eyes flicked between them all, jaw clenched so tight it looked locked in place.

The silence pressed in around them, filled only by the soft stamping of horses, including Glon's runaway stallion, and the wind sweeping dust through the air.

Finally, Vallas stopped and turned toward Lusa.

"You disobeyed orders."

Lusa met his gaze. "I saved us."

"You endangered the mission."

"We were already in danger. I made a choice."

"You made *your* choice."

"Because no one else did."

Glon stepped between them. "Maybe wait till the bleeding stops before we tear into each other."

His voice strained, a muscle ticking near his jaw. Blood had already dried in a line down his bicep, dark against the torn sleeve. He'd tried to pop the shoulder back in himself. She could tell from the tremor still running through his hand. He looked at Jarion—bandaged, bloody—and said nothing else.

Noreena finished binding Jarion's arm and stood, brushing grit from her knees. "We're not a unit," she said. "But in the chaos, we moved. Uneven maybe, but we're all still breathing."

Uneven was the only word for them. Not by number but by nature. Six edges that didn't quite fit, scraping against one another hard enough to spark. Sparks were fine. Sparks meant life. But unity? That was something else entirely. Lusa let out a slow breath. Her hands still shook faintly from the spell. She looked back toward the narrowing path, where golden dust still hung in the air like smoke.

"We need to keep moving," Vallas said.

No one disagreed. Lusa wasn't sure how they'd made it out mostly unscathed. They weren't trained together. They weren't a unit. But when it mattered, no one ran. Even Jarion had drawn his bow and fired.

The wyvern's roar was gone, but something of it remained—in the dust, in her bones, in the way they all stood just a little closer.

CHAPTER 11

Merravale

Dusk had all but bled dry by the time they crested the final ridge. The town of Merravale lay nestled in the crook of the hills like a secret tucked away on purpose. Slanted rooftops leaned into one another as if whispering, their outlines etched in soot-gray against a dimming sky. Lamplight flickered in a few narrow windows, offering only the faintest pulse of life. Lusa pulled her cloak tighter. Gone was the dry heat of the plains, replaced by something cooler. Damp. Clinging. Scentless, yet the Aether felt different here, enough to raise the hairs on her arms.

The group said nothing as they entered the town. Even the horses seemed hesitant, hooves clopping softly against uneven gravel. Doors stayed shut. Shutters clicked into place. A few faces peeked from behind curtains but vanished just as quickly, like sprites retreating from a flicker of dark magic.

Beside her, Glon rode with a stiff set to his shoulders. His arm hadn't moved much since the wyvern attack, and she'd noticed him shifting more carefully over the past day. He hadn't complained. He wouldn't. He struck her as the sort who'd carry the weight until he collapsed under it.

"Friendly lot," Dak muttered under his breath.

"Keep riding," Vallas ordered. His posture remained taut as ever and she couldn't help but wonder if the man ever knew how to relax.

Jarion trotted up beside her on his tan mare, pale and wide-eyed. It looked like all the blood had drained from his face, though she wasn't sure there'd been much color there to begin with. He adjusted his pack, careful of the bandaged arm, flexing it enough to wince.

The main road curved sharply between two buildings and deposited them into a small square. A weathered well stood at the center, its stones chipped and moss-covered. Beside it was a statue so eroded it was impossible to tell if it had once been a hero or heretic… only that whatever it had been, it was forgotten now. It had no head. She hopped off her horse and moved closer.

"It feels like a town that already gave up," she murmured, brushing dust from the crumbling plaque, its lettering faded to near-nothing beneath her fingers.

The general remained on his steed while the others dismounted, taking in the square with the same wariness.

"Or maybe," she added, her voice softer, "they stopped trying because whatever took root here… never left." She pressed the sooty dust between her fingers and glanced around the square once more. Even the Weave seemed snagged in the square, a net pulled too tight.

"Wrong. Towns that give up don't keep sending messages," Vallas corrected. He said it with that maddening tone of superiority, a little too pleased to prove her wrong, and it needled under her skin.

Lusa clenched her jaw. She hadn't meant it as a conclusion, but a warning. The amulet at her neck warmed. The Magics pressed forward, nosing at the edge of Kaden's ward like wolves scenting blood.

Let us speak, They whispered, velvet-soft and far too eager.

She swallowed them down, but the heat behind her temples didn't ease.

Vallas finally dismounted, flinging his cloak behind his shoulders with his typical air of arrogance. "Which means there's still something here, and it's our job to gather information."

"Think they'll actually give us any?" Dak asked.

"No."

Jarion and Noreena handed off their reins to the boy who appeared, silent and barefoot, from the shadows of a stable alcove. He took the horses without a word and disappeared again, as if rehearsed. Too smooth. Too practiced. Like someone who'd grown used to strangers vanishing. She found herself wondering, not without irony, just how many extra horses a town like this kept on hand from the ones who never returned.

They crossed the square and stepped into the inn, a squat slate-roofed structure that looked more like a converted barn than a place meant for rest. The common room wasn't empty, but it may as well have been. The moment they entered, silence claimed the space. Locals sat at tables along the walls, nursing mugs, their eyes following every step. Stares full of suspicion and questions… the kind probably born of too many vanishings and not enough answers.

The Magics writhed at the edges of her mind, eager to bare Their teeth in answer to the suspicion. She clamped down hard, forcing Them back. The effort left a sour taste on her tongue, her temples throbbing with the dull ache she'd come to know too well. Nausea stirred low in her gut, symptom of keeping Them caged for too long. Even the hairpin seemed weakened by Their constant prodding, like a dam cracking under pressure.

Vallas didn't flinch under those gazes, but his hand strayed to the hilt of his sword before he caught himself, fingers curling once against the leather. Lusa couldn't blame him. The silence here wasn't absence—it was pressure, the kind that prickled the back of her neck.

The innkeeper stood behind the bar; a relic left too long in shadow. He had his arms folded, posture hunched but rigid, and his face was carved with the kind of wear that didn't come from age, but from enduring. His sunken eyes tracked them with the quiet scrutiny of someone who'd seen too much to trust what came through that door.

"We need rooms," Vallas said.

The innkeeper grunted. "Four Eldras. We only got two available."

Vallas laid his coins down without flinching. "Will two Izaers cover it?"

Lusa's fingers brushed the pouch at her hip. It was still full of Myttican coin. Once, that had meant something. But with the massacre at the Temple and the Magi all but gone, her coin had become dead currency.

The innkeeper took the money, reached under the counter, pulled out a pair of keys and placed them down with no labels or explanation.

"Anything we should know?" Vallas asked.

The man paused, fingers still pressed to the counter. His jaw twitched. Without looking up, he muttered, "Don't go past the trees to the west."

Lusa started to speak, but he'd already slipped through the back door.

Noreena shot her a sideways glance—one that echoed her own thoughts. Vague and cryptic. That seemed to be Merravale's way.

"Well, there's our subtle clue for tomorrow," Dak sighed, eyeing the villagers who clearly didn't care they were staring.

Glon almost folded his arms across his broad chest, probably forgetting for a split second one arm would scream in protest. "At least it gives us somewhere to start."

Jarion nodded, eyes flicking to every shadow, and somehow ended up right beside Lusa. She could feel the tension rolling off him like heat from a forge.

Noreena took one of the keys from the counter and jerked her head toward the stairs. "You boys take one. We'll take the other."

Dak groaned. "Please tell me I'm not sharing a bed. I'd rather sleep in the stables."

"The general's being frugal, and for good reason." Glon followed Noreena up the stairs.

Dak mumbled something under his breath.

Noreena didn't miss an opportunity. "Great idea, Dak. The stables sound like the perfect place for a pampered mule like you."

Dak smirked and called after her, "Jealousy doesn't look good on you, Nori."

She didn't stop but the tightening of her shoulders said she'd heard him. The rest followed up the stairs. Lusa stayed a moment longer, her gaze drifting to the high-beamed ceiling, to the candlelight in its glass holders. Something about Merravale felt… hollow. Not broken, exactly, but maybe a place that had stopped expecting to be saved.

She scanned the faces still watching her and wondered how many held answers and how many had simply lost someone. The thought provoked her mother's face to surfaced paired with that helpless ache of not knowing where to look when someone you love disappears. She shoved the memory aside and followed the others upstairs.

The girls' room was narrow and spare: two small beds, a single cracked basin, and a window that refused to open. The walls held the scent of dust and burnt stew, but the sheets were clean.

Noreena moved with her usual precision, leaning her spear next to her bed, setting her pack down, and unrolling her blanket across the thin mattress like it was part of her routine. Efficient. Measured. Silent.

Lusa sat on the edge of her own bed, eyeing the other woman as she tugged off her boots. Of all the soldiers, Noreena was the hardest to read. No idle chatter like Dak. No quiet loyalty like Glon. Cool competence and a look that skimmed over people like facts in a battle report.

"You've been with the general a while?" Lusa asked, keeping her tone light.

Noreena shrugged, still facing away. "Long enough."

Right. Closed book.

Lusa gave it another go. "And the captain? I think I heard him mention fighting beside you during the Battle of Izier."

Another small nod. Noreena pulled her blanket over her shoulder, clearly finished with the conversation.

Lusa shrugged off her cloak and laid it at the foot of her bed, fingers brushing the fabric a little longer than necessary. She wasn't sure why it mattered—getting to know Noreena. Maybe it didn't. But it felt like something she should try. She hadn't had many female allies in her life, not since the academy, and the last ones had ended in flame and blood and names she didn't let herself say out loud.

She didn't want to think about that now.

She took a breath and tried one last time. "You think Merravale's hiding something?"

This time, Noreena paused before finally speaking. "Villages don't go quiet without a reason."

A fair answer. Not a warm one.

Noreena extinguished the stubby candle next to her bed, and Lusa waited for her eyes to adjust to the faint spill of moonlight peeking through the shutters. It had been more than a moon's turn since she'd slept in an actual bed. She blinked up at the ceiling, but her eyes were already losing the fight. The Treatise seemed to call to her from her satchel. She'd meant to study it again, trace every faded line until she made sense of it. But her head pounded with the day's efforts, and her body felt too heavy to move. Tomorrow, she promised herself. The lines still drifted at the edge of her thoughts, the cadence etched too deep to forget even as sleep claimed her: *When Light and Dark as one align, the path shall wake the wrath divine…*

Lusa startled awake to a dull thud from across the hall, followed by a scuffle and a low groan. Noreena was already on her feet, calm but focused. She crossed to the door and pressed her ear to it.

Another thud. Some muffled cursing.

Noreena gave Lusa a look, more muscle memory than alarm, and unlatched the door. Lusa swung her legs out of bed and followed her into the hallway.

Noreena knocked twice. "Everyone alive in there?"

A pause. Then Dak's winded voice, "Define 'alive.'"

Noreena pushed the door open.

Jarion was already standing, awkwardly adjusting his tunic with his hurt arm and avoiding eye contact. Dak was on the floor, brushing dust off his shoulder with the kind of irritation only someone who'd fallen out of bed could muster.

"Shoulda' gone with the stables," he muttered.

On the far side of the room, Glon lay on his back in the other bed, his good arm folded across his chest, eyes closed like he'd decided the situation didn't merit getting up.

Vallas stood near the washbasin, fully dressed, ignoring the situation while rolling his sleeves. The blanket from his bedroll was folded perfectly in the corner, and a pillow from one of the beds had clearly been used on the floor.

Noreena made a small noise, just shy of a sigh, and shut the door.

"Tenderfoots," she spat under her breath. "I'm surprised they've made it this far."

By the time they rendezvoused downstairs, the men had managed something resembling decency, even though Dak's hair stuck up on one side and Jarion limped like he'd aged a decade overnight.

The common room was nearly empty, save for a single man seated near the hearth, hunched over a bowl of something grayish and steaming. He looked up as they entered, spoon paused midair. His eyes lingered a moment too long before he shoved the last bite into his mouth, scraped back his chair, and left without a word. The door clicked shut behind him with a soft finality that didn't feel accidental.

Dak arched a brow. "Do we smell, or is that just the usual reaction around here?"

"Probably both," Lusa answered, brushing past him as she tucked the last of her braid behind her shoulder and repositioned her hairpin so it fit more securely.

The innkeeper didn't reappear, but a scrawny kitchen girl emerged with a tray. She set down a loaf of flat, uneven bread, a pot of bitter-smelling tea, and bowls filled with a pale mush speckled with what might've been dried herbs. Or mold. Hard to say.

Dak slumped into the chair across from her, eyeing his bowl. He prodded it once with his spoon. "Better than meat sticks."

Lusa watched Glon take a full bite without hesitation. He met her gaze and smirked behind his chew. "Waiting to see if I keel over first?"

She smirked back and braced herself for the first bite. The texture landed somewhere between porridge… and regret.

She rolled the stiffness from her neck and let her gaze drift toward the window.

Across the gravel road, beneath a crooked tree, someone stood, shadowed, half-swallowed by the morning mist. She almost mistook the figure for another statue… one that hadn't lost its head. It didn't move like a villager going about their morning, or a traveler passing through. The figure stood there, staring straight at the inn.

Lusa's brow furrowed, trying to figure out why someone would stand there, like they already knew who was inside.

Beside her, Jarion had gone still, his bowl untouched. He'd seen it too.

She looked again. The figure was gone.

Vallas cleared his throat. "We'll divide and gather information. There's a tradesman's lane along the north edge of town. Captain, take Dak and begin your investigation there. Jarion and I will take the woods to the west."

"That's the direction of the Citadels," Glon said behind his hand as he wiped his mouth with a napkin. His bowl sat empty. Military discipline, no doubt. She figured Jarion was the exception to that standard.

Lusa glanced at Noreena. "Guess that leaves us and the square."

"Lucky me," Noreena said flatly.

Lusa offered a tight smile. "I could always trade with Dak."

Dak raised his spoon midair. "Hey."

Noreena stood, fastening her cloak. "I'd rather take my chances with the mage."

Lusa blinked, unsure whether to feel mildly honored or vaguely insulted. She took one last sip of the bitter tea, trying not to grimace. The moment she stood, her thoughts flicked back to the figure outside. The space under the crooked tree was still empty, but her skin hadn't stopped crawling.

Vallas stood, wiped his hands on a cloth, and placed one zael on the table with a metallic clink. "Reconvene here at dusk."

He looked directly at Lusa, holding her gaze a beat too long. "No magic," he warned under his breath.

The words scraped. The Magics rattled against the pin, Their hunger thrumming in her skull. Her stomach turned, bile tang at the back of her throat. It took everything she had not to double over, not to let the pain and exhaustion show as she fought Them off. She forced a thin smile instead, biting down on the nausea as if that could make it vanish. Hairpin or not, Their intentions were getting louder than Their voices.

Glon grimaced and gave her a look—half apology, half *my hands are tied*—and followed Vallas out. She hadn't planned on using magic. But now? She almost hoped for an excuse.

Lusa exhaled slowly. One problem at a time.

Glon and Dak headed out with barely a word between them. Vallas and Jarion set off in another direction, the general already listing off instructions before the door even closed behind them. Lusa and Noreena stepped out last.

The air hit them like wet cloth—thick with humidity, cool but sticky. A light fog still clung to the ground, beading on leaves and curling around their boots. The sky was gray and dull, the kind of morning that couldn't quite decide whether to rain or burn off.

Noreena adjusted the spear slung across her back and scanned the street. "The square should be that way." She nodded with a flick of her chin.

Ahead, the road forked. Vallas and Jarion were already heading west toward the woods, while the path to the square curved southwest.

Lusa hesitated. "Before we go… I saw someone earlier. Out by that twisted tree. Just standing there. Watching. And then gone."

Noreena's eyes flicked toward the tree Glon and Dak were passing before looking at Lusa. "And you're just telling me now?"

"I wasn't sure it meant anything."

"It always means something," Noreena grumbled, already moving down the street.

Lusa fell in beside her. After a few steps of fog-thick silence, Noreena added, "Next time, lead with the ghost. Saves me guessing how we'll die today."

CHAPTER 12

Children of the Vanished

Mist still clung to the cobbles as they made their way down the narrow lane. The square held a small crowd, but it was hushed in that way Lusa was beginning to recognize as Merravale's natural state. A few merchant stalls were set up, though none looked particularly eager for business. The absence of voices shouting deals and enthusiastic bargaining was nonexistent. Merely dull eyes and the slow rearranging of goods that didn't seem to need moving.

Noreena's boots barely made a sound as she scanned the edges of the square. She carried herself like she was still on patrol.

"We split up or stay close?" she asked, tone clipped.

"Probably safer together," Lusa said, though it wasn't the kind of danger she was worried about.

They moved from stall to stall with their questions, but the answers were the same: shrugs, vague responses, eyes that slid away before Lusa could finish a sentence. She noticed the way people tensed when Noreena spoke. Her soldier's cadence seemed to shut down any hope of openness. They'd gotten bits and pieces. Four people missing since the last fortnight, but no names, details, or patterns were divulged. Only hints. Getting even that much felt like pulling teeth from a corpse.

It wasn't until the fourth merchant, an older woman with silver-threaded hair and dirt-stained fingers, that Lusa caught the flicker of something useful: a pause.

She leaned in slightly, keeping her voice low. "You've lost people, haven't you?"

The woman didn't answer. But she didn't deny it either.

Noreena shifted beside her, about to cut in with the kind of question that sounded more like an accusation than a plea. But a small figure stepped out from behind the edge of the stall, catching them both off guard.

A barefoot girl, maybe no more than ten full turns. Her tunic hung from her shoulders like it had once belonged to someone twice her size. Beneath her stringy light brown hair, dirt streaked her cheeks and clung to the hollows beneath her hazel eyes. She said nothing, simply stepped forward and held open her palms, fingers splayed, asking without asking.

Something tugged at Lusa. Pity, perhaps? The girl did look like she'd seen her fair share of hardships. She shook it off and reached into her pack, pulling out a dense travel roll. She offered it, but the girl's gaze didn't follow the food. It drifted upward… to Lusa's hair. To the pin. The girl pointed.

Lusa's fingers brushed the silver blooms without thinking. "This?" she asked softly. "It was a gift."

Still, the girl didn't move or speak. She just stood there with her hands open, eyes fixed not on the bread, but on the shimmer of silver.

Lusa looked down at the roll, then back at the girl's pale, thin-lipped face, caused by too much hunger. She reached into her pack again and added a smoked meat stick atop the bread.

That did it.

The girl took the offering with both hands, gave one small nod, and turned away.

Lusa watched her cross the square, weaving between puddles and discarded crates. She stopped behind a broken cart and knelt beside two younger boys—one no older than four, the other barely more than a toddler. She broke the roll in half, gave a piece to each, then carefully tucked the meat stick into a cloth pouch at her waist like it was something precious.

"She's one of them," the old woman said quietly from behind the stall.

Noreena turned slightly. "One of who?"

The woman didn't look up from the roots she was pretending to sort. Her hands moved without purpose; more habit than function. After a beat, she muttered, "Children of the Vanished."

Lusa turned, watching the girl settle beside the boys. Her thin arms curled protectively around them as they ate. A strange ache cut through Lusa's chest. She'd been a child left behind, too. Her mother vanished without a word, only to be found again carved hollow by the Magics, nothing left but a shell They could wear. Looking at these children felt too familiar. Survival without protection. Hunger without hope.

Now that she had a name for it, she began to see the pattern: a boy crouched behind a half-barrel, two girls whispering on a crumbling stoop, another child tucked into an alcove near a boarded shopfront, his bony arms pulled close around his knees.

In the background, a cart creaked along the far edge of the square, drawn by a thin, aging horse and steered by a stooped man. Crates were stacked high in the back, wobbling gently with each bump in the road. One of the wheels dipped into a shallow rut with a metallic groan.

Lusa's gaze returned to the stall.

"How long have they been disappearing?"

As expected, no answer.

Noreena leaned in, her face drawn in hard lines. "You said she's one of them. That means you know what's happening."

Silence.

Noreena's voice dropped into a low growl. "Where are they going?"

The woman's fingers stopped mid-motion. Her mouth thinned.

"Fine." Noreena pulled a zael from her pouch and slapped it on the stall's edge. "The roots. Wrap them."

The woman blinked, as if dislodged from the wall she'd built around herself, then nodded. She pulled out a scrap of cloth and began bundling the vegetables with practiced hands.

"It started more than a turn ago," she said at last. "Before the last Lady Ice."

Before the temple massacre.

Acid burned in her throat, stinging her stomach with the memory she forced back down.

The old woman handed Noreena the bundle without meeting her eyes. Behind them, wagon wheels thunked heavily over the cobbles. A few nearby merchants had begun to stare.

"We're trying to help," Noreena added, voice tight.

Lusa stepped in, softening hers. "Please. Your village chief hasn't stopped sending messages to the empire. That's why we were sent. To investigate. If we can understand what's happening, maybe we can stop more children from losing their families."

The woman's dull eyes lifted, meeting Lusa's. Searching for a lie.

Finally, she spoke again. "At first it was travelers. Then it was our own. Young men. Mothers. A few elders. One of the blacksmith's sons, nearly grown. No one under ten. They'd go near the west woods and just… never come back."

Noreena's stance eased slightly. Her gaze shifted past the stall, toward the tree line that bordered the square. Somewhere beyond those trees, Vallas and Jarion were already searching.

"That's where they vanish," the woman said, voice lowering to a whisper. "Out past the watch stump, near where the old road breaks. You don't go past that line. Not unless you've got a death wish."

A loud clack cracked across the square.

Lusa and Noreena spun.

The same cart jolted as its wheel struck another pothole. The horse reared slightly. The old man shouted, yanking hard on the reins. Crates teetered, one near the top sliding sideways, tilting—

—and beneath it, far too close to the cart's path, sat the girl and her brothers.

The top crate tipped.

"Para nor!" Lusa shouted, lifting her arm.

The word cracked like a whip through the square. The crate froze mid-fall, suspended in the air, trembling faintly, as if confused by its own momentum.

It wasn't just the crate that stopped. It was everything. The square fell into a stunned stillness. Merchants, villagers… their eyes were on her. All of them. A sea of stares that burned hotter than any flame.

Noreena spun toward her. "What are you doing?" she hissed under her breath.

Lusa rushed forward, the children still frozen beneath the hovering crate, wide-eyed with shock.

"Move!" she urged, flailing her arms to direct them. "Now—go! Get out of the way!"

The girl's eyes widened, but she reacted. She lifted her toddler brother with one arm, reached for the older boy's hand, and ran.

The crate crashed to the cobbles with a deafening crack, splinters flying. Squash and pumpkins exploded or rolled across the square. The noise snapped whatever had held the crowd still.

Gasps rang out. A murmur broke. A word. Then another.

"Mage." "Dangerous." "Sent to wipe us out."

The words dug under her skin, deeper than nails, deeper than knives. She felt them brand her—monster, curse, weapon—every name she had feared since the Temple fell.

She wanted to shout that she hadn't asked for this, that she had saved those children, not harmed them. But the words shriveled before they left her mouth. Would it even matter? To them, she wasn't a woman in a square but every story whispered in the dark. Proof that their nightmares were real. Under her ribs two tides ran crosswise—heat and cold, push and pull.

Ignoring it, she watched as the girl set her brother down and rushed to Lusa, arms flung wide, and wrapped her in a sudden, tight hug. Lusa crouched to catch her, stunned by the contact, heart still racing. The girl wrapped her arms around Lusa's head and gave one tight squeeze, held a beat, and then rushed back to her brothers. She hoisted the toddler again, and together they vanished between two crooked buildings without another glance.

Lusa straightened slowly, still catching her breath. The crowd shifted. Some backed away. Others leaned forward, their fear curdling into something darker. Hatred. Panic.

A crow burst from the rooftops, its wings slashing the air as it veered toward the shadowed line of the west woods.

Noreena moved to block their view of her, spear in hand. "We need to move. Now. Before someone does something stupid."

Cold shot through Lusa in an instant, knifing behind her eyes. Searing. The Magics ripped through her veins like molten fire cracking stone, free. Their voices no longer whispers but a thousand jagged mouths. Her limbs spasmed, her throat filled with a hum that wasn't hers. She could feel Them taking her—sliding beneath her skin, bending her muscles, trying her voice on for size.

Let us speak.

Make them kneel.

Silence them.

Noreena said something, but Lusa couldn't hear her over the roar of Them. Her nails bit into her palms, rage consuming her. These villagers wanted to fear her? To brand her a monster, just because of what she was?

Then let them see one.

Shadows bled at the edges of her vision. She turned, chest heaving, gaze narrowing, already seeing it: the square swallowed whole. Silence. Every mouth sealed. Every body bent to her will.

One word: obedience.

One thought: submission.

Hands seized her shoulders. Noreena spun her hard toward the trees.

"Move!"

Shouts. Boots. The square erupting. The crow's harsh caw pierced the air above her as they passed beneath its branch. Noreena stayed tight at her side, hand gripping her arm. Fog swirled low, cold on her ankles. She narrowly missed a tree. Bark snagged her sleeve. She barely felt it. All she could feel was Them—thrumming, gnashing, dragging her inward no matter how fast her body ran.

"Keep moving!"

And then—pain. A flare through her chest, white-hot. One numbing thought drowned out Their voices: *They're helpless. Ignorant. But innocent.*

The Light lanced through her. Seared every nerve. The Magics shrieked, wildfire ripping through her core, fury ravaging her from the inside out.

In a breath, she was caught between them. Body taut. Ribs ready to crack. Head splitting. Two powers tearing her apart, each clawing for dominion.

Her knees buckled. Noreena's grip tightened, hauling her forward. Her eyes squeezed shut, scream trapped in her throat.

She let Noreena pull her, because if she stopped, she wasn't sure which side of herself would win. They pushed deeper into the trees, feet pounding damp soil. Two powers warring inside her head and all she could do was to focus on the one less likely to kill everybody.

A sudden rustle overhead. A dozen crows burst through the canopy, black shapes scattering into the gray sky. Noreena pulled them behind the thick trunk of a half-dead tree, catching her breath and giving a quick glance behind them.

"I don't think they followed."

Lusa reached up, pressing a hand to her temple, trying to still the spin of her thoughts. Her braid had loosened, damp strands sticking to the sweat at her neck.

She froze. Her fingers searched, frantic, combing through the plait. Empty.

The pin was gone.

Her chest cinched tight.

"No," she whispered. Her hands swept through her braid again, harder this time. "No, no—"

Noreena turned. "What?"

Lusa didn't answer. Her fingers wouldn't stop moving, desperate to find the weight that wasn't there. The cool pressure at her temple. The silent shield she'd come to rely on.

Kaden's vow echoed in her mind, *No one's gonna touch ye'r mind again, not while I'm breathin'.*

But the ward he'd given her was gone. The realization slammed into her chest like a blow. Of course—Their surge, Their frenzy, why every step out of the square had felt like drowning in Them. Without the pin, she was wide open. And They knew it and ripped through her mind with unbridled hunger.

Noreena frowned. "What are you doing?"

Lusa looked at her, words choking before they could form. How could she explain what the pin truly was? What it caged back?

She shook her head. "It's gone."

"Your hairpin?" Noreena blinked. "You can get another."

Lusa's head whipped toward her, the retort snapping loose before she could stop it.

"You don't understand," she snarled, venom burning through the cracks in her restraint. "It's not just a pin."

Noreena flinched—subtle. Her eyes narrowed, soldier-sharp, weighing threat versus defense.

Breath ragged, Lusa turned away. Her fingers fumbled through her braid again, searching as if the pin might still be there, hiding, waiting to be found.

"I need to find it." She spun on her heel, already moving toward the square.

"Wait, what?" Noreena caught up, planting a firm step in her path. "You can't go back. That mob is on edge. One wrong move and they'll come for you."

"Let them try."

"I won't be able to hold them all off."

Lusa snorted. "You won't have to. Stay here if you want."

Noreena stepped in front of her, boots set, spear raised horizontal across her chest.

"Don't make me choose between protecting you and stopping you." She spoke through clenched teeth. "You're not in your right mind."

The Magics pounced on the words, seizing control.

Strike her down. Show her who commands power.

Lusa's fists clenched. The image flashed, intruding all other thoughts: snapping the spear in two, driving Noreena to the ground with nothing but a breath of spellwork.

It faltered. The vision guttered, strangled by something quieter. The second force flared in her chest, cutting through the din.

This isn't who you are. Don't become what they fear. Don't give Vallas the satisfaction.

That last phrase seared more than any other. She would burn before letting him be right. She swallowed hard, forcing down the urge, the ache, the fury. Closing her eyes, she dragged in a steady breath and forced her pulse to slow until the Magics receded to a sullen hiss.

"I know you don't understand." When she opened her eyes, Noreena was still there with her spear braced, weight forward, ready to strike the moment she slipped. Lusa hated how much she respected her for it. She really didn't want to fight her.

"The reason I'm like this… is because of that pin." She sighed. "It… keeps Them back."

Noreena didn't lower the spear right away. Her eyes swept over Lusa like she was mapping every weakness. Finally, she shifted, lowering the weapon inch by inch until it rested in the grassy earth—but her grip never eased.

"I still don't get it," she said. "But maybe that doesn't matter."

She glanced back through the thicket of trees that separated them from the square. "We'll find it. When the town cools. Assuming no one's already pocketed it."

Her hardened gaze returned. "Can you handle the west woods? Or am I walking a liability into the dark?"

Lusa hesitated. The Magics prowled at the edges of her mind, pressing harder. Without the pin, she wouldn't keep Them quiet for long. But falling apart wasn't an option. Not with vanishings to investigate, and not with Merravale already sharpening its pitchforks.

"I'll manage."

Mostly true.

A soft drizzle started to fall, the canopy overhead barely shielding them. Before long, rain ticked against the leaves, a steady drumbeat against her frayed nerves. They stepped into the shadows of the west woods. If memory served from the brief glimpse she'd had of the General's map, this was the same direction that led toward the Mage Citadels.

Above, a lone crow perched in the branches, feathers slick with rain. The silence pressed close, listening. It felt… expectant. Uneven. As if the Weave and the Magics inside her were biding their time, waiting to see which power inside her would claim her first.

CHAPTER 13

The High Canopy

The trek from Izier had been long, slow, and too quiet for Kaden's liking.

He told himself he hated the silence. But the truth? It was easier than what waited in Aeonia. All those tight smiles. Perfume-laced lies. The kind of talk that made your skin itch even when the words sounded sweet.

At least the silence didn't pretend to be anything else.

They'd crossed the northern passage of the Glydales beneath a canopy of brittle leaves and frost-laced pines that hadn't belonged to Lady Fira. Trees yellowed and withered out of turn. Rivers once swollen with spring melt ran thin, exposing bone-dry riverbeds. Even the winds blew strange—hot one moment, freezing the next, like it couldn't make up its mind.

Anadine had offered no answers, only cold welcomes and tighter patrols. Every province along the route had shown signs of strain. Wilting crops, restless citizens, soldiers who watched too closely but spoke too little. Now, in Aeonia, the air buzzed with the sharp tang of politics and paranoia. Kaden didn't need to tune into Resonance to know something unnatural was unraveling across the realm. He saw it in the silence of the forests, and he felt it in the soil. The wind had the wrong pitch. Even the little chimes the Aeonians hung in border trees, tuned to their Harmonies, kept slipping off-key.

Caelithia kept him close, but not out of camaraderie. He didn't give a damn what they thought of him. Most days, he almost believed that. But sometimes, late at night, their silence scraped worse than words… like he'd already been written off, same as his father.

Over time, Kaden had learned the layers beneath elven courtesy. To most of the Aeonian court, he was a necessary nuisance. Half-human, half-elf, and wholly unwelcome. The soldiers didn't bother hiding their disdain. Whispers carried when they thought he didn't know their language. He did. He just didn't give them the satisfaction of reacting.

All but for Commander Thalor.

Older, white hair in braids, and sharp silvery eyes, Thalor was the only one who addressed him by name without venom in his tone. He'd fought in the Eastern Wars, knew the cost of alliances, and treated Kaden less like an obligation and more like a comrade. Over firelight, he'd even shared a dry joke or two—rare currency among elves.

Still, respect was hard-won, and Kaden wasn't in Aeonia to make friends. While the others rode with noses in the wind and hands on hilts, Kaden rode with a blade on his back and soil beneath his nails. Every village they passed, he'd stopped to collect samples: wilting clover, rot-veined ivy, sickly marigolds that shouldn't have bloomed this far north. The others saw dead plants. Kaden saw a pattern. Roots that twisted the wrong way. Leaves that responded to no sun. Spores too aggressive for the season. Something was spreading, and it wasn't just political decay.

The Aeonian palace wasn't a place he'd ever stepped foot in, being not welcome until needed. Built into the high trunks of elderwood trees, its silver walkways spiraled like spider silk through branches thick as towers. The bridges weren't lashed so much as resonant—slender ribs of elderwood set to a quiet hum he felt more than heard. Sunlight poured in from leaf-filtered skylights, golden and cold. He'd barely had a day to unpack his satchel and get a general lay of his area of the palace before the summons came.

He stood in a chamber of polished root and woven vine, Caelithia sitting ahead of him with her fingers steepled like judgment.

"You've been... busy. Collecting samples. Inspecting village soil. Speaking with farmers."

"Someone's gotta be," Kaden replied, arms crossed, boots still dusted with dried lichen. "Isn't like the land's gonna fix itself while they argue in circles 'bout who gets to point fingers."

Her eyes narrowed a hair. "You presume much, for a guest."

"I'm here 'cause y'er crops are dyin' and y'er skies don't know what season it is. If that makes me a guest, it's a damned frostbitten welcome."

Silence stretched like tensioned bowstring. Behind her, a breeze stirred the hanging silk drapes, carrying the faint, sweet scent of cedar and rot. She finally rose from her seat.

"You speak plainly. That may be your charm in Izier. But in Aeonia, diplomacy is not optional. You'd do well to remember who granted you audience."

He'd considered softening his words. Playing the part. But Aetherealm didn't have time for politeness, and neither did he. "And you'd do well to remember who's tryin' to help you."

Caelithia let the silence linger long enough to sting, then turned away. "You'll address the king and queen at tomorrow's convocation," she said. "Keep your findings brief. Do not speak of rumors, and do not provoke alarm."

Kaden's jaw flexed. "Truth's already bubblin' under their feet. I'm not the one stirrin' it."

"You are a representative of Izier," she replied without turning back. "Behave like one."

She swept out, guards falling in behind her like shadows, leaving Kaden alone with the hush of leaves and the soft creak of timber underfoot. He exhaled through his nose. Fancy words and finer robes wouldn't fix what was coming.

Later, in the guest wing nestled between two colossal trunks, Kaden knelt on the floor, satchel open. Dried sprigs of brittleblade and frost-curled fern lay arranged on a woven cloth beside samples he hadn't dared share with the Aeonian archivists. One in particular caught his eye. A thread-thin root, pale as bone, pulsing faintly under the lantern light.

He hadn't noticed that before.

He leaned closer at a low hum on the edge of hearing. Not sound exactly, more like a vibration that resonated faintly in his Seryn—that small, half-formed well of energy the elves claimed sat behind the heart. His was weaker than theirs. He only felt it when he was still enough, quiet enough, to let the pulse of the world brush against his own.

He reached for another sample from a village nearly twenty leagues away. Same root. Same shimmer. Same faint pulse.

He set them side by side. They matched exactly. That shouldn't have been possible. Different soil, different climate, and yet both throbbed with the same rhythm—like echoes of a single breath.

He hesitated, then spread his hand over the first root and let his breathing slow. Let that dormant part of him stir… the piece of his blood he rarely touched. The Aeon within.

When he was young, his father had told him the Aeon was the world's Resonance. The harmony that bound all living things, a weave of pulse and pattern that could be felt through one's Seryn if you listened closely enough. He'd never cared for it much—the hymns, the hand-signs—but he still knew it in his bones. Everyone in Aetherealm did. Whether they called it magic, Resonance, instinct, or something holier, the Aeon threaded through them all.

He focused enough to send warmth into the root with intention. His hand shifted through the motion he still remembered from his father's lessons—fingers curved and drawn together, palm turned inward. The Aeonian sign for harmony.

It felt foreign now, like a language his body still spoke but his heart no longer trusted. He held the shape steady until the warmth stirred from his Seryn, threading down his arm.

Gradually, the pulse in the root slowed, the shimmer along its edge flickering out. The faint hum in his Seryn quieted, leaving only stillness.

Kaden exhaled and scratched at his chin, uneasy. The Resonance had answered him then gone still. Huh.

A knock at the door broke his focus.

Kaden rose and opened it to find Thalor leaning against the frame, arms folded, white braids damp from night mist.

"You're up late," Thalor said, eyes drifting toward the cloth. "Trying to outthink the court?"

"Diplomacy never saved a dyin' tree." Kaden stepped aside. "Come in."

Thalor entered without ceremony. His gaze landed on the root that still pulsed under the lantern light.

"Glowing roots. That's new."

Kaden picked it up with tweezers. "Same root showed up twenty leagues apart. Different provinces. But this?" He nodded toward the faint shimmer. "Isn't natural. And I'm pretty sure it's spreadin'."

Thalor looked again, slower this time. "Never seen anything like it."

"But you've marched through rot before. Famine. Blight. Does this feel the same?"

"No," Thalor said. The answer came too quickly to be anything but honest. "This is definitely something else."

Kaden gave a dry huff. "That's what I thought."

He set the sample back down and rubbed a hand over his face.

Thalor studied it a moment longer. "The song's always lived in the roots," Thalor said at last. "This feels like someone changed the key."

"Yeah. That tracks."

They both fell quiet.

Thalor finally turned and moved to the table, pouring himself a cup of the tea left out by the stewards. "You'll be addressing the court tomorrow?"

"Yeah. Caelithia wants me groomed and grateful. Smile like I don't know better."

Thalor snorted into his cup. "Careful with that smile. This court's got more cracks than stonework."

Kaden glanced over. "Who do I need to worry about most?"

Thalor took a slow sip, then leaned one hip against the table. "The Crown Prince's bold but impatient. Talks about reform, but what he's shaping serves a narrow few. The second prince clings to the old ways. Thinks tradition's enough to hold the cracks together."

Kaden raised an eyebrow and moved over to pour himself a cup.

"The princess is… young. Bright, but some say naïve. Could be a façade. Either way, she's caught between brothers with too much to prove." Thalor set the cup down. "The queen's father doesn't speak often, but when he does, the whole court leans in. Doesn't need a crown when half the trade routes, and council members, run through his pocket."

Kaden nodded slowly, squinting at the tang left by the tea. "And the king?"

Thalor didn't answer right away, instead staring at his cup like the words were somewhere at the bottom of it. "He's held this place together longer than most expected. But there's wear in him. Deep."

A pause. Then, more quietly: "When he steps down, if he does, it won't be a peaceful handoff."

Nobles here liked to pretend their blood kept time with higher Harmonies. Kaden knew what that meant in practice: closed doors. His attention drifted back to the root.

"Sounds like a snake pit."

Thalor followed his gaze. "Then maybe you're the poor bastard who brought a stick to poke it."

Kaden smirked, but it didn't last. "And what exactly do they want from me?"

Thalor finished his tea before answering. "Truth. Or leverage. Depends who's asking. Just be careful what you give them."

After Thalor left, Kaden didn't sleep. He stayed at the table, candle burned low, sorting the samples again with slower hands. When he reached the one he'd touched with Resonance, he paused. The shimmer had returned, jittering along its edge like a nerve misfiring. Kaden frowned. So much for healing. He hadn't expected a miracle, but he'd hoped it'd last longer than an hour.

He wrapped it and its twin from another province in oilcloth and tucked it into the leather-bound folio Caelithia had scowled at during their first meeting. Most of the others were brittle now, curling in on themselves, edges browned and frayed. He cataloged them anyway, jotting notes in cramped script: village names, weather at the time, soil color, anything that might matter later.

He placed the folio into his satchel, noticing a dried flower, half-crushed beneath a fold. Faded red petals, delicate veins like spun glass. It hadn't withered yet, but was dry enough to hold its shape, as if clinging to the memory of Lady Fira, trying to hold onto its youth. He'd plucked it the morning he left Izier. Didn't even know why, at the time.

But he knew now.

He remembered her that night at the Lady Fira festival. The way those deep red-gradient solovine blooms had been pinned in Lusa's hair, vivid against her dark curls and catching firelight as she moved. A few had come loose by the end of it, drifting down to catch in the soft ripples of her gown.

She'd cursed the shoes. Complained about the gown's length. Threatened to stick blossomfire toffee "where it counted" if she caught one more person staring. She'd hated every part of the pageantry. And something about that made her the most radiant thing in all of Aetherealm.

It still sat wrong with him that they hadn't said a real goodbye. Not really. Both of them too damn stubborn to say what needed saying. She'd been too mad to watch him leave, and he'd been too hardheaded to look back when it might've mattered.

By the time he did, she was already gone… a blur of wind and hooves, hunched low in the saddle like she couldn't get away fast enough.

A glimpse. That's all he got.

Kaden turned the pressed flower between his fingers, let out a slow breath, and wondered if the ward was holding, if she was still safe. Still angry. He wrapped the solovine in cloth, careful to keep it from crumbling, and tucked it into a fold inside the breast of his tunic. It was just a flower. Once it started to crack and crumble, he'd toss it. That's what he kept telling himself, anyway.

Morning in Aeonia came quiet as snowfall. Kaden followed the steward through the winding corridors, every footstep muffled by moss-lined runners and petals scattered with a perfectionist's precision. He caught a faint scent beneath it all, sour and wrong.

The trees were sick. He could feel it now that he was listening. The woven bridges between towers creaked too much for a place that never swayed. A carved lantern flickered in daylight, its flame moss dull and gray at the base. Even the air hummed wrong, like a string pulled too tight.

A few stewards passed wearing guard-rings that chimed softly with each breath—Seryn monitors, Thalor had called them once. Elves treated a Resonance out of tune like a fever.

They passed balconies that overlooked the forest canopy, and for a moment, the weight of the court ahead eased just enough for him to breathe deep. But it didn't last.

The steward stopped in front of a tall, root-twined archway guarded by two soldiers in green-etched silver.

"Wait here, Ambassador," the steward said with a bow. "The High Canopy will summon you shortly."

Kaden nodded once and, as he waited, his gaze drifted again to the vines. They weren't just wilting. They were curling in the wrong direction, toward the stone.

The doors opened with a hush, not a creak. Aeonian craft didn't creak. But the silence that followed felt colder than it should've. The High Canopy, the royal family and their court, was carved into the living heart of the forest. The central tree rose like a sacred spine through the vast chamber; its massive trunk wrapped in centuries of memory and judgment. Branches arched into vaulted ceilings, and woven platforms hovered in the air, tethered by thick chains of root that pulsed faintly with age-old Resonance.

Some of those platforms jutted like hanging balconies, suspended from the upper limbs. Nobles clustered there in threes and fours, draped in forest-dyed silks and sharp glances, looking down on the chamber like birds from a high perch.

Kaden stepped onto the circular dais below the throne tier, boots echoing too loud. The king sat at the highest point, his crown a tangle of silver and vine. Eyes heavy. Beard braided with ceremonial jade. He looked like he hadn't slept in a season.

Beside the king, Queen Valenne watched with a cool, calculating gaze. Pale lashes framed golden eyes that probably missed nothing. Her near-strawberry-blonde hair was towered high and tight, not a strand out of place.

Flanking the throne were the three heirs, each as different as the stories claimed. All far too aware of the eyes on them.

Crown Prince Eldarion stood tall and rigid, hands clasped behind his back, tension evident in his narrow jaw. A leader in the making… or trying to be. Prince Vaelar lounged half a step behind, all polished disdain. His silver robes gleamed like ice, eyes colder still.

Between them sat Princess Siraen, younger by several decades if the air around her was any measure. Light seemed to favor her—platinum-white hair catching every glint, gold eyes bright with open curiosity instead of caution. While her brothers postured, she swung one foot idly beneath her chair, studying Kaden like he might be a riddle she wasn't supposed to solve but wanted to anyway.

Behind the throne, cloaked in the gallery's shadows, stood Lord Laerynth—the queen's father. Regal. Motionless. Like he'd grown from the same elderwood as the dais itself. And farther off, near the wine table, leaned Prince Lorenthar, the king's brother. At least he guessed as much. His arms were crossed, and he was smirking between a thin goatee, gold-flecked silvery eyes gleaming with too much charm and just enough warning.

Thalor stood nearby, arms behind his back, unreadable. But Kaden caught the faintest nod. The king's voice broke the silence, low and worn but still carrying the weight of a sovereign.

"Kaden Everwyn. Son of Laerien of Aeonia and Princess Anora of Izier. You have come far to stand before the High Canopy. Speak now of what you have found."

Laerien. Anora. Names he hadn't heard together in decades. It wasn't grief, but something colder, lodged beneath the ribs. His mother's laugh, distant and wind-soft, flickered in memory. He pushed the thought down. No time for ghosts.

Holding up the leather folio, he opened it slowly. "Somethin's wrong with y'er land. And it's not just the weather."

He reached inside and drew out a sample, one of the pulsing roots swaddled in cloth, its strange shimmer dulled but still present. Whispers stirred the air.

"I've seen this same rot in three different provinces," Kaden said, voice level. "Spread across leagues. It isn't natural. Isn't seasonal. It's growin' where it shouldn't, in soil that shouldn't be carryin' it."

He paused, then added, "I'm no scholar. But I know plants. And I know when the ground's bein' poisoned."

He let the silence stretch. No point in dressing it up for people who only heard what they wanted.

Crown Prince Eldarion was the first to move. A silver circlet rested on his brow. Lighter than the king's heavy vinework crown, but no less binding. Its branches curled upward like small antlers, catching the sunlight with every movement.

"Are you suggesting Aeonia is poisoning itself?"

"I'm sayin' whatever's happenin' out there isn't chance," Kaden replied. "The soil's turnin' on itself. Roots drawin' from the wrong veins, like the Weave's pulse got tangled."

Eldarion's mouth twitched—almost a smile, but not quite. "Spoken like one who's learned his craft in soil, not in song."

"No, y'er highness," Kaden said evenly, meeting his gaze. "Spoken like someone wonderin' how a people so attuned to the Aeon haven't noticed the discord in its song."

A sudden murmur rippled through the chamber. Courtiers shifted, silks whispering like hissing leaves. One counselor actually gasped, the sound thin and scandalized.

Eldarion's jaw flexed, but before he could speak, Vaelar stepped forward, silver-strawberry blonde hair pulled back into a tight ponytail beneath a thin silver circlet.

"You tread dangerously close to insult, half-blood," he said. "This is fearmongering. You bring us weeds and omens as if they're evidence. Superstition paraded as insight. Aeonia does not shape policy on folk wisdom."

Kaden looked up at him, slow. "You ever held a shovel, y'er highness?"

From behind the prince's, Princess Siraen let out a sharp exhale. Close enough to a laugh that she caught herself, raising her goblet to hide the curve of her lips.

Queen Valenne's voice sliced through next, calm and controlled. "You speak boldly, Kaden Everwyn, for someone who stands between two legacies and belongs wholly to neither."

There it was.

His mouth opened with a retort already forming, but he caught himself. He'd learned a long time ago that survival wasn't about being right but about knowing when to shut up. Still, the old Aeonian creed crept up in memory: purity keeps the Seryn clear. Convenient creed, if you needed a reason to look down.

He exhaled slowly, then dipped his chin in the smallest nod. "Majesty," he said, tone even. "I only mean to serve the land. Same as your court."

King Theron raised a hand before another word could spark. His eyes were heavy with weariness.

"You have offered your warning. Your findings will be examined by the Court Alchemists and the Grove Keepers. Until then, you remain a guest. Conduct yourself accordingly."

Kaden gave a slight bow. "Your Majesty."

As he stepped back, the king's brother finished a sip from his wine and finally straightened. His voice rolled out smooth, unhurried.

"Fear alone serves no kingdom," said Lorenthar. "Perhaps we give this scout the chance to prove his claim… quietly. The health of our land deserves inquiry, not indignation."

Another murmur rippled through the courtiers—some surprised, others suspicious. Kaden watched Lorenthar a beat longer. Of all the elves, he hadn't expected sense from that corner of the room. And yet… the king's brother was the only one who sounded like he didn't care enough about politics to bother masking his words.

Maybe that made him honest. Or just dangerous in a different way.

CHAPTER 14

Fruits of the Crown

The corridor beyond the High Canopy thrummed with the aftermath of politics, every breath still measuring the cost of what had been said. Kaden moved quietly over the moss-lined stone as he turned toward the guest wing, his pulse finally settling back to normal.

He wasn't three paces from his door when Thalor stepped out of the shadows beside a carved support column.

"Walked right into a nest of thorns, didn't you?" The commander smirked, leaning his shoulder against the column.

Kaden rubbed the back of his neck. "Yeah well, I didn't do much to diffuse the situation either."

Thalor uncrossed his arms, glancing once toward the guards posted farther down the corridor behind Kaden.

"You made an enemy today," Thalor said. "Maybe more than one."

"Wasn't tryin' ta' make friends."

"That's clear." Thalor's tone wasn't mocking. If anything, it carried the edge of approval.

He moved closer, voice dropping. "Laerynth's already talking. You embarrassed Vaelar. And Queen Valenne doesn't take kindly to anyone who challenges the shape of her world, least of all someone not born into it."

"They asked for truth. I gave it."

"No. They asked for false harmony. You handed them dissonance."

A beat passed.

"Just watch your doors," he added. "And your food. This court may be rotting from the roots up, but the fruit still bites."

He turned to go but paused mid-step. "They'll come at you in layers. Flattery, questions, silence. Don't confuse patience for peace."

Then he was gone, footsteps swallowed by the living wood beneath them. Kaden turned to his door, hand halfway to the latch, when a soft voice interrupted him.

"Apologies," said the steward standing at the opposite end of the corridor from where Thalor had left. He held out a scroll sealed in deep green wax, the crest a faint etching of interwoven vines. "Prince Lorenthar requests your company. He asks that you bring your satchel."

Kaden's eyes narrowed. "Now?"

The steward bowed. "At his leisure. But I'm told the wine is already poured."

Kaden let out a quiet breath through his nose and looked at the door. So close. He adjusted the satchel on his shoulder. "Lead on."

The steward guided him through a narrower wing of the palace, past a spiral staircase that arched up into a closed balcony chamber overlooking the southern edge of the canopy. It was quieter here, thick with hanging plants and golden light from the sun, already beginning its descent into dusk. The air itself seemed tuned. Aeonian halls were built to hum in resonance with the canopy above, their architects claiming the right balance of light and breath could steady the Weave around them. The kind of place where secrets could steep like tea.

Lorenthar waited near the far edge, lounging with one leg crossed over the other on a crescent-shaped bench. In his hand, a glass of wine gleamed plum red, catching the sunlight like a drop of blood in crystal.

"Everwyn," he said smoothly. "Didn't think they'd let you out of the throne room alive."

Lorenthar lifted the second glass from the vine-carved table beside him and held it out without rising.

"Luthira," he said, as if that explained everything. "From the eastern boughs. Rare this late in the season."

A smile played at the corner of his mouth. Silver-blond hair hung loose, catching a ray of light through the canopy slats above. The dark velvet of his tunic absorbed the glow, layered beneath a half-cloak of brushed leathers. He looked less like a prince and more like someone who belonged to the shadows between politics.

"And with the way things are going," he added, "I expect the price'll double soon."

Kaden took the glass, letting its weight settle in his hand.

"These vines don't thrive when the land starts to sour," he continued. "The resonance is off. You can feel it, can't you? The Aeon's breath falters, and the roots lose their song. Most of the court pretends it's just drought. Easier than admitting we've forgotten how to listen."

Instead of drinking it, Kaden brought it close enough to his nose, pretending to admire the aroma, but really testing for any trace of bitterness, rot, or something too sweet to be trusted. He didn't catch anything unusual.

Lorenthar gestured to the seat across from him. "Sit. You've had a long day offending half the kingdom."

"You didn't call me here for the wine."

"No," Lorenthar agreed easily, swirling his own glass. "Though I'd like to think I have a better reputation than most for hospitality."

He set the glass down with a soft clink, then reached for a scroll at his side tied with old twine.

"Tell me," Lorenthar started, unrolling it onto the table, "What do you know about the Old Grove near the southern canopy rim?"

Kaden stepped closer, eyes narrowing. The map was hand-drawn. Trails not marked on official palace routes based on what he'd seen in the Archives when he'd first arrived. A cluster of trees were marked with small, inked runes.

"I know it wasn't on any of the maps the archivists let me see."

Lorenthar almost laughed. "Of course not. They stopped charting the grove properly about a century ago. Claimed the area was 'unstable'. Landslides, weakened bridges, all very tidy excuses."

"And what do you think?"

Lines deepened around Lorenthar's golden eyes as he studied the inked map. "That grove hasn't bloomed right in years. Missed two seasonal cycles. No birds, no fruit, no interest from the court."

Kaden didn't answer right away. His gaze held on the map, something tugging at the edge of memory. An unease he couldn't name. "And what do you want from me?"

Lorenthar shrugged, casual as ever. "Nothing. Just thought someone with your… inclination for roots and trouble might find it worth a look."

He leaned back, lifting his glass again.

"Of course," he added, "you didn't get this from me."

Kaden finally took a sip of the Luthira. The flavor bloomed fast. Sharp at first, almost floral, then mellowing into something earthbound. Notes of spice and forest fruit clung to the back of his tongue, sweet without being soft. The kind of wine that took its time ruining you. He set the glass down, slightly off-center, and let the silence stretch long enough to study Lorenthar properly.

The king's brother didn't look dangerous. All that loose hair and relaxed posture and a smile that seemed to reach his eyes more often than not. He wore charm like a second cloak, but Kaden had known too many bounty marks who smiled the same way, as if knowing what came next. There was no crown on his head, but the room still bent around him… like it knew who held the real gravity.

Kaden nodded once to the map. "I'll look into it."

Lorenthar tipped his glass in acknowledgment. "Safe travels, Everwyn."

Kaden didn't thank him, turning to walk back the way he'd come, his mind pulling tighter with every step. By the time he reached his quarters, the sun had dipped behind the canopy. Inside, the air was still. He crossed to the table where he'd left the samples and unwrapped the oilcloth bundle.

The root he hadn't healed was gone. Not stolen, but not crumbled or rotted, either.

Dust.

A smear of it clung to the cloth, the last trace of whatever it had been. Ancient. Spent. As if time had reclaimed it in a blink.

The other healed root still remained. But its pulse was faint now, and the shimmer along its edge was flickering like a dying ember. The magic hadn't cured it. Just slowed the inevitable. Kaden stared at them.

Since leaving Izier, everything had pointed in one direction: sick land, erratic weather, crops gone sideways. The palace ignored it. The court called it rumor. And now Lorenthar handed him a grove that hadn't bloomed in years.

The land was trying to say something. No one wanted to listen. He reached for his notebook and scrawled a fresh line beneath his last entry:

Magic delays decay. Doesn't fix it.

He let the quill hover a moment, then added:

Lorenthar knows more than he says. And that map wasn't a favor.

Kaden leaned back in the chair, eyes trailing to the high window as the moon drifted into view. The rot wasn't just in the roots. It was in the palace walls. In the silence. In the people who smiled too easily. And if he didn't start digging soon, someone was going to bury the truth for good.

He glanced around his quarters—modest by palace standards. One bed, neatly carved from elderwood and tucked into the curve of the wall. He sat at the small writing desk, worn at the edges but polished clean. A basin for washing, a single lantern overhead, and a view of nothing but filtered green light from the canopy beyond the lattice window.

Kaden capped the ink bottle as another knock came at the door. He stared at it for a beat, hoping if he pretended he wasn't there, they'd go away.

Another knock. A little more insistent. He sighed, ran a hand down his face, and crossed the room and opened the door. The steward from before waited outside, scroll in hand. This one was sealed in pale green wax, the soft imprint of leafwork curling along the edges.

"Princess Siraen requests your company," the steward said. "In the Aevian Garden. If you're available."

Kaden raised a brow. "She always summon right before supper?"

"She prefers dusk," the steward said. "It's when the blooms open."

Oh, well then of course that makes sense. He held his tongue and took a sweeping glance at his room, at the satchel resting on the chair, at the quiet that kept getting interrupted.

He thought of Thalor's warning. *Flattery. Questions. Silence.* And the king's tired voice echoing somewhere in the back of his mind: *Conduct yourself accordingly.*

He turned back to the steward, tall and fine-boned like the rest of them, with pale golden hair swept back in a neat twist, and silver-flecked eyes that never quite met Kaden's for long. Dressed in layered linens of sage and ivory, he moved like wind through reeds. Graceful, silent, and detached just enough to remind Kaden where he stood. But there was something about how he lingered a beat too long, how he watched without watching.

They always see more than they let on, Kaden thought. He muttered under his breath and grabbed the satchel.

"Lead on," he said, already regretting it.

The Aevian Garden wasn't like the austere halls below. It perched high in the canopy's uppermost ring, bright and breathing, where light pooled through the leaves like poured gold. Every flower looked hand-tended, every path curved with intended grace. Even the air smelled new—like rain caught in petals. Ivory-laced planters cradled blooms in shades of silver, pale blue, and mint. The petals stirred with the breeze, timed to open with the fading light as if the garden bowed only for dusk.

Princess Siraen stood by a low table of stone, a porcelain teapot gleaming beside two delicate cups. She turned one slowly in her hands, as if deciding whether to drink or simply watch the steam curl.

Her gown shimmered in layers of mint and ivory, fabric so fine it moved like mist when she shifted. Diaphanous sleeves fluttered with the evening air, the bodice cinched just enough to hint at form without demanding attention.

A silver circlet rested across her brow, slender and leaf-patterned, catching the last rays of sun that filtered through the treetops above. Her platinum hair fell loose around her shoulders, touched with the same glint of moonlight that softened the whole garden.

Kaden slowed as he approached, taking it in despite himself. She was, objectively, stunning. When she noticed him, she looked up with bright eyes, like someone who hadn't yet learned that not every smile was safe to give away.

"Ambassador," she said, a hint of relief beneath her formality. "You came."

Kaden gave the barest dip of his chin. "Wasn't much of a choice."

"That's not true," she said, motioning toward the seat across from her. "I just wasn't sure you'd come. Most people don't when I invite them."

He didn't sit. "You in the habit of invitin' people ta' gardens when they're under suspicion?"

The princess smiled again—an unguarded thing, warm and earnest. In that instant, he understood Thalor's assessment of her. She wasn't foolish, not exactly. Probably untouched by the edges of the world.

"No," she said lightly. "Just the interesting ones."

Kaden's gaze flicked to the teapot, steam curling gently from its spout. Two cups. One already poured. He stepped closer and lowered himself into the seat opposite her, careful not to let his satchel slide too far from reach.

Siraen poured the second cup without asking. Mint and something faintly floral hit the air between them.

"I hear you've taken an interest in the land," she said, setting the pot aside. "So I thought I'd show you a corner of it few ever see. The Aevian Garden's been mine since I was old enough to wander it. I used to think it belonged only to me."

He took the cup but didn't drink. "Didn't think royal gardens were open to half-blood guests."

She blinked, then frowned slightly, thoughtful. "They aren't," she admitted softly. "But that seems rather dull, doesn't it? A garden that never meets anyone new?"

A light breeze stirred between them, catching the loose strands of her hair. She brushed one aside, fingers lingering on a silver-petaled bloom that had begun to open to the moonlight.

"You speak so plainly," she said after a moment. "It's... refreshing. Most here only talk to be heard. I think even the trees have learned to pretend."

He raised a brow. "That supposed ta' mean somethin'?"

"Only that I envy you," she said, folding her hands in her lap with the smallest of a smile. "You've seen more of Aeonia than I ever will. The rivers, the roots—the parts no one writes songs about. I read about them in the archives, but words never smell like rain or sound like wind."

Kaden leaned back, studying her. "So what is it ye're really after, Princess?"

"Maybe I just wanted to know what the world looks like to someone who's actually touched it."

A pair of birds flitted through the branches above, their soft whistles trading calls between the leaves. Kaden studied her across the table. There wasn't calculation in her tone, no polished edge of diplomacy. It was quiet wonder… the kind that didn't belong in a court like this.

He'd met plenty of royals who spoke of the world like it was a story written for their amusement—King Nargone and his four broods of heirs chief among them. But she wasn't performing. He felt certain the words weren't bait, but belief, and that made her dangerous in a different way.

Naïve hearts didn't last long in places built on politics. They either hardened or broke. He wasn't sure which fate suited her more, or why he suddenly gave a damn which it would be.

Kaden took the pause as permission and finally tried the tea. Cooler than expected. Mint first, then something faintly floral with a hint of sweetness that lingered on the tongue. It wasn't what he expected. Refined, but simple.

"You listen more than you speak," Siraen said, brushing a petal from her sleeve. "That's rare here. Most people only wait for their turn to sound clever."

Kaden's mouth quirked. "Guess I missed that trainin'."

She laughed—soft, free, like it hadn't yet occurred to her that laughter could be used against you. "Maybe that's why I wanted to meet you."

He didn't know what to do with that, so he took another sip. The tea really was refreshing.

Siraen studied the steam curling between them. "Do you think the land is unwell?"

He blinked. "Unwell?"

"The stories say the Aeon runs through everything that grows. But lately, the air feels… tired. The blooms don't open as wide. The roots don't hum like they used to. Maybe it's us. Maybe we've asked too much of it."

Kaden set the cup down. "You always talk like that?"

Her brow creased. "Like what?"

"Like ye're still hopin' the world's better than it is?"

She tilted her head. "Someone has to."

He looked away before she could read the thought that flickered across his face. That kind of unarmored hope wouldn't last long in a place like this. And he wasn't about to be the one to crush it.

He leaned forward, elbows on his knees, fingers curling around the cup again. "What's this really about, Princess?"

Siraen hesitated, her eyes dipping to the swirl of tea in her cup. When she looked back up, her voice was quieter. "I wanted the company of someone who doesn't treat questions like trespass."

That pulled something faint across his chest. Pity, maybe. Or understanding.

"You're not like them," he said finally.

Her lips parted in surprise before smiling, eyes twinkling as if he'd just given her the biggest compliment.

"No," she admitted. "But I've learned how to move among them without losing myself."

He nodded once, slow. She might think herself untouched by the court's rot, but it was already brushing her edges. Sooner or later, she'd have to decide whether to become callused or broken.

Kaden rose, the chair's legs scratching against stone. The breeze stirred through the garden, carrying the faint sweetness of the blooms and the shimmer of her loose hair in the dimming light.

"Thanks for the tea," he said, setting the cup down. "And for seein' the cracks instead of pretendin' they don't exist."

"Let me know what you find," she said softly. "Before someone else decides what it means."

He almost smiled. "Careful, Princess. Sounds like ye're startin' to sound dangerous yourself."

Her laugh followed him as he turned down the path, far too free for a place built on restraint. At the archway, he caught sight of her lady's maid waiting beyond the vines with hands folded and gaze lowered. Not close enough to hear, but close enough to have timed it perfectly. The meeting hadn't been an accident. Whatever Siraen wanted from him, it hadn't been idle curiosity.

Still, as he walked away, a thought struck harder than the politics or the plotting.

He'd meant it when he said thank you.

Kaden rubbed at his nose, half a grimace, half a sigh. He was tired, hungry, and more than ready to get back to something that made sense—soil, roots, anything that didn't smile like that. He hadn't gotten answers. But he'd been seen. And in Aeonia, that was either a blessing or a curse.

CHAPTER 15

Invisible Threads

The further they moved into the west woods, the more the trees seemed to close in. Drizzle thickened to mist. Mist to clinging vapor. The sodden earth muffled each step as they moved.

Lusa rolled her shoulders. Deep tension had settled there. She sent out tendrils of magic—threads of the Weave drawn through her center. The Aether shivered, the living current through which all things breathed and answered, and she felt it.

Something was out there watching, waiting… but shielded. No matter how many times she probed for this… entity, she failed. It knew exactly how to keep just beyond reach. Her magic hit a wall of nothingness. And yet, something stared back. Throat dry, she glared into the woods. Whatever it was, it saw her.

They walked another ten steps, Lusa gathering her Magics to try one last time to pin this thing down, when a sharp crack shattered the stillness.

A broken branch.

Lusa's heart slammed against her ribs as she spun, instincts flaring too fast for control. The spike of adrenaline cracked her focus and the Magics took Their chance. They surged in before she could brace, twisting the Aether's current into Their own design. Her vision blurred. Eyes inked over. The world tilted sideways.

She felt herself move, but it wasn't her. Trembling fingers lifted. Arms rigid, aimed like weapons. Her power pooled in her palms, seething, ready for release.

She tried to fight Them. Tried to will her body to obey her, not Them.

Jarion cried out.

His face flashed through the haze: young, pale, eyes wide and horrified. He stumbled back, hand twitching toward his bow, but didn't draw. Couldn't, frozen in shock at what he was seeing. He looked like a child. Terrified. Helpless.

Vallas shouted. "Stand down!"

His sword was drawn, ready to strike. His feet braced, his jaw locked. But it was fear Lusa saw, not rage. They felt it too. And They fed on it.

Lusa grit her teeth, forcing her arms down though every muscle screamed under the weight of a thousand stones. Every tendon screamed. The Magics thrashed inside her, howling for release, twisting her bones like They could shatter her into submission.

Let go, They hissed. *Let us end this.*

They promised safety. Power. Freedom.

But Jarion's fear cut through the noise. So did another face… Tryston. His smile. His blood. The weight of his body against hers when she'd been too late. She should've saved him first…

The pain tore through her chest. Lusa gasped, and in the space between breaths, she reached. Not outward.

Inward.

Toward the quiet magic beneath it all. The Light. It flickered in response, faint but real, like sun behind storm clouds. While she couldn't figure out how to gather enough to burn Them out, she summoned enough to resist.

Squeezing her eyes shut, Lusa shoved downward, pressing with everything she had. The pressure cracked behind her eyes and she cried out.

Slowly, the black began to recede. Color bled back into her vision. Sound returned in echoes. Her knees buckled and she caught herself on a low-hanging branch, chest heaving, head pounding.

No one moved.

Lusa stayed hunched, one hand braced against the branch, the other trembling at her side. The air around her still crackled with leftover magic—hot, bitter, wrong.

She didn't look up at Vallas, whose sword gleamed, still ready. Or Jarion, whose hand hadn't moved from his chest. The brittle silence dragged on until Noreena addressed the general.

"There've been four disappearances in the last fortnight. No one older than ten."

Lusa blinked. Her vision was still focusing. Her ears rang. She shook her head and stood a little straighter.

"She used her magic to freeze a crate midair. Saved some children," Noreena continued, all debrief. "Now the whole village wants her head. She started slipping after she lost some hairpin."

Vallas's eyes never left Lusa. He didn't blink or, more importantly, lower his sword. He was probably weighing how simpler things would be without her. Kill her now, bury the truth in the trees, report that the mage had lost control. No interim Sorceress, just another tragedy.

Maybe he was replaying Myttica. The sprites. The inferno. The way she'd lost herself to Them. Even if she'd saved his life afterward, it hadn't been enough. He didn't trust her and probably never would.

Still, he wasn't a fool. If anything, his silence now suggested he was already considering his next move. Maybe he'd tread more carefully, at least until he figured out how unstable she really was. Or perhaps the decision had already been made. A spell gone wrong. A mage undone by her own power. The report would practically write itself. And with her gone, he could sleep easier, no longer waiting for her to lose control again. The silence between them was suffocating. Mage and general, caught in a standoff.

Jarion shifted, the quiet crunch of a boot breaking the stillness. "Are… are you okay?"

Lusa flinched. It wasn't the question that made her, but the intention behind it. Genuine. Her eyes met his. The fear was still there, buried beneath the surface, but what surprised her was the concern layered over it. She'd nearly flayed him alive, and he wanted to know if she was okay?

"I'm fine," she lied, barely above a whisper.

Vallas lowered his sword, only a fraction, and turned to Noreena. "Go. Find Glon and Dak. Bring them here. This clearing. We can't go back to the inn."

She gave a short nod and slipped into the thicket without a word.

"You're with me," Vallas said to Jarion. "We're going to find that pin."

He looked at Lusa when he said it, and she realized then that he understood. He hadn't asked about the pin, but somehow, he'd put it together. It wasn't just a trinket, but a tether that helped keep the Magics at bay. And without it, she was losing the fight.

Lusa raised an eyebrow. "So what, you're leaving me here?"

"I'm giving you space, not trust. Don't confuse the two."

Jarion gave her one last glance, following the general into the trees. Before they disappeared back to the square, Vallas glanced back over his shoulder.

"Don't kill anyone while I'm gone."

"No promises," she muttered under her breath, watching them fade into the fog.

Lusa stayed still, letting her eyes adjust and the throb in her head recede. Her heartbeat was slowing, but the Magics hadn't settled. It felt like They were pacing beneath her skin, winding through her veins, testing for cracks. They weren't whispering anymore.

They were growling.

"You're not in control," she chided them.

We are you, They replied, slick and immediate. *We're the part you keep locked up. The part that wins.*

"You're the part that kills."

We're the part that survives.

Lusa sank to the damp earth, her back pressing against a tree. Leaves clung to her boots and palms, but she barely noticed.

"I didn't survive just to become another monster."

But you already are, They purred. *You felt it, didn't you? The power. The clarity. You could've crushed them all.*

"I didn't."

You wanted to.

She closed her fists, nails biting into her palms, and held her breath. They needed to shut up.

Inside, she reached for the warmth she'd felt earlier. The Light didn't demand. It required effort. Focus. It was will shaped into magic, not magic running wild. The warmth spread across her chest, and it felt like her lungs had opened to the most refreshing breath of air.

"You feel that?" she whispered. "That's strength too."

Weakness, They spat in Their hundred-tongues. *Softness wrapped in false hope. You think peace will protect you when the world turns on you again?*

"It already has. And I'm still here."

They hissed, recoiling but not retreating.

She touched her chest, fingers brushing the amulet beneath her tunic. It thrummed in time with the two rhythms battling for space inside her. Closing her eyes, she held onto her Source.

The amulet had become more than protection. It was a conduit. The reason words no longer mattered when she cast. The reason her magic struck harder, moved faster, bent greater things. Once it had glowed with pure white Light. Now it shimmered bronze, where creation and ruin shared the same pulse, tempered by the Dark Magic she'd forced through it.

Light and Dark, bound in one vessel. Just like her. Her other hand brushed the leather pouch at her hip, where the *Treatise of the Dual Flame* rested. She hadn't yet understood all of it. But its importance? That, she felt just fine.

As the forest settled in around her, something shifted. A presence. It wasn't the growling in her veins or the simmer of magic beneath her skin. This was colder. The prickling sense of being watched crawled up the back of her neck again. She searched the clearing.

Across the way, a figure stepped out from behind a tree. He didn't speak or take further steps. He simply stood, waiting to be noticed.

Lusa stiffened, every muscle pulled taut. The Magics cycled through a storm of threats and promises. She gripped that sliver of Light hard enough to hold Them back.

The stranger kept his hands visible. Empty. His stance… calm. Almost calculated, as if he knew not to startle her. As if he'd been watching.

She rose slowly, scanning him as she moved. He'd likely seen forty Lady Firas, with worn clothes and a weather-beaten face carved by hard labor and too little rest.

"Who are you?"

He didn't answer right away. His expression flickered a hint of desperation. Or fear. Or something worse masquerading as both.

"I need help," he said at last.

"You were outside the inn earlier."

He fit the shape of the figure she'd seen beneath the crooked tree, watching. Still half-shielded behind the trunk, he gave a slow nod.

"I won't hurt you," she said, stepping carefully toward the center of the clearing. "Why are you following me?"

"I am not," he said quickly. "Not trying to. I saw your group arrive in Merravale last night."

His voice was dry. Worn, like it hadn't been used in a while. "You were sent by the Empire?"

She gave a single nod but remained in the open. A subtle invitation for him to step forward and show himself fully. Her tactic worked. The man hesitated, then slowly stepped out from behind the tree, keeping at the edge of the clearing.

"My son," he said, voice cracking on the word. "He has been missing for days. No one will help. Everyone here just shrugs and turns away."

His hands flexed at his sides, and he moved closer.

"They say it is the woods. Or that he ran off. Or that it is just how things are now. Like that is a reason not to do anything."

He stopped a few feet away from her. His eyes were a strange sort of coal color—flat, matte, almost dusty-looking. She'd seen plenty of odd traits among different races—silver-haired elves, golden pupils in desert traders—but something about his eyes still gave her pause. Maybe it was a Merravale thing. Maybe she was reading too much into it. Still, she couldn't help the way her pulse stayed elevated.

"I begged them. I shouted. I offered coin. They looked at me like I was cursed. Like my boy was already dead."

His face contorted. Rage and grief flickered through it like heat waves. "I do not care who you are. If the Empire sent you, if you are here about the disappearances—then help me."

"What's your name?" She tilted her head, trying to catch little details.

Something Kaden had tried teaching her. *The truth's in the edges, not the eyes.* A lie could smile. Grief rarely bothered.

His clothes were simple, worn at the edges. A fraying collar. Mud-caked boots. Stitches pulled tight on one sleeve, like it had been mended too many times. A faded patch sewn near the hem of his tunic, the kind of thing only someone who couldn't afford new fabric would bother with.

He looked like a father from a village on the edge of forgetting. A man who'd lost something he couldn't replace. She knew that feeling. The desperate ache. The search that led nowhere but deeper into loss. She'd followed it once too—chasing answers about her mother, about the pieces of herself she couldn't remember. That ache had started everything.

She eased a little, though the Magics still hummed under her skin.

He took a breath, shoulders trembling as if speaking was effort. "They call me Blyven. I told them… about my son. About the traps. He was just going to check them. That is all. He is not the type to wander. They did not want to help."

Lusa nodded slowly. "When did he disappear?"

But the question seemed to bounce off him. His eyes flicked past her, jaw working. His voice picked up pace.

"They said it happens. That people vanish sometimes. That it is just the woods. As if that is normal. As if that makes it fine."

He took a step closer. Lusa didn't move, but her fingers drifted near her sword.

"They are all pretending," he went on, words tumbling faster. "Like he never existed. But he is real. He is mine. You understand that do you not? You know what it is like to lose someone. You—you look like someone who has lost something."

He took another step. Too close now.

Lusa narrowed her eyes. "Back up."

"They will not do anything," he said, ignoring her. "But you will. You have power. You came from the Empire, did you not? You can help. You *want* to help. I can lead you. I know the way. I have seen the signs—"

"Stop." She raised a hand, the other now gripping the hilt of her sword.

He kept going. "You have to do something. You *have to—*"

The Magics rose, seizing the opening as the man's words blurred into noise. *Draw it,* They purred. *Cut him down. You're faster. Stronger. End the noise. End the threat.*

Lusa's fingers twitched on the hilt.

No one would blame you, They coaxed. *He's not sane. You feel it. Let us help you.*

The pulse behind her eyes throbbed. Her body was already tense, heart thudding in sync with the hunger in Their voices. Her hand clamped down on the hilt, pulled it out, aimed it. Blyven's eyes went wide.

"No," she whispered, sheathing it with all the force of a punch. Blyven turned to run.

Coward, They hissed as her hand lifted to cast instead.

"Somnaris." Her sleeping spell snapped through the clearing. Blyven dropped like wet moss, the breath in his chest evening out as he crumpled at her feet.

Lusa exhaled sharply and let go of her sword.

The Magics grumbled behind her temples. *You should've let us finish it,* They sneered. *But fine. Take your crumbs.*

Ignoring Their voices, Lusa gave Blyven a once-over, then stepped back, rubbing her temple. Something about him still itched at her instincts but she chalked it up to nerves and exhaustion.

She glanced at the trees where Vallas and Jarion had gone, the fog swallowing everything. This wasn't what she'd imagined when she agreed to help Izier. If agreed was even the right word. She hadn't exactly been given options—just expectations. A title. A task. An empire's worth of weight dumped on her shoulders.

And no one waiting to catch her when it finally crushed her.

CHAPTER 16

Light Breaching the Dark

The clearing around her was eerily still. No birdsong. No rustle of creatures in the underbrush. Only Blyven's soft, arrhythmic snore, and the distant hush of wind against wet leaves. Clouds blanketed the sky overhead, casting everything in silver-gray. The world felt subdued. Paused. The spell had worked a little too well. Not that Lusa minded. Silence was a rare luxury, and she knew better than to expect it to last.

She stood on the far side of the clearing, half-shadowed beneath the tree line. A cluster of low-hanging fruit had caught her attention: smooth-skinned, sunset-hued, their scent syrupy and ripe even in the misty air. She'd plucked one without thinking, now mid-bite when something darker pulled her gaze.

To her left, an ancient tree hunched over the underbrush, its form almost skeletal. The bark was split and blackened; its limbs twisted into crooked angles. Only a few brittle leaves clung to the uppermost branches, shivering in a wind that didn't reach her skin. Veins of rot spidered up the trunk, a slow disease that had ruined the tree into decay. Chewing slowly, she studied it.

The murmur of boots brushing wet earth broke the spell of stillness on her left, across the clearing, where three familiar figures cut through the haze. Glon, Dak, and Noreena stepped through the mist, ducking under low-hanging branches and immediately froze at the sight of Blyven sprawled motionless on the ground.

Lusa swallowed too quickly, the bite of fruit catching halfway down. She winced at the awkward lump in her throat and raised a hand before any assumptions could root.

"He's just asleep," she said quickly through coughs.

They exchanged looks. Lusa figured Noreena had already debriefed them about her earlier... episode.

"I swear," she said, stepping forward and motioning toward Blyven. "The man wouldn't shut up. He was spiraling—on the verge of a full panic. I figured if he kept going, I'd kill him. Or… *They* would. So, I did the next best thing."

Glon moved first, his long strides carrying him ahead of the others. He watched the subtle rise and fall of Blyven's back before turning to her. There was concern in his gaze… but it was tempered. Guarded.

"You okay?"

"I'm fine." She took another bite of fruit, a bit of juice dribbling down her chin. She wiped it with her forearm and nodded toward Blyven. "His son's one of the missing."

Noreena gave the clearing a slow, tactical sweep while making her way to them. Dak, meanwhile, zeroed in on Lusa's fruit, mouth falling slightly open.

"Is that…" he started, narrowing his eyes. "By the Empress, is that *honeypear*?"

He reached for it, and she jerked her hand away.

"Hey. Get your own. There's a tree with a few left—somewhere back there." She jerked her thumb over her shoulder and took another bite.

Dak looked stricken, like she'd just denied him a family heirloom. "But how? Those only fruit in Flora, and…"

He trailed off, muttering about how it was his favorite, how rare it was this far south of Izier, disappearing behind some trees.

Ignoring the fruit spectacle, Noreena approached Lusa. "What did he tell you?"

Lusa sighed, licking a bit of juice from her thumb. "Said his son went missing while checking traps. Claimed the village wouldn't help. Was practically frothing by the end."

Glon crouched beside Blyven, checking his vitals with a practiced touch. Lusa noticed the way he favored his good arm. His injury still bothered him.

"He's breathing fine," he said.

He sat back on his heels, rubbing his shoulder absently. Lusa tucked that detail away. She hadn't seen him flinch much since the wyvern attack, but now the stiffness was obvious.

Noreena leaned into her space. "Anything else?"

"He said he saw signs. Offered to lead us. I knocked him out before he could start convulsing." Lusa arched a brow. "You're welcome."

Dak returned, holding a misshapen piece of fruit like it was a prize chicken egg.

"Found one," he said, cradling it like a relic. "Only one good honeypear. The rest are rotten. They never last long… why they're so pricey up north. But here?" He held it up with theatrical flair. "Bit bruised… but free."

Lusa blinked, then glanced toward the gnarled tree as if seeing it for the first time. A question stirred in her mind… not about fruit, but about choice. Up close, the sickness looked worse. Veins of decay spiderwebbed through its bark, the soil around its roots soft and sour-smelling. She reached out, brushing her fingers against the brittle surface.

A dull pang rose in her chest. Maybe it was exhaustion. Maybe it was the memory of Jarion's horror-stricken face as he'd stumbled away from her in the clearing, like she was something demonic. The mermaid's trembling form flashed through her thoughts, her breath rattling in Lusa's arms after the healing spell had taken. That moment had shifted something. A sense that maybe her magic didn't only destroy.

Maybe it could give something back, now.

And this dying tree wasn't so different from everything else she'd broken. Everything she still wanted to fix. Those thoughts swirled in her head, making the choice easy. But how? Healing herself was simple, second nature for a Dark Mage. She'd dabbled a little at the temple, but she'd never been able to mend another living thing without Light Magic. Now… it was different.

She was different.

Her mind reached for the information.

To mend the living, one must listen first. Healing is not forced. It is offered. Given. And only where life still answers.

Lines from the *Book of Magics*, words she'd skimmed on the way here, but never truly absorbed. Before the war, before the massacre, healing had belonged to other people. Menders. Mothers. Those with something left to lose. But now?

Now she had names. Faces.

Kaden's voice in the dark.

A mermaid recoiling in pain.

Jarion's wide, terrified eyes.

Her gaze drifted to Glon's still-sore arm.

People worth healing.

Her Master's margin note returned to her: "Don't grab the Weave. Press the Aether through it and let the cloth answer."

Magic prickled beneath her skin. The current rose in her as a double beat, out of step at first, then close enough to move her hand without shaking.

She took in a slow, meditative breath. This wasn't about Dak's rotting fruit. It was about proving she could choose which part of her to listen to. Which part to channel now that there was more than the Dark Magics.

She pressed her palm against the trunk, just above a deep knot choked with rot. Warmth grew with her focus. It came slowly, like sunlight through fog. No incantation. Only the memory of green things. Wind whispering through branches. Life rising from soil. And she pushed it outward.

Into the bark. Into the brittle veins.

Return, she urged, sending the current along the smallest living vein she could find.

The tree didn't shudder. Didn't crack or burst or bloom. But something shifted. Subtle. Like the tilt of a solovine reaching for a sliver of new light. A faint lift in the air around her fingers. A shimmer of gold threading through blackened grain. Her Master had a word for that first answer: the Weave's "take." If it took, you kept feeding. If it didn't, you stopped before you broke more than you mended.

Behind her, Glon's voice came low and uncertain. "What are you doing?"

She kept her eyes closed, focusing on images of new growth. Noreena shifted somewhere near, probably uneasy. Dak had gone quiet. The only sound was the hush of wind through trees and the soft hum of magic sinking into wood. And under Lusa's palm, the faintest pulse answered. Not hers.

The trees.

A soft crack came from the tree, like the first splinter of ice beneath Lady Flora's thaw. Lusa flinched but didn't pull away. The tree groaned. Bark shifted beneath her palm, creaking and splitting along the deepest veins of rot. But instead of falling away, it began to seal. Threads of gold light stitched through the cracks, mending the broken bark like a wound closing over fresh skin. The black faded, replaced by rich, earthen browns flushed with undertones of green.

The change continued. Brittle limbs above her quivered, flexing like muscles waking from sleep. Knots smoothed. Branches straightened. From the skeletal twigs, buds erupted, then unfurled into fresh leaves of emerald and jade. A gust of wind caught them, and they shimmered in the pale light like glass kissed by the sun.

Lusa stepped back, the breath stolen from her lungs by what she'd set in motion.

The blush of color startled her. After so much gray and rot, the sudden bloom felt almost violent, like the world had been drained and repainted in an instant. Peach-colored blossoms opened in waves. Soft petals trembled, golden centers winking in the dim light. And then, before the last petals had even stilled, they began to shift. Centers thickened. Petals curled inward, dissolving into fruit. Smooth-skinned orbs swelled and ripened in seconds, glowing with the warm blush of sunset. Honeypears, fat and perfect, bowed the branches like an orchard in full bloom.

Behind her, soft gasps of awe or surprise.

Lusa stood there, chest rising and falling, eyes locked on the miracle she'd wrought. At last, she pulled her hand away and stared at her palm—the fine lines, the dirt smears—and marveled at the fact that this time, the magic hadn't broken something.

She'd made it whole.

Somewhere behind her, Dak exhaled a reverent, "By the stars…"

Lusa barely heard him. She turned, feet quiet on the damp ground, gaze already fixed on Glon. He was still staring at the tree, jaw slack. Before he could speak or raise a single protest, she stepped close and pressed her palm gently to his shoulder.

A faint light spilled from her touch. Gold, then white, then clear as spring water. Glon hissed once under his breath. A twitch of surprise, and then it was done. Flesh took the current differently than nature—shorter path, quicker close—so long as the Aether didn't snag on fear or pain. She pulled her hand back, and he flexed his arm, brows knitting.

"You didn't have to."

"I know."

A shuffle of boots turned their heads toward the far end of the clearing. Vallas and Jarion emerged from the mist. The general moved with his usual clipped authority, the other a shadow trailing behind, eyes flicking to the group with quiet unease. Hope sparked, eyes searching for a glint of silver, but Vallas came to an abrupt stop the moment he spotted Blyven's crumpled form.

"He's not—" Lusa began, lifting a hand.

"What part of *don't kill anyone* did you find unclear?" Vallas's fingers were already on his sword hilt.

"He's not dead."

"He's asleep," Glon added, voice even.

Vallas crossed the clearing in long strides, Jarion following. Lusa couldn't look at him. Not after the clearing, seeing the terror on his face.

The general crouched beside Blyven, studying the rise and fall of his chest with clinical scrutiny, as if verifying that Glon hadn't been glamoured into defending her. When satisfied, he straightened to speak—but stopped.

His gaze flicked past her to the tree.

In the haze and gloom of the clearing, it looked like something torn from a painting. Lush. Impossible. Wrong, in a way that beauty sometimes was when surrounded by decay. Dak stood beneath it, cradling a honeypear like it might float away. Glon flexed his shoulder once, absentmindedly. Lusa said nothing.

"You did this?" The general's brows pulled low.

Before she could answer, Blyven stirred. He didn't groan or blink blearily. He sat up too quickly, spine stiff. His eyes swept the clearing. He didn't seem confused. He seemed calculating. He looked from Vallas and the others behind him, to the vibrant tree, and then Lusa.

Something in his expression flickered. Irritation? No—gone too fast to be certain. Replaced instantly by dramatic, wide-eyed fear.

He scooted back, boots scraping against the damp earth until his back hit the base of a scraggly tree. Then, in one fluid motion far too smooth for a man in distress, he scrambled to his feet and bolted.

"Hey!" Glon called, taking a step forward.

Blyven vanished into the woods, swallowed by mist without a single misstep.

Dak let out a low whistle and shifted the fruit in his arms. "Guess he's bashful."

"That's him." Jarion's voice was taut. He turned to Vallas, pale beneath his freckles. "That's who was following us."

Noreena's brow twitched. "You had a shadow?"

Jarion nodded. "During patrol this morning. I figured it was just nerves… but now?" He flicked a glance at the honeypear tree, then toward the place Blyven had disappeared. "That was him."

"He was the ghost watching us at the inn," Lusa added. She met Noreena's gaze, then steadied herself against a tree trunk as a wave of dizziness blurred her vision. She masked it quickly, fingers curling against the bark until her balance returned.

"You said he was panicked earlier?" Glon shook his head. "If he wanted help, why run?"

"Like I said, bashful." Dak dug into his satchel and started offloading hard rolls and meat sticks into Jarion's hands, who looked both confused and concerned.

"Maybe," Glon said. "Or maybe he wasn't here for help."

Vallas turned to Lusa, arms crossed, voice flat. "What exactly happened while we were gone?"

Lusa sighed and pinched the bridge of her nose, the bark behind her grounding more than she wanted to admit. "He said his son was missing. Claimed no one in the village would help and begged me to do something about it. He was frantic. Kept talking in circles. I figured if he spiraled any further, he'd pass out—or make me do something I'd regret."

She let her hand fall and met Vallas's gaze, holding it.

"So, I put him to sleep. Thought it was the safest way to keep him conscious… and alive."

Vallas's jaw ticked. "Assuming you're telling the whole truth, he's not running blind. He's heading somewhere."

His eyes turned toward the looming stretch of forest ahead, where the trees thickened into a wall of shadow and moss-draped limbs. The light faded fast under that canopy, swallowed by the tangled weave of trunks and wet branches.

"The Citadels."

Silence rippled through the group. Old wards left odd currents; near a Citadel the Aether snagged in places, slid too fast in others. History you could feel with your hands.

He scanned them, voice clipped and cool. "We were going that way anyway. If he's heading there, we'll catch him on the path. Two targets, one strike."

Dak raised a brow. "You mean killing two hares with one snare?"

"Same thing," Vallas corrected, already moving.

They followed.

The air thickened as they passed beneath the deeper wood, heavy with damp earth and the scent of decaying leaves. Ferns brushed their legs, and mist clung low along the pathless ground. The sky vanished above them, replaced by a weave of gnarled limbs and moist leaves.

Dak stuffed honeypears into every available pocket, sack, and fold of fabric he could reach, muttering about sacred fruit and divine providence. Jarion trailed beside him, arms awkwardly full of discarded rations, looking like he'd been tricked into hauling offerings to a feast he wasn't invited to.

Lusa fell in step beside him.

The underbrush was dense, and they had to duck under branches. The light, when it came, dappled in green and gold, filtered through veils of moss and moisture. She glanced at Jarion's bandaged arm and hesitated before saying anything. He noticed, his eyes flicking toward her with a hint of wariness.

"I didn't mean to scare you," she said, her voice barely above the squelch of their boots. "Back in the clearing."

Jarion didn't answer at first. His gaze dropped to the uneven ground, to the roots curling like veins through the mud, minding the foliage that grew higher.

"I've just never seen magic up close," he whispered. "Not like that."

"It wasn't supposed to be like that," she replied, softer. "I didn't… I didn't mean to lose control."

His grip tightened on the bundle of rations, knuckles paling. He kept his eyes ahead.

"Are you in pain?" she asked, nodding toward the bandage.

"A little," he admitted. "But it's manageable."

They walked a few paces more, shadows deepening.

"I could fix it," she said carefully, keeping her tone even. "If you want."

Jarion looked at her again, slower this time. His throat bobbed. His green eyes, too young for the things they'd probably already seen, showed no fear but no trust either. Only the quiet weight of a choice he wasn't sure he should make. After a pause, he gave a single nod.

Lusa stepped a little closer, careful not to rush him. She raised her hand, not yet touching, and waited. "You sure?"

He held his arm out, offering it. "I'm sure."

The bandage was crude, dark with dried blood and fraying at the edges where Noreena had tried her best. The skin beneath was raw. Bruised. Too much pain for a boy just beginning to bleed for this war.

A wave of faintness swayed through Lusa's head, blurring her vision slightly.

But she pulled deeper.

The Light rose beneath her skin, drawn not by command but by choice. She reached for Jarion's arm and pressed her palm gently over the bandage. Her fingers warmed. Magic flowed from her hand into Jarion.

Color returned to the boy's cheeks before the wound ever mended. The bandage curled loose. New skin bloomed beneath her hand, whole and pink and smooth.

Jarion stared, speechless. He looked at her and she offered the faintest of smiles.

"Better?"

He nodded. Lusa glanced over, realizing they were being noticed by the others. She quickly started up again. The forest pressed close, dim and quiet. The last reserves of Magic she'd scraped together now burned low and her knees buckled before she could stop them.

A firm hand caught her.

She looked up, startled. Vallas. His grip was tight, his expression unreadable. The second she found her footing, the moment passed. He withdrew his hand and moved on, like nothing strange had happened.

Lusa stayed for half a breath longer, her hand brushing the tree beside her. The bark was damp. Real. She needed that. Something to anchor her.

Her thoughts scattered, slipping like water through fingers. It took a moment to remember why she'd even been alone in the clearing. Blyven—his panic. His talk of traps. His son. His sudden flight into the woods.

But that wasn't why she'd stayed behind.

The others had gone searching. Not for Blyven.

For her pin.

Her stomach dipped.

She turned her head and spotted Vallas already a few paces ahead, gaze fixed on the path. She pushed off the tree and caught up to him.

"Did you find it?" she asked. "The pin."

Vallas glanced at her, then gave a curt shake of his head. Her heart sank. Dread didn't crash—it crept. Slow. Heavy. It settled into the hollow places her magic had emptied. Without the pin, she was exposed. To Their desires. Their manipulation.

But They were just as drained as she was. Her well was drying up, and if she had nothing left to give, neither did They. Still, They waited, patient. Resting. Waiting to twist whatever power returned. Her limbs felt leaden. Her head throbbed from the effort of healing. And without the pin, she was vulnerable.

Glon's hand landed on her shoulder. "Come on," he said quietly. "Let's get you to your Citadels."

"I'd hardly call them mine." The thought was absurd.

Dak juggled a precarious pile of honeypears between his satchel, an overstuffed pouch, and the crook of his arm.

"You realize what this means, right? An actual honeypear harvest in the wild?" He held one up like a sacred relic. "This is fate. A gift from the Ancients. I will not let these beauties rot like the last batch. No honeypear left behind."

He sidled up to Noreena, who was tightening the straps on her spear, and held one out with an eager grin.

"Just one bite. They taste like honey-glazed starlight."

Noreena didn't even turn her head. "I'm not eating tree magic."

"Your loss," Dak muttered, biting into one with exaggerated reverence as juice ran down his chin.

Lusa walked behind Glon. She watched his shoulders, the way his eyes scanned the shifting dark between branches. The farther they moved, the quieter things became. Even Dak's fruit commentary faded.

The forest narrowed. Branches knotted overhead. Even the mist thinned, as if it knew better than to trespass here.

Lusa kept pace with Glon, but her feet felt heavier with every step. Not from exhaustion—though that still buzzed under her skin—but from memory.

They were close now. She could feel it. The way it pressed tighter with every breath. The Citadels weren't just ruins. They were remains. Carved out by fire and violence and the echoes of the Asbanese, who'd she'd allowed the Magics to kill in her effort to get to Lazorious.

She remembered the first time she saw the black tower after the Glorious Ones had transported her and Kaden. The path of ash and blood she carved to get inside. Lazorious's body burning. That image would forever be branded behind her eyelids, but it haunted her dreams less than it should. Because it wasn't the sorcerer that haunted her.

It was her mother.

A scream torn from a throat that barely sounded human. Warped by possession. Emptied of soul. The Dark Magics had already hollowed her out by then, twisted her into something unrecognizable. A puppet of Their will.

Lusa had been the one to stop her. Not save. Stop.

That was the cost of entering the tower once.

And now she was returning.

The other Citadels had been just as lifeless. Cold stone. No wards. No voices. No light. Only dust and silence where the Magi had once stood. And now Izier wanted her to take up the mantle. Interim Sorceress Supreme. Rebuild what had been lost. Lead what remained.

But what remained? What had happened to the Magi? Why had they vanished? Why was she the only one left?

Lusa's fingers twitched. Even though her magic was spent, something inside her stirred. Whatever waited beyond the west woods remembered her. And she wasn't sure she was ready to face it.

CHAPTER 17

The Return to Mage Haven

The canopy dulled the light so thoroughly, the time of day was impossible to guess. Time had become a suggestion in this part of the forest anyway, swallowed by mist and drizzle. Lusa's feet ached with each step, the soft earth sucking at her boots. Her cloak stuck to her tunic, saturated hours ago, the damp leather chafing her shoulders.

The sprinkling of rain had started as a blessing. Dak claimed as much, swatting lazily at the buzzing insects that had grown more intense. He didn't seem to mind the steam rising around them as humidity clung thick to the undergrowth. His damp hair curled with the moisture, and his sleeves were rolled up, pace undeterred.

Lusa envied his ease. Every few steps, she could feel the leyline beneath this part of the forest tug and stutter, like a pulse misfiring. Something about the West Woods made the Aether nervous.

Ahead, General Vallas hacked through tangled brambles with merciless precision. What they decided passed for a trail earlier had long since vanished beneath thorn and vine, and now each foot of progress had to be carved by hand. He didn't complain. He didn't even speak. But the tightening of his jaw and the growing aggression in his strikes told Lusa enough. This terrain was testing his patience.

The blade. The stride. The silence. All of it stirred something half-buried in her chest. She wiped her wet face in vain and blinked away the vision of Kaden.

Her first memory of him was a sword, lowered but ready. Mud-slick grass crushed under his boots. His voice—gruff, steady, not quite unkind—asking if she was the one who'd bent the swamp path. She'd nearly set him ablaze for it. She could still feel the tension in her palms, the Magics surging wild and hungry, and his maddening calm as if her fury didn't rattle him at all.

She had hated him.

She had wanted to burn the smirk from his mouth.

And yet now, in the hush of drizzle and ache of solitude, all she wanted was to hear that voice again. She wanted the brush of his cloak at her shoulder, the quiet assurance that he was walking beside her again. He wasn't here. And that shouldn't have hurt as much as it did.

Lusa blinked hard, wiping at her face again. He wasn't here, and neither was the luxury of distraction.

Next to Vallas, Noreena moved like a forest ghost. Something about the way she walked, all stealth and silence, was impressive. Her short coils were plastered to her scalp, and she made no attempt to speak, as per usual. But she kept pace with Vallas, occasionally slipping ahead to point out safer footing or a better route through the muck. If the rain bothered her, she didn't show it.

Somewhere behind them, Dak groaned. "You know, Captain, sure would be nice if your sister could come up with some kind of rain-proof cloaking. My spine's starting to mold."

"She's working on it," Glon replied, matter-of-fact. "But she keeps saying the fabric either breathes or repels."

Lusa smiled faintly. "She said the same thing when she fitted me for this." She plucked at the edge of her soaked tunic, which now clung to her arms like a second skin. "Though I think she warned me not to wear it through a forest during a three-day drizzle."

Glon smirked. "You did ignore the weather briefing."

"If only we could control it, maybe we wouldn't need a briefing," Dak muttered, ducking under a dripping branch.

"She could," Jarion said suddenly.

His tone wasn't teasing. It was almost blunt, and so out of character that Glon and Dak traded a look. Vallas and Noreena had already moved ahead.

Lusa slowed. With how curious Jarion had been back in the canyon, and how quickly he'd recovered from her almost losing control, she supposed she shouldn't be surprised.

Dak caught her glance. "Wait… can you?"

She paused at a fallen tree before answering.

"I can feel it. Sometimes shift it. But it takes… a lot."

She didn't offer more, keeping her eyes on the path ahead, heart beating faster—and not from the climb. Storms were Aether in its rawest form: living currents, unanchored and unwilling to obey. Only a mage with immense core power could reach for one without unraveling. The danger wasn't in calling the storm, but in holding it. Aether pushed back, and every bit of resistance pierced through one's core like a needle through fabric.

Lazorious had done it—summoned storms that battered the horizon for months, hammering cities until they drowned or bent the knee. He had been powerful… and she had destroyed him. What did that make her?

The Magics stirred in the quiet of her mind, brushing against her thoughts with silken arrogance.

It takes power to destroy power. Their velvet whispers aimed to stroke her pride.

Jarion stumbled over a half-buried root, nearly pitching forward. Lusa caught his arm on instinct, steadying him, grateful for the interruption. She kept hold of his sleeve a moment longer than necessary.

"You ask a lot of questions about magic," she said quietly. "Where'd you learn so much?"

He blinked, wiping rain from his face and shoving his matte of curly orange hair out of his eyes. The drizzle hadn't let up.

"Temple scraps," he said. "My uncle salvaged whatever was left after the ban. Stuff that should've been burned. He kept most of it. I read whatever he didn't sell."

"Was it your uncle who made you enlist?" Dak asked, squinting up at a brief opening in the canopy. He missed the flicker of pain that crossed Jarion's face before he masked it.

"He enlisted himself," Glon answered.

Jarion said nothing.

"That's a brave thing to do," Lusa offered. Her look snapped to Dak—dry, pointed, and leaning toward lethal. The kind of look that said *change the subject* with all the subtlety of a thrown dagger.

Dak held up his hands. "Didn't mean to poke anything sore. Just making conversation."

Jarion's voice came soft, almost too quiet to hear. "My mom died when I was little. And my dad… he fought for Izier."

Glon shook his head. "You don't need to explain anything to this dimwit."

No one spoke after that. The rain filled the quiet, pattering through the leaves. Boots squelched through mud, branches creaked overhead, and the moment passed. Not forgotten, merely folded away.

Lusa's magic hadn't fully returned. She could feel it somewhere deep within, but no spark came when she reached for it. Meditation had been impossible with the rain and marching and Vallas barking commands. Still, she was no longer empty. That was something. The rain finally began to ease as the trees began to thin.

Lusa didn't notice it at first. The change came slowly… branches loosening their hold overhead, the canopy breaking apart, letting slivers of light through the mist. Rain softened to a fine veil, silvering bark and stone. Dusk.

The path widened into what remained of an old road, though that was little more than a suggestion, half-swallowed by moss and root. That's when she saw them.

The Citadel walls.

Tall and worn, the stone lined the clearing like a fortress surrendered to time. Ivy crawled through its cracks, scrawling across the surface. At the center, rusted iron gates stood bent open, shivering with every gust that found them.

Lusa exhaled, surprised by the tremor in her breath. She tried to will it away, but facing this place again pressed against her. Vallas stepped forward and shoved the gate open with one hand, the other still gripping his sword.

They entered one by one over the wet stone. The rain had stopped, but the air clung with vapor. Every hand stayed close to a weapon. Blyven had never returned, and none of them knew what he wanted.

A jittery pressure built in her chest: part anxiety, part dread, part fractured memory. Childhood echoes and battle-worn fears braided together into a cocktail of emotions. The kind of heavy feeling that swallowed all the space inside her. The courtyard stretched wide before them, rimmed with crumbling columns and overgrown gardens. Mage Haven.

Once the heart of mage life with practice grounds, teaching circles… a place of gathering. Now moss claimed every edge, and shattered tiles lay slick with overgrowth. Rain dripped from the broken eaves and wild plants that clung to half-toppled archways. Mist hung low across the ground, hiding fallen debris and curling around their drenched boots.

Glon stepped up beside her, wiping his brow with the back of his wrist. He surveyed the courtyard, then muttered, mostly to himself, "This isn't Lady Fira's weather."

He didn't need to say more. The gray sky said enough. Lusa watched the captain study the clouds with narrowed eyes, his usual friendly face tinged with concern.

Vallas moved toward the center of the square and scanned the perimeter, checking every shadow like an officer entering hostile ground. Noreena circled wide in stealthy silence. She bent briefly near a stone basin filled with rainwater, dipped a hand in, and took a drink. Dak plopped down on the edge of a broken bench, wringing out his cloak with a grunt.

"Woah," Jarion breathed.

His gaze had caught on the towers rising beyond the mist. Chunks of white stone lay scattered at his feet—remnants of the Citadel of Light. Lusa remembered the way the bolt of lightning came for the tower like a curse. Slowly, she turned around to face the towers. Three of them, each one different. Each one so familiar it made her chest ache.

To the left: the Citadel of Light, its golden spires dulled now by time and rain, but still catching the last edge of dusk. Her training had begun there, back when it breathed with healing and order, before Lazorious claimed it with lightning and left only ruin behind.

To the far right: the Citadel of Dark Magics. Its walls were black as coal, impervious to the sun's reach even at mid-day. A place of ancient, terrible power. And even worse memories.

And at the center: the gray fortress of cobblestone and mortar. It stood shorter than the others… but this was the seat of balance. And balance, though often overlooked, was never without weight. The seat of Neutral Magics, built for those who didn't belong to either end of the spectrum: imps, sprites, a few among the elvenkind, and creatures whose gifts walked the middle line.

The Magics restlessly stirred inside her. They were waking, slow but insistent, and she didn't know how long she had before They rose to full voice again.

"Jarion," Vallas said, sheathing his sword with a clean motion and unhooking his waterskin. "Patrol the perimeter. See if our shadow's lurking somewhere. He has to be close."

Jarion gave a stiff salute and ducked back out through the iron gates. Lusa stood there debating whether to wring out her cloak first or eat. Vallas caught her attention with a tilt of his head, nodding her over with all the warmth of a summons to the gallows. So much for choices.

She stepped carefully over the slick stones to meet him beneath a broken arch.

"You know why we're here," he said, skipping pleasantries. "But Arcturius wanted you to understand what comes next."

Lusa folded her arms. "I assumed he'd left the hard parts to you."

Vallas didn't rise to the bait. His gaze stayed fixed ahead. "There's a scroll. It's supposed to be stored inside the Citadel of Light—sealed, hidden, maybe warded. It contains the last known records of the Magi. Names. Territories. Survivors. If there are any left."

That tugged at her. Survivors.

Vallas continued. "Arcturius said retrieving it is the first step. If the towers recognize you, if the scroll yields…

then we proceed. Until then, you're not interim anything. You're a candidate with a long road ahead."

She nodded slowly, the word *recognize* echoing in her ears. "And if they don't?"

Vallas finally looked at her. "Then we turn back."

"What about the Vanished?"

"The scroll comes first," he said. "But yes… Arcturius suspects the disappearances in Merravale may be connected to something here."

He didn't look at her again, scanning the shadows pooling beneath the broken archways like something might crawl out of them.

"So, we split our focus?"

"No. We keep our eyes open. But your focus is the towers. The rest we handle after."

She hadn't realized how badly she'd wanted to find survivors until the possibility had been dangled in front of her… and snatched back by uncertainty. Before Lusa could ask more, a strangled yelp tore through the courtyard.

"Oh no—no, no, no!" Dak's voice cracked like a boy mid-puberty, pitiful enough to echo off the broken walls.

She and Vallas turned sharply, blades half-drawn. Glon hadn't moved, already beside Dak with arms crossed, watching the scene unfold with mild amusement. Noreena spun, spear lowered in a ready stance. Dak, however, stood cradling his open pack like it held the corpse of a dear friend.

"My honeypears!" he wailed. "They were right here. Ripe, perfect—"

Glon reached inside and pulled out a blackened lump. It crumbled in his hand to a fine, silty dust that scattered to the ground.

"Strange," he muttered, brushing his fingers clean.

Vallas's gaze flicked toward Lusa. Noreena followed, quiet but sharp-eyed.

Lusa didn't respond. She looked at her hands instead—turned them over, palms out, then in, flexed her fingers like she might feel the truth in her skin. But nothing explained it. The warmth she'd summoned. The intention. It hadn't been wild or desperate. It had been gentle. Controlled.

So why had it turned to ash? Her chest tightened. The Magics stirred faintly in her mind, but not in accusation or glee. Was it Them?

No. She'd kept Them at bay. She was sure of it. She had tried to do something right. Was she broken? Was the Light rejecting her now… or had it never really been hers at all? Or maybe it was something completely unrelated to her. One could hope.

She swallowed hard, the questions digging deeper than Vallas's stare.

"Stick to the meat sticks, soldier," he said to Dak, though his eyes never left her. "Told you not to trust magic."

Dak grumbled something indistinct, still shaking out his pack.

Lusa turned away, ignoring Vallas, the Magics and Their soft snickering, and her own voice whispering that maybe even her best intentions were destined to fail.

CHAPTER 18

Master of the Strings

Jarion jogged back through the iron gates, rain sliding off his sleeves in rivulets.

"Nothing out there," he called. "No sign of—"

He faltered, slowing to a stop as he caught the look on everyone's faces.

Noreena had just settled on the edge of the broken fountain, one leg outstretched, her hands braced behind her… but now she sat upright, stiff as stone. Glon rose from his crouch in one fluid motion, hand drifting to the hilt on his back. Dak had frozen mid-bite, his meat stick held halfway to his mouth. Vallas stepped forward like a blade unsheathing, gaze locked on the figure behind Jarion.

Lusa's stomach dropped.

Just beyond the gate stood Blyven. His cloak clung to him, drenched and pale, the hood hanging low over his face. But the shape of him—those too-long limbs, the hunched stance—left no doubt. His eyes were hidden, but Lusa could feel his stare.

Jarion turned, confused by their sudden alertness. The moment he caught sight of Blyven, he stepped back toward the group, drawing and nocking his bow in one fluid motion.

They stood like that for magics knew how long. Weapons drawn, bodies stiff. A gust of wind swept through the courtyard. Mist slithered in its wake, curling between them and Blyven. No one moved.

Blyven didn't raise a hand or even speak. He staggered. And then, without warning, collapsed face-first into the mud.

Dak blinked. "Uh…"

Glon reached him first, flipping the man over with one boot, then crouched, checking for breath.

"Unconscious."

"I don't like this." Noreena rose from the fountain, grip tightening on her spear.

Neither did Lusa. But she barely had time to register the others' reactions. Something shifted in the Weave. A crackling tension that wasn't weather, or nerves, or even fear.

Magic.

Powerful magic.

She whipped toward the source as a sharp *crack* split the courtyard, louder than thunder. A streak of dark blue light, arcing over the wall like lightning with a mind of its own, sliced toward them in a whip-fast blur.

She didn't think. She reached. The Weave thrummed under the courtyard like capillaries through stone; the Aether carried it, bright and cold. Her core caught, the amulet warming as it bridged the pull. A gold film curved up from her palm in a breath, doming over the group like starlit glass.

The blast struck.

The shield flared.

And held.

Wind and debris splashed against it and then scattered, the blue light dispersing back beyond the walls. Lusa's heart pounded. Magic still thrummed at her fingertips, the shield pulsing with her breath.

"What are we fighting?" Vallas snapped, stepping in beside her as the group fell into a tight battle stance.

"I don't know."

The Magics crescendoed into a mind-splitting chorus that tore through her skull. She cried out, clutching her head.

"Lus!" Glon vaulted over a pile of broken stone, shield raised, landing at her side with practiced ease.

The iridescent dome flickered as her focus slipped. Vallas shouted something she couldn't understand. Jarion's bow was drawn, arrow ready, eyes locked on the gate.

Somewhere, a bird shrieked and went silent. And Noreena was gone, already moving beyond the wall.

"Stop!" Lusa called out to her.

The Magics quieted enough for her thoughts to clear. Her voice rang out again, this time aimed at the only one who needed to hear it.

"Stop, Noreena!"

But the soldier had already vanished through the gate.

"We're stacked like siege dummies in the yard," Vallas growled, eyes scanning every shadow.

"Let's get out of here then," Lusa snapped. The shield tightened around them as if responding to the rise in her voice. "Stay inside it. Follow me."

No one questioned her. Even Vallas, grim and skeptical, fell in line behind.

She moved toward the gates, splashing through shallow puddles, each step a battle of will. The iridescent dome shimmered around them, light refracting in golden hues.

Inside her, the Magics screamed.

Leave them. Useless shields. Take the storm to its throat. You know what waits beyond—power to match your own. To test it. Claim it. Burn it.

Visions struck her like lashes: Vallas turned to bone, Dak screaming in silence, Glon collapsing with smoke in his lungs. The courtyard, slick with blood and broken stone.

She winced, trying to breathe, sweat prickling beneath her soaked collar. Her hands shook from fighting against Them. But then came the other presence. A flicker of something warm at the edge of her core. A knowing brushing against her minds-eye. She needed to protect them. She had to, or she'd lose more than just control.

Lusa blinked hard, throat tight. The shield wavered before surging stronger, drawn from that aching thread of light she wasn't sure she deserved to hold. She couldn't let it go.

"Keep tight," she gasped. "If I drop this shield, you're as good as those honeypears."

They passed Blyven's body, unmoving beside the gate. Beyond that, the air crackled. Lusa's vision narrowed into a tunnel, hoping she could cover Noreena in time as she walked out the gate and turned the direction Noreena had left. Whatever power was coming, it was close. Close enough that the Magics writhed like hounds on a leash.

Gritting her teeth against Their desires, Lusa pushed forward, splitting herself down the middle just to hold the line.

"Call her back, General!" she shouted, the shield flickering with strain.

But the words barely left her lips before a spear came slicing down, cracking against the iridescent dome with a sharp *clang*. The force knocked Noreena back several steps, but she recovered fast—eyes wild, teeth bared.

She lunged again, straight for Lusa.

"Stand down!" Vallas barked.

But she didn't slow. Didn't blink. There was something wrong in her gaze. Something blank. And suddenly, it clicked.

"This isn't Noreena," Lusa said, bracing the shield as another blow rang out across its surface. "She's not in control."

"Nori! Stop!" Dak shoved past, intercepting the next strike with a clash of steel.

"Stay in the shield!" Lusa shouted, her voice cracking. "Get her in here!"

Glon was already moving. He stepped into the arc of Noreena's next swing and slammed the flat of his shield into her temple. The hit staggered her long enough for Dak to catch her arm and haul her inside the dome's protection.

Lusa dropped to one knee, the barrier branding her skull from within. Every breath scraped. Every heartbeat thundered, her core pulsing hard to keep it intact. When she looked up, her eyes adjusted from the haze of her dome, and she saw their threat.

A tall, poised figure emerged from behind the distant wall, watching. Keeping the shield up with one hand, she hurled a fireball with the other.

A casual flick of his fingers sent the flame scattering like dandelion seeds in the wind. His hand shifted, fingers aligning in a deliberate pattern. Sigils flashed violet along his knuckles like ink called to light before pulsing at his index finger. The air bent around him. A ribbon of dark-blue energy unfurled from his palm, sliding along the wall before slamming into her shield with a loud crack.

The world pitched sideways. Shouts rang out—Vallas cursing, Dak yelling, and then a scream cut through the chaos. Lusa spun, sword drawn, shield barely clinging to life with her other hand.

Jarion was half-outside the dome, boots scraping through mud, eyes wide in horror.

Blyven had him. His face was slack. His grip tight. He moved like a puppet, strings pulled by something unseen. A blink of violet light at the center of Blyven's forehead, there and gone, like a sigil burned from inside his skull.

"Levista tellum!" Lightning erupted from her fingertips, a lance of bluish white. It struck Blyven square in the chest, hurling him into the trees with a wet snap.

But it cost her.

The air imploded with the sound of shattering glass. The shield broke. A brittle hush fell over the group as they scrambled for footing, breath ragged in their throats.

The shift came before she could blink.

Steel caught the light as Vallas turned, blade already raised. Glon took a step forward as his eyes clouded over. Dak's hand went to his hilt. Noreena lifted her spear to strike.

Not one of them looked confused.

Not one of them looked like themselves.

Lusa staggered back. "No, wait—"

Steel hissed past her ribs. She dodged. Another blade came. She barely parried, her shoulder screaming from the cut. An arrow sliced the air near her ear.

Panic overwhelmed, but she couldn't afford it. Couldn't breathe it. Couldn't stop. They weren't attacking her on their own. She could see it in the glaze over Glon's eyes, in the way Dak's grip faltered a breath before his strike.

They were being controlled.

The Magics laughed, drunk on the bloodlust humming through her veins. *Let them fall. They're already lost.*

"Shut up," she growled, ducking as Glon's shield came crashing down, narrowly missing her.

A spear clipped her ribs. She cried out, staggering as pain bloomed bright and hot. Blood welled between her fingers where she clutched the wound. She dropped, rolled, came up behind Vallas, and tore the sword from his hands in one practiced move… only to find Noreena already turning, spear leveled, her gaze vacant and wrong.

Why fight? the Magics purred. *Use us. End this.*

"No," she snarled through clenched teeth.

Her fingers twitched as she reached deep, gathering what strength she had left. Light swelled in her chest, unstable, weakening. She released it in a burst. An invisible force rushed them like a gale, throwing all five of them back. Some hit the ground hard. Others skidded through mud and stone.

Lusa dropped to her knees, chest heaving, blood hot on her palm. Everything was spinning, and the Magics wouldn't shut up.

But when she lifted her head, she saw him again.

A shadow, moving along the stone wall. Smooth, calculating. Closing the distance with the calm precision of a predator. His long black hair hung in partial braids. His robes rippled around him as dark as thunderclouds. But it wasn't her eyes that told her what he was.

It was the Magics.

A Dark Elf.

Lusa's mind raced through every magical attack she knew, only to run headfirst into the wall of his likely defenses. He'd see any spell coming and have time to counter it. But he was weakening. Just like her, his power had limits. And mind control? That cost almost as much as bending the weather.

She needed to get clever.

Drawing in a shaky breath, she shifted her focus to the rain-slick earth beneath her. Mud clung to her skin. The smell of wet grass filled her lungs. Lusa pressed her palm into the ground and growled, "Levista tellum."

The spell flashed straight for him through the wet soil. His hand-conjured shield flared to life too late. Electricity snapped through the space between them, and though his barrier caught most of it, enough got through to stagger him. He fell back, shoulders jolting with impact.

Lusa gasped, chest burning, her hand still planted in the mud. She turned—

And saw the others stirring.

Groans. Curses. Hands clutching heads.

They were waking up, blinking against the fog that had clouded their minds. She had to get them out of here.

"Quick, into the woods!"

Vallas shook his head hard to clear it, reclaimed his sword, and glared past Lusa at their enemy. "You're not in charge here."

"Oh, for Magic's sake, stop with the male pride parade," she snapped, shoving damp hair from her face. "Even if you had a full battalion behind you, you'd still be scraping what's left off the mud when he's through. That thing is a Dark Elf. You want to throw your ego at him, be my guest. But you won't win. Not with steel."

That got his attention.

Vallas glanced down at her, something shifting in his eyes—but she was already moving, hurrying past to help Jarion to his feet. She readjusted his quiver with one hand and jerked her chin toward the tree line.

"Go."

"He'll just follow us," Noreena said, rubbing her temple and glancing back at the elf, who was slowly pushing himself upright.

"I'll hold him back. Just need to buy you enough time."

She moved with them quickly toward the woods, glancing over her shoulder every few steps. The Dark Elf was still dazed but recovering. Fast. She wanted to send out a probe, a small flicker of magic to test how much he had left. But she didn't have enough to spare.

Glon reached for her, hand gripping her shoulder to say something—but when she turned, pain lanced through her side. She hissed, doubling slightly.

"You're hurt."

He tried to stop her, but she slipped free of his grasp, shrugging him off with a wince.

"I'm fine." Lusa clenched her jaw, her arm pressed tightly to her bleeding side. She didn't have time for this.

Closing her eyes, she summoned the thinnest thread of Light. This was worth sparring for. It shimmered beneath her skin, resisting at first, then softening under her will. Her fingers glowed gold-white as she pressed her hand to the wound.

Glon watched in stunned silence, his sword lowered, the glow reflecting in his eyes. She opened hers.

"Tell Arcturius it's a Dark Elf. He's behind the missing villagers."

Vallas started to protest, but she cut him off. "Just go. I'll be right behind you. Soon as I knock him out."

Jarion stepped forward, still pale, still shaken. "You've used too much. That kind of magic… healing, shielding, casting… you're burning through it."

"So is he," she said flatly, wiping mud from her cheek. "I'm not the only one running on empty."

"Lusa—"

"Go."

"Watch out!" Dak hollered.

She spun to face a dozen conjured, shadow-glassed arrows soaring through the air, straight at them. Dak threw himself into Noreena, knocking them both to the ground. Vallas and Glon raised their shields just in time.

Lusa reached for Jarion, shoved him sideways—

A scream tore loose as the arrow punched through her shoulder. It felt like her arm had been torn off and stitched back on with fire. Her knees buckled. The arrow jutted from beneath her collarbone, blood soaking her tunic in waves.

Lucky. It had gone clean through.

"Lus!" Glon was at her side in an instant.

"There's no time," she gritted out.

Grabbing the shaft, she brought her sword down hard, screaming the pain out in full fury. "Get it out!"

Noreena moved fast. One smooth pull. The pain nearly blacked her out, but Lusa reached inward, clawing at the remnants of her well. She forced magic up from her core, but only enough to stop the bleeding from the gaping hole in her shoulder.

The Magics shrieked. Clawing. Tearing. Hungry.

Dark flooded her veins like poison. Her vision blurred. Her pulse stuttered. Somewhere in the mess of her mind, a voice—hers, but thin and far away—whispered *no*. A flicker of Light tried to surface, feeble and flickering like a dying flame.

But They laughed at it. Smothered it.

Faces surrounded her—Glon, Noreena, Jarion. All staring. Blood draining their faces. Frozen. She could feel it now—they weren't just afraid of the enemy.

They were afraid of her.

"Go!" she roared.

Her voice wasn't fully hers. Not anymore.

The Magics spun her around, hijacking limbs she could barely feel. Thoughts cracked apart as visions poured in—violent, glorious, terrible. A hundred ways to end the Dark Elf, and not one of them clean.

They didn't wait to see if the others fled. They didn't care. The elf stood across the soggy ground, weakened—but not broken. Yet.

They studied him, the way predators study prey. High cheekbones. Tapered jaw. Obsidian eyes too calm for a battlefield. Ink-dark hair half-braided with silver clasps. Golden-olive skin that gleamed like metal pulled from fire.

They loved a beautiful target.

Lusa watched from somewhere deep under the surface, screaming inside her own skull. But her mouth was already twisting upward.

The Light inside her tried again, desperate to rise. It flared, swimming through her limbs like a gasp of clarity. Her body jerked. A violent, involuntary twitch as if her muscles didn't know which master to obey. She was caught in the middle, pulled taut between Light and Dark, a thread stretched to snapping.

With a sweeping surge, They devoured everything and took control. They lifted her arms, one hand clutching her sword, the other flexing with anticipation. They ignored the pain engulfing Their host. Black-veined lightning crackled at her fingertips, laced with blueish smoke. A warning. A promise.

They could crush his lungs. Silently. Or boil his blood until his eyes melted and his mouth spilled black. Perhaps jade shards conjured from thought—one to each eye, another to the throat, the last to the heart. Theatrical, but effective.

They stepped forward through her, feet sinking into the mud, and outstretched her hand like a priest about to cast judgment.

The Dark Elf smirked. A navy leather band circled his brow, framing a gaze far too steady for someone nearly out of power.

But he knew it. Oh, he knew.

The weight of his power was fading, but it didn't matter. His smirk wasn't mockery. It was anticipation.

He wants this, the Magics whispered. *He's been waiting for someone worthy.*

The elf tilted his head, measuring her, measuring Them, like a swordsman savoring the moment before steel sings.

Let him.

He would learn what it meant to challenge Them.

They struck first.

The ground heaved beneath the elf's feet, cracking open a sliver as a wave of force rushed upward to knock him off balance. He skidded back, cloak snapping and threw up a magical shield with a quick hand formation. A lash of fire curved bright and hot toward him from Lusa's fingers, barely blocked.

Another strike, an invisible blast of compressed air, slammed into his chest. He stumbled back, retaliated with a shock of violet lightning. It tore through the space They'd just left, harmless.

He's faltering, They hissed.

Lusa felt it, too. The Dark Elf was skilled, dangerous, but tiring. They closed the distance. Her sword flashed up from her side, already in motion. The elf blinked, caught off guard. He hadn't even drawn his blade.

He thought he wouldn't need it.

He stood a full head taller. Muscles taut beneath his robes as he shifted to brace himself. Steel sliced through air, missing him as he jumped back, his fingers twisting for another spell. They slashed high, forcing him to duck. The blade hissed past his ear.

He snarled. The cutlass came out.

Now it was a fight.

Their blades crashed, fast and furious. Sparks flew with every impact. He drove forward, taller and heavier, trying to overpower with sheer weight and reach. The Magics didn't know swordplay… but she did. They reached inward, scrambling through her memory, pulling every movement, every drill, every sparring match into Their control. They turned his strike, twisted his wrist, slipped under his guard, using Lusa's training to its edge and beyond.

He barely evaded.

Their magic flared again, channeled through her core. They hurled a paralyzing spell at his chest. He barely twisted away. The spell hissed past, skimming the edge of his sleeve.

He rebounded, flinging his own strike in a clean arc toward her ribs. They ducked, pivoted, drove the sword low toward his thigh. Steel met steel with a crack. His cutlass held.

Lusa hated Them. Despised every second of being controlled. But right now, Sardan help her, she wanted Them to win. To finish it. End it.

They pressed against his blade, twisting for an opening. The sword began to rise, tracking toward his throat—

Then the elf raised one hand and blew something from his palm.

A sudden cloud of white powder burst into the air, momentarily blinding.

Lusa flinched. It settled on her skin, her face, her mouth. Drowsiness hit like a crashing wave. She staggered. Her limbs filled with wet sand. Her sword slipped from her grip. The Magics screamed in protest, but They were fading, pulling back, Their hold unraveling.

No, no, no…

Her knees buckled. The excruciating pain returned. Panic clawed up her spine.

He stood over her now. A faint smile of satisfaction curling one corner of his mouth.

Get up.

Get up.

MOVE.

Nothing.

Though darkness devoured her, she was still conscious enough to know… he could do anything. And there was nothing she could do to stop him.

CHAPTER 19

The Secret Grove

Kaden kept to the shadows, boots soundless on the mossy path as he followed the hand-drawn map Lorenthar had pressed into his hand two nights ago. The prince had called it a gift, but Kaden didn't believe in gifts from nobles. Not without a price, anyway.

The Old Grove lay beyond the southern arc of the palace past the gardens, past the sentinel pines, and into a stretch of forest that had quietly fallen out of memory. No lanterns marked the path and there wasn't a guard in sight. He figured it wasn't out of being forbidden, probably just forgotten. Left to the hush of time and nature.

The deeper he went, the more the quiet settled. The air hung with the kind of calm that came from being undisturbed for years. Just as Lorenthar had said, the trail forked where it shouldn't. Kaden slipped through a false thicket, ducking under branches feathered with pale moss. The leaves were cool to the touch—cooler than they had any right to be in the tail end of Lady Fira.

The grove opened before him. A natural ring, cradled by ancient roots that jutted from the earth like ribs half-buried in loam, sat in the center of the small clearing. The place lacked flowers or birdsong. It felt as if it had been left untouched for generations.

He took one step into the clearing before freezing. There, a little off-center where the shadows thickened, stood the Crown Prince, speaking to a hooded figure half a head shorter, their face hidden beneath the cowl.

"Keep this between us for now," the prince said, voice low but resolute. "It serves our greater purpose."

Kaden narrowed his eyes. The princes' phrase reeked of convenience. He silently shifted behind the gnarled trunk of an old elder tree. He could slip away. Fade back into the brush and pretend he'd never come this far. Probably the safer choice. Better to avoid looking like he'd been trying to overhear something he shouldn't. But he might not get another chance like this. If this grove was what Lorenthar hinted at… if it really was being scrubbed from records and avoided on purpose, Kaden needed eyes on it. His eyes. Besides, sneaking off now meant risking suspicion anyway. Better to make it look accidental.

He angled his heel above a fallen limb and let it drop. The branch snapped clean beneath his boot. He cleared his throat, loud enough to carry.

Eldarion turned sharply, the hooded figure retreating into shadow.

"Ambassador," Eldarion called, voice smooth but clipped. "Out for a walk?"

Kaden stepped forward slow, palms visible. "Didn't realize this path was restricted. Must've taken a wrong turn."

Eldarion said nothing for a breath. Then, with a flick of his fingers, the hooded figure swiftly vanished into the trees.

Kaden let his gaze linger on the retreating shadow before returning it to the crown prince.

Eldarion stepped forward, hands clasped behind his back. "Strange, isn't it?" he said. "How often one finds themselves exactly where they're not supposed to be."

"Aeonia's got plenty of paths," Kaden said stoically. "Hard ta' tell which ones are frowned on without a signpost."

A faint curve touched Eldarion's lips, though it held none of the warmth a smile might offer. "And yet you chose the one no one walks."

Kaden tilted his head, unbothered. "Didn't think anyone was walkin' it. That's why I came."

They stood with little more than a patch of earth between them—bare moss, twisted root, and the hush of old branches bearing witness. Eldarion's gaze, cold and pale as starlight on snow, did not waver. He studied Kaden like one might study a relic from another age, weighing whether it belonged in use… or in memory.

"You walk under the Empress's favor," Eldarion said at last. "But even guests of great standing would do well to tread lightly. Aeonia forgets little and forgives less."

"Funny. From where I'm standin', seems she's forgotten a fair bit already."

Another beat of silence stretched between them.

"You believe the land is sick," Eldarion stated.

Kaden studied him. "I believe what I see. And I see a grove that hasn't bloomed in seasons, with roots curlin' like they want outta the ground."

Eldarion's smile returned, thinner now, more shadow than shape. "Some rot is natural. It clears the way for growth."

"Or it spreads. Kills what still had a chance."

Eldarion let that hang until the silence felt unnatural, then turned and walked back into the trees. "Be careful where you dig, Ambassador," he said over his cloak.

Kaden watched the Crown Prince until the forest swallowed him. He stayed like that for a bit, unmoving, making sure he was truly alone. A trail of insects scurried up the bark of the nearest tree, their tiny legs quick against the quiet.

The wind didn't pass often, but when it did, it stirred a scatter of brittle leaves across the grove floor—dry and whispering like the aftermath of Lady Ice, not the heart of Lady Fira's season.

It should've been warm here. Lush. At a glance, the rest of Aeonia sweltered under full bloom, branches heavy with sun-fed green. But this grove? It was hollowed out. Lifeless. As if the trees had bowed out of Fira entirely.

Dead. That was the only word for the flora encircling the grove. Kaden scratched the back of his neck and pulled the map from his satchel. Lorenthar's hand marked the grove in fine script, with a small note scrawled beside the border:

Old elven ritual glade. Curious spot. Forgotten.

Kaden had read that line at least a dozen times since the prince gave him the map. At the time, it felt like a favor. A lead. A quiet nudge to look beyond the stone corridors and cold smiles of the Aeonian court. Lorenthar had seemed amused when he handed it over, as if it were nothing more than a historic footnote.

But now Kaden wasn't so sure.

He turned in a slow circle, scanning the grove with the eyes of a tracker. The foliage told more truth than any archive. He crouched by a dying bramble, ran two fingers along the stem, and scraped the bark with his nail. Dry all the way through. The leaves had gone dull at the veins first—a sign of severed life, not disease. Whatever was killing this grove wasn't natural. It was as if the land itself had been sucked clean dry of any life.

He stood and moved methodically, examining low grasses, fungal blooms, the discolored moss clinging in patchy rings along the bases of the trees. Each oddity he noted silently, intending to sketch them into his journal later. He hadn't brought it with him—hadn't expected to need it for a place Lorenthar had brushed off as nothing more than a footnote in a dusty scroll. Regret was an understatement.

Kaden had expected signs. Stones, bones—something tangible he could read. Instead, there was only the same slow rot he'd seen on the road to Aeonia. The same dry foliage and withered bark. He blew out a slow breath and rubbed his jaw, layers of doubt tightening across his shoulders.

Something strange prickled along his spine and he froze. A tug… soft, gentle, not on his limbs, but on something far quieter. It pulled at something deep within the marrow of him. His Seryn stirred, the hum so faint it could've been mistaken for muscle memory.

But it wasn't.

He swallowed and focused, narrowing his senses to the faint vibration at the edge of his awareness. Cautiously, he reached for his satchel and pulled out the folded oilcloth from the other night. The last of the strange twin roots rested inside, its companion long since reduced to ash after his failed attempt to heal it. The smear remained, a dark echo of what had been. The surviving root pulsed faintly, casting the faintest glow through the fabric. A hum trembled from its center, barely audible.

Kaden bent closer, gingerly picking it up with the tips of his fingers. It cracked in half with a dry whisper and fell apart in his hands.

"Sardan's spawn," he cursed under his breath.

The slivered remnants of the root spilled through his fingers and drifted away… but not by gravity or wind. They shifted as if guided by the Weave, trailing across the grove's floor in a slow path toward the heart of the clearing… but curiously, the air around him hadn't moved at all.

The remnants stopped at the base of a shallow rise. The dirt was dry and bare. Even fungus didn't grow there. Kaden crouched. The hum in his chest returned—subtle, but clearer now. Less a vibration than a beckoning. He brushed aside the splinters of the old root with the edge of his hand and began to dig with careful fingers, peeling back layers of soil.

Soon, his knuckles scraped stone. He cleared more away, revealing the wide face of a circular slab, mottled with age but unmistakably carved. Seven concentric rings, faintly etched, spiraled outward from its center like ripples frozen mid-motion.

Kaden exhaled and rocked back on his heels, muttering a low, "Huh." He hadn't seen anything like it before. Not in Izier. Not anywhere. He tugged the map from his satchel once more, scanning its weathered surface for any symbol or scribble he might've missed. But there was only the faint crease from where he'd folded it and Lorenthar's looping hand scrawl at the margin.

With a short sigh, he tucked it away and let his eyes fall back to the stone. Now that he wasn't digging, he could feel it again. That peculiar vibration. And it felt like it was calling to him. He narrowed his eyes and leaned in, brushing the dirt aside.

As soon as his skin met the stone, a low beat thrummed in his ears like it had been lying in wait. The forest vanished behind the sound—a wall of pressure and pulse. He fell back, jaw clenched, trying to shake it off. The hum inside him surged in response. He blinked hard, licked his dry lips, and stared at the stone.

This wasn't just old. It was *alive*. Or at least, it had been. He gave a sweeping glance through the grove anew. The decay. The silence. The way the roots seemed to recoil from this very spot. He'd seen land starved before. Drought, plague, even salt-poisoned fields… but this was different.

Kaden reached for his satchel out of habit before cursing softly, forgetting momentarily he'd left his notebook back in the guest quarters. With a frustrated sigh, he leaned closer to the slab, tracing the etched rings with his eyes. He followed each curve, each line, committing them to memory. The spacing. The depth. The way the spiral converged inward, like a tether pulling toward a single, hidden point.

He didn't know what it was, but it felt like a capstone. Like something meant to seal. Capstones were stabilizers of the Weave, said to anchor the Aeon's flow through the Network. The Seryn in every elf was a thread of that same system, a living node meant to keep the Harmonies steady.

He still didn't have any clear answers as to why the earth was dying and the seasons were confused, but he'd bet a hefty bounty this was the kind of secret people killed to keep buried.

He dusted his palms clean and headed back toward the palace with the map tucked away and the stone's song still ringing in his ears. In his quarters, he set out a single sheet and began to write.

He noted the abandoned grove; the carved slab buried at its heart; the way the roots there seemed to pulse and then recoil; the hush of a place that hadn't bloomed in seasons; Eldarion's secret to serve some greater purpose. He added what he'd seen on the road in: brittle leaves and frost where Lady Fira should have held, rivers run thin, winds swinging hot to bitter in a single afternoon, villages strained and watchful. He listed his samples—the repeat of that pale, pulsing root found leagues apart—and his failed attempt to steady one with a touch of his Resonance.

Then he set down the politics as plainly as the soil. Queen Valenne cool and cutting. Eldarion bold and cunning. Vaelar boastful and clinging to the old ways. Laerynth speaking rarely but moving the room when he did. The king worn thin. Thalor steady, if blunt. Lorenthar amused and useful in equal measure. Rations already a fight. Cracks in the court growing faster than anyone would admit.

His pen hovered for a breath. There was one name he could have added. One voice that didn't belong in the web he was mapping. But he left it off. The princess didn't deserve to be part of this.

He read back over the report, the words sitting stiff on the page. Talking through trouble he knew; writing it for a court half a realm away was another thing entirely. Before sealing it, he pulled his journal from the drawer and sketched the slab's spiraled rings.

His first full account since arriving. Roots and rot recorded alongside the people circling them. With luck, the Empress's court would treat it as more than a green ambassador's nerves. And if a reply came, maybe it would carry more than orders. Maybe even word of her.

He leaned back in the chair, eyes unfocused on the ink drying before him. It had been months, yet he could still imagine Lusa—the flare of her eyes when she fought, the quick, sure rhythm of her training blade against his. He'd thought about that last spar more than he wanted to admit. The way she'd smiled when she bested him. The heat of her body when she knocked him flat. The kiss that he dared to leave that afternoon. His, but never truly his.

He scrubbed a hand over his jaw, trying to banish the memory. It clung anyway. She'd been fire and will and every reason he'd ever had to stay close. He'd walked away because he'd had to. Because duty had teeth and he'd learned long ago what it cost to ignore it. But the silence since… it gnawed.

Slowly, he sealed the report, its wax cooling to black. The grove's hush still rang in his head, replaying how roots shriveled, and the earth became untuned. Aeonia had forgotten its harmony. And in some twisted way, so had he.

CHAPTER 20

A Banquet of Whispers

Kaden splashed cool water into his hands, the basin cradled in the hollowed heart of a living root. The surface shimmered faintly, catching soft blue light from the glowmoss braided through the chamber's rafters. Vines curled, woven as deliberate design with its growth. Even the floor—an ancient branch, wide enough to walk three across and smoothed by elven hands until it resembled polished wood—sat cool beneath his bare feet. The palace hadn't been built in the forest but coaxed from it. A quiet marvel of design, where every wall, floor, and frame grew with purpose.

Kaden cupped his hands into the leafstone vessel and doused his face, letting the water trickle down his jaw. The Grove's chill still clung to his skin… or maybe it was the memory of how that capstone had reacted to his touch.

He wiped his face on a cloth spun from spider silk and glanced at his reflection. The mirror wasn't glass like in Izier, but a stretch of silvered bark. Kaden stared at himself; eyes shadowed with the memory of stone rings and withered roots.

From the edge of the basin, he uncorked a small vial the elven steward had left and rubbed a few drops of shaving oil along his jaw. Light, pine-scented, probably made from pressed root or blossom. He didn't care. It worked. He drew his travel blade from its worn leather sheath and gave it a once-over. Nothing fancy, simply steel and edge, but it did the job. He dragged the blade along his jaw with practiced ease.

Shame his thoughts weren't as obedient.

"Let it remain in turmoil for now." Eldarion's words circled like gnats. His hands worked on instinct, but his mind kept snagging. What turmoil? The land rotting from the roots? The court tearing at itself? Or something he hadn't even clocked yet?

He rinsed the blade. Lathered again. Scraped downward.

The root had crumbled in his hands and then drifted away, straight toward that stone slab. There hadn't been wind. It was like something invisible had pulled at it. There had to be some connection between the pulsing roots and that capstone—a fracture in the Harmony itself, a wound where Aether had stopped breathing.

He set the blade on the edge of the leafstone and watched water drip from his chin. Whatever lay beneath that stone hadn't faded. It had been pushed into shadow. And now that shadow was pushing back.

He wiped his jaw clean, fingers pausing at his throat.

Growth, Eldarion had said. As if rot itself were the strategy, a patient reclaiming rather than decay. And the hooded figure…Whoever it was, they hadn't moved like a court pet. They moved like someone trained. Someone used to shadows.

Jaw freshly shaven, mind far from settled, Kaden reached for the dark blue tunic folded on the vine woven bench. A formal cut, the Empress's colors, embroidered in silver thread. He held it up for a beat, fingers brushing the collar. The banquet was in honor of Lord Laerynth's birthday, the Queen's father and one of the oldest names in Aeonia.

His cousin would've felt right at home doing something like this. Nolanna had been raised in the Izierian court, taught to turn charm into a weapon long before she needed one. Banquets, diplomacy, ceremonies… she moved through it all like it was breathing.

Kaden wasn't built for that kind of grace. He wasn't meant to be a symbol. But here he was, the Izierian ambassador in a kingdom that barely tolerated his presence. He would've skipped the whole thing if he could. But after witnessing the Crown Prince speaking in shadows…

He was starting to think the rot wasn't just in the roots. Grabbing his sealed report, he tucked it away in the interior pocket of his formal coat. If Aeonia planned banquets like Izier, he'd be placed with his two envoys. One of those unlucky bastards would be the one to trek back to Izier with his report.

The chamber doors parted with barely a whisper. Smooth, vine-laced wood folded inward to reveal the heart of Aeonia's high court. A hush followed as his name was announced, the elven accent stretching the vowels just so, "Kaden Everwyn, Ambassador of Izier."

He stepped into the banquet hall, boots sinking into mosswoven carpet threaded with gold. Harps, flutes, some other instrument he couldn't place, rose from hidden alcoves. Tables grew outward from smoothed root, carved with elven script and spiraled like unfolding leaves. Petaled plates and blossom-cut glass shimmered under the biolight, each bearing delicacies that looked like crafted art as much as food.

And everywhere… green. Emerald silks, sage velvet, sea-glass gauze. Courtly robes rustled like leaves in a Flora's wind, elegant and almost fluid. Against it all, Kaden's imperial blue tunic cut a stark silhouette. He was one of only three souls cloaked in Izierian blue.

He'd stood in the marble halls of Izier's palace more times than he could count. Collecting bounties, facing nobility with blood on his boots… but this? This was something else entirely. The High Canopy didn't feel like a palace. It felt like stepping into another realm. One he was tied to by blood, but still didn't belong in. A massive tapestry dominated the far wall behind the royal dais; its golden threads worked into the ridges and rivers of Aetherealm. Decorative, meant to awe, but too precise to be art. The kind of thing a man might overlook if he weren't used to reading maps.

A quick sweep of the hall told him the two Izerian envoys were already seated near the outer ring of tables, watching him with stiff-backed patience. As he moved towards them, his gaze caught on hers.

Princess Siraen sat beside her mother near the dais, meeting his eyes with the faintest tilt of her chin and a barely held back smile—bright, unguarded, and far too pleased to see him. The kind of smile that didn't yet understand how dangerous it was to offer someone like him warmth in a room full of watchers.

She was the one who'd sent the invitation, worded in court formality. Maybe it was diplomacy. Maybe fascination. Judging by the looks he was drawing from the rest of the court—including King Theron, who sat between his sons—she might've been the only one who wanted him there at all.

Not that it mattered. He could've skipped the whole thing, kept to his quarters, or better yet, returned to the Grove while the court drowned itself in wine and niceties.

But something about the gesture… about *her*… made him show up. A strange sense of duty he didn't quite understand.

And he hated that it held.

Kaden finally made it to his table, noticing the conversations that faltered when he passed. Eyes followed. Some faces tilted in curiosity, others in veiled disdain. He kept his posture easy, practiced. Let them stare. He wasn't here to win friends.

Prince Lorenthar, leaning casually against the curved back of his chair, goblet in hand, offered Kaden a nod. Kaden returned the gesture, barely more than a lift of his chin, and took his seat, spine straight but gaze roving. The air was sweet with fruit-wine and blossom incense, but underneath it, he still caught the musky scent of decay.

The low chime of glass rang clear and reverent as the herald stepped forward.

"All rise for Lord Laerynth of the Verdant Line, Father to Her Majesty, Sovereign of the Southern Wealds, and Keeper of the Ninth Tree."

The court stood as one, a ripple of movement like wind across grass. Kaden rose as well, slow, studying the figure that emerged between the twisted columns of the dais arch.

Lord Laerynth walked without hurry, tall and wiry, his silver hair bound in a dozen thin cords, each looped with barked rings and woven beads that clicked softly as he moved. His gaze swept the hall once, sharp as a falcon's. He neither smiled nor acknowledged the room. And he didn't need to. His presence alone demanded homage. He reached his chair on the other side of the Queen and sank into it as the court resumed their seats.

By the time the first course arrived, some kind of honey-glazed root spiral with blossom-drizzled broth, his fellow Izierians had already started in on pleasant diplomacy.

"Lovely turnout this evening," murmured Envoy Ronus to the other, Whilm if Kaden recalled. His gray beard was trimmed neatly, and his tone carried the smooth veneer of someone who never stopped politicking. "You should commend Princess Siraen for extending the invitation. No small gesture."

Kaden dipped his head toward Ronus as he drew a linen from the stack and used the motion to pass the sealed letter into the envoy's waiting palm.

"Time-sensitive," he whispered. "Northeastern passes, if they're open. If not, the coast."

Ronus didn't look down. He slid the letter beneath his sleeve with ease and lifted his goblet. The men each took a long drink, taking in the essence of the High Canopy's show of wealth and power.

Glimmers of pollen-like luminescence floated in the upper air, pulsing faintly with each vibration of the music. It was Aeonia's version of Resonance made visible. Proof that even the air here responded to the Seven Harmonies. But even so, the light felt out of sync, its rhythm uneven.

Midway through the meal, the music changed—rising, lilting, the tempo shifting in a way Kaden could guess what was coming next. A ring cleared at the center of the hall, and into it stepped a circle of slender elven dancers, their dresses shaped like layered petals, soft as fog and bright as river glass. Their movements were otherworldly. Arms glided like reeds in water; feet barely seemed to touch the floor with each graceful move.

And yet Kaden only watched in pieces. Because just before the music rose into a climax, Prince Vaelar left the royal table. He didn't draw attention, but Kaden noticed anyway. His hair hung mostly loose, silver, shot through with hints of strawberry blond, half pinned back in braids. He made his way behind his family towards an exit.

The dance continued. Elven laughter trilled in quiet corners. Goblets clinked. Ronus was still talking about something with Whilm—treaties, maybe—but Kaden tuned him out entirely. Because by the middle of the dance, Lord Laerynth's chair sat empty.

Kaden hadn't seen him leave, but the seat was bare. Taking a slow sip from his goblet, he tried to catch any movement in the shadows behind the dais holding the royal family. Besides the missing royals, everything continued as normal, oblivious to the benefactor missing out. Three-quarters into the performance, Laerynth returned, silent and composed. He took his seat without comment, his fingers steepled before him.

Vaelar returned from the shadows as the final notes of the dance faded. Applause erupted throughout the hall while the prince walked the curve of the dais with the same unhurried grace, leaned in close to Princess Siraen, and bent close enough to murmur something in her ear.

She tilted her head slightly—enough to listen, not enough to show it. Her smile nearly slipped before she caught it, knuckles whitening on her goblet's stem.

Servants moved like whispers between the tables, clearing empty platters and setting out fresh wines laced with moonpetal or wild fennel. The formalities dissolved slightly as chairs were pushed back and the crowd began to shift, drifting toward the far end of the hall where the dessert pavilions awaited.

Kaden didn't move right away. He watched the tide pull nobles and dignitaries toward sugar-spun confections and pastries, the air filling with new scents: ambered citrus, roasted nutmoss, honey-laced berries still warm from a low flame. A dozen separate tables stood beneath their own sculpted canopies, each one themed around a different seasonal fruit, flower, or elven myth. Delicacies hovered an inch off their trays, enchanted to pulse faintly with light and give the first bite a gentle rush. Not quite drunkenness. Not quite aphrodisiac. Something in between.

Kaden stood and moved the way he did through any crowd.... unobtrusive but alert, a shadow given polite shape. The court was too caught up in their own laughter and delicacy-picking to notice him this time. He passed several dessert options before slowing near a vase of vineberry tarts, using this time to scan the room. Princess Siraen had made her way to one of the blossom tables, a half-finished petal-pastry in hand, nodding at something whispered by her attendant. Vaelar was gone again.

Instead of approaching her, Kaden picked up a tart, letting it warm the inside of his palm, and pretended to study the texture. He was aware of every movement behind him. Every flick of fabric. Every shift in sound.

Play the part. Wait for the opening.

The court may have written him off as an afterthought. An ornament from Izier, sent for diplomacy's sake. But they hadn't seen the way Siraen's hand had clenched her goblet.

And he intended to find out why.

CHAPTER 21

Aelenth

Kaden circled the tables with unhurried ease, the tart still warm in his hand. His gaze slid over silk trains and jeweled sleeves until he spotted the princess. But it looked as if Siraen had already spotted him and was pretending she hadn't. Kaden could tell by the way her gaze, deliberately distracted, kept drifting across the crowd. The almost imperceptible lift of her chin whenever she thought he might be looking. She wasn't subtle. Not even close. Her attempts at nonchalance were all soft edges and too-long pauses, like she'd memorized how intrigue should look but hadn't had to practice it before.

He should've ignored it. Should've turned back toward the other diplomats and played his role. But something in her persistence, earnest and unpolished, made him want to spare her the sting of being ignored. Besides, he still planned to learn what Vaelar had said to upset her.

When he finally moved along the dessert tables, she was conveniently already there. Fingers poised over a plate of glowing vineberry tarts she clearly had no interest in.

"Your Highness," he said, voice low enough to vanish beneath the music. "Didn't realize the dessert table doubled as a place to hide from watchful eyes."

Her head turned a little too fast. "Ambassador," she said, tone soft but brightening with relief that he'd spoken first. "I was just…" Her gaze darted down at the sweets. "Deciding which one looks the least enchanted."

"Bad odds, then. I hear they're all cursed ta' make a man forget his manners."

Her laugh came before she could smother it—light, unguarded, and completely out of place in a room full of people pretending not to breathe the same air. She bit her lip, realizing too late that she'd given herself away. "Then perhaps I should be careful which one I touch," she said, brushing her fingers near a glass of mousse that glowed faintly rose-gold.

Kaden caught himself watching that small, careless motion longer than he should've. "Depends who you're hopin' to enchant."

Her cheeks colored instantly. "I— that isn't—" She looked down, a smile breaking through despite her effort to compose herself. "You're teasing me."

"Maybe." He reached for the same mousse she'd hovered near and handed it to her. "But if ye're gonna walk straight inta' trouble, might as well taste it first."

Siraen took the glass, eyes flicking up through her lashes in a way that wasn't practiced, completely innocent. "You sound like someone who's already made that mistake."

"Once or twice."

She dipped her spoon into the mousse, slow, pretending to study its shimmer. "I heard you wouldn't attend any of these gatherings."

"Not my kind of hunt."

"Then why tonight?"

He almost smiled. "Seemed someone wanted me here."

Her grip tightened slightly around the stem of the glass. "And did you come because of duty… or curiosity?"

Kaden tilted his head. "You always this bold, Princess?"

"Only when no one's watching." She said it quietly—but her gaze held his for a long, lingering beat that pulled something taut in his chest.

He broke it first, glancing toward the dais where Vaelar now stood beside the Queen. "Your brother didn't seem thrilled with you earlier."

The flicker in her eyes told him he'd struck true. "He worries too much," she said lightly, swirling the mousse with her spoon. "He thinks every shadow hides a scandal."

"Maybe he's right to."

Siraen's lips curved, soft but mischievous. "And which do you think I am, Ambassador? A scandal or a shadow?"

"Neither," he said after a beat. "But both attract too much trouble for my taste."

She smiled at that—shy, proud, and a little reckless. "Maybe that's why I wanted to talk to you," she said, leaning a tad closer on the balls of her toes.

Something in her voice sank past his defenses, quiet and unassuming, like sunlight slipping through cracks. This wasn't politics or performance… it was pure curiosity. Directed straight at him.

Kaden cleared his throat, trying to bury the warmth rising beneath his collar. "Careful, Princess. Curiosity's a dangerous habit in realms like yours."

"So is pretending not to feel anything."

The air between them shifted, charged and still. Then she smiled again—bashful, as if she hadn't meant to say it aloud—and turned to set her goblet of mousse down.

"Enjoy the evening, Ambassador. I hear the desserts are enchanted to make one's heart race."

She left before he could answer, her perfume trailing behind her like something light and wistful. Kaden watched her weave through the guests, her grace still stiff around the edges but brave in a way that made something inside him twist. He wasn't used to this kind of pull—quiet, innocent, disarming in a way that felt far more dangerous than seduction.

He took an absent bite of the tart before realizing what he'd done. The sweetness hit his tongue and he froze, debating whether to spit it out. Pride won. He swallowed.

The effect was instant. A sharp warmth flooded through him, sparking low and fast, spreading heat in all the wrong places. His breath caught. Eyes—traitorous things—found her in the crowd, the sway of her gown, the soft line of her neck as she turned to laugh at something he couldn't hear. The pulse that followed wasn't from magic alone.

He blinked hard, grounding himself, and set the tart down a little too hard. "Damn enchantments," he muttered

When he looked up again, he caught Eldarion's cold gaze cutting through the crowd. The pulse that had been burning through him cooled in an instant.

Kaden straightened, schooling his features into something bland and unreadable. Let the prince think what he wanted. He wasn't here to compete for anyone's favor, least of all hers.

Still, when he turned away, he caught himself glancing once more toward where Siraen had vanished into the press of silks and lanternlight. Just to be sure she was gone.

At least, that's what he told himself.

The hall had slipped into that soft, drifting quiet between the last course and the first goodbye. The King and

Queen had retired. He hadn't seen Prince Lorenthar since his arrival and wondered if he'd left early. Courtiers eased into their second glasses of moonpetal wine and their third rounds of polite intrigue.

Kaden was already settled back in his chair, draining his goblet nice and slow. Might as well savor every drop of their fine wine while he had the chance. He doubted he'd be invited again, and the aggravated look on Eldarion's face made it all the more satisfying.

The guest of honor, Lord Laerynth, leaned in and murmured something to Prince Vaelar, who'd dropped into the seat beside him. Kaden watched over the rim of his glass, trying to read Laerynth's lips.

As if on cue, the old elf lifted a hand to shield his mouth, finishing whatever hushed conversation was passing between them. Vaelar's brows drew tight, his steely gaze cutting down the long table to the princess.

Siraen let out an obvious sigh, forced a polite smile, and rose from her chair.

"I'll say," Ronus slurred, blinking blearily at the dais, "your elven folk sure know how to throw a party." The man had knocked back more moonpetal than Kaden could count on one hand. He patted his swelled belly with a satisfied groan.

"They're not my folk," Kaden corrected, finishing the last of his drink.

Whilm slid in smoothly, trying to lighten the air. "And those dancers. I mean, they don't top the beauty of the empress, but it was like magic to watch, for sure."

An amused snort slipped out of Kaden before he could swallow it.

Whilm lifted his brows, affronted. "What? A man can appreciate grace, can't he?"

Kaden ignored them both and turned his gaze back to the dais, only to find Siraen and Vaelar both gone. Lord Laerynth hadn't moved. He caught Kaden's stare and lifted his goblet in a mocking toast, the gold cup barely hiding the sly curve of his mouth.

Kaden's fingers tightened on the stem of his empty glass. He told himself it wasn't worry about Siraen. He hardly knew the princess. No. It was Vaelar and Laerynth, and the way they looked when they thought no one was watching. He'd tracked enough bounty marks to know the look of men already plotting how the rest of them would lose.

He pushed out of his chair and excused himself to the envoys, as if he'd suddenly remembered somewhere better to be.

The corridor beyond the banquet forked in three different directions. Moss trailed from the rafters, and the walls pulsed with faint amber light from fruit-lanterns strung like swollen pods along the ceiling. He moved slow. The kind of walk that didn't draw eyes. Even in a palace this curated, people left signs: the hush of servants stepping aside too quickly, a trace of Vaelar's cologne warming the air. He'd tracked harder men with less to go on.

Somewhere deep beneath the wood, he felt it again. That faint, thrumming pull that had haunted him since the Grove. The underlying hum of Aeonia itself, what his father had called the Aeon's harmony, felt faint here. Like the world was running on a memory instead of its full breath.

After a few turns of the path, he found a doorway carved into the base of a trunk. The door was shut, but he heard faint voices. Kaden exhaled slowly, sinking into that quiet part of himself where instinct blurred into something older. His senses were already enhanced, an inheritance of the elf blood he'd never asked for. But the door was too thick and the voices too soft.

He slipped into the shadow of a trunk column and closed his eyes. He hated leaning on that part of himself—the elven side he'd spent half his life wishing he could carve out. But it was a gift he could respect when it served a purpose.

With careful focus, he called on the Resonance that lived under his skin and let it sharpen his hearing until the world beyond the door began to take shape.

A heartbeat. Two.

And then the voices slipped through the wood like sap bleeding through fresh-cut bark.

"…He wants more time," came one low whisper.

"He's had years," Vaelar replied. Tighter now. "The binding thins by the cycle. It's spreading beyond the Grove."

Silence.

Then: "If the Aelenth is right, then the capstones—"

Footsteps rubbed out the rest of Vaelar's response. Kaden held his breath and slinked further into the column's shadow, watching the prince's steward approach the door. He waited, every muscle strung tight, as the man paused a bit beyond the threshold. A quick knock, then another, and the door opened.

From inside, Vaelar's voice trickled out, "…so we'll discuss then."

The steward stepped inside, and the door shut. As much as he wanted to stay and figure out what the youngest prince was up to, every instinct told him they were about to leave.

Kaden backed away in three careful steps, turned, and slipped into the nearest side passage. He didn't stop until he reached an archway opening onto the outer walk.

Aelenth. Was it a person? The word, or name, had never appeared in any ledger, archive, or half-remembered tale he'd heard. And how he phrased it… *the Aelenth.* A title, maybe?

The binding thins by the cycle.
Spreading beyond the Grove.
If the Aelenth is right, then the capstones…

He replayed each fragment, testing them against the histories he'd scraped together in taverns and his mother's bedtime stories. The Aeon. The Harmonies. The old belief that every realm sang a note in the world's balance. Maybe the Capstone had something to do with that—maybe not. But if those notes were faltering…

He rubbed at the back of his neck, uneasy. Whatever was happening out there, it wasn't just politics or bad harvests. It felt older. Wilder.

And what in Eldere's name was Aelenth? Or who? The way Vaelar had said it made one thing clear: it was tied to whatever was happening in Aetherealm.

He turned a corner and nearly collided with a steward hauling a tray of empty goblets. He muttered something close to an apology and kept moving, letting the quiet close around him again. When he finally reached his quarters, he shut the door with deliberate care. He'd gotten away clean. *This time.*

At first, he'd thought the blight, or whatever it should be called, was political. Tampered magic. Some petty sabotage meant to sour the alliance between Aeonia and Izier. But this felt bigger than that. Kaden knew better than to ignore words like that, especially when they came wrapped in shadows.

CHAPTER 22

The Vanished

She was underwater again.

Cold slammed into her chest. A thousand unseen hands dragged her down, nails biting her scalp. Her throat locked. No air. Petals drifted past her eyes: soft pink turning dark, curling to ash. She clawed upward for the surface, but it wasn't water. It was thicker, red-black, flooding her mouth, smothering her tongue in copper.

Above, something watched. Two eyes burning like coals. Martyaxwar. Her mother. Both. Neither.

Ours.

She tried to scream. Bubbles slipped between her teeth and burst into cackling voices. The water vanished, replaced by cold stone. She lay there; ribs cracked beneath Lazorious's boot. Pressure ground deeper, deeper, until something in her chest gave way.

"Not yours," she tried to say. Her jaw wouldn't move.

A hand… her own, rose into view, blue fire racing over her knuckles. It burned her from within.

Ours.

Atraun crawled closer. One arm hung twisted, fingers black with frost. Blood dripped from her mouth.

Mother.

She blinked. The shape changed.

Kaden.

He convulsed, eyes wide, mouth open in a scream she couldn't hear. His skin blistered under a blazing light. She reached for him, but her hand fused to the floor. Cracks split the stone around her fingers. Darkness slithered up her arm, threading through her veins.

Ours.

The martyaxwar leapt, jaws yawning wide—

Darkness swallowed everything.

Lusa's eyes snapped open, breath tearing from her in ragged bursts. The muted scream still burned the back of her throat. It took too long to understand what she was seeing. Pale strands of sunlight slipped through wooden slats overhead, catching dust that drifted like falling embers. She blinked again, and again, willing the world to focus.

Her heart wouldn't slow. Each beat thudded against her bruised ribs. She couldn't remember how she'd come here. Only the nightmare, the martyaxwar's eyes, her mother's broken body, the taste of blood…

Slowly, she shifted, realizing her wrists were pinned behind her, bound tight with coarse rope that bit into raw skin. Memory came in a stuttering rush: the forest, everyone suddenly turning on her, the Dark Elf. She'd tried to stop him, but the Magics were faster, hungrier. They had wrenched her under until she could no longer tell her own rage from Theirs. And when he had blown that white powder in her face, her will, her strength, everything had slipped away.

She drew a trembling breath, testing the place inside her where magic lived. Nothing answered her. No shrill voices hissing from the dark. No roiling cold. The Dark Magics were silent. Her core would need time to recalibrate before she could reach for magic again. Days, maybe longer. Until then, she was nothing but flesh and will.

But deeper still, beneath the hollow ache, she felt a small, stubborn flicker. A fragile warmth, like a single coal banked in ash. The Light? She curled her fingers as best she could, focus closing around that ember. If she needed to heal, it was all she had left.

Her shoulder throbbed in a slow, ugly rhythm that made her vision pulse. She shifted her arms, wincing as the half-healed puncture wound screamed in protest.

Despite it all, she was alive. Somehow. The thought didn't give her relief. Only a hollow dread. For all she'd been through, she still hadn't found answers. Why she was the last mage. Why she had both Light and Dark… and what exactly did that passage in the *Treatise of the Dual Flame* really mean?

Gritting her teeth, she pushed herself upright. Pain flared so bright she nearly lost consciousness again. She forced her eyes back open.

She lay on a pile of damp hay, tucked into the corner of a windowless hold. Crates lined the walls, scrawled with symbols she couldn't read. A lantern burned low on a barrel. The door was a hatch in the ceiling, iron bands crossing the wood.

Trapped.

She swallowed past the panic rising up her throat. A row of shapes huddled against the far wall. Three older women in patched dresses, hair braided tight and some streaked with gray. Two men: one with a split lip crusted dark, the other with a sleeve torn nearly away. A boy, no more than fifteen Fira's, his knees pressed to his chest.

Behind them, half-lost in shadow, another figure slumped on his side, unmoving. Face turned away, one arm twisted beneath him at an angle that made her stomach knot. Asleep. Unconscious. Or…

She couldn't tell.

They watched her the way you'd watch a snake in the grass, afraid to stir in case it struck. One of the older men shifted almost imperceptibly, his hand moving across the boy's shoulder as if to draw him back. She drew a slow breath, voice rasping past the tightness in her throat.

"Who…"

Before she could finish her question, a girl shifted behind one of the women and Lusa's chest went cold. Small. Narrow-shouldered. Tangled, light brown hair fell across her cheek as she looked up. The village girl. The same child she had saved from falling crates.

Lusa could only stare, trying to reconcile that memory with the bruises on the girl's arms, the hollow in her face. The truth pressed in with each awkward second that passed. She had become one of the vanished.

The girl's gaze met hers, then fell. Her hands twisted in her skirt as though she carried some hidden shame. Pity replaced Lusa's shock and she swallowed, trying not to wince and wondering how long she'd been out. With how dry her throat was, had to be more than a day.

"Where are we?"

No one answered. Only the dry shuffle of someone shifting. One of the men cleared his throat.

"We… don't rightly know," he said. His voice sounded as starved as the rest of him. "Woke here same as you. Couldn't say how long."

The man's gaze flicked to the others. "Most of us… we were in the woods. West of Merravale. Somebody said—" His jaw tightened, eyes glinting with grief. "Said they'd seen my boy. Told me to follow."

A woman nodded, her hands twisting. "Said they found my sister."

The boy didn't lift his head. His whisper was only a breath. "My da."

Lusa closed her eyes. A cruel trick. Lure them out with hope and vanish them until no one remained to notice.

"How long?"

The man shook his head. "Days? A week? Hard to tell. They don't come often. When they do—"

A groan of old hinges cut him off. Every head turned upward. One of the hatch doors shifted, a hairline of light widening across the slats. The rusted squeal set her teeth on edge, but she didn't wait to see who, or what, was coming.

She gave a warning look and shushed them in hopes they'd play along, sagging her body against the crates, her breath slowing to an even rhythm. Eyes nearly closed, she waited.

Boots thumped near the hatchway. Two pairs. Heavy. A curse muttered low as whoever it was climbed down. The air shifted, thick with sweat and something sour. The first figure landed, broad-shouldered, head shaved in uneven patches. A man, by the shape of him. A fraying scarf knotted around his forearm. His gaze swept the captives, measuring.

The second figure, also human, hopped down, buckets in hand. Water sloshed over the rims. He set them down, then dragged a crate down the ladder. Rations?

Lusa let her lashes flicker. Hard rolls. The stale reek of fish. One of the women flinched, and the first man turned with a snarl.

"Calm down."

"Any trouble since last meal?"

"Nah."

She felt his gaze pass over her. She lay still, her breath thin and measured.

He moved on.'"tay know betta'."

She tried to place their accents but honestly had no idea. A bucket thudded nearby.

"D'ink up. Oon fill. Nuh more."

The crate scraped as they worked down the line, dropping bread and gray lumps into waiting hands. The last roll fell with a dull thump. The man with the scarf spat near the slumped figure and turned for the ladder. At the hatch, he paused and looked back.

"'Ta' mage wakes, 'member'n, she kills. Best'n yoo tell us."

Lusa stopped breathing, every muscle tensing in anticipation of a betrayal. Her ears strained to pick up on movement, breath being taken that warned of confessions. Every plan of escape raced through her mind, but it was pointless. She wasn't in any shape to fight, let alone run.

But no one spoke. The hatch swung shut and she noted the lack of a lock or chains. She stayed unmoving, waiting for the screech of a bolt that never came.

Breathing a little more regular, she opened her eyes. They hadn't locked it. She doubted it was because they'd forgotten, more likely because they didn't need to. Lusa took in the weak stares around her.

The boy clutched his bread as if it might try and escape. One of the women began to weep. Those men believed none of them were brave, or foolish, enough to try and escape.

Perhaps, she thought bitterly, they were right. But that certainly wouldn't be the case forever. Not with her around.

Lusa flexed her bound hands again, testing each finger, each pulse of pain. She swallowed the last of the panic and forced her mind to settle on what she still had: her memory, her will, and that flicker of Light.

She needed answers. She needed to know where they were, who had taken them, what waited beyond that hatch.

But she also knew that questions wouldn't matter if she couldn't even stand without blacking out.

Drawing in a breath that tasted of salt and old straw, Lusa let her eyes drift shut, not from surrender but from purpose. That ember of Light, buried beneath the bruises and exhaustion, waited. It wasn't enough to break her bindings, or to fight. But enough, perhaps, to begin mending the damage she had no other way to heal.

She let her awareness sink into it but didn't dare try to draw on it fully. If she emptied it now, there would be nothing left. But she could coax a trickle to ease the worst of her pain, to keep herself from tipping into unconsciousness again if she moved too quickly.

The warmth responded, hesitant, like a half-tamed creature unsure if it could trust her. Her thoughts flashed to the girl in the corner, to the boy clutching his bread, to the slumped figure unmoving in the shadows. She wasn't the only one here who needed strength.

A thin line of heat pulsed through her shoulder, dulling the throbbing ache. She swallowed, tasting blood and determination in equal measure. She would not die here.

A rustle of straw drew her attention, and her eyes snapped open. The girl had shuffled away from the older woman she'd been clinging to, head bowed as she crept a few paces closer. The movement was halting, like she expected to be struck for daring it, but she kept going until she was near enough that Lusa could better see the bruises on her arms in the lantern glow. They seemed a few days old, greenish-yellow streaks like fat fingers had gripped too tight.

Lusa let her breath out slowly, her pulse still quick from the sudden break in silence. She wanted to speak, to ask why she was approaching her, but the girl didn't lift her gaze. Instead, she held out one small, dirt-smeared hand, clenched tight around something she hadn't let go of.

Lusa blinked. She looked from the girl's bent head to her closed fist. The girl lifted her eyes, searching Lusa's face for something—permission, forgiveness, understanding—before dropping her gaze again. A tremor went through her shoulders before she slowly uncurled her fingers. Even before the light touched it, Lusa knew what it was.

The hairpin.

Silver gleamed in the dim glow—delicate, shaped like a spray of gypsophila blooms. The marcasite glinted soft and dark between the petals. Lusa could only stare, the sight of it doing something strange to her chest, an ache that was more than pain. Looking up, she met the girl's eyes. She had taken it. At some point during that moment in the square when Lusa had lifted her out of harm's way, or when she had clung to her afterwards, she'd slipped it free.

All this time, Lusa had assumed it had fallen, lost to the mud and the broken crates. And as much as she wanted to be angry, wanted to scold the girl for the trouble she'd caused, she couldn't bring herself to do it.

Because the truth was, she was relieved. Relieved it hadn't been abandoned somewhere in Merravale, trampled and forgotten. Relieved it was here, in the hands of someone who, for reasons she couldn't name, had kept it safe.

She offered a weak smile. "I can't take it."

The girl looked up at her, eyes wide and questioning. Tear tracks streaked down her dirt-smudged cheeks.

"My hands are bound," Lusa explained, lowering her head so the girl could reach. "You'll have to pin it yourself."

A beat passed. Lusa ignored the pinch in her shoulder and waited. Maybe she wouldn't follow through, maybe she was too timid to dare it. But Lusa remained patient.

At last, the girl crept closer. Her small fingers lifted the pin and clipped it into Lusa's tangled, dirt-matted hair, securing it. Relief washed through her and she sat a bit straighter.

"Thank you."

The girl nodded, so slight a gesture Lusa nearly missed it.

"What's your name?" she asked.

"She don't speak," the older man from before said. "Least, she hasn't since she was taken."

The woman the girl had hidden behind earlier fussed with her long braid, debating whether to chime in. "Her ma called her Tessanee."

Lusa studied the girl's face, trying to gauge her age. She remembered the old merchant woman in the square insisting none of the vanished were under ten. Tessanee looked close to that line. Her slight frame suggested nine or ten, but her eyes—and the way she held herself—felt older. She'd learned too soon how to shoulder burdens.

Lusa's throat tightened. She wondered how long Tessanee had been the one to watch over younger brothers, how long she had waited for a mother who never came back.

"Thank you, Tessanee," she said softly. "And thank you all…for not telling them I was awake. I won't hurt you."

But even as she said it, a realization settled over her as she watched their reactions. Maybe they hadn't stayed silent because they trusted her. Maybe they were more afraid of her than of the men above.

Every wary glance and bowed head said as much. A few pairs of eyes flicked, almost involuntarily, to the unconscious figure slumped near them. Lusa shifted, wincing, and tried to see past the crates and shadows. The hair, the length of the body, the angle of the jaw—

Her stomach lurched, sourness flooding the back of her throat. Memory flashed: lightning crackling from her fingers, striking Blyven in the chest. The way he'd staggered back, eyes wide, before falling limp. She'd thought he was dead. But now…

"He was going to hurt my friends," she said, the words spilling out in a rush. They sounded so small, so thin—like some sad excuse she'd whispered to herself to feel better.

But they didn't understand. How could they? Had any of them ever watched someone they knew turned into a weapon? Had they ever seen that blank stare when a mind was stripped away for someone else's purpose?

She hadn't learned much about the Dark Elves at the academy. They barely earned a footnote in the old histories—always framed as a warning, never a people. Elves who broke from the Aeonian house after the First Eastern War. Elves who turned from the Aeon's song.

That was all she'd been taught.

There were whispers, too—lessons delivered with lowered voices that their magic no longer followed the same Resonance. That it twisted it. They could press against another's will and bend it, a violation the Aeonians would never forgive. Anything beyond that blurred into assumption.

Power taken too far always carried a cost. Depletion. Hollowing. That much she knew. What she didn't know—what no one had ever bothered to teach—was how much they'd lost… or what they'd gained in return.

Her gaze drifted once more to Blyven's motionless form. What if he never woke? What if she had done more than drive the Dark Elf out? If the Magics were still here with her, they'd scoff. Wouldn't be the first life lost because of her. The Temple and Tryston's lifeless face flashed behind her eyes.

She swallowed hard, pressing the knot in her throat back down where it belonged. It all made her head circle back to the one unanswered question that haunted her. In all the searching, not one mage had been found. Was she just lucky, or had she been spared—and if spared, then for what? The prophecy circled her mind, but she couldn't find the strength to go down that path.

Lusa looked away. There would be time to answer that question… and to answer for it, if she survived long enough. She pressed her bound hands against the straw behind her, feeling the rope cut deeper into tender skin. The pain was grounding. Real. They might be trapped. Weakened. Afraid. But she was still here. And so was that small ember of Light, waiting.

Lusa lifted her chin enough to see Tessanee watching her. The girl's expression hadn't changed, but something in her eyes had. A glimpse of something that might have been hope. And despite her sorry state, and the fact she didn't owe any of them promises, Lusa couldn't help the words that slipped past her dry, cracked lips.

"I'll get us all out of here."

CHAPTER 23

Fathomless

Lusa didn't know how long she'd been down there. Hours, maybe more. Her wrists burned from the ropes, her shoulder throbbed, and the floor kept tilting in ways that made her want to retch. She pressed her bound hands flat against the wooden floorboards, trying to steady herself, but the room still seemed to move. Something was off.

Maybe it was blood loss.

Maybe it was magic.

Maybe she was losing it.

She forced her focus back to healing. The Light barely answered, more a whisper than a flame. But she tugged it forward, again and again, enough to close the worst of the gash and steady her hands. She didn't dare go deeper. She could feel the edge of herself thinning.

Tessanee had returned twice—once with a crust of bread, once with a small palmful of water. No words, just wide eyes and quiet courage. The girl had even tried the knots once, before giving up.

Lusa couldn't place her concern for the girl for the longest time. Perhaps it was the way Tessanee moved, quiet and careful, like the dark might bruise. Once, when she thought Lusa was asleep, she pressed a damp cloth to her head, fingers trembling but determined. Lusa wasn't sure what she'd used to wet the cloth, and figured she was probably better off not knowing. Hopefully water.

The girl never spoke, but her presence said enough. She stayed longer than necessary, constantly glancing toward the hatch as though she knew she'd be caught but couldn't bring herself to leave. There was no pity in her eyes—no fear either—only a fierce, silent loyalty that felt far too large for someone so small.

Why?

The question circled Lusa's mind.

Guilt over the stolen hairpin?

Or something else entirely?

And Lusa, who had lost too many and trusted too few, felt something shift. Not much—but enough to know that if it came down to it, she wouldn't let anything happen to that girl. Not if she had a choice.

She didn't have a plan, merely three rough ideas and one painfully sore shoulder. All of them stupid. All of them dangerous. She turned each one over, not like a strategist but like someone who had run out of time.

First: fake unconsciousness. Wait for a ration drop. Surprise the next brute who got too close. Jam her pin into an eye or a throat before he could blink.

Second: try the hatch. Climb if her shoulder held… *if*.

Third: keep sawing her wrists against the crate behind her, fray the rope, break free. Then heal, fight, improvise—light a fire, throw a punch, hurl moldy fish if she had to. Whatever it took to get out and drag the others with her. Assuming they'd trust her enough to follow… and she didn't get them all killed in the first five minutes.

More time lapsed in the dank silence of whatever this holding space was. The rope was nearly worn through. One more drag—harder this time, skin stinging—and it snapped, falling away like shed snakeskin. Lusa froze, her heart punching her ribs. Free. She was free.

Around her, the captives shifted uneasily. A hush settled, dense as silt, filling every corner of the hold. The older man—Purdue, she'd learned earlier—watched her with a wary gaze.

"What are you planning to do?" he asked.

Lusa didn't answer. She pressed her palms to the floor, testing her balance. Ribs ached. Shoulder throbbed. But she'd survived worse. The dungeons of Izier, Lazorious, the Magics…

She could survive this.

She pushed herself upright slowly, swaying as the floor rocked beneath her. The movement twisted her gut, but she planted one hand on a crate and breathed through the nausea until her head cleared.

Glancing up at the hatch, she counted the steps. Considered the risk. Her gaze snapped to the crates. Not a strategy. A reflex.

She staggered toward the nearest box and started dragging it—sloppy, clumsy, desperate. A barely thought-out trap to be ready for when the next bastard came down.

Tessanee moved to help without being asked, tiny hands straining to shift one side. They shoved together. A few inches were enough. The boy, bordering on being a man, broke from his guardian's grip and joined them.

Lusa grunted out a breath. "Thanks."

They lifted another crate, stacked it crooked. She planted her palm on it, sweat soaking her brow, and looked around at the captives. All of them looked exhausted, trembling, helpless.

"Whatever happens," she said, her voice low and fierce, "I won't leave you to die in here."

She'd always planned to get them out. But plans didn't survive real blood, real bruises. This window… this one sliver of a chance… was hers alone. No one else had the strength, the reach, the sheer rage to pull it off. If she didn't make it topside, no one would. So, she'd go first. And then she'd come back. Sardan help anyone who tried to stop her.

The Magics pushed past the edge of the pin's ward with a hiss of disdain, newly returned and contemptuous. *Leave them. Their fear will feed us.*

Shutting Them out, she looked up as bootsteps creaked overhead and dust rained down through the cracks. Tessanee clapped her hands over her mouth. Lusa waved the children back, mouthed *shhh*, and slipped behind the stacked crates, heart pounding in her ears.

The hatch groaned open. Iron rungs clattered down. Then came the boots, two pairs like before. She crouched low, watching shadows stretch and shift across the straw as the men made it down the ladder.

"Git up," a voice barked.

Without warning, Lusa hurled herself into the stack, ignoring the ache in her shoulder. The crates exploded forward, slamming into both men right as they turned.

Limbs tangled, grunts and curses erupted. Before they could recover, she vaulted over the mess, stomped one man's back to gain height, and lunged upward—fingers catching the third rung.

Her shoulder screamed. She gritted her teeth and kept climbing. One leg over. A shove. A twist. She threw the ladder free, heard it crash below, and slammed the hatch closed with a kick before the men could reach it.

Shouts roared up from below. Blood soaked through her tunic, the wound torn wide again. She stood, turned, and all breath escaped her.

Not a hallway.

Not a chamber.

Endless black and the soft roaring of water. Wind hit her face. Salt on her lips. Deck planks beneath her boots, rocking gently…

A ship.

She staggered back, heart crashing in her chest.

She was on a ship.

The realization sent her mind reeling. She'd never been to sea. The closest she'd gotten was Glon's childhood stories about his father gutting fish by lantern light. And now here she was. Bleeding. Trapped. Miles from land and no idea which direction home even was.

A flicker of thought broke through the panic: The Dark Elf. Had he handed her over? Sold her like cargo while she was unconscious? She clenched her jaw and shoved the thought down.

The hatch thudded loudly behind her. Someone slamming something into it from below. She swallowed hard and stepped over to the nearest barrel, spine pressed to the cool iron bands as she crouched in its shadow, willing herself to breathe.

Movement caught her attention across the deck. Someone coming. What she could only think to describe as a pirate-looking man emerged near the mast. His cutlass gleamed in the moonlight, and a thick beard reached halfway down his chest. His gaze swept the deck, pausing on the sealed hatch.

If anyone was going to kill her, it sure as hell wasn't going to be some greasy pirate with missing teeth and worse breath.

Lusa bolted from the barrel's shadow, boots skidding on wet planks. Her hand shot out mid-sprint, grabbed the nearest coil of rope, and flung it straight into the pirate's face.

He grunted, swearing, batting it away with one thick forearm, but it bought her time.

She slipped past him as a blur of chain swung toward her from the right—a rusted hook screaming through the air. No time to duck. She caught it.

Metal slammed into her palms, jarred her bones, but she twisted, growled, and sent it flying back the way it came. It cracked across another pirate's skull with a satisfying *thwack*. He reeled, blood painting a dark smear across his temple.

A third brute charged toward her from the far end of the deck; cutlass raised like this was a barroom brawl and she was his last coin purse.

Sweet Magics, were they breeding in one of the cargo holds?

Lusa spun in place, eyes scanning for a weapon, anything. A broken plank? A chunk of railing? A net?

There.

Lantern. Hook. Swinging. Just low enough to grab.

She ducked under the pirate's sideways slice, snatched the lantern mid-arc, and smashed it into his face. Glass burst, oil sparked, flame licked his jaw. He screamed, staggering back, hands flailing at the fire.

Lusa spun again, disoriented now, feet slipping. Her heel bumped against a bucket. She kicked it. It flew across the deck and slammed into the next man's shin as he lunged. He cursed and went down hard.

The railing ran along her right side. Beyond it, dark rolling waves reflecting the night sky. Could she survive the fall? Could she even swim?

She didn't remember learning. Then again, she didn't remember *not* learning, either—which hardly boosted her confidence.

A furious roar snapped her back into motion. She twisted around in time for the pirate's cutlass to rake across her good shoulder. Shallow cut. Hot pain.

She hissed and dropped to one knee, caught his wrist, and twisted it between her palms until something gave. His blade slipped free and clattered across the deck in a trail of salt-slick droplets.

Bracing one hand to the boards, she drove her heel into his chest with everything left in her body. He went down, she shoved to her feet and ran, doing her best to ignore the pain threatening to take her out.

Sprinting across the deck, her eyes locked on a narrow staircase cutting up toward the back of the ship. She climbed it two at a time, hair plastered to her face, chest on fire.

There was a room of some sort, one door dead center, built into the rear wall like it was meant for her to find it. The captain's quarters?

Didn't matter.

She had no plan or backup, only plenty of wounds and a gut-deep instinct that said *pick the door, not the sea.*

Maybe she could bar it. Catch her breath. Think.

Her hand flew to the handle—

But it swung open first.

A fresh wave of dread washed through her. There, framed by soft lanternlight and shadowed wood, stood the Dark Elf. His fathomless eyes locked on hers, lips curving into a thin, expectant smile.

A pressure slid into her mind, subtle at first, then insistent—like a key testing every lock.

Give in.

The ward flared, cold and taut across her thoughts, snapping the intrusion shut. The pressure broke off, leaving only the dark echo of his presence.

Lusa stumbled back a step. The Dark Magics flinched against the ward, still weak from depletion. They snarled at the touch. She could feel the imbalance, the sluggish pull of her core trying to recalibrate after being emptied.

His onyx gaze never left hers, and she tried to read him. Her fingers itched for a weapon. She hated the way he looked at her like this was already decided, like he'd already won. And the worst part was, she believed it. That scared her more than she wanted to admit. But she'd swallow glass before she let him see it.

CHAPTER 24

Survive

The Dark Elf stood framed in lamplight, taller than she remembered. Midnight hair spilled over his shoulders in sleek braids, silver clasps glinting like flame moths. His face—long, sharp, unnervingly perfect—was all cold marble and shadow. A statue carved to unsettle.

"As if you could simply... walk away," he said, his voice a quiet reprimand.

Lusa's fingers tightened on the railing. She risked a glance behind her and her stomach dropped. The three pirates she'd fought off were back on their feet, glaring, blood-streaked, and angrier than ever. A fourth man herded the two she'd trapped in the hold into view.

The Dark Elf didn't take his eyes off Lusa as he raised his voice, just enough to carry. "Bring them forward."

"Yes, m'lord," came the reply, the man shoving them forward like the disappointing failures they'd been.

Not captain, she thought numbly. *Lord.*

The scent of scorched cedar drifted in his wake as he moved down the stairs. Lusa turned to track him—watched him approach the pirates like they were stains he meant to scrub off his deck.

A second figure slipped out of the captain's quarters behind her—smaller, wiry. Another dark elf, though the comparison barely seemed fair. Where the tall one's skin gleamed like sun-warmed bronze, this one looked almost sickly—sallow where he should've glowed, his hair limp and unbraided, his robes hanging like they belonged to someone else.

The taller elf didn't glance at the men. He simply extended one hand and made a small, precise motion. He lifted two fingers, then a twist of the wrist, like turning an unseen thread.

The pirate with the ragged scarf twitched. A faint violet light flared at the center of his forehead, pulsing once like a heartbeat before disappearing. His pupils dilated, went glassy, and locked on something she couldn't see.

"Step over," Malvian said softly.

The smaller elf stiffened. "But my pr—"

A single look cut him off.

"Malvian," the smaller elf corrected. "Shouldn't we… keep all our resources? It would… " His words trailed off, swallowed by Malvian's piercing stare.

He turned his attention back to the pirate, fingers still poised midair as though balancing a note only he could hear. The man's body moved, loose-limbed and vacant.

Lusa's stomach turned as he obeyed, walking forward until he reached the railing and stepped over. A splash followed, sealing his fate.

The second pirate let out a strangled yelp, confusion flickering across his face as his limbs started to tremble. The same violet glimmer ignited between his brows, and he began moving toward the railing.

The smaller dark elf tried again. "But—"

"Veyrin," Malvian murmured, tone still mild. "If you question me in front of the crew again, I will peel the tongue from your head."

Veyrin's throat bobbed. "Understood."

The pirate no longer fought against whatever spell Malvian held over him. His body swayed once before pitching forward, over the rail, and into the abyss below.

Malvian exhaled as though he'd merely set something back in order. His eyes turned to her. A dozen thoughts slammed into her at once, but only one stuck, piercing and terrifying all the same: What if he made her his?

Not killed. Not tortured.

Controlled.

Like Lazorious had. Like the Magics still tried.

Break her down and twist her until she was just another empty thing in his arsenal. Moving, killing on command, helpless to his every whim, her body no longer her own while some shredded piece of her still watched from the inside, screaming, locked behind her own eyes, powerless to stop it.

Her stomach pitched. Her fingers shook. She gripped the railing harder to keep them still. Malvian's gaze pinned her in place. The effort to summon anything at all sent shards of pain through her core. She was more than half-spent, and he knew it.

"Now," he said softly, "shall we discuss your punishment, little mage?"

Her breath caught somewhere between her chest and throat. She wasn't a vessel. She wouldn't let him crack her open and crawl inside. She had the pin. It had shielded her from the Magics. It would shield her from him.

Wouldn't it?

Her powers had barely started to recover. Her sword was gone. The pirates blocked the stairwell. The captain's quarters stood behind her like a coffin with a doorknob. She had no way out. All she had left was fight.

She shifted her weight, knees bending, ready to launch forward. If she was going down, she'd go swinging—barehanded if she had to. Make him earn it.

But his hand came up, fingers spreading eerily before her. She flinched.

"Somnaris," he whispered.

And just like that, the fight drained out of her. She hated herself for it. She knew that spell. She'd spoken it herself in the West Woods. Had watched Blyven's eyes dim and close beneath it.

Only a heartbeat passed as her thoughts spun. He shouldn't know that spell. He had to have read it from her *Book of Magics*. It'd been with her during the fight at the Citadels. This was payback. A neat little symmetry, using her own magic to drag her under like she had when he'd been inside Blyven's mind.

The last thing she saw before the dark rushed in was Malvian's face, tilting ever so slightly. That same calm, unbothered smile. Like he'd just proved a point.

When awareness returned, it came in aching fragments. Pale dawn kindled at the edges of the sky, smudging the waves in hues of gray and washed-out rose. Her arms were drawn high above her head, wrists bound tight to the cold curve of the mast. Rough wood bit into her spine, indifferent to her shivering.

She swallowed. Her tongue was dry as sand. Every inch of her body throbbed with bruises she'd lost count of. Beyond the rails, the sea stretched smooth and brightening, gilded by the slow crawl of morning light. Her eyes slipped shut again. It didn't help. He was still there behind her lids—dark eyes, that indulgent smile.

And worse, he hadn't killed her. Not like the others. He could have. A flick of his hand, and she'd have gone over the rails, forgotten before she hit the water. But he'd chosen this. Left her here, bound and on display. Her wrists rubbed raw against the mast. The wind stole warmth with every breath. Why? Her thoughts circled, restless, and always came back to the same answer.

Power.

He didn't want her dead. At least, not yet. Was it because there was still something he needed? Some use she still had to him? A vein he could tap or a crack he could wedge open?

She'd let the Dark Magics take her before she gave him so much as a sliver. The thought alone sent a ripple through her head. The Magics stirred, slow and sinuous, brushing the inside of her mind with the barest trace of interest.

Yes, they whispered. *Let us show you what power really is.*

Warmth flared against her chest. The amulet reacting to Their hunger? Or the Light, shoving Them back? Lately, every time she cast, she could feel that space inside her split. Two rhythms beating just out of sync. Maybe it wasn't exhaustion. Maybe something inside her really had… changed. The thought should've terrified her. Instead, it hummed with dangerous possibility.

The words of the Dual Flame resurfaced: When Light and Dark as one align, the path shall wake the wrath divine.

Whose wrath? The gods'? The Magics themselves? If she was the path, then what exactly would she be waking? A weapon? A reckoning? Every time she touched the Dark, she felt what They wanted… to burn, to unmake. Was that the wrath the prophecy warned about? Or was the Light no better, only waiting its turn to scorch the world clean?

If Light and Dark were both alive in her, maybe she wasn't chosen at all. Maybe she was the error the prophecy was trying to warn against.

No. She couldn't go down that path now. She squeezed her eyes shut, shoved Them back, and forced her focus outward.

Below, the deck rocked beneath boots and bare feet, the crew weaving between coils of tarred rope and crates held down with fraying lines. They spared her only the briefest, wary glances before looking away. As if she were already something less than human.

Malvian was nowhere to be seen. Probably ensconced in his fine quarters, content to leave her lashed here, half broken and half watched, until he decided she had nothing left worth taking.

The sun was nearly swallowed by the horizon when rough hands wrenched her upright. She didn't fight them. Couldn't. The world tilted in slow, nauseating arcs as someone sliced through the rope binding her to the mast. Blood surged back into her arms, flooding her fingers with hot, prickling pain.

Two pirates dragged her across the deck, boots scuffing against sun-warmed planks. She caught one glimpse of the sea before the hatch yawned open and she was shoved forward. She stumbled and fell, striking the boards below with her shoulder. A bright flare of pain momentarily blackened her vision, and the hatch slammed shut.

Silence poured in behind it, too heavy, too complete. She stayed there with her cheek pressed to the boards. The air was stale, tinged with old fish and damp rope. She told herself to breathe, to count the lines between planks, to stay in the present. But the dark didn't care where now was.

The dungeons of Izier consumed her before she could take her next breath. Her mind slipped, unmoored, the dark curling tight around her with its talons. The same hush pressed in here. The same suffocating quiet that had filled every inch in that cell. No footsteps. No voices. Only her own ragged breathing to prove she was still alive, and the scurrying of her cellmates, hungry to taste her if she fell asleep.

Her ribs strained with each inhale, too shallow to ease the ache in her lungs. She shook her head, trying to clear the trauma creeping into her mind, into her limbs, into her shallow, erratic gasps. The wood beneath her palms was rough and splintered, and she curled her fingers against it until her nails bent.

It didn't help.

All she could see behind her eyes was that void of all devouring blackness she'd barely survived in the dungeons. The cold drip of water she could never find… the sense that time itself had dissolved, leaving nothing but her body withering away.

Hours passed. Or days. Lusa didn't move, trapped in her head, paralyzed in irrational fear. Once, she thought she heard someone breathing near the crates. Felt the shift of weight, the slight stirring of air, but when she looked, there was only darkness. When she slept, it was in thin, broken fits that left her worse than before. She dreamed of the martyaxwar's eyes, of Malvian's voice controlling her every move.

The next time the hatch opened, a tin bowl clattered to the floor. She blinked down at the remains of the pale, lumpy slop that hadn't sloshed out. It barely resembled food, but her hands reached for it anyway, trembling so badly she nearly upended it.

Sometime later, there was another creak overhead. A cracked cup followed, water sloshing inside. Enough to keep her alive and nothing more. If only she had her pack still, the reagents Arcturius had given her. She could conjure some sort of feast, enough to satiate her for days.

She drank without thinking, and the taste hit—brine-bitten, warm. Stomach-clenching. She let the cup slip from her hands. It hit her lap and rolled off, forgotten. Caught in the cycle of fear, Lusa remained there, reliving the hours she'd spent wishing she could die, only to count her breaths just to prove she still existed.

Another day of this, and she'd start to slip.

Her heart fluttered wild, frantic, trapped.

Lusa shut her eyes. No. She would not surrender. She needed to find that place inside her the panic couldn't reach.

The Light had gone quiet. Dimmed to a coal she could barely feel. But it was there. It had to be. She focused—tried to remember the warmth of it. The way it used to hum beneath her skin. The way it had once risen to meet her like a sunrise.

Her breath shook on the way out.

Heal first.

Her body was a ledger of hurts. The reopened gash at her shoulder. Bruises on top of bruises. The raw bite of rope around her wrists. She touched each pain one by one to catalog it.

And somewhere, under all that ache—

A flicker answered.

Relief threatened to undo her, but she held steady, gripping the thread of Light with care, coaxing it out of hiding. It pulsed, faint as a heartbeat, gradually growing a little stronger.

Time stretched or folded. Hours, maybe. Or a single breath caught in a loop. All she knew was the Light was there, and she had it. A slender tether wrapped tight in her fist. The dark lost some of its bite. The walls of the hold receded, softened, blurred into something distant.

She drifted deeper and, in that hush, something returned. Not power. Not strength.

A memory… of not being afraid.

Warmth stirred in her chest. Slow. Shy. Like dawn easing over the bones of the earth. It spread through her ribs, slid into the burning rawness at her wrists. Each soft pulse whispered a promise: She was not what they'd made of her. Not just a prisoner forgotten in the dark.

Pain eased by degrees, loosening its hold. She didn't rush it, drifting in that space between waking and sleep, where thoughts moved like tides and nothing hurt quite enough to pull her under.

She could almost believe she was elsewhere. Some quiet groves at the edge of Lady Flora, where the air smelled of rain and new leaves. A place untouched by iron, salt, and the memory of screams.

For a while, she stayed there. And when she came back to herself, it was like surfacing from a long dive. Oxygen filled her lungs without splintering pain. Her shoulder no longer burned with every breath. Not whole, maybe. But closer. Closer than she'd been in longer than she could name.

Slowly, she opened her eyes.

The dark was still there. Still deep. Still waiting. Hunger gnawed. Thirst rasped. But her hand lifted, trembling, and pressed flat to her chest. Her heart pulsed beneath her palm in a calm, steady rhythm.

Still here. Still herself.

And as long as she could hold to that…

She would not break.

The quiet stretched on, all but for the dull groan of timbers shifting under the weight of the sea. She tried to keep her thoughts anchored to the slow rise and fall of her breathing. But exhaustion pressed closer with every hour, flattening time into something shapeless.

Eventually, she slept.

When the hatch creaked open again, a new tin bowl clattered to the floor, another serving of sloshing greyish lumps she guessed passed for food in this floating dung heap.

So generous, she thought, grim annoyance flickering up through the haze. They'd spared no effort. Whatever this was, it looked exactly like it had already been eaten and regurgitated.

Only after she scraped the last gluey mouthful from the rim did she let herself think of magic again. Testing it was a risk. But better to know what power she had left than to pretend she was helpless when she wasn't. She didn't dare reach for the Dark Magics. Not when every inch of her still simmered with the urge to burn something to the waterline.

The hairpin was still tangled somewhere in her snarled, salt-ridden hair. That would keep Them quiet. For now. Carefully, she settled her back against the crates and closed her eyes.

"Illumina."

A soft glow flared at her fingertip. She lifted it higher, letting it spill across the hold. Pale light washed over every squalid detail she'd only guessed at in the dark. Barrels stacked haphazardly to the ceiling; some so rotted they sagged under their own weight. A mat of straw damp with mildew. Rusted hooks dangled from overhead beams, crusted with salt and old rope. A dark smear, blood or something fouler, stained one corner.

The smell was worse when she could see it. She let out a slow exhale, not sure if she felt better or worse. But the test was enough. Her Magics had returned. Not to Their full extent, but enough to get her mind working like gears on her next plan.

She pinched the light out between her fingers, plunging herself back into the dark.

When that hatch opened again, she wouldn't be cowering behind crates. She couldn't escape the ship, but she could make them regret every bruise and every hour they'd left her stewing. If she couldn't get free, she'd settle for something else: Wreaking as much havoc on this miserable tub as she could. And if she was lucky, she'd make them wonder if she'd ever been worth the trouble.

The time finally arrived, and of all the things she could have been feeling—fear, dread, bone-deep exhaustion—she was giddy.

Giddy.

She nearly laughed, though it would have come out cracked and wild. The hatch creaked open, flooding the hold with sunlight so bright she had to squint against it.

A pirate leaned down, peering into the gloom. She didn't give him the chance to do much else. Her focus slipped into the amulet's quiet gravity, and the magic obeyed her thought alone. An invisible force seized him by the front of his shirt and yanked him off his feet. He tumbled down with a strangled yell that cut off with the bruising impact.

"Para nor," she whispered hoarsely, hoping the spell would hold long enough to keep him still… and quiet.

With a small hop, her boots found purchase on his back, and she vaulted for the hatch.

Sunlight exploded across her vision, blinding after so long in the dark. She staggered once, before her eyes adjusted enough to see two hazy pirates turn and freeze, staring straight at her.

Her hand twitched. Power pooled in her palm, but not all at once. She had to be frugal. The Magics weren't fully recovered. A dozen feet away, a tangled stack of rope began to slither. It moved fast, a sudden rush across the planks. The two pirates barely managed a shout before the cords whipped around their legs, climbing higher in relentless loops.

With a final snap, the ropes yanked them upside down, leaving them dangling from the lowest sail like trussed hens. Their muffled curses cut short as their own headbands tore free and wrapped tight across their mouths.

Lusa smirked and drew a shaky breath, vision swimming. The amulet beneath her tunic radiated that familiar, reassuring heat.

Quickly, she slinked across to the other side of the ship, eyes darting for any sign of movement. She dropped behind a barrel, the stink of pitch clogging her nose. No bell. No shouting. Her heart hammered as she risked a glance.

She squinted—then blinked.

A black shape crested the horizon, sails billowing in the breeze. Even from a distance, the sigil stamped across them stood out: a gnarled tree, roots jagged as lightning, ringed in silver.

Her stomach twisted.

Slowly, she lifted her gaze to the sails above her head.

Same symbol.

Questions could wait. Survival couldn't.

She needed her *Book of Magics* back before Malvian used another scrap of it against her. Her reagents and the *Treatise of the Dual Flame* was in that same pouch. The thought of him flipping through those pages—pages that hinted of something ancient, impossible, and very likely living inside her—made her teeth grind.

Staying crouched, she shifted her weight and peeked around the barrel. Every part of her ached, but her mind felt clear. Clearer than it had since the night they'd dragged her onto this cursed ship.

He humiliated her… thought he could break her. There was a price he'd pay.

The shadowed quarterdeck was only ten paces away now. Voices drifted across the deck, men talking or barking orders, but she couldn't see any of them from where she crouched.

After one last glance to be sure the path was clear, she crept along the crates, timing each step with the wind's gusts to drown the scrape of her boots. At the base of the steps, she hesitated, listening to be sure no one had moved closer.

Nothing.

She climbed up, slow and careful, and pressed her back to the wall below the quarterdeck rail. A long, measured breath slipped past her lips. From here, when she peaked out, she could see nearly the whole length of the deck. Pirates moved in circuits, hauling ropes, checking crates, arguing in low voices. No one was looking up. Good.

Her gaze tracked the deck, cataloging every detail with a calm she almost didn't recognize in herself. A line of captives was being marched out of the aft hold, wrists bound together with thick rope. Her eyes widened. Others must have been kept in different holds. At least a dozen more than she'd seen when this nightmare began.

Purdue's broad shoulders were hunched; his face covered in fresh bruises. Tessanee shuffled beside him, hair a matted curtain hiding her small, bowed head. Two of the older women she'd met trailed behind. Pirates flanked them front and back, herding them toward the port side where more crew wrestled a massive plank into place. The thing looked twice the width of any boarding plank Glon had ever described, and heavier, too—like a slab meant for siege engines, not ships. Lusa could only watch, acid rising in her throat. *Slaves? Something worse?*

Near the prow, Malvian stood with his hands folded neatly behind his back, observing the grim procession like it was a spectacle arranged for his private entertainment. As the line shuffled past, he tilted his head. Lusa squinted, tracking his gaze.

It landed squarely on Tessanee.

A chill feathered down her spine. Malvian leaned a fraction closer to Veyrin, who stood behind him. Though she couldn't hear over the wind, she saw the slight movement of his lips—calm, almost conversational. Veyrin nodded once and slipped away to speak with one of the pirates.

The thought of Malvian's attention settling on that child made something cold and furious knot in her chest. She wanted nothing more than to tear the hairpin free and let every last scrap of her power burn them all to ashes.

But the fury cooled into something sharper. She couldn't help the crooked smile that twitched across her mouth.

Thank you for the distraction, she thought wryly. If they were busy with their wretched hand-off, she could slip inside unseen. All she needed was the right moment. She waited, body tense, until a gust of wind snapped the sails overhead and a dozen heads turned to watch the plank settle across to the other ship.

Now.

Lusa slipped across to the cabin door. She quickly pressed down the latch and, as she pulled it open, kept her gaze fixed on the horde of pirates. No one turned. She slid in sideways through the narrow gap, never taking her eyes off the deck until the last ray of daylight vanished behind the click of the door.

CHAPTER 25

How to Ruin a Pirate's Day

The closed door muted the world outside. Lusa pressed her back against it, scarcely breathing. Her core thrummed unevenly, but her magic felt stronger. Maybe recalibrated. Her well wasn't full, but there was enough to fight if she needed.

The space around her was richly adorned, almost arrogant. A map lay half-unfurled across a side table, weighted with inkwells. Thick drapes swayed gently beside narrow windows that looked out over the sea. And in the center, like an altar left waiting, was a long table piled with fruit, bread, and soft white cheese.

Her stomach cramped on instinct.

She hadn't eaten in—Magics, how long? The mere sight of food made something in her gut twist and snarl. A nectarine, overripe and glistening, sat like a sun-tinged jewel among darker berries and quartered figs. A heel of bread slouched beside a dish of spiced oil, dusted faintly with flour.

She shouldn't. She knew that. But her body moved before logic could protest. One hand shot out, grabbed the fruit, and she sank her teeth into it. Juice burst down her chin. She didn't care. It was real, and sweet, and she was starving. She devoured the rest in three savage bites, wiped her mouth on her sleeve, tore a few bites from the loaf with her teeth, and stuffed a handful of berries into her pocket.

A half-drained wine flask rested beside a folded cloth. With a mischievous smirk, she swallowed the bread, snatched it and drank the rest, hoping it was the last pleasure of his—rendering him one luxury poorer on this forsaken ship. She cast a quick glance at the door, straining for the sound of boots on the stairs. Nothing yet. Setting the flask down, her eyes caught on the far table. Beneath the sway of the lantern lay her book. Seeing it here, open and unguarded, felt like sacrilege.

She stepped forward, pulled by instinct. The *Book of Magics* lay open to a familiar page, but the margins were lined with ink that wasn't hers. Neat, angular script. Observations. Corrections. Possibilities, maybe. She didn't know the language. But it seemed he hadn't only skimmed it. He'd studied it. Desecrating a relic most of Aetherealm pretended no longer existed. She shut the book harder than necessary. As if he had the right to annotate her magic. Holding it to her chest, she turned—only to kick something on the floor.

Spilled from her torn pouch lay the *Treatise on the Dual Flame*. She tucked the *Book of Magics* under one arm and knelt, gingerly cradling the smaller tome in both hands. The worn cover seemed untouched.

Relief slipped out of her in a quiet sigh, and she sank onto the edge of a bench, shoulders curling in, one hand gripping the Treatise, the other still tacky with nectar, both books pressed close like armor. But she didn't have time to sit, or the luxury of pretending everything was fine now that she had most of her things back.

Lusa pushed to her feet, packing everything back into her pack, double checking her reagents were still inside, and securing it. Pulse beginning to climb, she started to pace. Her thoughts spun fast—feral, reckless.

Set the ship on fire.

Too risky. The captives were still onboard. She couldn't trap them in a blaze just to make a point. Or could she? No, choose a different path.

Cut the sails? Smash the rudder?

They'd still be at sea. Still under his command.

She cursed under her breath, turning sharply at the edge of the table, and froze. Her gaze landed on the map she'd barely noticed earlier. She stepped closer, frowning. Her fingers ghosted over the chart, tracing a marked path. The ink arced from the southern coast of Myttica, just below Merravale, across open sea toward a small scattering of islands near the map's jagged edge. The name was scrawled in sharp, almost thorny script she *did* recognize:

The Isles of Velkher.

They weren't familiar to her. But the shape of the route, the direction, the absence of other known ports… it wasn't hard to guess. This was a dark elf ship. And they were heading home.

A noise cut through her thoughts: voices, shouting. Instinct shoved her into motion. She turned toward the door and stopped cold. In the shadowed corner, partially hidden behind a chest of scrolls and wine crates, stood her sword. Crossing the space in two quick steps, she seized the hilt. The leather grip felt good back in her hand. She nearly sagged with relief but didn't have the time to savor it. Shouts echoed again, this time with a small cry.

Tessanee.

Lusa crept toward the door, blade tucked low, her shoulder brushing the frame as she pressed her ear to the wood. Nothing distinguishable… movement, raised voices, boots pounding on planks. Slowly, she eased the latch and cracked the door open a sliver to see—

Chaos.

One of the pirates had Tessanee by the arm, dragging her toward Malvian. The girl kicked and twisted, but he held fast. Purdue and two of the women from the hold were shouting. Pleading, maybe. Lusa couldn't hear the words over the din. One of the women threw herself forward, striking the pirate with a clenched fist.

He backhanded her without even looking.

Lusa's breath hissed between her teeth. Her fingers tightened on the hilt of her sword until her knuckles ached.

Veyrin stood a few paces back, arms folded, watching. And Malvian—Sardan curse him—stood near the rail, posture relaxed, expression unreadable. He didn't move; eyes fixed on the girl.

A heat rose through Lusa, thick and blinding. She didn't have a plan. Didn't have an opening. But she had a sword. She had her magic. And if he thought she'd let him touch Tessanee without consequence, he was about to find out just how much fight she had left.

Every instinct poised to lunge, to burn, to cut something down. She no longer had the luxury of restraint. She was halfway out the door when Malvian moved.

Not toward Tessanee.

Toward the pirate.

His hand lashed out in a blur. A sharp crack echoed across the deck as the back of his palm collided with the pirate's cheek. Lusa froze mid-step, blade halfway lifted. The man reeled, stunned more by shock than the blow itself. Gasps stuttered through the captives, and the crew went silent.

Malvian didn't even look at the others. He stepped forward and knelt before the girl. Tessanee shrank back at first, trembling, but he didn't grab her or bark a command. He merely said something. Lusa couldn't hear the words. But his tone… didn't seem cruel. Wasn't loud. His hand moved slowly, fingers brushing the hair from the girl's face. He reached for her like someone soothing a startled deer.

Lusa's jaw clenched so hard her teeth ached. No. She wasn't falling for it. Whatever this was—kindness, mercy—it reeked of performance. A new tactic. A new pressure point. He wanted something. And if he thought she'd sit quietly while he used that girl to soften the game…

She stepped fully into the light, magic pulsing to her fingertips. But Malvian didn't glance her way. Instead, he turned to Veyrin.

"Take her hand," he said at normal volume. "Guide her across."

Veyrin blinked, clearly caught off guard, but obeyed. He reached down to Tessanee with fumbling fingers. The girl hesitated, then let him take her hand. They began walking toward the plank that bridged the ships, the rest of the captives already being herded in that direction. Only the small group from her own hold remained behind, shaken from the skirmish.

Malvian rose slowly, smoothing the fur lining of his coat with the kind of casual grace that made Lusa want to punch him square in the face. He moved to follow them, but a pirate sprinted up from the starboard side.

"Sir—m'lord—those men—!" He pointed toward the far rigging, where Lusa had left those two pirates dangling upside down and gagged.

Malvian stilled. Then pivoted, fluid as a blade finding its mark, eyes sweeping the deck with lethal precision.

And found her.

This time, Lusa didn't flinch.

His gaze narrowed, catching the sword in her hand, the quiet fury in her stance, the faint glow threading her fingers. The performance was over.

She offered a wicked smile. "Miss me?"

A glint of… amusement? Before a mask of annoyance fell over his features.

"Para nor!" The spell leapt from her hand and a whoosh of gray streaked for his chest.

Malvian flicked a quick formation with two fingers. Her spell veered off course, slamming harmlessly into the mast behind him.

"Disappointing," he murmured.

Chaos erupted before the word even faded.

Veyrin yanked Tessanee further across the bridge, both landing on the other ship and turning to watch. The captives from Lusa's hold were shuffling across, still bound wrist to wrist, bridge groaning under their weight. Lusa moved, eyes scanning for threats. Three pirates were peeling off from the deck crew, blades out, charging toward her.

"Levista tellum!"

Lightning tore from her fingers and slammed into the first man's chest. He flew backward with a strangled cry, smoke already curling from his tunic. The bolt split. Zapped the second pirate's arm. His sword spun loose, clattering across the deck in a burst of sparks.

The third didn't make it that far. He dove for cover, rolling behind a barrel as smoke and light ripped across the planks, burning the air between screams.

Lusa's heart pounded, magic sizzling under her skin, wild and hungry, eyes meeting his. Malvian lifted a hand, the command stopping the advancing pirates. He said nothing but shifted his fingers the slightest degree, like dismissing a servant. They backed off without question, and she wondered if it was free will or his mind control.

He wanted her to himself.

Lusa didn't care. She welcomed it. A strange sensation pulled at her mind. Probing invisible fingers. He was trying to get in.

She didn't think. Her body moved first, legs propelling, blade slicing the air. Another spell curled from her lips, "Flarentia!"

A ring of heat burst to life around her blade, spiraling along the steel. She slashed wide, sending a streak of flame crackling across the deck.

Malvian flicked his wrist, a pulse of energy snapping from his palm to smother the blaze. His hand followed through, fingers locking into pattern. Violet light flared. A lash of shadow tore toward her.

Lusa ducked, rolled, and came up swinging. Her blade caught his coat, splitting the fabric clean through.

He stepped back, answering with a streak of blue energy. She met it midair, her shield flaring white-hot before it shattered his second strike.

The blast sent them both reeling.

They circled each other, magic sparking between them, her steel catching the blazing sun overhead. Each spell met another. Each blow answered in kind. She wasn't winning. But she wasn't losing, either.

Another pirate, clearly slower on the uptake, rounded the corner with a snarl and a blade raised high.

"She's mine!" Malvian shouted. Not calm this time. Not quite in control. And that, more than anything, made her smile.

But the rogue pirate didn't slow.

Lusa twisted, sword snapping up just in time. Steel met steel, the clang rattling up her arm.

The pirate lunged, sloppy but fast. She parried once. Twice. Forced him back. He swung low. She dodged. Too slow. Her shoulder slammed into the mast. Pain flared. Her hairpin clattered to the deck.

The world snapped to black.

The Magics burst from her core, engulfing her like wildfire. Their voices were a chorus of angry desire. Her head jerked back. Her vision darkened. Ice cold prickles webbed down her face.

The pirate in front of her hesitated, sword raised. They closed her eyes, savoring the feel of control, the smell of blood, the rush of power as Their magic flooded her limbs, her mind, her bones. Spells she hadn't meant to think crackled at her fingertips. Heat. Ice. Death. Control.

They opened her eyes, staring hungrily at Their opponent. The pirate took a step back.

Wise. But too late.

They didn't lift a hand. Didn't utter a word. A single thought wrenched the world around the man's throat. A sickening snap echoed across the deck, and he crumpled, lifeless.

Screams followed. The other pirates scattered like insects, shoving each other aside in their rush to flee the thing now wearing Lusa's face.

Malvian threw a spell—a bright crackling tether of shimmering force. A powerful one. Complex. They tilted her head and waved it off like fog. But something pressed behind her ribs. They weren't alone.

Light.

It curled like gold thread through the shadows, small but determined, trying to tether her soul back to her body—back to herself. They flinched.

No.

The Light pulled. In her mind, Lusa reached, and for a heartbeat, the Dark Magics struggled.

She broke through—gasping, choking on the weight of Them—and grabbed for the fallen pin, fingers scrabbling across the planks. A rush of energy singed the air. Malvian again, faster this time.

She dove and rolled, the spell obliterating wood behind her in a thunder of splinters. Her sword slid across the deck. Old wounds ripped fresh, new ones screamed for attention, but her fingers stayed locked around the pin. Lusa jammed it back into her nest of hair, fingers trembling. Their voices screamed once more before being silenced.

She lay there, gasping, palms braced against the deck, heart trying to restart itself.

She was back.

But Malvian was still standing.

And he looked… intrigued?

"Malvian!"

Both she and the darkling jerked their focus toward the source of the voice.

Standing at the center of the plank bridge—one boot braced forward like he owned the sea itself—was a broad-shouldered and sun-burnished man, with salt-and-pepper hair swept back in waves. Scars laddered one forearm, the ink of old tattoos half-faded beneath them. His coat, open at the chest, flapped behind him.

"What in the name of Sardan is going on?!" His gaze swept the deck until it landed on her. "Is…"

Something flashed behind his eyes, but he caught himself before she could register what it was. She arched a brow and sat up. Guess he wasn't used to seeing mages lying flat on their backs.

Malvian barely shifted, but she caught it. The slight dip of his shoulder. The twitch of his fingers near the pouch at his belt.

Not this time.

She sucked in a breath and snapped the words the same instant he flung the powder.

"Windosa Nu!" Wind exploded from her palm, reversing the arc of white dust midair.

The swirling cloud slammed into his face. His eyes widened enough to register shock, then rolled back.

"Sleep on that, darkling," she muttered.

He dropped like a sack of robes, out cold.

Lusa propped herself on one elbow, satisfaction curling at her lips. Finally, something on this cursed ship was going her way.

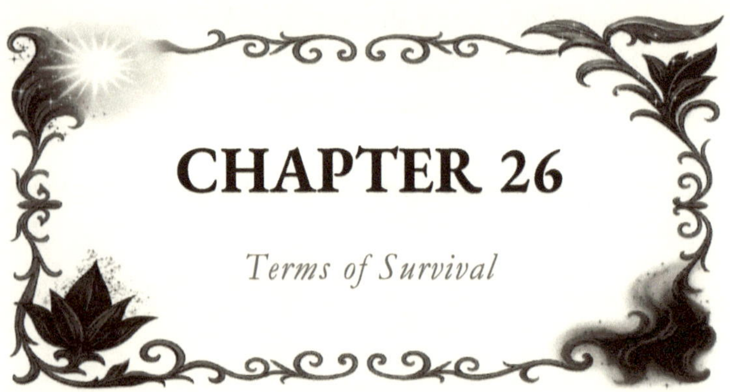

CHAPTER 26

Terms of Survival

The new ship pitched under her, every sway a knife through her ribs as she fought to stay upright. She pressed a hand to her side and limped across the deck. Crates clattered. Chains rattled below. The sea stretched in all directions, gray and endless.

The other ship was already shrinking into the horizon. Back to Merravale, maybe. Or wherever they planned to collect their next victims. Either way, she hoped she'd left it crippled enough for the ruin to fester in every course they tried to chart.

She scanned the deck. A few pirates shouted at each other, some hauled crates, others herding the captives below. A few glanced her way, but their eyes slid off quickly, none of them apparently eager to stir whatever storm they imagined she'd unleashed on the other ship.

Her grip hadn't loosened its hold on the hilt, even though the captain of this new ship had offered a temporary truce. No shackles or threats. Merely a silent concession as she'd limped aboard, bloodied and seething. Kindness meant nothing from a man who trafficked in stolen lives.

With that reminder, she peered through every shadow, watched captives, hoping to spot Tessanee. But the girl was nowhere. Doubt flickered in her chest. Why did it matter so much? Tessanee wasn't family. Wasn't even a friend. But… she was a choice Lusa had made, a life she'd fought for. A tether to something in herself that hadn't gone dark. Letting Tessanee slip away now felt like letting that small spark of Light burn out.

The darkling had been dragged belowdeck, unconscious, robes trailing like a fallen banner. Part of her had wanted to follow… to finish what she'd started and end the dark elf's miserable existence. But her body was wrecked. Her magic, threadbare. And no one on this ship was worth losing her soul to the Magics.

She spat blood and grit over the rail and turned her eyes toward the man who'd granted her passage. Captain, yes—but he hadn't offered mercy, only a stay of judgment. A silent truce born of calculation. He'd seen what she could do. Knew she'd crack the hull in half and drown them all if he didn't step in. Letting her aboard hadn't been a favor. It was self-preservation.

He wasn't like the others shouting orders across the deck. His movements carried a soldier's precision, not a smuggler's slouch. The chain at his wrist caught the light when he turned. Tokens, maybe. Oaths kept or broken. His coat snapped in the wind, frayed from years or battles. Probably both.

She limped toward him.

"Keep the lines tight! If one of you drops a crate, you'll swim for it!" he barked, then turned, voice lowering, calm as surf. "You're bleeding on my deck, mage."

"You're the one running this," she said, voice teetering on venomous. "The vanishings. The slaves."

He assessed her once with his piercing blue eyes. He looked like a man who'd stared death down more than once… and probably asked it for a drink after. Amusement ghosted across his face.

"We trade. We survive."

"You sell people."

"You burn them," he countered. "Difference is, mine live long enough to regret it."

Her fingers twitched near her sword. "You think that makes you noble?"

"No," he said, and his voice softened, dangerous. "It makes me alive."

His accent wasn't Myttican, or Izierian either—something older. Coastal, worn thin by wind and war. She'd heard of pirate captains like him once, long before mages were outlawed—men who swore by sea oaths older than any king's law.

"What do you get out of it?" she pushed. "Kidnapping kids, selling people like sacks of flour? I'll see you in Sardan's Hell before I let you bind me in chains."

"You're no prisoner, lady. You're insurance. I keep you; I keep the board steady. Lose you, and the pieces scatter."

Worse than a captive. He was keeping her for a purpose, and the hunger to know it gnawed at her.

His gaze narrowed, lingering on the scar by her cheek as if trying to read a face he half-remembered. Then, with an odd, courtly tilt of the chin that felt almost out of place on a pirate, he said, "Captain Aleric. And you?"

Lusa blinked. Of all the responses she expected—a threat, a sneer, a backhand—that wasn't one of them. She gave him a long, incredulous look. Since when did pirates bother with names?

"You smuggle people like livestock, and now you want introductions?"

"Names matter," he said.

"Not to pirates."

"Especially to pirates."

Lusa folded her arms and responded flatly, "I didn't come here to make introductions."

Aleric's gaze sharpened a fraction. "I'm allowing you to live. Seems the least you could offer is a name."

Her mind ran the angles. He had a point—what was her so-called freedom worth? He could have left her to drown. Could've ordered her tossed overboard. But he didn't.

Which made her trust him even less.

"What do you want it for?" she asked finally, eyes narrowed. "Something to scribble on a manifest? Carve into a cell door?"

Aleric didn't rise to the bait. He simply watched her.

"You offering trade?" she went on, shifting her tone darker. "Because if you're thinking I'm part of the inventory you move belowdecks, I'll burn this ship to ash with every last breath I have."

"Easy," he said. "I'm not interested in owning you."

She didn't relax. Not even a fraction.

Then he added, almost offhandedly, "But the girl you keep looking for? She might not survive another stunt like the one you pulled earlier."

Lusa stiffened. She hadn't said Tessanee's name aloud. Hadn't asked after her since first climbing aboard. But something about her—maybe her gaze, the way her head kept turning when new prisoners were marched past—must've given her away. Or it was a very accurate guess.

Damn him. She hated how fast her pulse jumped. Hated that he'd seen it. Tessanee was her weakness.

She hadn't wanted to admit it. Had told herself she just wanted to make sure the kid didn't die because of her. That it wasn't personal. But it was. She could feel it, a hook buried deep. Part of her wished she could let the Dark Magics rise. Let them burn it out, cauterize the soft parts, make her immune to this. But she couldn't afford that. If she gave Them so much as a breath, she was in no state to keep Them in check and prevent herself from spiraling. So, she dragged her attention back to Aleric.

"Fine," she muttered. "Lusa."

Aleric's nod was faint, the kind that carried verdict. His eyes stayed on her as though measuring how much effort her death might cost him. Then he looked back to the sea as if the conclusion had already been reached and filed out of mind.

The corner of his mouth twitched, not quite a smile. "Didn't think it'd be that easy."

"Don't get used to it."

"Wouldn't dream of it."

They stood in silence a beat, the crash of choppy waves swelling between them. Wind tugged at the rigging above. She shifted her weight, careful not to show how much it hurt.

"You said you're not interested in owning me. So, what do you want? And who is Malvian to you?"

"For starters? That you don't sink my ship."

"I told you. I'll burn it down if you make me."

"And I told you," He replied without turning, "I'm not looking to start a war." A pause stretched before he added almost under his breath, "But I'm not above finishing one."

One wrong word and this whole conversation could ignite. She kept her tongue in check. The breeze kicked up again, flinging tangled bands of her raven hair across her face. She resisted the urge to cross her arms and keep the chill from biting.

"Don't mistake survival for surrender."

"I don't. Which is why you're still alive."

Every word with him was a negotiation. But she'd learned to play games like this back in Izier. He wasn't going to give her the information she really wanted, not willingly.

A flick of his fingers summoned a passing pirate—grizzled, one brow split by an old scar, eyes dulled from too many years squinting at the sun.

"Your sword. The bag, too," Aleric said, tone even. "Consider it collateral."

Lusa's jaw clenched. Her fingers twitched at the hilt, reluctant to let it go.

"A truce," he added, "still needs terms."

She stared at him, then at the pirate's outstretched hand. Not surrender but a pause. A breath between storms. She could keep fighting until there was nothing left of her—or she could regroup, regain strength, and maybe, just maybe, scrap together a plan. Reluctantly, she loosened her grip on the sword.

"Try anything funny and I'll take back my blade one vertebra at a time."

One brow arched, the pirate went to snatch her things but quickly added, "And tell your crew not to touch my books unless they want to sprout boils in unfortunate places."

The grizzled pirate blinked, clearly weighing the risk of cursed boils against the orders he'd been given. He glanced at the sword in her hand, then to her blood-streaked face, and finally to Aleric, as if silently asking if this was truly worth it. Aleric's mouth curved, approving.

With a grunt that sounded more like a whimper, the pirate stepped forward and carefully took the sword and pouch of books like they might bite him. He held them at arm's length, muttering something under his breath in a dialect Lusa didn't recognize—but she caught the word "mage" in the middle of it.

The ship groaned under the strain of its sails, pitching the deck, and he didn't even sway. A man made for the sea.

Aleric turned to go, but tossed over his shoulder, "You'll earn your keep or lose your place. Just like anyone else."

He waved down to the main deck. Another pirate—scraggly, long-haired, and vaguely bored—scrambled up the steps.

"Let's see if she's worth the deck space," Aleric said, already descending.

The newcomer barely spared her a glance. "Grab a scrubba' an' a bucket. Clean ta deck. Supplies're ova' t'ere."

Lusa blinked. "You want me to mop the floor?"

"You wanna breathe t'morrow?"

The pressure beneath the pin pressed harder, her Magics prowling. Even silent, she knew what They whispered for her to do. But Tessanee was still somewhere below—Magic's knew why she kept caring—and Lusa was outnumbered, outmatched, and running on fumes.

The man left her to it, and she limped toward the pile lashed near the mainmast and crouched, prying a crusted scrubber free from a coil of rope. The bucket reeked of fish and iron. Saltwater bit into her knuckles, stinging the raw rope burns. A reminder that no matter how powerful she was, she still bled like the rest of them.

Mages weren't supposed to bow. That was before the Hunt—before the world decided their existence was a threat worth erasing. She'd survived dungeons, imps, a crazed sorcerer… and now she was cleaning plankboards. Izier would've laughed her off the citadel steps.

Her stiff shoulder protested as she hauled the bucket toward the rail, but she didn't stop. Pride wouldn't keep her alive. She scrubbed until the motion blurred into rhythm, and her mind, no longer stuck in survival, began to drift.

To Kaden.

She could almost hear his dry, exasperated voice teasing her for not playing it smarter. For not ducking sooner. For charging in with half a plan and a full heart.

"You always go for the jugular, Lusa. One day that fire's goin' ta' burn you up."

And yet, he'd always stood beside her when the flames rose.

She scrubbed harder, like the ache in her chest could be scoured away with brine and grit. It wasn't the bruises.

Was he safe? Had he made it to Aeonia? Had the others sent word of the ambush, and he was assuming the worst?

Her hand slowed. The amulet beneath her tunic still radiated faint warmth. It had always pulsed with power but now, it felt heavier. Like a tether. Every time it flared, he'd been there—close enough to reach, close enough to steady her when the world tilted.

She pressed her palm against it, searching for more than magic. Trying to make sense of the hollow ache lodged beneath her chest. She'd missed people before, sure. Her mother, after the Temple. But this… this was different.

It wasn't about safety. Or comfort. Or even hope. It was deeper. Stronger. Like she'd grown used to walking with a second heartbeat beside hers… and now, in the silence, her own stumbled.

Her fingers slipped beneath her tunic, closing around the pendant's smooth edge. She drew it out, cradling it in her palm. Once, it had been a weapon. A well of Light. Now, it carried something else.

The weight of his absence.

She let out a breath and sagged back on her heels. The deck rolled gently beneath her, the sea murmuring against the hull, and it seemed the world stopped asking anything of her for a moment.

She stood, stretched her aching back, and leaned her arms across the railing. The stars had begun to blink through the dusk. Wherever he was, she hoped he could see them too.

A creak behind her. She didn't flinch. Too many days expecting danger had trained her body not to react until it was time. Slow steps climbed the quarterdeck. Probably another pirate drawn to the helm. The sea had a way of calling to men nursing bruised egos.

She kept her gaze on the stars… until the steps stopped. The sudden stillness hooked into her, forcing her to turn. Dread gripped her heart and squeezed.

Malvian stood a few paces away, hands limp at his sides. His fingers twitched—caught somewhere between disbelief and bloodlust. Eyes locked on her, and in an instant, confusion curdled to rage… then to the stillness that comes right before a kill. His world narrowed to a single point: her destruction.

Someone moved behind him. Relief caught in her breath at the flash of silver-streaked hair—Aleric, striding up the steps. But it vanished the moment Malvian's hands lifted. Violet light burst from his palms and slammed into her chest, hurling her backward.

"No!" Aleric's voice cracked through the air. "Bring her back!"

The railing caught her for half a heartbeat before gravity tore her loose and the cold, brutal sea took her.

CHAPTER 27

Tides of Borrowed Time

The sea took her without mercy. Breath stolen. Dusky light fractured into ribbons as the deep swallowed her whole. The stars vanished in a churn of salt and shadow.

She twisted, grasping for anything, but found only endless water. Up blurred into down. A thousand needles of ice bit into her, crushing her chest until her lungs convulsed. She had never learned to swim, never needed to—now her body floundered like a thing already dying.

No. She hadn't clawed through fire and blood to be taken by water.

The Dark Magics slammed against the pin's ward, violent and relentless, straining to take the reins. But something inside her didn't just resist—it split. The familiar burn of Light collided with the Dark's pull, two forces clawing for dominance. The clash sent a shock through her chest, like her magic couldn't decide which half of her it belonged to.

They didn't care about her pride—only about keeping Their vessel alive. But her limbs turned heavy, her vision dimmed. Each heartbeat slowed.

Memories flared: wildflowers and her mother's laughter. Nellis's grin in the Temple corridors. Tryston, offering an apple. Kaden—the heat of his arms, the ache of their last kiss. Tessanee… small, afraid, still counting on her.

I can't die yet.

But her kicks slowed. Her arms floated at her sides, fingers slack, the ache in her chest unfolding into something almost peaceful, and just like that, the fight slipped out of her.

This was how it ended. Not in fire or steel or the wrath of Dark Magics, but in water, quiet and merciless, sealing her in its grasp.

The thought cut deeper than the cold: she'd never see Kaden again—never hear his laugh, never feel the wind whip around them on griffin wings, or touch the warmth of his hand in hers.

Her lips parted, the first burn of water spilling in—

Hands clamped around her arms. Lips crushed to hers, forcing air into her lungs in a rush that shocked her back into herself. Her eyes flew open.

Malvian.

Revulsion and rage tangled in her gut, turning her stomach harder than the sea ever could. Of all the people to reach her in the deep, it had to be him. She'd sooner drown than take his breath. She tore against his grip, magic surging through every nerve.

Windosa Nu! The words ripped through her mind, and the sea obeyed. A gale burst from her, hurling him upward in a spiral of bubbles. The backlash punched her deeper.

Her ears roared. Water pressed in from all sides, stealing her sense of up or down. She kicked—once, twice—legs flailing against the heavy drag. Her scream escaped, releasing bubbles that spun away toward the unreachable surface. She clamped her mouth shut, lungs burning. And then, from the dark, a faint, haunting sound reached her.

Not the moan of the current, nor her thundering pulse, but a song. Soft, strange… winding through the water until its familiarity brushed against her memory.

The mermaid in the Northern Sea, injured. Her own trembling hands pressing against slick, bloodied scales. Magic spilling forth—not Dark, but Light. It had been the first time the Light had truly answered her, filling her with warmth, peace… power. Lusa closed her eyes and reached for that same Light and clung to it.

Air, she thought.

A spark ignited at her core. A gentle warmth, small but mighty. The amulet floated before her, chain taut at her neck, glowing. The ache in her chest dulled the moment a shimmer of light flared into a translucent sphere of air. She curled inward, gasping in greedy gulps. Her eyes still burned. She was still suspended in the sea's cold, endless dark… but now, she could breathe.

Lusa twisted gently inside the sphere, forcing her sluggish limbs to move. Which way was up? The water distorted everything. Her fingers brushed the top of the sphere, the bubble thinning slightly near the upper curve. That way.

She kicked, if it could be called that—stiff legs and graceless flails, arms mimicking strokes she'd only ever watched, all motion without momentum. The glimmering amulet, still looped around her neck, floated in front of her.

Disoriented as she was, she could still make out movement in the murk. Something too big to be a fish. She narrowed her eyes, calling up what magic remained to sharpen her sight.

A net. Wide. Weighted. And Malvian was guiding it. He drifted beneath the mesh, expression focused as if he expected to recover a corpse. Her glowing air-sphere made her far too easy to find. When he noticed her, disbelief flickered, then suspicion… before sealing behind a blank mask. She wasn't supposed to be alive.

She definitely wasn't supposed to be glowing.

Lusa shoved the Source beneath her tunic. The edges of the sphere blinked a warning. It wouldn't last. Her legs were numb. Land wasn't in sight. The net floated mockingly, her only escape to the surface, and to the enemy hauling it.

Survive. Make him regret letting me live.

Growling, she grabbed the frozen netting and glared at the darkling. His earlier fury was gone, intent on ignoring her. He looped a rope around his waist and tugged.

Above, wood groaned. The net jerked, rising. Water rushed past her ears as it pulled her toward the surface. The sphere shattered as they broke through and the night air whooshed into her lungs. She welcomed it with rapid coughs and deep breaths all while the Light steadied her and the Dark seethed beneath it. Two halves of a heartbeat, never in rhythm.

The net sluggishly crested the side of the ship before slapping on the deck. She collapsed inside, shivering so hard her teeth ached.

The darkling climbed out without a glance, robes dripping, long hair plastered to his body. The crew parted for him. Good. She didn't have the strength to waste hating him properly.

Another shadow blocked the wind. A heavy wool blanket dropped over her shoulders, smelling faintly of smoke. She blinked up through drenched lashes at Aleric, his expression unreadable, coat snapping in the breeze. Chest heaving, she stared right back. The sea had tried to kill her. Why drag her back? This wasn't mercy. Mercy was clean. This dripped with conditions.

Lusa turned her head away, teeth chattering. The cold had sunk in marrow-deep, and every inch of her screamed.

Her fingers were pruned and trembling, her knees knocking under the blanket.

Tired of shaking, she closed her eyes, ignoring the pathetic men surrounding her, and scraped together the last spark of Light she could find. It flickered beside the Dark Magics. She could feel the divide now, the way one pulse fought the other for room inside her ribs. The Light swelled, weak but steady, seeping through her veins until it pushed back the worst of the tremors. It didn't erase the exhaustion, nothing could, but it kept her from folding where she sat. Barely.

As she recalibrated, her core felt... off. Heavier. Larger, maybe. Like it had split and doubled when she wasn't looking.

Her head slumped against a coil of rope. She didn't see Aleric's signal, didn't hear the order—only felt the rough hands hauling her semi-upright.

"This way," came a gruff voice.

She was half-led, half-dragged across slick planks, every step sending jolts up her legs, down a steep ladder into wavering lanternlight. Hammocks hung there like cocoons. A few pirates looked up, but most didn't bother.

The one guiding her pointed to a low-slung canvas sling tucked near the wall, apart from the others.

"That one's open. Try not to puke in it."

Lusa didn't answer. Didn't have the energy to glare. She climbed in like someone crawling into a grave. Curled on her side, clutching the blanket tighter, letting the ship's slow sway drag her toward unconsciousness.

For now, it was the closest thing she had to peace. And she hated that. Sleep never held her for long. Not with the snoring, the uneven but constant sway, and the muffled groan of the sea in its bones. Every creak, every shift of the hammocks was a reminder she wasn't here alone and that Tessanee was still somewhere frightened in the dark.

The moment her eyes opened, the cold was waiting for her. Salt-stiff clothes rasped against her skin, her hair a tangled snare. She checked for the pin by habit, fingers finding it buried in the mess. Still there. Still humming. Still the only thing keeping the Magics mostly quiet. The only good thing about her hair turning into a bird's nest was that the pin hadn't shaken loose in the depths.

Quietly, she slipped from the sling. The air was thick with sweat and tar, the slow sway making the lanternlight crawl across the walls. Moving between hammocks, she kept her shoulders low, each step measured. She didn't have a plan yet—only a name in her head and the hold in her sights.

Every step made her socks bunch uncomfortably, and she had the unpleasant sense she'd be walking in damp grit for days. She pulled the blanket tighter, and began weaving between hammocks and crates, each shadow a possible set of eyes.

The ladder waited ahead, pale in the faint spill of starlight from above. She glanced once toward the sleeping crew, then started up, slow and silent.

Once topside, the ship's pitch and roll swayed her toward the wall, but she let it—better to look like part of the motion than fight it and make noise.

The path in her mind was clear: Purdue's group, funneled past the foremast into a hold. If the groups stayed together, Tessanee would be there.

She guessed even in the dead of night a ship was never truly still. Lanterns swung faintly from hooks along the bulkhead, throwing sickle-shaped shadows across the passage. Somewhere above, a rope clinked against a mast. One wrong step, one pair of watchful eyes, and she'd be caught before she even reached the hatch.

The aft section rose ahead, pale lanternlight glinting off the seams of the captain's quarters. She moved quiet, steps matching the ship's slow roll, until a low murmur snagged on the wind. Aleric's low cadence and Malvian's deeper rumble.

Lusa stilled and cast a glance over her shoulder, but the passage behind lay empty. Timbers creaked under the push of the sea and rope clanked somewhere above. Safe enough. She edged closer, fingertips grazing cool wood. Through the seam where two planks didn't quite meet, the voices bled clearer.

"… yet to give me a reason," Malvian said, each word clipped with restraint. "Every day she breathes, the risk grows."

A pause. The faint rasp of paper being rolled.

"We need her." Aleric's tone held the kind of calm that felt chosen, not natural.

"For what?" Malvian shot back. "She is not the Dreadstar's crew. Nor is she bound to the goods. She is a mage. The only one we have seen in nearly a year."

Her pulse hit harder. Nearly a year. No wonder she was thought to be the last one left. Between the Empire's decree and Lazorious's magehunt, they were also being kidnapped and smuggled?

"The quota is not met," Malvian continued, realization in his tone. "She ensures it will be."

"The yield's greater near the lines. Rushing it here would be wasteful."

She frowned. *Quota?* That was for the captives. So, they did intend to make her one of them. And *lines*… she wasn't sure, but she highly doubted they meant rope.

"She is unpredictable. That is worse than being dangerous."

That's right, be afraid, she thought, lip curling in contempt. The darkling made it easy to hate him. If only she could figure out what in Sardan's name they were talking about.

"You think I'd keep her without a leash?"

Her stomach knotted. She already knew the leash. Tessanee's face flickered in her mind, wide-eyed and scared. The tittering of the Magics grew and her fists tightened.

"Keep what matters to them where they can see it. And where you can take it away." Aleric sounded a little too confident.

Footsteps creaked across the floor as he continued, "We don't usually take children. Slows the trade. Complicates the work. Makes it harder to keep the crew from getting sloppy. I'd have thought your men sharp enough to notice one wasn't the right age for the ledger."

The air shifted, charged. Malvian spat the next words. "You'd use the girl as a leash?"

"If it keeps the mage in line."

Lusa's jaw tightened. Let them think they held the leash—she'd be the one to cut it and wind it around both their necks. A chair scraped hard across the boards.

"She is not—" Malvian broke off.

The pause stretched. Her heartbeat rose with it. The quiet wasn't empty; it was listening. And no sooner than she realized she'd been discovered, the door burst outward on a violent surge of purple Resonance, slamming her shoulder into the opposite wall.

Malvian filled the doorway, strands of hair plastered damp against his cheeks, the thin leather band at his brow catching the light. The power humming in the narrow space clung to her skin, stealing her breath. She straightened, rubbing the sore spot, and met his glare without flinching.

Behind him, Aleric lounged at the captain's table, a hand wrapped lazily around a glass.

"Eavesdropping?" he asked, the word almost pleasant.

"I was walking."

"And stopped. Conveniently. Here."

She kept her face neutral.

He set the glass down with a whisper against the desk. "Everything on this ship has a purpose. The moment it doesn't, it's gone."

Her voice dropped to a grumble. "And his?"

Aleric glanced behind her to the darkling, then returned to her. "To keep you in line."

A snort slipped out before she could stop it. "And mine?"

"You'll know soon enough. Even the storm has its place… until it blows itself out."

Lusa's fingers curled against her sides. That's all she was to him—something to steer until it smashed against the rocks. She pictured the cramped hold below, the stifling dark, the reek of sweat and piss, the eyes that flinched from the lantern's flare. Tessanee's among them. Small. Afraid. Waiting for freedom that might never come.

She took a step closer. "If you want the Dreadstar to stay afloat," she said, emphasizing the name enough to keep his attention, "the captives get treated like people, not livestock. Put them to work, same as me. More hands means more work finished."

If there was even a sliver of pride in running a tight, efficient crew, she'd find it and twist it to her advantage.

His eyes narrowed. "What makes you think you're in a place to bargain?"

"If you want this ship ending up like the Seafang, keep running it the way you are."

His jaw ticked. "They'll drag the pace."

"Give them work that keeps them out of the way."

"They'll turn restless."

"I'll keep them busy."

"They'll need watching."

"Half your crew's asleep in the rigging—put them where they're worth the rations."

"Rations we don't have."

"Let me worry about that."

Aleric's gaze lingered, head tilting enough to look slightly perplexed. "We'll see how loud your mouth is after we make landfall." He took a slow drink. "If one thing goes wrong, one item goes missing, one drop of blood hits my boards, every one of them will pay for it, starting with the girl. And you'll watch before joining them."

He could keep his threats. She'd keep her vow.

This was her chance to be more than the villain they feared her to be.

CHAPTER 28

The Archives

Weeks had slipped by since the banquet, marked less by summons and more by the weather pushing harder at Aeonia's walls. Lady Ice had come swift and merciless, laying frost over the groves before harvest. Villages whispered of empty bins. Farmers lit fires in their orchards in desperate attempts to keep the frost at bay. Outside the palace, people endured; inside, the cold was answered with fur-lined cloaks and arguments over ledgers—numbers sliding across parchment while the land starved.

Kaden kept his distance from the bickering. He'd already sent his first report home with the envoy. Now he waited for a reply that might never come. If the passes closed, the message could be snowed under until Flora. And with it, any word of Lusa. The court gossiped she'd been named interim sorceress, but no confirmation had reached Aeonia. That silence gnawed at him more than the frost.

So, he buried himself in the archives.

The chamber walls were ribbed with shelves of bark-bound tomes and pressed leaf scrolls. Resin tablets leaned in crooked stacks between narrow rows of tables. The air was dry with sap and dust, heavy with memory—and heavier still with the sense that none of it had been meant for the likes of him.

He read what he could, though half the phrasing tangled itself in idioms never meant for outsiders. The Aeonians wrote their histories like riddles—half poetry, half code—and despite the blood he carried, he hadn't been raised with the keys to unlock them. The more he read, the more it struck him that they didn't record history. They wove it.

Their words were less about what happened and more about how the realm remembered. Every age bent back toward the Aeon, the unseen pulse they claimed bound all things. To them, the world wasn't built but sung into being. Maybe that was why every page felt alive with something he couldn't quite touch.

Culture, memory, the unspoken knowledge passed through generations… all of it lay beyond his reach. He tugged his cloak tighter against Lady Ice's bite and turned one brittle page after another, piecing fragments that hinted at meaning but never added up.

One ancient Elvish symbol kept surfacing. At first, he wasn't sure of the translation, but the more he stumbled across it, the more he convinced himself it could only mean 'capstones'. Always paired with images of seasons and rivers, skies and roots. The sort of word scholars would twist into riddles while men like him just needed someone to spit it out straight.

He moved to one of the oblong tables and pulled a sheet of bark tucked in the tome like a marker, slipping off a fur-lined glove so he wouldn't tear the edges. Circles and lines sprawled across the surface; runes repeated with near-obsessive care. Could've been a map. Could've been some bored scribe killing time. Hard to say. Still, the spacing tugged at him, familiar in a way he couldn't place, even if the symbols didn't mean a thing. He flipped it over, hunting for a key, some scrap of explanation, but the back was bare. Only the bold Elvish mark at the top gave it a sense of importance… it was the same symbol he kept finding.

By the time he shut the tome, a dull throb pressed behind his eyes. His breath fogged in front of him before fading into the rafters. Whatever truths the archives held, they weren't meant for him. He rubbed at the ache in his temple with cold, stiff fingers, muttering under his breath. If he wanted answers, he'd need someone willing to cut straight instead of talking in circles.

Lorenthar was exactly where Kaden expected him—legs stretched out in an alcove, boots crossed at the ankles, a cup of wine dangling in his hand, pale hair loose over one shoulder. Lady Ice had claimed everything, even here, her breath seeping through the carved walls and frosting the rim of his goblet. He looked like a prince with nowhere else to be, which meant he was probably watching everything.

"You've been haunting our archives," Lorenthar said, eyes still fixed on the frosted window. His neatly trimmed goatee framed the curve of his lips as he smiled. "Half the court thinks you're trying to turn scholar."

Once, Kaden might've ducked his head, played the guest. Lorenthar was still a prince, still dangerous, still an elf with more power in his smile than most carried in a sword-arm. But weeks of sly maps, whispered warnings, and wine-paired truths had worn down the formal edges between them. Lorenthar knew Kaden wasn't about to polish his tongue for anyone, and Kaden knew the prince didn't want him to.

So, he dropped the sheet of bark onto the low table. "Not tryin' ta' be anythin' but sane. You make sense of this or not?"

He shoved the tome after it, open to the page the bark had marked and tugged his cloak tighter. "I don't need a song about roots 'n seasons. Just tell me plain what the hell I'm lookin' at."

Lorenthar finally shifted his gaze from the window, golden eyes dropping to the sheet Kaden had thrown on the table. He let the silence hang, long enough for his smirk to settle deep.

"Blunt as ever," he drawled, lifting his wine as if to toast the bark. "My ancestors loved their riddles. They thought themselves clever, but most days I think they just liked the sound of their own metaphors."

Kaden snorted. "Figures. I don't speak the tongue proper, and even if I did, sounds like they still wrote it sideways. It's of no use when I need answers, not poetry."

A low laugh rolled out of Lorenthar, smooth as the wine on his tongue. He set the cup aside and tapped the bold symbol at the top of the bark with one long finger.

"Ah… the Aelenth. Capstones set where the leys cross. Without them, nothing in this realm holds." He leaned back, eyes glinting.

"Some bloodlines tuned keener than others," Lorenthar added, almost offhand. "In old records, they called it a vessel. Most of those lines are dust."

The name 'Aelenth' slammed into place, but Kaden kept his face neutral, cloak tugged close against the draft. Weeks of chasing a ghost through the archives, the word dropped from Prince Vaelar's lips with all the weight of a secret, and he'd found nothing. Because it hadn't been a word at all, just a mark. Bold, simple, staring back at him the whole time.

The slab in the grove rose sharp in his memory… the hum that had rattled through his bones, the roots curling as if pulled to its center. All of it pointed here. To these capstones.

If the realm once leaned on a vessel when the lines frayed, then somewhere, now, it had done the same.

He forced his jaw loose, kept his eyes steady on the parchment, and gave Lorenthar nothing.

"So then these—" he began to trace one of the lines, the overlapping circles.

"Ley lines," Lorenthar supplied easily, almost bored. "The veins of the realm. You'll find references scattered across half a dozen tomes if you know where to look. Most don't."

He reclined again, eyes glinting. "Of course, the archivists won't tell you this. Not directly. They prefer their riddles. Keeps knowledge in the hands of the right people. But here you are, Everwyn—holding the kind of truth men kill to keep buried."

"Why tell me?"

"Because you asked. And because half the court is too busy sharpening their talons on one another to notice where you dig. Consider it a curiosity."

He finished his drink and gestured toward the decanter in silent offer. Kaden ignored it, scooping up the bark of symbols and scrawlings, eyes narrowing as he studied it again.

"So it's a map."

Lorenthar inclined his head, the faintest nod. "Of the capstones, yes. And the leys that bind them. Knowledge best left buried, if you ask the rest of my family."

He leaned in and poured another goblet of wine for himself, casual as if they weren't speaking treason in miniature. "Most here wouldn't recognize what you've laid on the table. My ancestors liked to keep their secrets wrapped tight. Some, though… still know how to read between the lines."

"Like you."

A smile drifted across Lorenthar's mouth. "Like me. And a few others with more patience than sense. Laerynth, for instance. My brother-by-law has never met a secret he didn't want locked under his thumb." He swirled his wine lazily. "And my nephew Vaelar… well, youth always thinks itself cleverer than it is. Laerynth keeps him close."

"Sounds like he isn't walkin' on his own feet."

"Oh, Vaelar walks. He just doesn't always know who's setting the path beneath him."

Kaden tucked the Aelenth in his satchel. He'd wrung what truth he could from the prince, even if there were still more questions than answers.

Lorenthar tipped his goblet in a half salute. "Walk carefully, Everwyn. Knowledge has a way of drawing eyes. And eyes aren't always friendly."

Kaden left him to his wine, the word 'Aelenth' clinging colder than the frost at his heels. The hall toward his chamber was quiet, lit with the pale glow of flame-moss.

He had nearly reached his door when a figure stepped from the shadows. Envoy Ronus, cloak still dusted with frost, bowed just enough to count as courtesy. In his glove was a sealed parchment stamped with Izier's crest.

"A rider arrived an hour ago," Ronus said, breath fogging with every word.

Kaden stared at the seal, pulse kicking hard in his throat. Finally. Word from Izier. Word of what they thought of his report—of the rot, the court, the capstone. And maybe… word of Lusa.

Inside his chamber, he dropped the tome and satchel onto the table with a thud. The letter felt heavier than its slip of wax and parchment had any right to. He pulled off his gloves, cracked the seal, and unrolled it flat. The script was clipped, the hand familiar.

Your observations regarding Aeonia are received. The matters of root, crop, and climate remain under review. Proof beyond words will be required. Secure what you can. Evidence speaks louder than ink.

As for the one you inquired after, her voice has not yet reached our halls. The accounts out of Merravale are conflicting. Some insist she was lost in the retreat, others that she parted from the company and has yet to return. None can speak with certainty. Until word comes from her own hand, we cannot confirm. For now, her absence is acknowledged, and the council holds steady in the interim.

The lines blurred before he reached the end. Lost in the retreat. Has yet to return. Absence acknowledged? Retreat from what? His grip tightened until the parchment crinkled, edges folding under his fist. In that brief moment it read like a death notice, dressed in polite ink.

He forced himself to read again, slower. *Conflicting accounts. Has yet to return. Until word comes from her own hand.* Not a death announcement. Someone had chosen those words carefully, leaving cracks wide enough for truth to slip through.

Lusa's face rose in his mind: pale as ivory, iron-blue eyes burning with passion, fury, fight. Solovine blooms pinned in her hair as she muttered curses at her gown. The same woman who'd stood unyielding at the Citadels, meeting everything Lazorious hurled her way. She had saved him there at a cost he still couldn't measure. And the last glimpse of her stayed longer than the rest. Her, bent low over the saddle, riding hard, never looking back. He should've called out. Should've gone after her.

No. He wouldn't let his mind dwell on the should'ves.

Kaden folded the letter, the crease biting into his palm. She wasn't gone. Couldn't be. Not Lusa. Not after everything. Dead or turned… he'd believe neither without proof. Until he saw her with his own eyes, every rumor was a lie.

He sat on the edge of the bed, letter set aside, the chill bleeding through stone and timber until it settled in his bones. Silence closed in and he dragged both hands over his face like he could tear through it. Dark thoughts pressed at the edges of his mind, but spiraling into them wouldn't change a thing.

The letter gave him nothing he could use and everything to turn circles around. He wouldn't sit here and pick apart what-ifs about Lusa, not when the words gave him nothing solid. Thinking of her lost to one fate or another—that was the thought that gutted him. Better to bury himself in finding evidence to send of the capstones and ley lines, even if it meant wading back into the High Canopy with all its games and courtiers. Sitting still only let grief root deeper. He pushed himself up, forcing motion before it pinned him to the bed.

He moved to the desk and pulled his journal free from the drawer. The rough sketch of the capstone filled a page near the back, lines crooked from haste, but it was enough to bring the slab into focus again. Proof he hadn't imagined it. Proof something was buried out there, waiting. He snapped the journal shut and slid it into his satchel. Answers weren't in ink. They were in the grove.

Kaden locked the letter away in a small box and shoved it deep in the drawer. With a sigh, he dragged on his heavier, fur-lined cloak, shook the frost from its stiffened hems, and cinched his gloves until the leather bit at his wrists. The chamber gave nothing back but silence, so he stepped out, boots carrying him into the hush of the corridors. Each strike felt too loud against the wood, the sound chasing him all the way to the outer walkways where Lady Ice's breath cut hard across his face.

Snow dusted the canopy bridges, catching in delicate fringes along the vines. The air hung raw with pine, each breath stinging his lungs. Far below, the forest sprawled in silence, its branches bowed under a hard crust of ice, no birds daring to stir. Aeonia should have been basking in Lady Fira's warmth. Instead, the realm lay caught in a season gone astray.

Kaden drew his hood and pressed on.

The trail toward the southern rim narrowed between snow-coated sentinel pines. Each step carried him deeper into stillness, the world shrinking until only the rasp of his breath and the crunch of frost remained. He pulled Lorenthar's map from his satchel, the inked lines a faint guide in the pale light, and matched memory to parchment with care. The fork in the path, the hollowed stone, the dip of the ridgeline… it all led him back to the place that waited.

The place that hummed.

The grove lay hushed beneath a shroud of white. What had once opened like a hollowed ring was now nearly swallowed, snow banked high against its roots, the clearing blurred into sameness with the forest around it. He might have passed it by, had it not been for the hum that began low in his Seryn. A vibration deep in the marrow, faint as breath against glass, tugging him forward. It was like remembering a song he'd never learned. The resonance built, threading bone and breath, rising until it felt like the ground itself had a heartbeat—and his was trying to match it.

He stopped where the pull grew strongest and dropped to one knee. Frost burned through his gloves as he swept snow aside, scattering it until the hard curve of stone emerged beneath. But the capstone was no longer bare. Dead vines had claimed it, woven into a brittle snarl across its face. They had wormed into its grooves the way ivy sinks into old walls, clinging long past life. Hollow stems cracked beneath his grip, but several refused to let go, as if the stone itself might deliver them from dying.

Kaden tore the vines away in fistfuls. The hum in him climbed with every pull, thrumming harder, like the stone was answering… or calling for something he couldn't give.

Lorenthar's offhanded word struck back through him: vessel. The capstone was reaching, but not for him. It was waiting for the vessel it was meant for—the lock fitted to its key, the match the realm itself seemed certain must exist.

The roots clung stubborn as he allowed his thoughts to circle back to Lusa. Was she safe? Had the pin held against Them? His jaw locked until the muscle ached. He shoved Lusa from his mind and fixed on the capstone. This he could face. This was solid.

At last, the spirals reemerged, carved shallow but clear. He wiped the last frost away with his sleeve, staring until the pattern burned into him. Concentric rings tethered inward to a single point.

He dug into his satchel and pulled out the bark parchment he and Lorenthar had studied. The faint circles and lines had teased him before, but set against the spiral etched in stone, they blazed with clarity. This wasn't metaphor. It *was* a map. The ley lines drawn as veins through the land, the capstones set to anchor them.

The image snapped together in his mind: the parchment's scrawl, the location of each capstone, and the golden-threaded tapestry of Aetherealm hanging in the banquet hall. They'd flaunted the truth in silk and gold, and he'd walked beneath it blind.

For a moment he forgot the cold, forgot the throbbing ache in his chest. This wasn't riddle or rumor. It was the realm itself, drawn twice over: scrawled in ink, threaded in gold. He still couldn't tie the dying crops or the erratic skies straight to Aeonia, not yet. Too many gaps, too many pieces missing. But with Vaelar whispering about it in corners, and the Aelenth staring back at him with the same bones as Aetherealm's own map… that wasn't chance. That was design. Maybe even the proof Izier had been waiting on.

Kaden pushed to his feet, breath clouding in front of him. Enough guessing. If the map still hung in that hall, he'd have his confirmation before the night was through.

CHAPTER 29

Stitched in Gold

Hours ago, he'd been knee-deep in snow, tearing dead vines from a stone that thrummed. Now he sat in a hall filled with wine and venison, golden threads of a vast tapestry gleaming above the murmuring crowd. The warmth didn't reach the bones of the hall. Magic or memory, whatever bound Aeonia to its roots, felt off here. He could sense it in the air, the same imbalance that had shivered beneath the capstone hours earlier. And if he, half-blood and half-tolerated, could sense it, then every pureblood elf in this hall sure could, too.

Officers in green and silver uniforms claimed one table, junior courtiers another. Servants moved with practiced quiet, carrying bowls of root-stew and platters of venison. The smell was rich but thinner than he remembered from the banquet. Lady Ice had pared down the harvest; even here, in the High Canopy, luxury tasted lean.

He sat near the end of a long table, draped his cloak on the bench beside him, and took a leisurely drink of wine. Across the wall, the golden-threaded tapestry of Aetherealm stared back at him. Rivers, mountains, coasts rendered in gilt. To anyone else, a work of art, a map of pride and place. To him, something else entirely.

He fixed on it the way a starving man fixed on bread. He wasn't seeing a map of pride, but anchors. The same placements as on the bark parchment. Myttica. Izier. Aeonia. Velkher. The bones of the realm laid bare, disguised as art. He felt the same chill as in the grove—that sense of something reaching, not for him, but for a vessel it had once been promised. A match the realm itself refused to forget.

His gut tightened. All this time, the truth had been stitched above their heads, paraded as decoration while the land starved beneath it. He forced his gaze down into the stew again, taking a slow sip. Can't stare too long.

Thalor dropped onto the bench opposite, settling like a man who'd already put in a long day. He reached for a bowl, steam curling toward his broad face.

"A strange season," he said, tearing some bread. "Lady Ice never comes this early. Not in my memory."

"Maybe memory's the problem. Seems this realm's forgot its own seasons."

Thalor chuckled under his breath. "The Aeon keeps balance. The rest of us just hope she remembers we exist."

Thalor studied him across the rim of his bowl, offering a smirk. "I hear you've been haunting the archives," he said it mildly, but his eyes didn't quite match his tone. "Some say Izier sent us an envoy. Others, a scholar in disguise."

Jest or test? Hard to tell.

Kaden tore off a piece of bread as well. "Better that than freezin' in circles with courtiers."

Thalor focused elsewhere momentarily, and Kaden let the silence stand, keeping his focus on the bread soaking in broth. Better to say little. He let his focus drift up again, dancing over the gold stitches.

A faint stir rippled near the doors. Courtiers tilted their heads, voices dipping. Kaden returned his attention to the bread in his hand, but the air shifted around him, taut and expectant. He finished it in one bite, chewing as the savory warmth grounded him.

At the next table, officers straightened, laughter cut short. Even Thalor's posture stiffened. It only meant one thing: royalty had entered.

Bootsteps carried through the hall, purposeful—until the rhythm faltered. Kaden swallowed his food down and turned just as Prince Vaelar came into view, silver cloak scattering frost in his wake, two young officers flanking him. He was mid-conversation, voice smooth, but it broke when his gaze landed on Kaden.

The prince slowed. "Ambassador Everwyn." A faint smile touched his lips. Polite enough to pass for civility, thorns beneath the veneer. "Eating with soldiers suits you. Easier than untangling Elvish you'll never truly grasp."

Conversations at nearby tables quieted, but Kaden didn't flinch. Princes, predators—it was all the same. Show weakness, and they tore in deeper. He'd bled in worse pits than this hall, steel at his throat and no velvet to soften the threat. And now he wasn't stumbling blind. The grove, the bark parchment, the tapestry stitched in gold… all of it pointed to truths the High Canopy wanted buried. Maybe he didn't have exact proof yet, but he had enough to know he wasn't the fool at the table anymore.

He dipped another piece of bread in his stew and ate it slow before answering. "Ya dress yer' words like yer' court… pretty, but empty underneath."

Everything turned painfully silent. The prince's smile fell. "You speak boldly for one living on borrowed courtesy." His tone carried enough for the whole room to hear. "Perhaps too boldly."

Thalor shifted, but Kaden caught his warning glance and shook it off. He stirred the soup with his spoon. "Or maybe not bold enough. Seems ta' me the real problem's starin' everyone in the face, but half the court's too busy polishin' mirrors ta' notice."

The snickers that had rippled from Vaelar's followers died quickly. The prince's eyes cooled, but he didn't rise to the bait.

"Careful, Everwyn," he said softly, almost pleasant. "Mirrors cut if handled poorly."

With that, he turned and strode on, his attendants falling in behind him like shadows.

Kaden let out a breath through his nose and reached for his wine. "Snake pit," he muttered.

Thalor's mouth twitched again, more grim than amused. "And you keep walking through it barefoot."

"Rather walk through it than lie down in it."

Kaden eyed the tapestry again. Every gilded thread was a lie polished into beauty. The elves called it harmony. He called it denial.

Eventually, he finished his wine, the tapestry constant in his periphery. Proof or not, hungering for it here was a good way to get more attention than he wanted. He managed a small nod at Thalor. A show of friendship, or at least tolerance. Whatever else, it cost him nothing to keep the elf close.

"Maybe I'll take your advice and stick to scrolls," he said, pushing his bowl aside. "Safer company than princes."

Thalor gave a low chuckle, though his eyes searched him and Kaden had to wonder if it was sincere concern or calculations. Kaden shrugged and reached for his cloak. He'd had enough stew, enough stares. Best to quit the hall before curiosity turned into trouble. The wine's warmth faded as he stood and tipped his head to Thalor.

"Stay warm."

As he pivoted toward the exit, he glanced once more to the tapestry. The Aelenth was a key to the capstones and ley lines of Aetherealm. Now he only had to learn who was meddling with them enough to twist the seasons and leave the fields in ash. And he had a pretty good hunch. The thought followed him out, heavy as the frost-laden air.

Kaden's boots thudded hollow across the hanging bridge, the wood creaking under each step, frost crunching where ropes had gathered it in stiff knots. The cold bit sharper out here, wind dragging at his cloak, the forest dropping away into black beneath. He kept his head down; teeth set against the sting in his lungs.

Halfway across, a figure moved into his path. White fur caught the moonlight, hood drawn close, a strand of hair escaping at her temple. Princess Siraen. Her maids trailed behind, their footsteps hushed, but as soon as she noticed him, she lifted a gloved hand. They stayed at the bridge's mouth.

"Ambassador," she said, her voice carrying a nervous sort of excitement. "You walk alone. It's terribly cold for a walk."

Kaden slowed, hands still in his cloak. "Your Highness," he returned, the words rougher than intended.

The moonlight framed her, lashes edged in frost, the chill painting her cheeks with a muted rose, and her golden eyes steady on his. Too striking not to notice. Only a fool would miss it. He wasn't blind, only stubborn enough to pretend otherwise. He dipped his chin in bow, his eyes holding hers longer than was wise.

"I've heard," she started, stepping closer, "that you've been haunting the archives."

That phrase again. He almost smiled. Maybe they really did hold briefings in order to keep their stories straight about him. But her tone was more curious than accusatory, like she'd stumbled upon a secret and couldn't wait to share.

"Is it true you found something? Something… important?"

Kaden let a careful breath fog between them. "Ya shouldn't be out here askin' that," he said quietly. "Bridges have ears."

Siraen's brows lifted, the faintest crease forming as if she'd been scolded. "I just want to help. Everyone pretends the realm is sound, but I can feel it—the air, the frost… even the light feels wrong."

Her sincerity caught him off guard. She wasn't playing court games; she genuinely believed she could make a difference just by caring enough.

"Yere not wrong," he said. "But the less ya talk about it, the longer ya get to keep that pretty head of yours clear of worry."

"You talk like everything's already lost," she said, almost pouting. "Every problem has its solution. I am not one to give up that easily."

Kaden huffed out what might've been a laugh. "That kind of optimism'll get you eaten alive in a place like this."

"Then you'll just have to keep me safe," she said before she could stop herself. The words tumbled out, bright and unguarded. The flush on her cheeks deepened instantly.

Kaden looked away. "That's not my job."

"Maybe not," she said quickly, "but you look as if you'd be rather good at it."

The wind stirred between them, ruffling the edge of her hood, and the world seemed to narrow to frost and breath and the faint creak of ropes beneath their boots. He shifted back half a step, trying to reclaim the space she kept closing.

"You should go, Princess. Eyes'll be on ya before long."

Her gaze stayed on him, steady in a way that didn't belong to court manners. She leaned closer, her voice barely carrying over the wind. "Be careful, Kaden."

The sound of his name in her voice landed warmer than it should have. He didn't like that it did.

Siraen looked at him as if deciding whether to say something more. Her expression slowly lifted with a kind of bravery.

"Perhaps tomorrow, you might join me for tea? Just to warm your hands after studying in the archives."

He blinked, caught off guard. "Tea," he repeated.

Her smile faltered briefly before she recovered. "If it's not too improper," she added, though the hopeful lilt in her tone gave her away.

Kaden sighed inwardly. Eldere help him, he couldn't stomach seeing her look disappointed. She was too delicate for this world. All lace and light and no armor to speak of. The last thing he needed was to be the one who dimmed that brightness.

He rubbed a hand over his jaw. "Don't think I'd fit in with yer' crowd, Princess," he said, aiming for gruff instead of gentle.

"Then I'll have them fit around you."

The wind caught her cloak again, sending a stray strand across her cheek. She didn't seem to notice.

He did.

She dipped her head, the motion more grace than farewell, and motioned for her maids. Kaden shifted aside, bracing against the rope rail. The bridge wasn't built for comfort; two could pass, but only just. When she did, her shoulder brushed his, the faint scent of crushed petals trailing after her. The contact was fleeting, and he honestly couldn't tell if it was deliberate or not. Her maids fell in behind her, whispering, skirts swishing across the planks.

He stayed where he was until the last hint of white fur disappeared into the night. The bridge groaned under him as he finally exhaled. She had no idea what she was playing at—too soft for politics, too open for deceit. And still, she'd left him rattled. Maybe she knew what she was doing… or maybe she didn't.

It didn't matter. He couldn't afford to want warmth, or company, or a princess's gaze. Want dulled edges, and dull edges wouldn't cut through a nest like this. Still, he'd seen too many bright things dim under the darkness of this world and he wasn't eager to watch it happen again, least of all to her.

CHAPTER 30

The Mage, the Darkling, and the Maelstrom

The days blurred together, one rolling wave after another. A week, maybe longer. Lusa had stopped counting after the third sunset bled into the sea. Out here, time wasn't measured in sun and stars but in boots on wet planks, ropes squealing through calloused hands, and wood groaning under wind and the strength of the sea.

Her Magics had returned—not the ragged scraps she'd clung to after Malvian hurled her overboard, but a steady thrum beneath her skin. They hungered for freedom, but her will and the hairpin held the leash tight.

A tarnished brass plate was nailed to a barrel, warped but reflective enough. Lusa caught her likeness—braids yanked tight against her scalp, the silver hairpin snug at her temple. Tessanee's handiwork. Thin plaits from every lock until her reflection looked more like the darkling than herself. She hated it. The girl had giggled through the whole ordeal, hands gentle, eyes bright. Lusa had let her, only because Tessanee had so little else to smile about. And because—Magics help her—something in the girl tugged at her chest, as foreign as the Light inside her. She was just glad Tessanee hadn't been locked away in one of the holds. Malvian's strange attachment to her had kept her living comfortably above deck.

A sharp gust of wind slapped her face, tangling loose ends of her braids. Tessanee gasped, glancing up. Colder now. The scent was different. Rain. Lusa shifted, scanning the horizon. Clouds gathered heavy, bruising the sky.

"Is it going to rain?" Tessanee's voice was almost carried away by the wind.

Lusa flicked her a sideways glance. The girl had found her voice again somewhere between Lusa making sure the captives weren't penned like animals and Malvian's… watchful interference. It was a relief when she found out she hadn't been put in a hold with the rest of them.

She gave a curt nod and turned back to the skies. Seafaring wasn't her skill, but she'd learned enough from the crew's grumbling. The weather had been wrong. When the sea didn't behave, men looked for someone to blame. Their eyes always found her.

She heard their mutters, the way talk cut short when she passed. Calm seas at the wrong time of year—an omen, they said. And with a mage on deck—worse, a female—every foul wind and snapped rope was her fault.

The crew had barely stomached her bargain with Aleric. Watching her walk the deck in daylight, captives trailing behind, seemed to unsettle the 'old order'. Some spat when she passed. Some muttered threats. Others merely waited, knives ready, for a chance. A ship was a world unto itself, and worlds like this did not forgive disruption.

So, she kept her head high. Agency, however small, had to be taken and held like a blade, because when the order broke, as it surely would, she wasn't sure if her Magics or her bargains would save her.

"Tessa." Malvian's voice carried across the deck.

The girl's hands stilled in Lusa's hair. Then she gave a quick squeeze at Lusa's shoulder—half a hug, half a thank-you—and darted toward him, light-footed despite the ship's roll.

Lusa's mouth flattened. Of course. He only ever spoke when it was to her.

Malvian's gaze brushed Tessanee, then lifted and caught on the plaits woven tight against Lusa's scalp. His expression shifted, darkening like the storm bank gathering at the horizon.

Almost worth it, Lusa thought. Almost worth letting Tessanee fuss over her hair until she looked like the darkling, just to see his face sour.

With a sigh, she pushed to her feet. Movement across the deck caught her eye—Aleric, watching from the quarterdeck rail, hand easy on the wood, gaze heavy on her.

The captives shifted below, their muffled movements carrying up through the planks. She'd fought to win them air, scraps of daylight, the right to stand on deck instead of rotting in the hold. But they weren't hers. Not her kin. Not her burden. She had no reason to care whether they lived or starved.

And yet—

Her chest tightened, a tug she couldn't name. Strange, unwelcome. Like a thread of Light weaving through her, soft where she was hard, insistent where she wanted to be indifferent.

Lusa ignored the looks as she crossed the deck. One sailor sneered. Another muttered under his breath. She kept her chin high, fingers brushing the pouch at her hip. Not reassurance—habit. A reminder of what she'd reclaimed in secret, and what no one above deck could know.

The hatch yawned dark, and she slipped below. The air was damp, carrying the stink of salt, unwashed bodies, and despair. Lanternlight guttered, shadows swaying across the low ceiling and stacked crates. Lusa's steps slowed. She let her eyes skim the corners, the faces that turned toward her. A cough in the dark, a shuffle of boots—her hand drifted to the pouch at her hip. She kept her back angled toward the wall, never leaving herself open.

Purdue, the old man, sat hunched near the bulkhead, his hands folded like he was praying to a god who had long since stopped listening. He wasn't the only one who looked up when she entered. Subtle shifts ran through the hold—the captives straightened, lifted their heads, hope flickering across their faces like a spark catching on wet tinder.

Lusa's throat tightened. She crouched at a crate, loosened the pouch, and drew out a pinch of juniper and a dusting of pearl powder. Her hand hovered as she murmured the words softly. The amulet against her chest pulsed awake.

Light shimmered. The reagents folded in on themselves—gone in a blink. In their place, warm and whole, sat a round loaf of bread as wide as her chest.

Steam curled from its crust. The smell of baked grain filled the hold, drowning out sweat and salt.

It wasn't much. One loaf, no matter how big, wouldn't feed so many. A crust here, a crumb there, only enough to take the edge off hunger, to give stomachs something to hold. But when she looked at their faces, saw the awe and gratitude shining raw in their eyes, something twisted in her chest.

Why? Why did she care if they ate or starved? They weren't hers. She owed them nothing.

But that something inside her that shifted at their looks, at their reliance, snagged. Was it satisfaction? Power, thinly disguised as kindness? Or a hollow place in her chest being filled by borrowed need?

Did she crave importance because she'd been dismissed all her life? Did their dependence soothe an ache she wouldn't name—gratification in place of love, family, the one thing she'd never had: to be chosen for herself, not cast aside for the magic inside her?

No one but—

Her chest ached, Kaden's face pushing into her thoughts where it didn't belong. With a sharp breath, she tore the loaf into rough pieces and handed them out. It didn't matter why. It only mattered that she could.

Later, she coaxed the captives up onto the deck. As fresh as the air could be on a ship full of unwashed men, it was still better than the damp hold. The sun hid behind a gray veil, skies heavy and unwelcoming, but the captives didn't seem to care. Purdue closed his eyes, lifting his head as if the chill in the wind were blessing enough. They remained bound wrist to wrist, a condition she couldn't bargain away with Aleric. Freedom had limits.

When the deck quieted for the night watch, Lusa restlessly paced the planks. Thunder rumbled far off, tugging her gaze toward the dark horizon. Tessanee slipped to her side, as she always seemed to, unless Malvian had claimed her company. She said nothing until her gaze snagged on a sailor's whetstone. The scrape was sharp, grating, and Tessanee flinched, her fingers seizing Lusa's sleeve.

Lusa told herself it wasn't her problem. The girl wasn't hers to protect, wasn't hers to shape. But the sight of that fear burrowed under her skin, unsettling, and the thought continued in its cyclical nature.

Why did she care so much?

Her gaze flicked to the mast, to the memory of Malvian's face when he'd seen her braids. How it would gall him to see Tessanee learning from her, not him. The thought almost made her smile, decision settled.

"All right," she said, stepping away from the rail. "If steel makes you flinch, you need to learn how to make it work for you."

"I don't want to fight," Tessanee whispered.

"This isn't about fighting."

Lusa scanned the deck and pulled a short wooden pin from its rack, the kind she'd seen pirates jam ropes around to hold them fast. She turned it over, testing the weight, before handing it to Tessanee.

"It's about protecting yourself. Knowing you can." She steered the girl toward a quiet stretch near the stern, half-hidden by barrels and coiled rope.

"Wider," Lusa said, nudging Tessanee's feet apart with her boot. "Feel the sway. The ship isn't your enemy. Move with it."

A memory rose of Kaden standing over her with a wooden sword, besting her again and again until instinct finally cut through hesitation. *Too slow, Lus. Trust your hands, not your head.*

She swallowed hard and echoed him. "Strong grip, but not stiff. Let it move with you, not against you."

Tessanee jabbed at the air, the rod wobbling with every sway of the deck until her wrists shook. Her lips pressed tight in stubborn focus, but the harder she fought it, the more pathetic it became. Lusa bit back a huff.

"Not like that." She stepped behind her, adjusted the girl's grip, steadied her small hands with her own. "Better. Again."

The next jab was clumsy, but at least she kept her feet. A prickle climbed Lusa's spine. She didn't need to look to know she was being watched. She turned anyway. Malvian leaned against the mast, arms folded, braids shifting in the wind. His gaze wasn't on her. It was on Tessanee.

When the girl faltered, nearly losing her grip, he was suddenly there. His hand closed over the rod, stopping it clean. "What are you doing?"

"Teaching her not to stand there helpless while the world decides she's easy prey."

Their eyes met. Iron striking flint. Hatred. Challenge. Tessanee shifted between them. Malvian looked away from her, focusing on the girl instead. His voice lowered, his hand shifting hers with careful precision.

"Loosen here. Don't choke it. Let it move."

Tessanee's breath steadied. The next swing cut cleaner through the air. A smile flickered across her face. She trusted him for this, adored him for it—and the sight dug at Lusa, somewhere between outrage and emptiness.

When the girl managed a clumsy parry, Lusa forced her voice softer. "That's better."

Tessanee lit up, gripping the rod with new determination, readying herself to try again.

Lightning split the sky, a jagged crack that bleached the deck in white. Lusa's heart lurched to her throat. Thunder followed close, a shuddering boom that jolted all three of them where they stood. Tessanee cried out, the rod slipping from her hands. Malvian's head snapped toward the horizon. The Magics stirred from Their slumber, eager and hungry.

A gust of wind tore across the deck in a screaming gale. Sails snapped like whips, rigging wracking against the masts. The ship jerked hard to starboard, pitching Tessanee off her feet. The belaying pin rolled, lost to the tilt of the boards. Malvian snatched the girl by the arm to keep her from meeting the same fate.

Another jagged bolt flashed. Thunder chased it close, booming so loud it rattled teeth. Men shouted over the noise, boots pounding as they fought the lines.

Aleric appeared in the chaos, cloak streaming, his voice booming above the storm. "Reef the sails! Secure the yardarm! Move, damn you!"

The deck canted beneath them, spray leaping over the rails. Lusa's hand shot out, catching Tessanee by the arm before she could slide, noticing Malvian still firmly held her other arm. The girl's eyes were wide, frozen in terror.

"Inside!" Lusa barked.

"Inside!" Malvian shouted at the same time.

Tessanee gawked at them as they both glared at each other, irritation sparking even as the storm roared.

The next wave struck broadside, sending men sprawling and water sluicing across the deck. The ship groaned like it might tear apart, every plank straining under the violence of the sea. Tessanee nodded at their twin command, stumbling toward the hatch—but the ship lurched again, harder than before. She yelped as her knees buckled, crashing to the planks.

Both Lusa and Malvian moved. His hand closed over the girl first. Lusa only rolled her eyes and turned away. Fine. Let him play guardian.

Malvian guided Tessanee toward the hatch, shielding her from the rush of water. Lusa turned to the storm, braids snapping behind her. Wind shrieked through the rigging, tearing at the sails until the canvas cracked like whips. Waves slammed broadside, drenching the deck in water that slapped over her boots. Men shouted, their words swallowed by thunder as they fought ropes that seemed determined to flay the ship apart.

A thrum in her veins matched the pitch of the waves… the Magics were stirring. The amulet at her chest vibrated faintly, hot even through her tunic. Her hand closed around it as a feral thought shoved aside all others: what if the storm bent to her will? What if she stilled the sea with a breath, silenced the thunder, ripped the lightning from the sky?

The Magics swelled at the idea, filling her chest until it was hard to breathe. Not survival. Not mercy. Dominion. Her grip tightened on the amulet. The storm seemed to lean toward her, waiting. A hand clamped on her arm and yanked her back.

Malvian. His face was inches from hers, braids whipping in the gale, eyes burning.

"None of your magic here, mage," he snarled.

The Magics bucked at the insult, answering for her before she could think. Sparks leapt from her skin into his hand, a snap of white-blue that lit his features. Malvian hissed and stepped back, fury flashing across his face, darker than the storm above.

He straightened, teeth bared, hand rising to strike her down—

"Your Highness!"

The shout tore across the deck. Veyrin—his ever-present shadow—stumbled toward them through the chaos, cloak plastered to his frame. "You must secure yourself! The storm—"

He didn't finish. Malvian's rage pivoted, a weapon seeking release. With a sweep of his hand, ropes lashed from the rigging, snapping around Veyrin's limbs. He slammed against the mast, bound in an instant. More lines twisted, winding tight, crossing his chest, his throat, climbing higher until his mouth was gagged in hemp.

Veyrin's eyes bulged in terror as the storm drowned his muffled cries. But the storm didn't care for Malvian's rage. It slammed against the hull with renewed violence, jerking the ship so hard a man was flung screaming over the rail. Another mast groaned, timbers shrieking

"Haul her steady! Brace the foremast!"

Aleric bellowed orders, rope in hands, pulling as though sheer will could keep the ship from breaking apart. But will wasn't enough. The storm hammered the ship, relentless waves slamming against the hull in a thunderous rhythm.

Heat channeled from the amulet and all through her body. Against her better judgement, she closed her eyes and let Them go. The Magics released like a floodgate breaking. Her vision swam, eyes snapping open to the inky black glimpse They offered her.

The wind shifted. Not much, but enough. A rope line held where it should have snapped. Rain suddenly shifted by mere thought, falling sideways. The ship slowed its wild rocking. She almost believed she had it.

But the Magics turned against her. Hungry. Violent. They heaved the sea higher, waves breaking across the deck with bone-rattling force. Wind howled sharper, snatching ropes from hands, hurling men into the belly of the sea. The storm raged worse, fed by Them. Her knees buckled, Their power ripping through her grasp.

Malvian's arm rose beside her. His braids lashed his shoulders, eyes blazing with rage turned to focus. He moved his hands in Resonance formations, and the storm shifted like it had always been his to command. Water curled back, waves bowing to his will.

Lusa spat rain from her lips, anger burning with each breath. It wasn't skill so much as inheritance. He was born to this—air and water bending like extensions of his own body. The elements didn't wrestle with a darkling. They obeyed.

And Magics curse it, he made her look like a child thrashing in the shallows.

Another crack of light split the sky, followed by a deafening boom of thunder. The Magics howled with it, hungry to drown the ship, her, everything. They were winning, always winning, because They had the reins.

But somewhere buried beneath Them lay the Light. She closed her eyes, dragged her breath steady, and reached for it. The act felt like tearing open her own chest. The Dark screamed, clawing to keep its dominion, but she dragged the Light upward anyway, forcing it into the fight. It wasn't summoning so much as splitting. Two pulses hammered inside her chest, discordant. She chained one against the other and hurled them outward.

The storm shuddered as the Magics reluctantly obeyed. Wind dropped, waves reeled, the deck steadied under her boots. Malvian's current slammed into hers, his mastery forcing its way into the gaps she couldn't hold. The two powers clashed as much with each other as with the sea—Dark Elf Resonance against those of a fractured mage.

Through the blur of rain and agony, she caught his stare, too fixed to mistake for anger. But the Light and Dark wrenched her attention back. The storm stuttered, caught between resistance and submission. Air thickened, pressing against her ears until every sound dulled and her nose began to bleed. But she wouldn't stop until she won.

Finally, the gale eased, sails hanging limp. Waves curled back. Malvian continued to pulse his Resonance outward with her magics and together they hammered the maelstrom into defeat.

Though the sea eased, the deck was wreckage. Rain thinned to a mean drizzle, dripping from torn canvas and splintered spars. Men staggered through the aftermath, hauling ropes, dragging bodies, patching what they could under Aleric's hoarse commands.

Lusa dropped her arms and fought to stay upright. Her chest felt scraped hollow, her veins raw where Light and Dark had torn through her like opposing tides. The emptiness should've felt familiar, the usual drain after battle, but it didn't. Beneath the ache, she could feel two throbs of emptiness. She pressed a hand to her sternum.

It wasn't possible. A mage couldn't house two cores; it defied every law she'd ever been taught. But she felt them. Distinct, unwilling halves, neither strong enough to silence the other. Thoughts swirled, one after another. What if they tore her in two next time? What if one lived and the other didn't?

A sailor glanced at her too long. She met his look with ice; he blinked and looked away. She clenched her jaw until her teeth ached, spine rigid, daring it to give. Weakness here was blood in the water. Her hand gripped the rail so hard her knuckles blanched. She just had to stay standing.

Malvian stood a few paces off, rain plastering his braids to his shoulders. His eyes were on her.

Veyrin sagged at the mast, rain streaking his face as sailors cut the ropes. She remembered then the title he'd screamed in the storm, thinking Malvian was something worth saving.

Her gaze slid to the darkling. How carefully he carried himself… how he snapped when anyone dared to use a title. He didn't want them to know what he was? Good. She'd take whatever little victory she could get, even if it was the kind of triumph only the desperate bothered to count.

A cruel smile edged past the pain in her body as she spat brine over the rail. "Your Highness."

Veyrin had spoken it in loyalty. She would make it his curse.

CHAPTER 31

When Light and Dark Align

The storm had wrung her dry. Fatigue draped her like a sodden cloak as she stood there relying on the railing, every muscle heavy from forcing Light and Dark to move as one. Her skull still pulsed with the echo of their struggle—except... maybe it hadn't been a struggle this time. Somewhere in the heart of that storm, They'd listened. For one impossible breath, They'd aligned.

Her hand drifted to her chest. Beneath the ache, she sensed them—twin cores, hollow and aching for recalibration. It wasn't balance. It was truce. Fragile. Temporary.

She'd began to sag and forced herself upright. Whatever she'd done, it had nearly broken her. And she wasn't about to let the darkling see the cracks.

Malvian stepped toward her. Power prickled in the air between them. She glared up at him, drained but ready to lash back. Tingling burned at her fingertips, her hand poised to fling fire into his face.

Then it came… the faint press at the edges of her mind, thin and wavering, but familiar. Him. She knew the shape of his will now. Overdrawn Light, the Dark's backlash, and his damned prodding all tugged at the same frayed thread. She smirked anyway, savoring the flicker of confusion in his eyes when he failed to breach her mind. The look only fed her satisfaction which she had no problem showing. His rage burned hotter, his hand rising as if the tempest still answered to him and she'd be flung once again into the sea.

Movement to their left. Malvian's gaze snapped where hers had flicked. Tessanee had stumbled onto the deck, hair a wild nest matted and plastered, eyes wide. She clung to the rail, shivering, a girl too small against a sea that had tried to eat them whole.

The fury in Malvian's face broke. His hand lowered, sudden as a blade sheathed. The air lost its charge. Lusa held her ground, chest heaving. Her own magic still simmered, begging release, but she curled her fingers into a fist and forced it down.

Tessanee looked between them. "Is it over?"

Lusa stepped first and crouched in front of her. "It's over. You hurt?"

Tessanee shook her head, lips trembling.

Malvian stepped between them and took her arm, firm but not unkind. "Come."

The girl glanced once at Lusa before letting him guide her toward the aft cabin the captain had ceded him, Veyrin dogging his heels.

Lusa's mouth twisted. Whatever. Let him play savior. If it gave her a moment to breathe, she wouldn't argue. She unclenched her fist, the Magics' crackle draining out of her, leaving only the ache beneath.

She lingered at the rail, before the rest of the deck forced itself back into focus. Sailors swarmed through the wreckage hauling torn lines, cutting away shredded canvas, dragging bodies beneath soaked tarps.

At some point her feet had started moving. She blinked, half-aware, and found herself weaving through the press of pirates. On the quarterdeck, Captain Aleric's orders cracked across the wind. His gaze swept the crew before catching on her… not just leverage. Something measuring, almost familiar, then gone. The moment she lifted her chin, his attention shifted, and he was already helping men haul a broken spar across the deck.

Her wandering feet carried her farther than she'd meant, and before she realized it, she was standing at the entrance to Purdue's hold. Belowdecks reeked worse than the swamps of Nardonia. Waterlogged ropes, mold creeping up the boards, the sour tang of vomit crusted in corners. The captives had no privy, only a barrel shoved against the bulkhead that sloshed filth across the planks whenever the ship pitched. Sweat, piss, sickness. The stench seemed to singe her nose hairs until it felt like she was breathing their misery.

They looked up when she entered, sunken-eyed, wrists rubbed raw where hemp had chewed them. Some shivered, clothes plastered to skin that hadn't been dry in days. A woman whimpered. Purdue shifted, coughing into his hands.

Lusa pressed her palm to the hatch frame. Their stares burned through her, stripping her to the bone—every face another demand she could not meet. She had fought storms. She had fought Magics. And still their eyes asked for more: air, bread, freedom. Needs that didn't end when the spell did. Caring was a different weight; no fireballs to throw at it, only a slow draining of the rest of her energy. What remained of her was little more than a husk held upright by spite and habit.

A cold, small logic slipped in where compassion had previously been. She had stepped up because it had been the only thing she could do in the moment—because the Magics had given her the means and habit had taught her to act. But the thought arrived quick as a blow: she owed them nothing. Not her life. Not her future or the small warm pulse at her chest. If she kept bleeding herself out here, there'd be nothing left to bargain with, nothing left to use to buy her way off this ship.

She stood there until the lantern flickered and the hold went back to breathing. Then she turned away and chose the living thing she could save: herself. Let them stare. Let them beg. She would give a crust where it cost little, a kindness that left her intact. Her energy, her planning, her stubbornness… those she'd turn inward. Find a way to the stern, learn who owed whom favors, pry at the captain's routes and watches. Live long enough to make a choice that wasn't just reflex. Protect when it costs little, preserve when it costs everything.

The emptiness was all consuming. She dreaded it most here, among pirates and watching eyes, because it meant no Light or Dark to wield. Only steel in her hand, if it came to that.

Her skull throbbed, but not in the way she was used to after over-exerting her powers. Her thoughts wouldn't stay where she put them. They slid off, scattered, frayed. Every time she tried to focus on one thought, it slipped away. Fog. That's what it felt like. Fog in her head, thick and shifting.

Had she eaten today? She thought so. Or maybe not.

Rain pattered, steady now, not the storm's fury but not gentle either. Sailors shouted somewhere close, or farther off, she couldn't quite tell.

Was she at the stern?

Buckets, ropes, something clattering. None of them looked at her, or if they did, she missed it. Fine. Better that way.

She kept on, legs remembering what her mind fumbled. Move with purpose. Look like she belonged to the work. The companionway was there—had it always been that close? She blinked hard.

Each step jarred her head, vision sloshing, like her skull was waterlogged. She gritted her teeth, made herself steady. They couldn't see this. Not the pirates, or Malvian. Especially not him.

The shadows below closed in. Lamp oil. Mold. The scent grounded her for a moment, and she used it, hand skimming the wall as she went deeper, away from their eyes, before the fog swallowed her whole.

The hammock caught her body as she threw herself in, swaying with the ship, a poor excuse for safety, but the only one she had. Here, at least, she could let her shoulders sag. Here, the fog wouldn't betray her to watching eyes.

She tried to plan. Think ahead. What she'd do once they made land. How to twist her bargain tighter, how to slip the pirates' grip long enough to—

Supplies. Yes, supplies first. Or was it allies? No. Supplies. Then…

Her thoughts scattered, congealed, scattered again. The prophecy crowded in, the words she'd turned over a hundred times before.

When Light and Dark as one align, the path shall wake the wrath divine.

Her breath caught. That was it. It had to be. She'd done it. Forced Them together, chained Them in balance, and the storm itself had buckled. Maybe that was it. Balance rests in one alone… her alone? The idea flashed bright before quickly dissolving, smoke in water.

What had she been thinking?

Kaden's face shoved in where it didn't belong. Steady, infuriating, telling her to trust her hands, not her head. Her pulse jumped. No—wait. She'd just had it. The answer. The piece she'd been missing.

What had it been?

The line blurred, slipped sideways, tangled with Kaden's voice, with rain and ropes and screams. She clenched her teeth, rage sparking through exhaustion. It had been right there. Clear. And now it was gone.

Lusa shook her head, as if she could knock her thoughts into place.

Bread. Bread would be good. She'd used her reagents earlier… on the captives. Fool. She should've made a loaf for herself, and now she hadn't even a spark of Magic left to conjure so much as a crust. Oh, the glory of the selflessness.

A chuckle answered her. Warm, familiar. She glanced up—and there he was, Kaden, leaning lazy against the doorframe.

"Laugh all you want, you don't get any either." She crossed her arms and shifted deeper into the hammock.

Kaden only smirked, lantern-light catching the amber flecks in his almond-brown eyes. Eyes she could drown in.

"I want blossomfire toffee," she said, tucking damp hair behind her ears, suddenly aware she must look a wreck, but Kaden didn't seem to mind.

"Rest y'er eyes, love. Toffee'll be with ya later."

Her lashes dipped. When they lifted again, the room had changed. Men swung in hammocks strung close together, boots and coats piled beneath them, snores rattling the air. Sunlight needled through the gaps in the planks above, laying thin bars across the shadows.

Lusa jolted upright, the sway of her own hammock tilting her stomach. She blinked hard, certain only a breath had passed. But the lantern was cold. The ship had stilled to the rhythm of men at rest.

Her pulse hammered, but she shoved the ghost of Kaden's voice aside. Lost time. She'd wasted it on sleep she hadn't meant to take, and there was no catching it back. Plans wouldn't make themselves. She swung out of the hammock, boots soft on the planks, and climbed for the deck.

Morning met her with a slap of unusual cold. The sky stretched wide, yellow bleeding into pale blue with thin clouds strewn like torn sailcloth. The chill stung her skin raw; her nose ached, her cheeks prickled. She drew her damp cloak tighter. Useless. Plus, her hair was still damp, and the wind teased it free, nipping at her neck until her teeth clicked together.

The ship was hushed, most men still below, only a few watchful shapes moving slow across the boards. At the prow she saw them: Malvian and Tessanee, backs to her, the girl leaning close as he pointed out toward the horizon. His voice carried low, meant for the girl's ears alone.

Lusa drifted starboard, easy, unhurried, until she reached one of the tall supports that braced the rigging. She set her shoulder against it, body angled perpendicular and half-hidden. From here she could watch them without being seen. The wind bit sharper, but she held still, breath misting as she strained to catch his words.

His voice carried on the wind, spun more like a tale than a warning.

"…the sea wyvern sleeps beneath the waves, where the light cannot reach. Its wings are vast enough to shade a fleet, its scales brighter than the coins kings hoard. Sailors say it rises when the world is out of balance, when storms grow too fierce or when the sea grows hungry. Then it climbs from the deep, and all who see it pray their ship is not the one it chooses."

Tessanee leaned forward, breath caught, as if she might glimpse the creature herself.

Against her will, Lusa's eyes searched the horizon too. The brain-fog still clung to her, thoughts softened and drifting, making it too easy to be drawn into his words. She scanned the rolling water for a crest, a shadow, anything.

Would it resemble the sand wyvern she'd faced in the canyon? Its jaws split wide, hide thick as stone? Or something worse: a beast wrought of storm and tide, vast enough to swallow ships whole? Fascination and fear blurred together. For a moment she almost forgot she was eavesdropping, caught in the spell of the story.

A throat cleared behind her. Lusa stiffened, shoulder still pressed to the post. She hadn't heard Aleric approach, but there he was, presence cold as the dawn air.

Malvian stopped. He turned, Tessanee's head swiveling with his, both of them catching sight of the captain first—and then of Lusa, standing in his shadow.

Tessanee broke from Malvian's side, darted across the deck, and wrapped her arms around Lusa's midsection.

The air caught in Lusa's lungs. Her ribs ached from the storm, her muscles heavy with exhaustion, and for a beat she forgot what to do with herself. Then the warmth of the girl's small body sank into her, easing the frost that had crept through her damp hair and chilled skin. She let herself breathe into it a bit longer than she meant to.

Aleric's boots creaked on the planks as he came nearer, glancing between them. His voice was low, rough as the sea itself, but there was something else buried in it. Something she couldn't name.

"My thanks to the mage," he said, eyes resting on her a moment too long, "and to you, Malvian. Storm near split us in two, and yet here we stand. The ship floats still. For that, you've my gratitude… and my eye."

The words were plain enough, but they sat strangely in the air—half blessing, half warning. Malvian inclined his head, unreadable. Lusa couldn't decide if she'd been praised, mocked, or measured.

Aleric turned his face toward the horizon, the wind tugging his coat. Tessanee followed his gaze and gasped, fingers tightening on Lusa's tunic.

"Look!" Her voice carried high with awe. "The wyvern—"

"It's land," Aleric cut in, though his mouth curved faint, almost like he welcomed her mistake.

Lusa squinted past the light of the rising sun. At first it was only a dark smudge against the sweep of yellow-blue sky, but then the shape sharpened: lush green hills, cliffs crouched low over the sea.

Aleric's voice carried to the few men already stirring on deck. "Our first stop. A spit of rock off the main isles, rich with fruit and roots enough to feed us, streams warm enough to wash the salt from your bones. We'll take what we need, and no more. The island's too small to matter, but it'll keep us until the next leg."

The words drew a ripple through the crew—relief, anticipation, the restless stir of men long caked in salt and stink. Even Lusa's own skin itched at the thought of fresh water, of rinsing the filth and sweat from her hair, though she'd never admit it aloud.

The word *land* rippled through the crew, stirring them like a thrown stone in still water. Men leaned from the rails, voices filled with sudden energy. Relief rolled off them in waves—relief, and something else.

Lusa's gaze caught on a pair of eyes in the throng, then another. Cren, that was what they called him, loitering near the boat hooks, thumb on a rusted clasp he should've been oiling. When her gaze snagged his, he gave a grin too knowing for a man with half his teeth, then passed the look along to another sailor down the rail. It was quick, silent, like a language she wasn't meant to read. But she read enough. They were waiting. Watching. One slip, one show of weakness, and she'd find out what pirates did to burdens they couldn't profit from.

She turned back to the horizon, forcing her focus on the blur of green cliffs rising from the sea. Land meant food, water, a chance to scrub the stink from her skin. It also meant time to recalibrate, plan, and dodge the blaming glares. Being the only mage left meant taking the blame for every storm the world spat up.

CHAPTER 32

The Darkling Prince

Malvian had always hated the sound of anchor chains. Too much clatter. Too much surrender. Chains belonged on humans, not ships. He stood at the quarterdeck rail and let his gaze drift across the deck below. Sailors hurried to swing down the longboats, oars and barrels already piled inside. Half would row for shore. Half would stay. The captives, of course, remained caged where they belonged.

Amusing, that the mage had not wasted her voice on their behalf. He had expected some defiance, some plea, the spark she squandered so freely elsewhere. Instead, silence. Calculated, perhaps. Or cowardly. Either way, it spared him the nuisance of her voice. But the question of silence was nothing compared to the other matter.

Her mind.

He had pressed again during the storm, tasting the moment her will frayed thin. He had expected the door to splinter. Instead, it held. The sting of it lingered—some strange resistance against his birthright. No mage, no human, no elf of the Aeon-born had ever stood unbroken beneath his will. Among his kind, strength of mind was measured in

Resonance—the clarity of one's thread within the Weave. His had always been near flawless, tuned to precision to secure his father's regard. And yet, this small, inconsequential mage had come out of nowhere, disrupting the perfect structure he had crafted.

Tessa, wrapped in an oilskin too large for her frame, waited by the mainmast. Her eyes flitted toward the mage as if she could not help herself.

The mage stood below near the stern rail, hands folded behind her back, braids flinging in the wind. He scowled. Tessa had insisted on braiding her hair. On making it resemble his. He hated it.

"Can I go ashore?"

Malvian tilted a glance to the human child. Her voice held no whine, only the soft edge of wanting.

"No."

"I'd stay close to the boats. Just to walk. It's green there." She pointed out toward the rocky strip of island, where scrubby palms and leafy brush pushed against the sky.

He studied her a moment. The way she rocked slightly on her heels, chewing at the inside of her cheek. Small. Fragile-looking. But there was a tenacity beneath it. Elaren used to stand like that, asking for things she was not meant to have. A ribbon. A ride. A future.

Malvian looked away. "Too many things crawl in green places."

"I'd be careful."

"I know." His tone softened, barely. "But I have seen careful corpses. You stay aboard."

Tessa's shoulders slumped, and she folded her hands into her sleeves.

He almost said more. Almost told her that keeping her close was not duty but penance. He had failed Ela, promised her the world and couldn't even keep her alive. He would not make that mistake again.

Instead, he offered, "I will bring you something sweet."

"I don't want sweet." She said it like it embarrassed her to want anything at all.

He reached out and tucked a damp strand of light brown hair behind her ear with a gentleness that surprised even him. "Then I will bring nothing. But you will still be here when I return."

From behind the mast crept the gaunt and gray-skinned Veyrin. He looked less like a Dark Elf and more like something left too long in a sickbed. Malvian's lip curled before he could stop it.

"To her quarters," he ordered flatly. "Do not leave her."

Veyrin shifted as if to speak, one hand twitching toward some pointless question or defense. Malvian's glare cut it down before breath could meet voice. He turned away. The only reason the wretch still clung to him was because his mother had insisted he bring him.

Tessa followed Veyrin. That was one thing he liked about her. No wasted breath or bluster, but obedience tempered with a quiet curiosity that had yet to get her killed.

He watched them go before turning back to the deck below, narrowing his eyes on the head of black braids. It was not fascination. No. The mage had barred him, and for that, he would unmake whatever shield she thought could hold against him.

However, he could not dismiss what he'd witnessed: the storm bending to her hand, two magics fused where they should have warred. The brilliance of magic that did not belong to a Dark Mage.

He'd seen it once before when he'd flung her into the sea, certain he was rid of her… until ordered to dive in after. He'd blamed the glow then on some rare casting, a relic of Dark Magic lost to time. Uncommon, perhaps, but not impossible. Yet no Dark Mage could wield Light—and she had.

The thought needled inward. A convergence. Two magics repelling and fusing in the same breath. Impossible by every doctrine he knew. Still, it sharpened the blade of his resolve. He would break her. Strip her mind to sinew and shadow. Uncover what she was, why she was. When he had done that, he would own her.

Satisfied for the moment, Malvian descended the slick steps with his usual grace, boots steady despite the slant of the planks. Rain clung to the railing like a reluctant memory.

As Malvian passed the galley hatch, a pair of crewmen froze mid-conversation. One held a crate of pommans. The other's blade hung too casual for galley work. They muttered something about provisions, avoiding Malvian's eyes.

A splash drew his attention toward the davits, where one of the longboats swung gently above the water. A line of crew shuffled down the narrow gangplank, barrels and nets in hand. And there, waiting her turn to board a longboat, stood the mage. Every inch of him locked in place.

She was going ashore.

He had not been informed. Not been consulted. Her stride was composed, almost regal. Shoulders back, chin high. She moved like someone who had requested passage and been granted it. A muscle in his cheek ticked once, twice, tension bleeding into his shoulders. It was not her confidence that offended him. It was that Aleric had allowed it.

The captain had been too liberal with her freedoms. She wasn't here to be coddled. She was dangerous. And if what Aleric had said was true… if her powers could be siphoned into the capstone, then sending her ashore was not shortsighted. It was reckless.

If Aleric meant to keep making decisions in shadows and offering him only the scraps of his reasoning, then he had clearly forgotten who wore the crown-blood here.

The captain stood near the davits, one hand resting on the rail as the longboat dipped toward the water. He was silent, not directing his crew, but watching. And his attention pinpointed on her… and not in a way that one watches a prisoner.

Something inside Malvian snapped. He crossed the deck in a blur of motion, boots striking wood with punishing force. Crew scattered in his wake. If Aleric noticed, he masked it well.

Malvian stopped two paces short, voice low but flint sharp. "Tell me, Captain. When did it become custom on this ship to send volatile assets ashore without informing the one holding them in check?"

Aleric did not turn but let a breath pass and Malvian could almost feel the smirk forming on the captain's mouth. "You're holding her in check?"

Malvian's fingers curled at his side. "She is unbound. Hardly watched. Powerful. And you treat her as if she has rights."

"She earned dirt under her nails and blood in her teeth after that storm. She's filthy, half-spent, and cornered by suspicion. Letting her cleanup is not a kindness. It's a calculation." He finally turned his head, face clear of any emotion. "She's less likely to explode when she feels she's gained a little dignity. Surely even you can appreciate that."

"You are playing with fire."

"I know exactly what I'm playing with." The sun caught on the silver streak threading Aleric's dark hair. His hand rested too casually on the hilt of his cutlass. "I also know what we stand to gain if she lives long enough to reach your homeland."

There it was again. That same veiled promise he had used before. Siphon. Power. Aelenth. Malvian refused to believe most of it. But he could not ignore the possibility.

"If you're so concerned she won't return, go follow her."

Malvian's eyes narrowed. "You want me off the ship."

"I want the mage to come back. Send a crewman, she'll balk. Send you, she'll behave."

Malvian saw the trap for what it was—draped in logic, baited with command. Every move Aleric made tightened around his pride like a noose. This was not about the mage's return. It was about how far Malvian would bend to keep control.

Aleric cocked his head slightly. "You do know she's been watching you just as closely?" Aleric gave the faintest smile at Malvian's silence and turned his attention back to the longboat. "She respects strength. And you've made yourself hard to ignore."

It took every shred of discipline to hold himself back. One flick of his power, and Aleric's conviction would splinter like dry kindling. But he would not. Couldn't, actually. The storm had cost him more than sweat. Too much Resonance burned away. His Seryn still reeled from the pull of wind and current, rage and restraint. And even if he had the strength...

His mouth tightened. The contract forbade it.

A clause signed in silence between his father and Aleric: no bending of will, no royal compulsion, not upon him. The one man on this ship who most deserved it was the one man his bloodline power could not touch.

And the Captain knew it. To stand before a human and feel the old restraints of the Harmonies tighten around his blood was its own humiliation. He was born to command

Resonance, not bow to it. And yet every word Aleric spoke struck the chord of obedience hammered into him by centuries of elven order.

"A quiet shadow's all she'll need," Aleric said. "Let her see you watching. Make it clear she's not as free as she thinks."

Aleric was maneuvering again. Using him. Every suggestion came dressed in logic, cloaked in reason, but beneath it all was that same rot: the captain playing puppet master with royal blood.

"This is beneath you."

"On the contrary. This is exactly where I belong."

Wind shifted, pulling at the sails and scattering the damp salt of the storm's memory. Below, the longboat had begun to push off. The mage turned her head slightly, gaze lifting—not quite toward them, but near enough that Malvian felt the attention.

"Fine. But I am not going for your benefit." He turned sharply, snapping his cloak behind him.

"I'd never assume as much."

Malvian stopped and glanced back at the captain. "And when I return, you'll tell me why a pirate shows a mage such favor."

Aleric grunted his assent, and Malvian resumed his march toward the longboat. A gust of briny wind swept across the deck, carrying the ship's collective grime.

"And Your Highness, while you're ashore..."

Malvian paused mid step, jaw clenching with restraint at the captain having to have the last word.

"You might make use of the hot springs. The crew reports the sulfur masks even the most... persistent odors."

He inhaled once, then moved on without a word. Their next exchange would not end so cleanly.

CHAPTER 33

Hunting the Mage

The longboat scraped ash against rock and grass, and Malvian stepped onto the shore. The jungle rose ahead in uneven swells, thick with shadows that writhed even without the wind. The eager crew spilled out around him, clumsy and too chaotic for his taste. Pirates, no matter how seasoned, tended to fray when land returned beneath their boots. Some hauled nets. Others checked snares long forgotten along the underbrush. A few wandered with that half-lost look he had come to expect from men who lived too long at sea.

They barked to one another in low tones, none daring to address him, let alone look his direction. One laughed too loudly. Another caught Malvian's eye and quickly busied himself with a crate. Already they looked softer here. Less dangerous. As if the moment the tide carried them from the ship's iron discipline, they had begun to unravel.

Pathetic.

He scanned the tree line for the mage, only seeing the jungle stretched wide, green smothered in grey. Leaves the size of sails shivered against the chilled breeze. The air had cooled considerably since they anchored. The sweat at the base of his neck chilled against his collar and he frowned. It had been hotter not long ago. The change unsettled him, but the weather paid him no mind compared to what the mage was doing.

He pressed inward with his Resonance, focused, searching. There. A thread of power. An echoing of rhythm pulsing faintly through the Weave. Her magic. Weak still, like the sputtering flame of a lamp long untended.

He narrowed his focus. The pulse tugged toward the far right, deeper into the trees. She was moving, then. Unwise. The island was small, answered to him, and there were few places to hide.

His boots sank slightly into wet sand as he moved, the ground still saturated from the storm. Brine clung to everything. The smell of rotted kelp, damp wood, old blood. One of the pirates gagged behind him, stumbling off toward the treeline to relieve himself. Another followed with a rusted blade, whistling. Malvian barely spared them a glance.

They would all die here if she chose it. Even now, even weakened, the mage had more power than they could comprehend. And no one seemed to grasp that but him.

Or perhaps Aleric did. Which only made it worse.

He adjusted the fall of his cloak after another frosty breeze, scanning the terrain. Broken boulders sat like half-buried skulls. Insects chattered all around, unaware of the cold that would be accosting them. She had gone where shadows thickened, and direction lost meaning. Smart. He could still track her. But smart.

A pirate muttered something about water skins. Another pirate in a stained red sash passed too close, shouldering a net of crabs. Malvian caught him by the collar before the man had a chance to flinch away.

"Where did the mage go?"

The pirate jerked against his grip; eyes narrowed under the salt-scabbed brim of his hat. "Ain't me turn ta' babysit," he said, spitting near Malvian's boots. "Cap'n said she's your problem."

Malvian's fingers tightened. He could almost feel the tug of his bloodline magic at the edge of his control, the delicious thought of hurling this insolent fool across the rocks and into the surf. One brief expenditure was all it would take.

He let go instead.

The pirate stumbled back, rubbing his neck and cursing under his breath before hurrying off toward the treeline.

Malvian dusted his hands of the man's filth and started inland. Better to conserve what little strength he had after breaking the storm. If he needed his powers to return the mage, he would not waste it here.

He stalked into the brush, boots snapping vines brittle from the sudden chill. The air no longer felt like the sea's breath. It hung in his lungs like smoke that had forgotten how to rise. As much as Malvian tried to ignore how strange the island had become since his last visit, it sat wrong with him. He shoved the concern away and focused solely on tracking the mage. He was fairly deep into the jungle when his heightened sense of hearing caught voices.

He cut through a snarl of palms and caught sight of three pirates moving too carefully through the brush, blades drawn low. Their steps were too measured for men checking snares, collecting fruit, or hunting game. They slipped out of sight between the ferns. No matter. The mage took precedence. He would not allow her to vanish into the wilds.

The jungle thinned ahead. He followed the river's curve, its crystalline waters winding between slick stones.

Somewhere beyond, water struck rock in a steady, patient rhythm. A small waterfall across the bank.

He stepped through the foliage —

And immediately stopped.

Across the river, beneath the pale curtain of falling water, stood the mage. Bare.

Her back faced him, her arms bracing against stone as the cascade broke over her shoulders. Black hair, unbound, flowed down her back. The strands clung to her skin, shadow against the pale glow of flesh untouched by sun, tracing unguarded curves that mocked his restraint. She stood as though she belonged to the jungle, without shame or fear, as if the world itself bent around her quiet defiance.

His body reacted before his mind could. Heat spread through him in a sudden rush, swift and unwelcome. He had seen plenty of females—elven, human, mage—but this struck at something he did not have words for.

She was a wretched thing. A trivial thing. Yet his gaze clung where it should not. Treacherous eyes. Disobedient breath.

Malvian turned sharply, nearly stumbling back into the trees. The memory flickered of the taste of her lips in the sea, the forced breath between them. He'd done what was necessary. Nothing more.

Pathetic. He was a son of kings, heir of shadow. He had burned armies, crushed minds, unmade men with a glance—and now here he stood, heart racing like some untried youth who'd never faced temptation.

He shook the thought off and followed the riverbend until the spring thinned into a silver thread of water. It should have steamed with heat, but the surface shimmered with cold instead—an inverted spring, warm breath turned to frost. Even the mist felt confused, coiling upward like it no longer remembered what warmth meant. Another peculiarity.

Stripping off his cloak and shirt, he crouched to dip a hand in the stream. His fingers stung, but he did not flinch. There was blood beneath his nails, salt in his hair. The residue of the storm. The residue of failure.

He scrubbed at his arms, shoulders, neck. The water refused warmth. So be it. He stood, stared at the current a moment longer, then stepped in.

The water gripped him like the frigid dead. It rose to his ribs, his throat. He sank beneath the surface and let it strip the heat from his limbs. Let it leech the want from his chest. He was not here to feel. He was here to reclaim.

She would not escape. He would not allow it. And if the memory of her skin lingered longer than it should, he would burn it away like everything else that threatened to soften him.

The current whispered through his braids. Gravel bit his knees. The forest leaned closer—green, pulsing, aware.

As he surfaced, he let the chill embrace him. For the first time in weeks, there was no stench of salt, or creak of rotting timbers. Only clean water and the hush of living things. Even the birds had gone still, as if the island itself were listening.

He reached inward, toward the lattice of power beneath his skin—the hollow where Resonance once thrived. What remained answered, sluggish but alive. He let it breathe, and the island breathed with it. Something ancient stirred beneath the roots, beneath the stones—a flicker of recognition. The forest remembered him.

Ley lines beneath the island shifted, whispering through the Capstone lattice that tethered Velkher's heart to the Aeon itself. His blood resonated with it. He held a signature of the old heirs, the first-born who could command the elements. The response came like a sigh through the soil, acknowledging its prince had returned.

Malvian sank again into the freezing current, and in the hush between breath and water, memory stirred.

A courtyard of stone. Warm wind. The scent of myrrh, copper, crushed pine—the perfume of legacy and power. His older brothers stood shoulder to shoulder, gold-threaded tunics catching sunlight. Bigger. Stronger. The games had never been fair. That was the way of things.

The housemaid knelt before them, eyes glazed, lips curved in a smile that never reached her eyes.

"How long can you hold her?" Vaelith had asked. Sorien's smirk gleamed. "Longer than you."

Malvian—no longer child but not yet forged—had not looked away. He wanted to win. To prove himself worthy. So he reached into her mind and gripped tight, listening as her thoughts dimmed beneath his will. His brothers grew tired. He pushed further. When she fell, he did not understand the sickness in his gut or the strange swirl in his chest, only that something sacred had been broken, and it was his doing. He had won. Yet the triumph felt hollow.

The memory dissolved into the reality around him. He broke the surface with a gasp, hair slick against his brow, lungs burning with earth-rich air.

He had not touched the earth like this in years. Had not let the wild fold around him, nor heard its pulse as more than background noise. His kind were born of root and rock, shaped by wind and night—Aetherealm's first heirs, before steel, before kings. But the sea had dulled that edge. The ship had caged it.

Bracing against the riverbank, he welcomed the chill sinking deeper. Though his strength had not returned, he felt more himself than he had in a long time… a creature of earth.

He drew a deep, grounding breath, then rose. Water streamed from his skin as he turned downstream toward the trace of magic he could not ignore. His soaked trousers clung to him, heavy and cold, but he did not complain. Pain was discipline. Discomfort was inheritance.

He pulled on his shirt and cloak, fastening each button with precise care, as though the ritual itself could quiet the shame along his spine.

Not for what he had seen. But for how long he had looked. A prince does not gawk. He would not make that mistake again.

By the time he returned to the falls, the mage was gone. Malvian stopped at the edge of the clearing and watched the water churn in its basin, whispering against the rocks where she had stood earlier. His jaw tightened as his gaze swept the bank for signs of her direction.

"Fool," he muttered. He had let her escape.

He scanned the trees, casting his Resonance wide, reaching for the thread of her power. It shimmered faintly—fraying, retreating. He turned west and followed it into the undergrowth, his boots silent against the loam.

She thinks to lose herself in this wild. He scoffed. *Naïve.*

Did she truly believe she could hide on an island that whispered to him? He pressed his hand to a narrow trunk, the bark cool beneath his palm. Ivy recoiled in recognition. Roots stirred beneath his feet, shy but listening. The soil hummed faintly with life—nyora beetles nestled deep, the low congested snores of glassback drakes sunning beyond the reach of canopy. Even the veltrix vines, those spiteful, sentient creepers, bowed ever so slightly as he passed.

She was in his domain now. And he would reclaim what was his.

Commotion pulled his attention to the right. A rustle too loud. A snapped branch. Voices—two, maybe three—muffled but rough and low. Not the mage.

He stilled.

Footsteps, fast and clumsy, tore through the brush somewhere behind him.

Pirates. Not careful ones either.

But the thread, her thread, was wrong.

He turned east. The signature had weakened. Flickering. Nearly gone. No longer drifting like mist but strangled. He pushed forward, leaves slapping at his sleeves. The magic led him in a half-circle through twisted boughs and waist-high ferns until the trees broke open into a clearing scarred by churned mud and shallow drag marks.

Malvian slowed.

A scuffle, maybe minutes past. The undergrowth bore signs of struggle. Boot prints. A snapped leather tie. Strands of raven hair caught in a bramble.

His gaze dropped and a few steps ahead lay a pit.

Roughly carved, half-shrouded in veltrix, wide enough to swallow a full-grown man and at least twelve virens deep.

He stepped to the edge.

There, at the bottom, lay the mage. Unmoving.

Her body curled slightly on her side, limbs slack, hair a dark spill across the leaves. One arm tucked beneath her as though instinct had tried to break the fall before consciousness failed.

Here, he could sense the faint hum of her twin-core even stronger than before. The opposing harmonies ground against each other like fault lines beneath her skin. The imbalance called to him, wrong and beautiful, and he understood then why the island had stirred. She wasn't just another mage. She was an interference in the Weave itself.

For the first time in hours, his breath stilled. Not from panic or pity. But from the clarity of knowing some pirate had dared to strike what was under his command.

And for that there would be reckoning.

CHAPTER 34

Of Serpents and Indignity

She lay still, but she was not dead. Her magic flickered faintly, weak but intact. Unconscious. Vulnerable. To be undone by a pack of gutter-born pirates. He had expected more from the last mage.

Malvian paced the rim, eyes sweeping the incline with the detachment of someone assessing a problem, not a person. Nothing usable. Or at least, nothing that did not verge on desperation or idiocy.

His Seryn pulsed unevenly, Resonance misaligned since the storm. The imbalance grated. He did not want to waste what little he had on an insolent mage who'd managed to get herself trapped in a hole.

Options without calling on his Resonance… Climbing down was possible, getting her out again, far less so. He crouched, touched the rim of the pit, and calculated the drop with narrowed eyes. The depth would not kill on impact, obviously, but probably enough to break something if mishandled. A rustling of leaves behind him and he stilled.

Beyond the fronds, a low hiss bled through the silence, followed by the shiver of brush. Something heavy and large headed his direction. Malvian stood slowly, and out of the trees slithered death wrapped in scales.

The velkrithan—a serpentine giant, scales black as wet obsidian, horns curling back from its skull like a crown forged in bone. Its eyes glowed a sickly amber. Its tongue flicked once. Twice.

Then it struck.

Malvian pivoted, powers flaring to life through his hand formation. He quickly pulled on the Pulse Harmony, where motion and will became one. A weak blast of violet force met the creature's fangs mid-lunge, sending it skidding backward with a guttural screech. It recovered fast, tail whipping hard enough to crack bark from a nearby trunk.

Malvian moved faster. Energy coalesced at his palm, fingers slicing a sigil midair. The air rippled. Vigil, a command from the Fifth Harmony, the one that spoke to living root and stone. The pull tore at his Seryn, but he held firm. One more command. That was all he'd allow himself.

The ground heeded. Vines tore upward, their movement violent and sure, echoing his command through the Weave. They slammed the serpent sideways, binding three segments of its armored length. But it still fought, fangs bared, tail whipping.

Malvian stepped in to strike again. Mistake. It lunged.

Fangs pierced his arm. Hot venom seared through him like liquid iron poured straight into the marrow. He bit back his scream and twisted, driving his other palm against its skull, releasing the full force of his Seryn in a single, violet burst. The velkrithan spasmed and collapsed.

Malvian staggered back, panting, arm dripping blood down to his fingertips.

The effects hit fast.

His vision doubled. The trees tilted as the world spun out from under him. Stumbling, his feet met air, and he fell backward into the pit. The fall stole his breath; the irony not lost on him. As earth and sky traded places, he fell for the same folly he had mocked.

He was home.

The stone beneath him was cool and familiar, veined with fire-forged minerals and softened by centuries of veltrix creeping in from the arches above. Faint light filtered down from narrow slits in the cavern ceiling, casting the glow of dawn across the obsidian floor. His room, hollowed deep within the base of Velkher's dormant volcanic heart. The familiarity wrapped its sacred cloak around his mind, and he felt himself relax. He turned his head, sluggish.

There. The carved pillars. The basin of smoked glass his father had imported from Aeonia. The scent of pine resin and rain, wafting in from the upper spires. He should not have left his bed. Not with the fever rising.

His mother had said as much, her hand brushing his brow, her voice hushed but firm: "You may not see her. Elaren's illness spreads too easily."

But he had gone anyway.

And now...

His chest ached. The edges of the world blurred. His mother's hand returned, cool against his skin.

"Ela," he whispered hoarsely, though the words came out wrong, too dry. "Stay."

The touch did not pause. It moved from his forehead to his arm. Wet. A gentle pressure. He could not smell his mother's velvet root perfume. In fact, his mother never smelled like moss and earth. The arch above him did not arch. The light did not fall right. The floor now felt as dirt, not smoothed stone.

This was not Velkher.

This was not home.

He opened his eyes… and met hers.

The mage crouched beside him, hair damp from her wash in the falls but face not clean as it should be, smeared again with the dirt of the pit's floor. She held a strip of cloth torn from her cloak, soaked with muddy water, and pressed lightly to the bite on his arm. Her brow furrowed as she focused on the wound. Her fingers were steady.

His heartbeat was not.

It slammed back into him all at once—the pit, the serpent, the strike, the fall. He tried to sit up, only to have the world tilt hard left. Gritting his teeth, he let his head drop back again, glaring at the canopy of tangled green above.

"I told you," he rasped, "you would not escape."

She didn't look at him, still focused on laying some kind of mud-leaf mixture along the punctures. He jerked his arm away from her touch, breath shallow, lips drawn tight. The movement cost him, his vision swam, but pride barked louder than pain.

"Do not touch me."

The mage sat back on her heels, wiping one hand on her trousers. Her other arm cradled against her midsection.

"You're welcome."

"I did not ask for your help."

She rose, crossing to the opposite side of the pit. "Honestly, I only did it because I didn't want to listen to you dying."

He glared, but his body sagged against the earth, traitorous in its weakness. His arm still throbbed, and an ache needled between his eyes.

"I suppose I should be thankful you landed on the other end," she continued, rummaging through the ferns. "Otherwise, we'd probably both be dead."

She returned with a handful of leaves, reached for his arm again, and he flinched so hard that a bird burst from the rim above.

"For a darkling, you sure are—"

"Finish that," he growled, "and I will forget you saved my life."

The mage stared at him a second, a possible smirk daring to form. Then, without warning, she pressed the wet leaves into his wound.

He ground his teeth at the white-hot sensation slicing down his arm. The skin was swollen, flushed an angry red, and streaked with something darker beneath.

"Lucky I remembered this root," she said, more to herself than to him. "Forsenth-something."

He found something useless to glare at, because striking her, or admitting how much it hurt, would have been a greater defeat.

She smeared the thick, bitter-smelling pulp across the wound, fingers quick, efficient. Her touch wasn't gentle. She didn't try to make it so. He closed his eyes and let out a slow, murderous breath.

"This changes nothing."

She stood, wiping her palm on her thigh, and he filed away her preference of that arm. The other remained clinging to her midsection still. The pit was wide enough for maybe ten paces across, damp as a grave, with gnarled roots crisscrossing the upper lip and water pooling near one edge. Every so often, soil crumbled from above, disturbing nyora beetles that scurried into crevices.

Malvian forced himself upright with a grunt. The mage crouched again, pulling one of the root bundles closer.

"Not likely Aleric would leave without us. Give it a few hours, someone will find the hole." She did not look at him, but he felt her words land like stones.

Us.

He almost spat.

Dragged from a jungle fight with a venomous beast, only to be rescued by the one person he'd rather see burn than bind his wound. And now he was meant to sit in a pit, bruised and humiliated, waiting like some castoff while her voice filled the silence.

"If I can recharge enough," she said, pressing two fingers to the dirt, eyes narrowing, "I might be able to lift us out with a spell. Assuming the magic holds. Which—" her lips twisted slightly "—is not exactly a guarantee."

She did not sound afraid. Simply… resigned. The same way she had spoken of poison, worked on his wound, strategized a way out. A curl of his lip betrayed him, and he turned away.

The canopy shifted, filtering shafts of dusk-gold light into the pit. A beetle scuttled across Malvian's boot. The air felt wrong. Still chilled, still off-kilter.

She crossed to the far side of the pit. Wise of her, and frankly, preferable. She remained silent, though her magic still flickered faintly under her skin like a threat that had yet to learn its place.

The mage seated herself cross-legged on the ground, spine straight, hands resting lightly on her knees. She closed her eyes and took a deep, meditative breath. She was recalibrating.

Malvian watched her through the pulsing throb in his skull. The pain had dulled, but its rhythm stayed, humming in his bones. Why heal him at all?

She could have left him to the venom. To the fall. To rot at the bottom of this pit, forgotten.

And yet, here she was. Mud on her once washed skin. Leaf paste drying on his arm. Eyes closed like she wasn't in a hole with someone who would snap her neck the moment he had gathered his strength.

His Seryn strained against emptiness. He forced his body to remain upright, resisting the pull of sleep that threatened behind his eyes. Every time he blinked, the jungle seemed to breathe differently. The walls of the pit no longer shimmered with dying light. It had grown darker. The vines heavier. The scent of wet stone and leaf mold stronger.

He set his palm to the earth. The chill sank into his bones, slow and invasive. Beneath it, deeper than soil, he felt the faint hum of the island's ley threads, the same rhythm that tethered his bloodline to the Aeon. He let his breathing fall into that cadence: inhale on the soil's rise, exhale on its retreat. Gradually, the ache behind his eyes eased.

He reached inward, coaxing what little of his power he could find to the surface. It was an ember more than a spark, the residue of Resonance left untuned too long. But as he breathed with the island, the ember caught, the first stirrings of Attunement. The hum sank beneath his skin, filling the hollow in his Seryn until it thrummed in answer to the island's pulse. Next time, he would not be caught unprepared.

The faint satisfaction of control faded as his attention drifted back to her. It made no sense. She should have let him die. But she hadn't. Which meant she had a plan—or she wanted something.

Or worse, maybe it was mercy. Unpredictable, without reason or strategy… and that was far more dangerous than intent.

CHAPTER 35

The Breaking Point

The silence had stretched long, broken only by breath and the slow return of power. He'd spent it the way a prince should—rebuilding, reclaiming, while the mage across from him did the same in her lesser way.

The sun's faint light barely reached the back of her half of the pit now, her figure a silhouette. Malvin went to close his eyes again only to jerk his head upward at a scuffle.

Foliage shifted. Branches creaked. A familiar, congested growl rippled through the twilight canopy, followed by the rasp of something heavy moving through underbrush.

Then silence.

Then—

A hiss that clicked on the edges of speech. A shadow moved above, tail lashing behind it like a whip of glass.

The mage's eyes snapped open. She rose in one fluid motion, already facing the sound. Her fingers twitched once at her sides, magic responding as a pressure shift in the air.

The creature stepped forward. A glassback. It was a long, lithe reptile gleaming with plates of translucent armor that shimmered faintly in the dying light. Its limbs were thick;

claws curved for climbing. Pale eyes blinked down at them with cold, hungry interest. It prowled the rim of the pit, sniffing the air.

The mage only waited, eyes following its every move.

The drake paused, tilted its head as its eyes focused on her, before it lifted its snout and let out a low, echoing set of clicks.

Malvian's jaw tightened. "She just called her pack."

"Of course she did." The mage's voice was dry as bone. But something in the air changed. The vines near her feet recoiled slightly, as if the earth itself sensed what was brewing beneath her skin.

He felt it, too.

Not the darkness that marked her. No—this was deeper. A split in the natural order. The image struck him again, of her twisting dark smog and silver light together, and of her beneath the waves, cocooned in a glowing sphere.

Dark magic did not glow.

This mage was a convergence. A weapon born of two opposing truths. A convergence would pull at the Capstones like a key against a lock.

Suddenly, she turned, as if sensing his scrutiny. Her iron-blue eyes fixed on him. He looked away too fast, breath catching. His mind betrayed him—flashing not to the magic, but to the memory of her beneath the waterfall. Skin pale as moonlight. Unmarked. Unclaimed. The image burned, shameful and vivid. He grit his teeth, willing the image away.

When she returned her focus to the rim, he watched again. The amulet at her chest pulsed—soft at first, then brighter. She lifted her arm.

Malvian sat up with a wince. "What are you doing?"

But it was already too late.

A flash of lightning cracked from her fingers, slamming into the drake. It fell with a heavy, twitching thud. Dead.

"Idiot," he hissed, forcing himself to his feet. "This will only enrage them."

She looked at him, expression blank—yet something simmered in her gaze now. A dark glint, as black as his own.

"You're just planning to remain helpless, huh?"

The provocation worked. His composure snapped, power flaring to his fingertips in a violent rush.

Naïve mage. This island bends to me.

With a curl of his finger, veltrix erupted from the walls, writhing and lashing around her, binding her arms. A cry broke loose as the arm she'd not favored was yanked against stone. Vines snapped taut around her legs, crossing her chest, pinning her hard to the wall. The earth itself claimed her.

One vine struck her head, tearing free something that glinted silver in the moonlight

And then—

Her mind opened to him. Wide. Unguarded. Resonance flared through his Seryn and bled into her with his seal of the Crown Harmony—forged when one mind subdued another. The thin trail of his violet light seared across her brow, shaping into a sigil that pulsed once before fading into her skin. A mark of command. He stepped into her mind like a predator into a sanctuary…

and immediately regretted it.

Overwhelming amounts of sound, scent, and light rushed him. The Dark Magics didn't escape so much as expand, pouring through him like a second bloodstream gone rabid. Voices shrieked in a hundred tongues. Sentience consumed his connection, wild and feral, devouring his focus.

A storm of thoughts that were not hers. Were not sane. He could barely breathe, barely think.

Malvian fought to contain them, to box them in—his Resonance straining to silence the chaos. He wove the strongest mental bind he could manage, locking the voices away. The sigil at her forehead flickered, answering the strain in his Seryn. It anchored his will to hers, a dangerous bridge, feeding on the friction between his Resonance and her pulsing twin cores. His strength swelled, somehow amplified by the unnatural harmony of their opposing magics.

But the box would not hold long. He felt it. The walls already thinning, the pressure building. He did not care. All he could think of was her mind—so carefully walled off, so infuriatingly out of reach— now split wide, laid bare. It was... exquisite.

He did not need to touch her to feel it. Her magic smelled of ozone and lavender ash—thick, humming, strange. And beneath, Dark and Light cores that should not coexist.

Standing in the wreckage of her unshielded mind, there was no denying it. She was not just a dark mage, but something else entirely. Something new.

And he had her.

The vines obeyed, slithering off her as if peeling from stone. Slowly, by his will, they released her so she could stand. And stand was all he would allow her to do. He held her mind like glass in his hand and he almost smiled at his victory.

Malvian stepped closer, pain forgotten. The jungle was alive above them, but he heard nothing beyond her shallow breath. She did not fight it, which thrilled him more than it should have.

He whispered through his Seryn.

Step forward.

She did.

And another step.

Her legs moved not of their own volition, but because he willed it. The subtle flex of muscle, the brush of her heel through the mud, the rise of her chest—he owned it all. The power of it sang through him like wine. Intoxicating. He could do anything now. Strip her mind clean. Have her speak every secret. Command her to dance, to kneel, to choke.

He could kill her with a thought.

His foot shifted forward. The gap between them narrowed. She was close enough that he could see the cloud of her breath, the faint rise of gooseflesh along her arms. Ideas whispered against the edges of his mind: *She is yours. Yours to bend. Yours to break.*

He could touch her. Taste her. Take her.

The image slipped passed his control—her in the falls, bare, skin white where the sun had never touched. He remembered the way her legs had disappeared beneath the water, the graceful dip of her neck, the curve of her spine. Heat surged where discipline should have lived.

Her earthy scent reached him, and desire knocked him sideways. He had never felt anything like it. Not in the rites. Not even in the maid's mind. This was no longer domination. It was hunger. It tightened low in his gut, tugging at what he'd thought long since forgotten.

A pulse fluttered at the base of her throat. He could see the trace of spring water on her skin, muddied and bruised, yes, but still burning with a life that tempted ruin. He allowed her breath to escape in a faint exhale, stirring the air between them.

And her eyes…

He blinked. They were not wide with panic, nor empty and glazed with submission as they should be. They shimmered, bright and defiant beneath the weight of his compulsion.

It enraged him.

It fascinated him.

No one endured him like this. For a century, he'd watched minds soften, that last spark of self extinguish beneath his will. But hers…

Hers burned brighter. Angrier.

His gaze trailed over her lips, chin, neck, the hollow of her collarbone. A quiet rage clung to her, wrapped in trembling flesh. Her body yielded; her spirit did not.

That defiance drew him closer.

Dryness seized his mouth. Heat curled through his chest, foreign and unwelcome. She was his prisoner, his puppet—so why did she feel like chaos made flesh, draped in desire?

A breath apart, her chest rose, lips parting at his command. His hand found her chin, jerked her forward until her breath ghosted against his mouth.

For an instant, she resisted—barely a shift, a tremor at the edge of his will—but he felt it. Every muscle in her strained against him, silent, desperate, finally fighting the command with everything she had left. She would willingly burn through her cores than yield to him, even if it left her hollow, broken.

Her eyes glistened, and a single tear slipped free.

He didn't understand why it broke his focus—only that it did. In his distraction, the barrier splintered. The box shattered. The feral voices of the Dark Magics tore loose, roaring through his mind. They clawed into him, wrenching open every corridor of power he'd spent years containing. Twisting buried memories. Laughing. Flooding him with their invasive chaos.

Pain speared through his skull. Blood welled and slid from his nose. He staggered back, clutching his head as his vision split in two. The hunger, the heat, the illusion of control… all of it ripped away in the pulse of his own undoing.

His strength was spent, reserves gutted by this mage he'd tried to break. He could barely stand, much less command, so he let her go.

She only stood there, chest rising unevenly, mouth parted but silent. No longer bound by his will but perhaps paralyzed by what almost was. In that tense silence, he saw her—nothing of race or blood, only the person beneath.

The mud on her skin. The tremor in her body. The wild pulse at her throat. A strand of hair, loose and matted with earth, clung to her scarred cheek. Her eyes met his, a mixture of shock and fury. There was fragility there, yes, but woven with something stronger, something that refused to disappear even when broken open.

She no longer resembled some inconsequential mage, an annoyance he'd been forced to keep in check. The shift was subtle, almost imperceptible, yet it left something unsteady in its wake. The world suddenly did not feel divided between captor and captive. It felt level. And it terrified him.

Malvian dragged a breath through his teeth and looked away, as if sheer will could shove the thought into some corner of himself that would never see light again. His fingers struck a formation, and the silver hairpin tore free of the mud, flying into his grasp.

He needed control. Something to command, or something that obeyed. The pin would do. More gently than he intended, he stepped forward and slid it back into her hair. The air stilled. Her Magics recoiled, muted and contained. His hand hovered a moment too long near her hair.

He told himself it was to ensure the ward held, not because the sight of her stirred something he did not recognize and would refuse to. He withdrew without a word. Nothing could undo what almost happened, and her burning gaze felt earned.

Malvian sat in the pit like a prince among rubble, his back against the cool earth, shirt damp and clinging. He stared ahead, past her, ignoring the constant throb in his shoulder. The jungle breathed above them, cold, rich with the stink of loam and drake blood. Night had not fully fallen, but the shadows had deepened, and the sky overhead wore a bruised hue.

The mage watched too long, still standing in the same place he had left her. He was tempted to say something but dismissed the idea before it could fully form. Eventually, she moved. Slow steps backward, eyes locked on him until distance offered the illusion of safety. She sank to the ground, spine rigid, injured arm cradled, and at last, her gaze broke away. Her fury, however, remained. He could feel it radiating across the space between them, seething.

His own power was still rebuilding, threads of Resonance crawling sluggishly back into place. Beneath the dull thrum, he sensed hers had fallen even lower… barely there. Strange, seeing as she had spent so much time meditating. Unless…

That was the reason her eyes had not dulled. Though he had locked away her Dark Magic, the Light still remained. He dropped his gaze to the amulet—that curious, faintly glowing stone nestled against her chest. Her Source, he was now certain. The conduit through which she wielded her monstrous gift without incantations.

They stayed like that until the moon had drifted to the other side of the pit. Malvian sifted through everything he'd learned of… Lusa. He had seen inside her, and what he found was not just power, but resistance. Survival, razor-sharp and threadbare, as if she had been holding back the flood for years and only now realized she was drowning.

The Magics—those voices, those things—were not separate from her. They were woven into her. They whispered always. She fought always. It was not control she wielded. It was containment. He wondered how long she could keep it up.

A branch cracked above them.

Lusa tensed, head lifting, eyes narrowing toward the canopy. He felt it too. The shift in the air, the hiss of breath not shaped for language.

The drakes.

Malvian pushed to his feet, muscles protesting, every nerve still alive with venom's residue. His cloak hung half askew, his shoulder throbbed, but his mind was clear. Lusa also rose, slower but ready. Leaves rustled. A low growl rolled over the rim.

And suddenly, the snap of a branch. A howl of pain, followed by a whimper and a thud. And then… voices. Men's voices. Familiar ones. Steel against scale. The twang of crossbows. A shadow crossed the pit's edge, and Aleric's scowling face appeared. Relief flickered there, unguarded for half a breath, before the mask returned. He barked orders. Ropes dropped.

Malvian moved first, reached for the rope, but stopped. After a measured breath, he gave the rope to Lusa, convincing himself it was strategy, not penance. She was clever. Dangerous. When her strength returned, she would not let this go unchallenged. The last thing he needed was her at his back.

Lusa grabbed it with her good arm and looked directly at him. A promise held in those fierce blue eyes. This was not over.

CHAPTER 36

Truth and Retribution

The longboat scraped the hull. Lines dropped, pulleys groaned, and the crew hauled them back aboard. Malvian stepped onto the deck first, boots steady despite the ship's rock. The mage followed, shouldering past him without looking back. He did not need to see her face to know what lived there. Hatred rolled off her in waves, so thick he could taste it. But there was nothing she could do about it. Not yet anyway. Her magic was guttered, little more than a dying ember. He could feel her residue in his mind, and beneath it, the echo of the Dark Magics.

The night air was frigid, filled with sweat and filth from the captives below. Lanterns swung with the roll of the sea, spilling fractured light across faces too cautious to meet his eye. Every breath of the ship seemed to wait for someone else to speak first.

Aleric's gaze swept the deck before landing on Malvian. "What happened?"

Malvian's lip curved in a humorless smile. "Your men set quite the trap. Shame they forgot to tell you." He kept Lusa in his peripheral vision, noting how she hadn't moved far from the center of the deck, back to them.

The men nearby stilled. Malvian watched, mildly entertained, as they exchanged nervous glances.

"Find out who's responsible," Aleric growled. "And if I don't have names by dawn, I'll hang three of you at random to remind the rest what loyalty means."

The deck stiffened. Men barked hurried orders, scrambling to look useful, to look blameless. Fear made them quick, not careful.

Malvian observed the chaos with detached interest, as one might study the spread of infection. Aleric's theatrics would yield noise, not answers. Pirates were creatures of impulse—able to grasp only what could be held or silenced with a blade. To them, the mage was a threat to be cut away, not an investment the captain had spared for purpose.

He let his Seryn brush the deck of men, enough to listen for guilt in the rhythm of their breath. He marked the faces worth remembering and would handle them in time. Quietly. Thoroughly. If anyone was to teach her what pain meant, it would not be a pirate suffering delusions of adequacy.

"Amusing, isn't it?" Malvian murmured. "You hang one, the rest grow bold enough to wonder who's next. Fear is a poor leash, captain."

Aleric turned on him, eyes narrowing. "To my quarters," he said, sweeping his arm in a mocking imitation of courtly grace. "After you, your Highness."

Malvian almost smiled. The gesture was so transparent it was nearly endearing. Let him play at command. He followed, the deck shifting slightly as they crossed toward the stern.

The captain's quarters were dim, smelling of salt and lamp oil. Charts sprawled across the desk, a dagger driven through one corner to hold it down, an inkwell at the other.

Aleric shut the door behind him as Malvian leaned against the map table, letting his silence do the work. He watched the captain circle like a wolf trying to convince itself it was the alpha.

"Since you seem to know my ship better than I do—what would you suggest?"

"Precision," Malvian answered easily. "A disease is not cured by cutting off the hand. It spreads from the blood."

"You forget whose ship you stand on."

"Hardly. I am merely reminding you it still floats because I've not decided otherwise."

An ugly silence pressed between them. He wondered if Aleric even understood the scale of what he carried… the thin thread between obedience and mutiny, between him and a prince who would slit a god's throat if it pleased him. Aleric's mouth twitched—something between irritation and reluctant respect.

"Stay out of my discipline, elf," he said.

Malvian's smile returned, thin and cold. "Then keep your men from forcing me to exercise it."

The pirates who lured Lusa to that pit belonged to him now. And he would break them before the captain ever laid a hand.

"I want truth, captain." Malvian folded his arms. "This fixation of yours… it is not just the capstones. You guard her as though she were more than a pawn."

"She is leverage," Aleric said evenly. "That is all."

Malvian let the silence stretch again. He studied the captain's face, every line, every twitch. Aleric was cunning, but no mask was perfect. He grabbed his glass, poured in some amber liquid and took a slow sip, peering at Malvian over the rim. There, at the corner of his mouth, a ghost of something softer.

"You—"

A shout from outside interrupted him, followed by a muffled thud, a scuffle, some yelling. Malvian and Aleric exchanged a look. Aleric's glass struck the table hard as he abandoned the drink. Both men moved at once, threw open the door—

And froze.

The deck was a battlefield.

Lusa stood at its heart, a cutlass swinging in the air as she drove back three men at once. Her hair whipped around her face, black and wild in the wind. The sound of steel on steel sang through the night.

Malvian felt it before he understood it. The violent impact of her power scraping against the edges of his mind. She was spent but burning, her emotions flayed raw. Not fury. Not madness. Retribution. She was chaos made flesh, and he had helped shape it. Watching her now felt less like rebellion and more like recognition… an echo of his own powers gone unchecked.

Her feet slipped in blood and saltwater, but she moved with the reckless precision of someone who had already accepted pain as the price of purpose.

"By the Abyss…" Aleric breathed beside him, awe laced with something dangerously close to concern.

Lusa's cutlass arced again, catching the light. One pirate fell, clutching his bloodied arm. Another stumbled backward into the mast, fear plain in his eyes. She moved without grace, without form. Instinct sharpened to survival. A knee to the gut. An elbow to the jaw. They would all be dead by now if it had been her Magics instead of the cutlass.

He caught movement behind the forward mast. Tessa crouched there, eyes wide at the madness unfolding. Malvian opened his mouth to order her below—

"Hold!" Aleric's bellowing command worked.

Lusa turned and her eyes found them.

The deck fell silent except for the groans of injured men and the hiss of the sea. She stood panting, hair tangled, blade trembling in her grip—but her gaze burned through him.

Something twisted low in Malvian's chest. Her expression was no longer shock or confusion but cold, volcanic wrath given form. The Dark Magics stirred beneath her skin. Her eyes inked over, black bleeding outward until nothing white remained. He felt the pressure of her intent before she even moved.

A sharp yelp to his right.

Lusa's head snapped toward the sound. Malvian's pulse hammered as he felt the spell gathering on her lips, the last scrap of her strength drawn tight. If not for the interruption, the ship would have burned from keel to mast. And part of him thrilled at the thought.

"Enough," Aleric growled.

Malvian looked to the captain holding Tessa by the shoulder, blade pressed to her throat. It was she who had cried out.

Malvian's vision went red. The world narrowed to the trembling child—Elaren's ghost reborn—and to Aleric, using her as leverage.

Before reason could intervene, he lifted his will into the Crown Harmony and raked it across the tether of their bargain. Breaking it in spirit, if not in word, Malvian unleashed the tide of his bloodline power into the captain's mind.

Release her.

Aleric stiffened. His cheek ticked and the blade lowered, the girl stumbling free. Malvian meant to withdraw, but the bond turned on him, ripping open what should have stayed buried.

Images flared:

A toddler on a forest's edge, sunlight raking through her dark hair. Her small hand clutching a silver compass. Eyes, bluer than sky, lifting toward him. Toward Aleric.

He knew those eyes. The child was Lusa.

He staggered back, air stinging his lungs. Hatred and revelation twisted together—two poisons made indistinguishable.

So that was it. She was Aleric's daughter. Whether his dealings with the Aelenth held truth or not, Malvian could no longer trust the man.

Aleric blinked, realization darkening his gaze… the contract had been broken.

At the same time, Lusa's focus shifted to the captain. Her chest heaved, lips curling into something malevolent. Her fingers straightened with the charge of a spell that would burn the ship, and everyone in it, to ash.

Fool mage.

Malvian drew on what little remained of his strength, dropped into Vigil, and let the ship's bones answer. A barrel tore free of its moorings with his command, flew across the deck, and struck her square in the temple. Her body pitched sideways, crumpling to the planks, and the cutlass clattered away.

The crew stared. Tessa whimpered against the rail. Aleric's sword had already vanished into its sheath as he hollered orders to drag the men back into line and bring him the mage.

Malvian steadied his breathing, drawing discipline over the wreckage in his chest. Rage and exhaustion blurred together until only restraint kept them from spilling outward.

He had crossed a line tonight. Not in defying the Captain—but in himself.

His father had built a kingdom on the certainty that power must be owned or erased. That anomalies were rot.

That mercy was inefficiency dressed in sentiment. Malvian had accepted that logic all his life because it worked. Because it made him strong.

And yet the mage had stood at the heart of the storm and refused to become either weapon or ruin.

The realization sat wrong. Dangerous. If his father learned what she truly was, there would be no study, no patience, no question of worth. Only consumption.

Whatever came next, he would not allow his father, nor the crown that bound him, to dictate when her truth was exposed. Timing was power. And power was his to wield.

The crew moved again, slow and careful, as though even breath might rouse her. The ship strained toward order. Ropes were drawn taut, and waves slapped against the hull… but the rhythm rang different. Malvian could feel the shift.

He could taste the metallic echo of her power on the back of his tongue—brilliant, ruinous, alive. She lay there, hair veiling her face, the faintest rise of her chest betraying death. He almost reached out to confirm she was actually breathing, but he stopped. Curiosity, he told himself. Nothing more.

But the memory of the pit pressed close. The heat of her breath, the raw want that had nearly driven him past reason. He told himself he had stopped because control was his nature. He refused to be ruled by impulse. Weakness. Yet even now, staring down at her motionless form, he could not quite silence the question of what would have happened if he hadn't.

As he turned his attention back to the crew, to Tessa, he mused on his earlier realization. The equation had definitely changed now, and he could not see where the balance would fall. This Lusa had become an unsolvable anomaly he was determined to master.

It took longer than it should have to calm her.

Tessa had gone still only after the fourth time he'd sworn the captain would not touch her again and that the mage would be okay. Even then, her quivering lip refused to stop. So, he stayed, crouched beside her pallet, voice low as he drew on a memory from a life that felt half a world away.

"My mother used to tell Elaren this one," he said. "When storms frightened her."

Her wide hazel eyes blinked up at him, glassy and uncertain.

"It is the tale of Thalara. The last of the Three," Malvian began. "Eldere made the light. Sardan, the dark. And Thalara… she walked the space between. She was meant to keep them in balance, but the gods grew jealous of what she could create from both. So, when they warred, she tore the world apart to stop them."

Tessa's lashes fluttered, the rhythm of his voice pulling her closer to rest.

"They say she knelt where the sea met the earth and drove her hands into the ground. Her touch split the continent. Mountains rose, waters roared, and the two halves drifted apart. The wound became the Strait of Thalara. And when it was done, she was gone. Her body, scattered across the lands. Her magic, woven through the air we breathe."

Tessa's small voice broke through, barely a whisper. "Did she die?"

Malvian hesitated, closed his eyes, replayed the image of his mother at Elaren's bedside. "No. She became what she'd made. The stillness between things. The quiet before dawn, the breath between heartbeats. That's Thalara's gift. To remind the world that balance always demands loss."

The girl's breathing slowed. Her hand unclenched against the blanket, her eyes finally too heavy to fight. The old tale sat with him, soft as the ghost of his mother's voice: *All power divides, but only sacrifice can keep it whole,* she'd said.

He sat there a while longer, elbows resting on his knees, fingers steepled against his mouth. The lantern swayed with the ship's motion, casting long shadows across the walls. Every groan of timber reminded him who slept, and drank, on the other side of that wall.

The calm he'd borrowed from the story began to dissolve, replaced by something darker. The more he stared at the lamplight, the more it felt like mockery… too warm for the cold that had taken root in his chest.

He rose, careful not to wake her. The air moved with him, rippling faintly as if recognizing the shift in his intent. He draped his cloak across the edge of her pallet, watching the soft rise and fall of her breathing one last time. Then he turned toward the adjoining door. The latch clicked beneath his hand, and he opened without a knock.

Aleric sat behind his desk, sleeves rolled, a half-empty glass of amber liquor catching the light. His expression did not change when Malvian entered, though his jaw worked once before he spoke.

"I wasn't going to hurt her."

Not an apology. A statement.

Malvian stopped inside the doorway. The latch clicked shut behind him. The lantern between them hissed faintly, its flame waving in the draft that followed him in.

If his power had not been drained to dust, Aleric would already be on his knees. His mind flayed open. His heart clutched in invisible fingers until it forgot how to beat.

Instead, Malvian stood perfectly still, his fury precise and soundless, the kind that filled a room without needing words. The air tightened, aware of him, the flame in the lantern drawing smaller as if the ship itself understood the danger of testing his restraint.

He moved closer. "You drew a blade on her."

"Lusa was losing control." Aleric's voice was almost weary. "I thought she had nothing left to give."

"You gambled on that."

"I calculated it."

"Call it what you like," Malvian said low, leaning forward until he met the captain at eye-level. "If I ever sense her fear again… if I so much as smell it in the air, you'll beg for the mercy I won't grant."

The captain's glass stopped midair. A slow muscle twitched along his temple. "You care too much for what isn't yours."

Malvian's mouth almost curved. "And you care too little for what is."

Confusion flickered in the captain's eyes before shifting to understanding. The color drained from his face.

Malvian straightened, the shadows bending subtly toward him, answering a power that hadn't yet returned but remembered him all the same. The ship shifted beneath them, creaking against the tide.

Aleric poured what remained of his drink, the amber liquid catching light as he swirled it once before speaking.

"We're nearing Velkher. You might consider what tale you'll feed your father when we dock."

"My father does not eat tales," Malvian said coolly. "He devours results. And he will expect proof that the Dreadstar's promises for the Aelenth were not pirate superstition."

"Then he'll have it," Aleric replied. "The mage lives. That's proof enough."

Malvian's gaze darkened. "Alive is not the same as contained. You saw what she did tonight. Imagine that unleashed in the king's sanctum, or near a ley line. If she breaks control before the siphoning begins—"

"She won't," Aleric said evenly.

"You cannot know that."

"I can." Aleric paused, some memory surfacing that darkened his features. Malvian watched, curious to what attachment the captain had for her since he had not outright claimed her as his child.

"Because she's survived everything meant to end her. Her mother's madness. The Empire. You." He met his eyes while licking any remnants of his liquor from his lips. "If she's still breathing after all that, it's because fate hasn't finished using her yet."

"You speak like a believer, captain. Dangerous habit for a man who serves King Draevyn."

"I serve his purpose," Aleric said. "And if that purpose means ridding the world of magic, I'll see it done."

Malvian's mouth curved, but not in amusement. "Even when the purge burns what little you have left to ash?"

"Magic took my wife," Aleric said, voice dark. "It can take everything else, and I'll still sleep easier for it."

Malvian considered him quietly. "So that's what drives you. Not loyalty. Not duty, but vengeance painted in royal colors."

"Call it what you like." Aleric lifted his glass and finished the contents.

Malvian leaned closer. "And what of the mage?"

Aleric's jaw tightened. "She's part of the plan."

"She's an anomaly," Malvian corrected. "And anomalies do not survive long in my father's hands. You of all men should know that."

"She'll serve her purpose," Aleric said, the words a weapon against himself. "And when it's done, maybe the world will finally have peace."

Malvian tilted his head slightly, reading him, weighing him, the way a wyvern studies another predator to decide which will break first. "You speak of cleansing as if it were mercy," he said softly. "But mercy is not something you've ever had much practice with, is it?"

Aleric's smile went thin and brittle. "Nor you."

He slid his glass away, glancing towards his chamber. Malvian followed his focus, noting Lusa laying there in the captain's bed, asleep.

"When we reach Velkher, my father will demand proof of her worth." He turned back to the captain and straightened.

"And you?" Aleric asked, voice calm, though the tremor in his fingers betrayed him. "What will *you* do when she stands before him?"

Malvian regarded him for a long moment, the faintest smile ghosting across his face.

"I will deliver what the crown demands."

Not what it deserves, nor understands.

Aleric's eyes narrowed. "And if command becomes cruelty?"

"It would not be my cruelty to question."

Before Aleric could reply, a shout came from the deck above—something about the winds shifting, sails catching. The ship had begun to move. The captain hesitated before turning toward the door.

"We'll finish this when we hit the mainland," he said, and strode out.

The door closed with a solid thud, leaving the room steeped in quiet. Malvian stood where he was, the faint tilt of the floor beneath his boots proof that they were already underway. He listened until the echo of Aleric's steps was gone.

He'd been consumed by the captain's maneuvering, by Tessanee's safety and what she represented—a debt, a promise, a complication. Only now, in the hush that followed, did he truly move towards what Aleric had left behind.

Lusa.

The cabin itself was stripped of warmth—charts nailed to the wall, an oil lamp wavering against the salt wind coming in through the port window. She looked wrong in it, emptied of the fiery determination that typically sat in her features, sleeping like someone who had burned herself hollow and survived anyway. That alone made her dangerous.

His gaze slid to the amulet on her chest, rising and falling with the slow rhythm of breath. He knew better than to touch it. Knew the rules carved into every text on magecraft. Yet curiosity, like pride, was a flaw he rarely fought.

He reached out and brushed the crystal with his fingers. A sharp jolt struck through him and heat knifed through his skin, precise as judgment. He hissed, yanking his hand back and sucked away the heat. Pain tingled through his fingertips as if the amulet had branded him for daring. Foolish. He should have expected no less.

He shook out his hand and studied her face again. The stubborn set of her lips that refused to relax even in sleep, the faint scar along her cheek. His hand lifted, tracing the air above the mark without touching. The motion steadied him. Reminded him what control felt like.

Outside, Aleric's voice carried through the walls, not a trace of the conflict that had shadowed him moments ago. Malvian didn't trust it. Aleric was many things, but predictable was not one of them. The man's loyalty had begun to fray the instant Lusa's secret came to light, he could sense it.

He drew a measured breath and folded the disorder back into place. Once they reached Velkher, he would place Tessanee safely in his villa, somewhere untouched by the currents already shifting beneath his feet.

As for the mage…

That question did not need answering yet. Truth ripened best under pressure, and his father had never been swayed by speculation. Malvian turned away, refusing the temptation to look back at her, and let the future remain unwritten—for now.

The corridor beyond was colder. He passed the small door to Tessanee's quarters without slowing. She would sleep. She was safe. That was enough. What waited beyond dawn was not.

Malvian climbed the narrow stair to the upper deck. Night pressed close, salt-heavy and still. Velkher loomed far off—a black seam on the horizon where sea and sky conspired. Somewhere ahead, his father's court waited, hungry for proof. For results. For her.

He told himself that was all this unease was. Anticipation. Duty. But as he looked west, the wind shifted, carrying a pulse of power so faint it might have been imagined. It hummed beneath his skin, familiar, taunting. Home awaited him.

Below, the tide dragged hard against the hull, straining as if resistance alone might change the ending. Malvian almost envied that illusion.

CHAPTER 37

Silver Tongues and Hidden Blades

Aeonians had always been proud and golden, but pride couldn't fill grain bins. Lady Ice had slipped through the carved spires and into the veins of every councilor's hand, a freezing presence even fire couldn't banish. The braziers burned low. Smoke and frost clung to the air, and beneath the scent of pine lingered the quieter reek of desperation.

Kaden stood within that brittle warmth as the outsider wrapped in borrowed fur. The chamber was different than the last time he'd stood before the crown. The walls bore not banners but maps and ledgers, and every face around the king's table shared the same weary expression: nobles trying to hide how close the cold had crept into their bones.

He could feel eyes track him—half-curious, half-predatory. It had been weeks since his last summons, weeks since anyone had so much as looked at him without agenda. He cleared his throat.

"Your Highnesses," he began. "We stand at a turnin' point. The disturbances in Izier aren't isolated."

He let that hang, scanning the council before finishing. The royal family sat on the other side of the table, two groups of counselors on either end. His gaze caught on

Caelithia, standing with the counselors nearest Laerynth's side of the table. Her silvery eyes watched him with the poise of someone already preparing to dismantle whatever he said next.

He hesitated. The words he was about to speak would ruffle every silk sleeve in the room. But holding his tongue had never saved anyone before.

Drawing in a small breath, he began, "Someone's tamperin' with the ley lines."

The high counselors shifted. Some remained cautious, others too smug for his liking. Doubtful mutterings passed among them. Someone was more than likely buying loyalty here. Maybe more than one someone. But that wasn't proof he could point to, and proof was all this court cared about.

King Theron's head lifted from the ledgers in front of him, looking at Kaden from under his heavy crown. The circles under his eyes spoke of sleepless nights, of rations divided too many ways.

"You are certain?" he asked with the fatigue of a man still trying to hold his kingdom together.

"I am," Kaden said. "It isn't just Aeonia sufferin' anymore. Recent messages say Izier's fields are just as frostbitten, the rivers thick with ice. Somethin's drainin' the life clean outta the realm."

Caelithia inclined her head. "The ley lines are constant. The capstones endure. Winter is not proof of tampering."

Another councilor nodded, adding, "We do not disregard your concerns lightly. We've seen many supposed crises come and go. Without clearer proof, it would be unwise to act in haste."

Kaden bit back the urge to sigh.

Queen Valenne adjusted the fur lining her cloak, the intricate braids of her pale orange hair holding her crown perfectly in place.

"You imply sabotage," she said arrogantly, eyes fixed on the map spread before her. "That would mean intent."

Laerynth shifted his cane, its tip tapping once against the chilly floor. "If intent were the cause, we would have evidence by now. What we have is panic, and panic makes fools of even the most loyal."

At the end of the table, Vaelar gave a faint scoff, strawberry-silver hair catching the faint light. "He speaks as if we've never seen a hard season before. Aeonia endures. We always have."

Eldarion, seated beside him, leaned forward with a frown. "Enduring doesn't mean ignoring."

Between him and Lorenthar, who bookended their group, the princess jumped in. "Ambassador Kaden has ridden the border roads himself," she said, a touch too fast. "If he says other realms are suffering, perhaps we should listen first and decide after."

Siraen had stressed the title *ambassador*. A not-so-subtle reminder to the room that Kaden wasn't some foreign vagabond, even if his rough dialect said otherwise. He briefly caught her eye, inclining his head in gratitude. Her expression softened into something shy, almost proud.

Sighing, Eldarion sat back and steepled his fingers. "If something truly is affecting the ley lines, the consequences would reach far beyond the frost. The realm's balance depends on them."

Lorenthar spoke at last, the only royal not wearing a crown. His tone was calm but edged. "Tampering of that scale would require access," he paused to smell his wine. "And knowledge. Neither of which lie beyond Aeonia's borders."

That earned a stir.

"You expect someone within our own court?" asked the King.

Before Lorenthar could answer, Laerynth leaned forward, smooth as ever. "My lord means to suggest caution, not accusation. Let us not turn inward when we already stand beset by hunger and fear."

Kaden's jaw tightened and he looked at Lorenthar, who only offered a tip of his goblet and a smile in his eyes. He knew a redirect when he heard one. He planted a hand on the map, letting his gloved finger drag a slow line between the capstones of Aeonia and Izier.

"You can call it fear, or coincidence, but the lines can't lie."

More whispers now, less of that smug certainty. Maybe he was finally cracking through all that silk and ceremony. Theron's council was split between his own loyalists and Laerynth's protégés.

The groan of the gilded doors behind him drew the court's attention. An attendant entered and bowed low, the chill from the corridor following him.

"Forgive the interruption, Your Majesties," he said, his voice edged with caution. "An envoy from Izier requests immediate audience on matters of the realm's welfare."

A current of murmurs followed. Queen Valenne's eyes flickered with a trace of concern, while Laerynth remained impassive, his gaze resting coolly on the attendant.

King Theron hesitated. "This council is private."

Princess Siraen spoke up, the fur of her lowered hood brushing against her cheeks as she turned to address the king.

"Father, if they've come all this way in such cold, they must have reason. Let them speak. Hearing them costs us nothing but turning them away might cost us more."

Laerynth's eyes flicked toward one of the council members seated to the left. The councilor, a thin elf with a hawk-like gaze, inclined his head almost imperceptibly.

"Your Majesty," the councilor spoke up, "while the princess's compassion is, of course, admirable, I must advise that we maintain the privacy of this council."

Caelithia added her leaf's worth, "Matters of such sensitivity should be discussed amongst trusted advisors alone."

A few other council members nodded in agreement, clearly taking their cue. But another voice, this one from a counselor on the opposite side, spoke up in quiet support of the princess's point.

"And yet, Your Majesty, the welfare of Aetherealm is no small matter. To hear them does not bind us to any course of action. It merely informs us."

Kaden kept his silence, though a part of him hoped she'd sway the king. Be a shame to see that kind of light put out so soon, even if she was too hopeful for her own good.

After a long silence, King Theron nodded and lifted an approving hand. "Very well. Let them speak briefly."

Siraen's eyes held the faintest spark of triumph and Kaden almost smiled.

The great doors opened again and cold swept in with the envoy. Snow crusted their cloaks, the wind swirling in a flurry of ice and shivers. Kaden's eyes immediately picked out the intimidating stature of Glon: the squared shoulders, the soldier's gait. Next to him, skin nearly blending in with her dark brown cloak, stiff posture and calculating stare, stood Noreena.

Relief was fleeting as unease quickly took its place. His gaze swept the trio once more, searching for the one face he'd hoped to see. Lusa wasn't among them. A swarm of energy tightened in his chest.

The third figure he recognized a second later—Dak, one of the guards assigned to Lusa's caravan. Whatever news they carried, it wouldn't be good.

Glon stepped forward, bowing low, his voice the tone of a man more used to orders than diplomacy.

"Your Majesties. Captain Glon of the Imperial Guard, bearing report from Izier." He remained bowed, waiting for permission to continue.

Kaden's attention flicked to the royal table. Queen Valenne watched with restrained impatience; one gloved hand poised at her chin. Vaelar half-suppressed an eye roll. Eldarion studied Glon with thoughtful curiosity. And Siraen—her gaze wasn't on the envoy at all. She was watching him. Kaden quickly looked away as King Theron gestured for Glon to proceed.

The captain hesitated, glancing at Kaden before choosing his words with a soldier's caution, though they tumbled out like he was reading it straight from memory. "We have reason to believe the Dark Elves of Velkher may be involved. I can't share all the details of how we learned this, but signs suggest their actions are worsening the disruptions. They may be using the chaos to their advantage."

Poor bastard. He'd probably practiced that speech the whole ride here and might just regret every word of it. The room that had chilled him minutes ago was about to turn colder. Skeptical whispers stirred across the chamber.

Vaelar, ever the picture of elven pride, gave a short, disbelieving laugh. "The Dark Elves?" he repeated, the corners of his mouth curving into something faintly cruel. "A people reduced to myth for a century? Hardly the masterminds of a crisis this scale. Assuming, of course, it is a crisis at all."

Laerynth brushed his trimmed beard, eyes landing on a few council members. "And yet," he said, voice a little too smooth, "perhaps we've underestimated them. If they've found a way to affect the ley lines from their capstone…" He let the thought dangle.

Vaelar, quick to catch the cue, shifted easily. "Yes—perhaps we've been too dismissive. Forgotten enemies do have a way of crawling back when the world grows weak."

The pivot was too obvious not to draw notice. Even Eldarion's brow lifted. The king's lips parted, but he said nothing.

Kaden's pulse ticked faster. Manipulation wasn't always an easy scent to catch in this court, but this—this was plain as blood in snow. He watched Laerynth carefully, tracing the noble's gaze across the chamber, cataloguing who nodded, who avoided looking at him.

"If Velkher's truly behind the disturbances," Eldarion said, his voice taut, "then we can't wait for word. The Strait's too far to receive word back quickly. We need eyes in the storm. Someone who can transport themselves through the Aether."

Whispers rippled through the council and glances passed between the royals. No one dared voice what they were all weighing. The power it would take. The exposure.

Laerynth was the first to break the quiet. "It would take one attuned to the Third Harmony, at least." His tone was deferential, but his eyes found Caelithia. "Someone who can step through the Aether and survive the Aeon's notice."

Vaelar leaned back in his chair, the corner of his mouth twitching. "Few in this room could do it," he said, feigning thought. "And fewer still who'd risk their Seryn for rumor."

Caelithia's jaw tensed. "Rumor or not, it concerns all of us."

"And yet," Lorenthar interjected softly, "such passage is no small feat. Even for one attuned as you are, Lady

Caelithia. The Aether strips the soul bare; it demands balance. A dissonance of the Seryn could take days to mend."

Empathy flickered in his golden gaze. "We would be asking you to cross the edge of exhaustion for a truth that may not exist."

Eldarion shook his head. "We can't afford blindness. If Velkher's tampering with the ley lines, this unending Lady Ice will be the least of our worries. It will unmake the balance the Harmonies depend on."

"He's right. And you know I can make the jump." Caelithia's posture straightened.

"At great cost," Lorenthar added.

"So be it." She met the king's eyes. "Better I fall to dissonance than we fall to ignorance."

The court fell silent again. None of the others spoke or offered to go in her place. None dared reveal what tier of the Harmonies they could truly reach.

At last, King Theron gave a weary nod. "Go, then," he said quietly. "But take care. The Aether has never been kind to the proud."

"Nor to the fearful," she replied.

Her dark green silver-lined cloak caught the light as she turned and made way. Kaden tracked her movement through the shifting crowd. Glon, Dak, and Noreena stood near the entrance, silent and stone-faced amid the sea of gold and silver. Their unease was plain. Glon's jaw was set hard enough to crack stone; Noreena's eyes flicked between Caelithia and the great doors, already calculating what her disappearance might mean. Dak shifted his weight like a man itching for action but too smart to move.

The council parted as Caelithia stepped into the open space before the throne. The air changed, thinned, like the moment before lightning strikes. She drew off her gloves and lifted both hands, fingers curving into a formation, each motion sharp and fluid, as if she were sculpting sound itself.

Silver threads flared beneath her skin. Her veins glowed faintly through the pale of her hands, tracing along her arms like ink. The light gathered at her sternum, pulsing in rhythm with her heartbeat until it coalesced into a sphere of shimmering energy cupped between her palms.

The court watched in silence as her breathing slowed. Even the braziers dimmed, their flames bowing as if to listen. The sphere brightened, its hue shifting from soft silver to the blinding white of molten glass. For one breath, her entire body was translucent—every line of her form suspended in that ethereal shimmer.

Kaden felt the pressure before the sound: a low hum that crawled through the floor and up his spine, the echo of power threading through the Weave like a note plucked from the Aeon's own song.

Caelithia's eyes opened, bright with reflected starlight. The glow spread, swallowing her completely. Then, in a single blink, she was gone—folded into the light.

Glon exhaled first. Dak crossed himself the old Izierian way. Noreena stared, her mouth parted, eyes still fixed on where Caelithia had been. Siraen exhaled a soft "oh," hands clasped to her chest, as if realizing for the first time that courage could be that simple.

"May the Aeon guide her path," Laerynth said.

Kaden turned back to the High Canopy.

"So that's our scout gone. What's the rest'a the plan?" The question broke the momentary awe that had captured everyone.

"We wait for her return," the king said, though the words carried no conviction.

"And if she doesn't return?"

Vaelar snorted. "You speak as though she were human."

"Everyone bleeds the same," Kaden said, keeping his tone even.

"Careful," Laerynth warned softly. "There are ears in this hall that do not take kindly to blasphemy."

"Blasphemy or truth—it's usually the same thing in rooms like these."

Some counselors shifted uncomfortably. Others pretended not to hear.

"Watch your tongue, outsider," one finally snapped. "You stand before the Aeon's chosen."

"Enough," Theron said. "We'll not quarrel over faith when ice eats away at our borders. Caelithia will send word when she can."

If she can, Kaden thought. He forced his shoulders square and gathered the crumbs of patience he had left. "And while we wait? The realms keep freezin'. The crops keep dyin'. Ya need more than hope ta' keep yer' people alive."

"Mind your tone, Ambassador," a different counselor warned, but Eldarion raised a hand, silencing them. His eyes narrowed, assessing.

"Then speak plainly. What would you have us do?"

"Prepare," Kaden said. "Quietly. If Velkher's reachin' across the Strait, you need ta' be ready 'fore it's too late."

"And risk war on rumor?" Queen Valenne scoffed.

"Risk survival," Kaden countered. "There's a difference."

The Queen's eyes flashed, but she said nothing more. Counselors nearest her father leaned into one another, whispering something.

Silence crept back before the princess added softly, more guarded this time. "Quiet preparations don't betray anyone. They protect us."

Theron's attention flicked toward his daughter, then to his eldest son. The crown prince hesitated, weighing his words.

"We can't afford blindness," he said finally. "If she finds proof, we act. If not, we still move. We can't let Velkher shape the song of the Aeon while we stand idle."

Laerynth looked briefly at his daughter, the Queen, before speaking to the king. "Then we prepare contingencies."

King Theron addressed the room. "Begin discreet arrangements for transport across the Thalaran Strait. We wait for her signal."

He paused, scanning the map laid before them, and next to it, the Aelenth. "When it comes, we act. Aeonia will not stand idle while the realm unravels."

His attention drifted toward the stoic figure stationed behind the council. "Commander Thalor, you and your regiment will lead our forces across the Strait. I want eyes that see what's true, and blades that strike only when they must."

Thalor stepped forward, fist to chest. "It will be done, sire."

"Ambassador, you and your men will represent Izier in this mission. You've seen the signs firsthand."

Kaden bowed his head. "'Course, Your Majesty. I'll send word to the Empress."

Queen Valenne shifted, her tone measured but laced with unease. "You send our best into uncertainty."

"And you'd rather send our worst?" Theron's voice carried no heat, only the brittle calm of exhaustion. "No one weaker will survive the crossing."

The Queen said nothing more.

Laerynth leaned back in his velvet chair, wearing that same look he always did—neutral on the surface, scheming underneath. "A joint venture, then. How… diplomatic."

"How necessary," Eldarion countered. "If Velkher truly stirs, the realm must answer as one."

Kaden had noticed the quiet rift between the crown prince and the queen's father for weeks. Laerynth's counsel always seemed to land just shy of deference, and Eldarion's replies carried the clipped restraint of a man tired of pretending patience. Tonight, that divide felt closer to cracking. Not that Kaden blamed him. If he'd had to share a table with Laerynth this long, he'd have drawn a sword instead of a breath.

Theron nodded once, final and absolute. "So it shall be. Preparations begin at dawn."

The council shifted, their voices a quiet current beneath the scrape of chairs. As Kaden bowed and turned to leave, he caught Glon's grim stare from the back of the hall. Noreena stood behind him, face drawn tight, Dak at her shoulder. Whatever message they carried had waited long enough.

CHAPTER 38

Where the Aether Bleeds

Kaden kept one hand on the rope rail as he crossed from the High Canopy to the guest boughs, frosted planks creaking under his boots. Wind cut through his borrowed furs, stealing the last warmth from the council chamber. Below, the canopy ghosted with snow, a white ocean rippling under moonlight. Above, lanterns swung in slow arcs, casting ribs of light across the path like bars of a cage.

Dark Elves. Convenient scapegoats—simple enough to make the frightened feel safe. Laerynth's faint smile had said it all: problem solved, blame assigned. It was the same tone the Empire once used when they talked about mages.

The guest bridge split around a cluster of silver firs and ran to three doors set into the ancient tree trunks. Guards posted at each end stamped their feet against the cold. The middle door stood ajar, lamplight pooling like warm honey across the threshold. He rapped knuckles on the half-cracked door then pushed it open.

Glon had already claimed the corner by the brazier. Snow steamed off his cloak on the back of a chair. He'd stripped to a linen shirt, one sleeve rolled, binding a long bruise along his ribs with the methodical efficiency of a man who'd done it on horseback more than once. Dak was on his stomach across the bed near the far wall, boots still on, chin propped in his hands, bone flute peeking out of a satchel. Packs lay open, contents squared and stacked with a soldier's geometry.

Both men looked up. Glon's mouth tipped up the slightest. "Ambassador." His voice always sounded like it had gravel in it.

"No titles." Kaden closed the door on the wind and set his gloves on the table. "You two settlin' in?"

"As much as anyone can settle leagues from the ground," Dak muttered, rolling onto his back. "I hate heights."

"You can always sleep on the forest floor," Kaden offered.

Dak made a face in sync with a full body shiver. "Hard pass."

Kaden's gaze slid over Glon's bandage. "You alright?"

"I've been worse." He tied the final knot clean and tight. "Noreena's next door. She'll want to walk the perimeter before she sleeps."

"Of course she will," Dak said. "I can't wait to be told the door is, in fact, a door."

The half-grin Kaden didn't intend found him anyway. It didn't stay long. "Ya didn't bring Lusa."

Glon's hands stilled. His eyes met Kaden's, and in them, a truth he wasn't ready to lay out in front of anyone else. "No."

Dak sat up, mouth opening, then thought better of it.

"Later," Glon added.

It wasn't evasion but a request. Soldier to soldier. At least that's how Kaden took it. With walls this thin and guards who listened as part of their duty, probably a good idea.

Kaden nodded. "Later."

From the middle room came a thunk, followed by Noreena's scolding sound. She opened her door two fingers wide, eyes already assessing the room. Her tight coils of hair were wilder than usual, thicker and grown out from nonstop travel.

"Ambassador," she said, taking him in, then the men behind him. "You all warm?"

Ambassador… the word still felt borrowed, like a title someone else had earned and he was just keeping warm.

"Just Kaden," he answered, rubbing the back of his neck. "Warm as this place allows. How's yer' room?"

"Window sticks. Draft under the sill. I've set a trip line at the balcony." She nodded her chin at Dak. "For the musician."

Dak blinked. "What—me? I wasn't gonna—"He cut himself off, muttering, "It was one time."

"Once was enough," she said dryly, disappearing long enough to reappear with a steaming pot and three wooden cups. "Tea," she said. "Before we freeze solid."

They gathered in Glon's room where the heat did its best. The tea tasted like pine needles and iron… Aeonia's idea of hospitality when honey had become a ration. Kaden wrapped his hands around the cup and let the sting of the warmth seep into him.

"Council went how we expected?" Noreena asked, pushing a second blanket toward Dak with her foot.

"Worse," Kaden said. "Or neater, anyway. They like a story with a clear villain."

Dak blew across his cup. "Velkher."

Glon set his tea aside. "They're definitely involved somehow. I just hope I gave the right information."

Kaden remembered the cadence of Glon's report before the court. He'd probably practiced a dozen times in the saddle. Public speaking had never been his strength, though he'd been forced to improve since his promotion to captain and the Empress started expecting full reports.

"You did fine."

"Did I?" Glon's mouth thinned. "Prince Vaelar laughed."

Dak slapped a hand on his shoulder. "He probably laughs at everything."

Steam curled from Kaden's tea, blurring his reflection on the surface. All he saw was the council table and the flicker of candlelight over too many calculating faces. Laerynth, too pleased. Eldarion, too careful. And Siraen, watching him with that bright, unguarded fascination she never quite managed to hide.

He wasn't sure which unsettled him more: that Velkher fit so neatly, or that Glon had known exactly when to hand them the name.

He lifted his gaze. "Where'd Velkher come from?"

"I'll walk the bridge," Noreena said as she set her cup down. "Two taps if we're clear. One if we've got company."

Dak frowned. "Company?"

"Ears." She slipped out, quiet as a fox in snow.

The room exhaled. The brazier hissed. Kaden watched the door a beat longer, then turned back to Glon.

"Alright," he said. "Where'd Velkher come from?"

Glon's face didn't change, but his shoulders drew a fraction tighter. "From me."

He didn't dress it up. He never did.

"Go on."

"We were at the Mage Citadels, west of the village. Rain, bad footing. Noreena got pulled by a compulsion. Vallas, Dak, Jarion, me… same. No control over our own heads. Lusa tried to shield us."

Kaden could imagine her there: mud, rain, defiance. Every time he closed his eyes, that image lived like a curse. She'd fought alone, and he hadn't been there to help.

"Then he showed himself," Glon continued, his voice a tinge darker. "Tall. Black hair in braids. Dark robes. Magic like a knife you don't see until it's in you."

Dak's fingers worried the edge of his blanket, silent for once. Noreena's two-tap signal sounded, all eyes glancing to the door a beat before continuing.

"He used our hands against her," Glon went on. "Turned us into weapons. She fought us off without injuring us, mostly, then said it plain: Dark Elf. Told us to run. To tell the Empress. She drew him off."

Kaden's mouth went dry. "And you left."

"We had no choice." No defensiveness, but a verdict he'd already passed on himself. "I tried to convince her. She's stubborn. You know that. Said she'd be right behind."

Noreena slipped back in, clicking the door shut behind her and quickly rubbed her hands together, blowing warmth into them.

Dak fiddled with his bone flute, twirling it between his fingers. "We went back to look for her. Trail ended at the shore."

"Not without traces, though." Noreena moved back to the chair, sitting in it with her elbows resting on her knees. "We found something. Dust. Gray, fine as ash, scattered through the muddy shore."

Glon sighed, finally trying the tea. "We gathered what we could. Figured the Empire's scholars might make sense of it."

Kaden's chest tightened. A shore. A handful of ash. That was what they'd brought back while he'd been half a world away talking politics. If he'd been there, maybe the trail wouldn't have ended at the water.

"Keep it close," Kaden said. "Until we know what's really goin' on, no one outside this room hears a word. The court's already lookin' for monsters under every rock. Don't hand 'em a name they can twist."

He stared into the brazier, seeing not flame but the shore Noreena had described with the ghost of Lusa's footprints dissolving into sand. If there'd been signs of a struggle, she hadn't gone willingly. She'd fought. She always fought. And somewhere, she was still fighting. He pressed his eyes close and took in a slow, deep breath.

The others' voices blurred, fading beneath the roar of his pulse. He'd search every frozen mile of this cursed realm if that's what it took. He'd tear through the lies of courts and kings, drag the truth out of gods if he had to, until he found her—or until there was nothing left of him to give.

"You think she's alive?" Dak's usual irreverence was gone.

Glon had his shirt back on, pulling it down over his bandage. "I think if anyone could make that bastard regret it, it's her."

"What's the Empire think?" Kaden asked.

"Velkher fits the truth close enough to buy her time. Laerynth didn't need to hear about a living mage on the run."

"Good call."

Glon's shoulders eased, but the grief behind his eyes didn't.

"She mention a connection to the ley lines?"

Glon blinked. "To what?"

Kaden hesitated, realizing his mistake. "Never mind." Humans weren't learned in the ways of magic.

Dak squinted at him. "Lake lions?"

Kaden sighed. "Ley lines. Not… lake lions."

Dak grinned, taking his opportunity to lighten the mood. "Oh. That would make more sense." He scratched his head. "I think."

Stretching out the kinks in his back, Kaden stood. "What about the rest of Izier? Or Myttica? Anything else strange before ya left?"

"Winter came hard. Fast," Glon answered, rubbing his chin. "Crops froze mid-harvest. Grainieries were half full at best. Vallas and Jarion stayed behind to manage rations and keep order. We were sent here to report conditions."

Dak leaned forward, elbows on his knees, same as Noreena. She noticed and instantly sat back, like sitting the same way might be contagious. Dak remained oblivious.

"Ice cracked the wells in three villages we passed," he said. "Saw livestock dead on their feet. Just froze where they stood. Never seen that before."

"Anything else?" Kaden pressed. "Somethin' that didn't fit. A smell. A sight. Anything."

Glon shook his head. "Just cold."

The tea leaves had sunk to the bottom of his cup. He took another sip, letting the heat spread down his throat and through his chest.

Dak's brow furrowed. "Wait." He snapped his fingers. "The honeypears."

Glon gave him a side look. "What about them?"

"They turned to ash." Dak sat forward, animated now.

Kaden froze, pulse quickening. "Ash," he repeated. "You sure?"

"As sure as soldiers swear and nobles lie. Looked like rot, but faster. Spread from the stem out."

"That was Lusa's tree," Glon said distantly, as if replaying a memory.

Kaden blinked. "Her what?"

"The woods outside Merravale. She healed a tree there. Looked decades dead. Went through its full life cycle right before our eyes with her touch. I thought maybe…" His voice trailed, uneasy. "Maybe her spell backfired."

Noreena's head lifted sharply. "No. That tree was still thriving when we left the Citadels. The fruit Dak found came from its graft." She frowned, the calculation already working behind her eyes. "If it turned to ash, then whatever killed it wasn't her magic failing."

Kaden's mind raced. Roots that pulsed. Crops turning to ash. The same quiet sickness threading north to south. He could almost see the invisible network bleeding energy out of the land. His stomach turned.

Glon was watching him. "You've seen this before," the captain said.

"Somethin' like it," Kaden admitted. "In samples I brought from the northern provinces. Roots shouldn't pulse or hum when they're dyin'. But they do."

Noreena stared hard at the floor, trying to fit the pieces. "The Weave?"

"Maybe," Kaden said. "But the Weave's only the surface—the threads that bind the spellwork of the world. This feels deeper. Like the Aether itself's bein' bled. The ley lines run through it… through everything. They feed the land, the weather, sometimes even the people. But if somethin's siphonin' them—" He stopped himself, jaw tightening. "You don't drain blood without killin' what's attached."

Kaden ran a hand down his face, the weight of it all pressing through his palm. The council's chamber. Laerynth's easy manipulation. Caelithia stepping into the Aether like she could outrun decay. Lusa's name still hanging unspoken in every silence. If the ley lines were dying, if the Aether was bleeding—then maybe it wasn't just the world unraveling.

Maybe it started with her. Or because of her. Or because she'd tried to stop it somehow.

He dragged in a breath, the icy air stealing what little warmth he'd borrowed from the tea. "Get some rest," he said, voice hardening. "Tomorrow, we start plannin' for the Strait."

No one argued. What was there to say? Lusa was missing, the Aether was bleeding, and they had no idea what was waiting for them at the edge of Aeonia. War seemed a word hiding just below the surface, and that was one fear none of them wanted to breathe into thought. The mood needed a little lightening, and Kaden knew just the man he could rely on.

He stood, rolling the stiffness from his shoulder. "And Dak?"

The young man looked up.

"No more lake lions."

Dak grinned. "No promises."

Kaden shut the door behind him, the sound of soft chuckling swallowed by wind and snow. Looking ahead at the bridge, he pulled his coat tighter. Waiting for Caelithia's return would be its own kind of suffering, and there was nothing to do but endure it.

CHAPTER 39

The Last Summons

Days had folded into frost. Aeonia did not wait with patience but with hunger—the quiet kind that gnawed beneath silk and gold, whispering of cracks beneath its calm facade.

News of Caelithia's passage into the Aether had spread through every corridor, leaving unease clinging to the air. Each dawn broke colder than the last, and hope thinned to something brittle enough to snap.

The High Canopy's dining hall gleamed beneath chandeliers spun of frost and flame. The scent of pine fought to mask the rot still rising from the lower boughs, a losing battle disguised as luxury. Tables curved in graceful arcs, silverware shining like captured stars—proof the kingdom still remembered how to pretend.

Breakfast was meager: thin stew, bread gone hard before the sun fully rose. Nobles ate with the grace of habit, though every scrape of silver on porcelain sounded like a small surrender.

Kaden and his companions sat at the outer edge of the hall—close enough to catch the hum of politics, far enough to feel the distance it implied. Thalor held his usual stillness near the head of the table, all poise and vigilance.

Across from Kaden, Glon and Noreena ate in silence while Dak somehow managed to talk, chew, and grin through the tension at once.

Kaden wasn't hungry. Hadn't been for days. His mind circled the same scraps: Glon's report, Dak's honeypears, the ash where life should've been, the ley lines draining. But always, it came back to Lusa. The world felt wrong in its skin, and waiting only made that wrongness cut deeper. He tore his bread just to have something to do with his hands.

"Strange season," said Ronus, spoon clinking softly against his bowl. "Lady Ice hasn't come this early in a generation."

Glon grunted. "Seems an understatement."

Thalor's attention slid toward Kaden. "You've been quiet this morning, Everwyn." His tone was light, but there was iron under it.

"Talkin's overrated," Kaden said. "Doesn't thaw the air or improve the company."

Dak raised his cup with a crooked grin. "Good thing you've got plenty of both."

The table managed a few thin laughs—the kind that lived and died out of habit.

Kaden set down his bread. "Heard the roads north are closin' faster than the reports claim. Cold's spreadin' in sheets. Anadine's passes're already gone."

Glon nodded. "Villages are emptying. We saw on the way here. Those who can, head toward the capital."

Ronus bit into his bread, winced, and checked his tooth. "Latest report says Lalimore's near abandoned."

Dak frowned. "Didn't hit Merravale that hard when we left. You think it's reached that far?"

The mention of Merravale drew a flicker between Glon and Noreena—one Kaden didn't miss. Dak must've caught it too; he pivoted quickly, flashing a grin. "Would be a tragedy to lose the honeypears. How would Aeonia survive such hardship?"

Noreena's look warned him off, and Whilm, eager to fill the space, leaned forward. "Three caravans gone missing along the Mire route last month."

At the far end of the hall, a crystal bell chimed. The nobles rose in a practiced wave, robes whispering like ghosts. Kaden was pulling on his gloves when the door burst open—wood against stone, breath against cold—and a young courtier stumbled in, frost clinging to his cloak and panic still fresh in his eyes.

"Lady Caelithia—she's returned."

The hall froze as one.

Thalor's chair scraped back. "Returned?"

The messenger nodded, breath coming in clouds. "Through the Aether Gate. She's alive… but—" His throat worked. "She bears the mark of the Aeon."

Thalor rose in a single motion, voice cutting through the stunned silence. "Clear the hall. Summon the council."

Chairs skidded, robes whispered, and the room emptied in a flurry of restrained panic. Kaden set his bread aside, pulse thrumming.

The mark of the Aeon.

He didn't know what it truly meant, but every whisper he'd heard about it ended in ruin.

Dak sighed, wiping his mouth on his sleeve. "Guess breakfast's over."

By the time Kaden reached the upper chamber, the council was already assembled.

Caelithia stood at its center, wrapped in a silence that didn't seem her own. Light touched her differently—too bright in some places, fading in others, as though the room hadn't decided whether to accept her return. Fine veins of silver traced along her hands, pulsing faintly with an internal rhythm. Whatever she'd brought back from the Aether, it had changed her.

"Something is happening in Velkher," she said. Her voice carried through the air like sound beneath water—soft, distorted, unearthly.

"Explain," said King Theron, his tone stripped of its usual tiredness. His long white beard hung in a neat braid, the silver in it catching the cold light as he leaned forward from his seat.

Caelithia lowered her gaze to the Aelenth on the table before her. Kaden narrowed his eyes and instinctively leaned forward to get a better look. The version he'd unearthed in Aeonia's archives had been inked on bark parchment, brittle and half-forgotten. This one was no relic. The ley crossings shimmered faintly, light flowing through its grooves as though alive. The royal family had kept it hidden, it seemed—guarding what was real. Now, they displayed it openly. That alone told him enough about their fear.

"The island feeds from the Weave," Caelithia said. "The lines twist beneath it like veins drawn too tight. Something is siphoning the flow. The Aether bleeds. The Aeon is stirring."

No one questioned the Aeon's existence. Only its awakening.

Queen Valenne's voice faltered despite her composure. "The Aeon hasn't stirred since the Divide. If it wakes…"

Caelithia met her eyes. "It won't wake kindly."

Anyone born in Aetherealm knew the story. The Aeon was no god, but a sentient current—the consciousness threaded through all creation. When awake, its awareness rippled through the world, shaping, correcting, unmaking. Its will was too vast for mortal balance.

It was the Eastern Wars that silenced it—the war between elves that birthed Aeonia and Velkher. When Light and Dark divided, the Aeon fell into dormancy, its stillness mirroring theirs. For the first time, creation steadied. The Aeon's silence became the truce that let the world endure. Its sleep was mercy.

Laerynth's dark amber eyes caught the light as he shifted his cane, voice smooth but sharp-edged. "You're certain this isn't mage interference? Some magic corruption or capstone decay?"

The old elf's gray-streaked hair was tied neatly back, his beard trimmed close. He looked every inch the diplomat—but the way he spoke made the question sound like accusation.

Kaden's jaw tightened before he could stop it. Disdain always came easy when the word *mage* entered the room. He wasn't one, but he loved one—and that would be enough to damn him in Laerynth's eyes. *Humans meddle. Mages destroy.* That was the Aeonian creed. He forced his hands to stay still.

"Does it matter?" Caelithia replied, unshaken. "The Resonance hums lower each hour. The Aeon's dormancy is failing, and Velkher sits at the fault."

Kaden's brow tightened. *Since when did she stop caring who to blame?* The Caelithia he knew had sharpened prejudice into an art form—pureblood this, human that, mage filth whispered behind tight frowns. But the elf standing before them now spoke without edge, stripped of judgment, like the words belonged to someone else wearing her face. Whatever mark the Aeon had left on her, it had hollowed something out in return.

Eldarion stepped forward before his father could respond, his silver circlet gleaming faintly in the chill. "Then we act before the decay spreads. The longer we wait, the harder it will be to contain."

Theron's hand came down flat on the table. The age in his face crinkled into something close to resolve. "Then it's decided. Commander Thalor will lead the Aeonian contingent. Ambassador Everwyn and Captain Glon will accompany him. You leave before dusk."

Caelithia's gaze lifted to him, her eyes distant but fixed. "Follow the fracture," she murmured. "You'll know it when you reach it."

He hesitated. She'd addressed him—not Thalor, not the king. *Why him?* He didn't ask. He doubted she'd answer anyway.

When the council broke apart, he fell into step with the others, the hush of boots on frost-slick stone following him out. He turned toward the guest boughs. Glon and the others were waiting for news none of them would like.

By the time Kaden made it to the second corridor, narrowing to the first bridge outside, a soft, familiar voice stopped him.

"Ambassador."

He closed his eyes briefly, gathering his bearings before turning.

Siraen stood by the frosted window, dawn breaking behind her in pale bands of gold and rose. The light caught her hair, threading it into strands of sun until she seemed almost ethereal. In her hands, she held something small and silk-wrapped, clasped as though it might disappear if she loosened her grip.

"Ya shouldn't be here," he said, gentler than he intended. The words came out more as mercy than reprimand.

"You're leaving."

"Looks that way."

Her fingers tightened around the silk. "Then before you do…" She hesitated, the formality of court language falling away. "I wanted you to have this. For the crossing."

She stepped closer, and he caught the faint tremor in her breath. The princess wasn't playing at anything. Not pity. Not politics. Just sincerity so unguarded it almost made him uncomfortable. Most nobles wore kindness like ornamentation—meant to catch the light, never endure weather. But Siraen's was untested, untouched by the cold edges of the world. And he almost felt sorry for her.

Kaden unfolded the cloth to reveal a pendant of gold shaped like a leaf, its veins spreading into seven delicate branches. A harmony charm. Old magic. Ancient superstition. Said to amplify an elf's Resonance when the Weave itself sensed pure, desperate need.

He stared at it a moment too long. "Ya realize this is wasted on me," he said, voice low. "Half-bloods don't have enough Resonance to stir a charm, much less the Aeon."

Siraen's gaze flickered, disappointment softening into something like defiance. "A princess can hope."

Her words landed, simple and sure, and he found himself envying such faith. Outside, a gust of wind swept the frost from the window, scattering it into motes of light. She stood there, so certain that goodness still held the world together.

"I'll bring it back ta' you," he said at last, his thumb brushing the charm's edge.

"You'd better," she replied, her voice briefly carrying something older than her years—an echo of the queen she might one day become—before it wavered into silence.

He slipped the chain over his neck. The cool metal touched skin, and for a fleeting moment, he almost believed it could protect him from what lay ahead. Almost.

When he looked up, she was already gone—her golden outline swallowed by the turning corridor and the soft rustle of her maids. Some people didn't learn how to doubt until the world taught them. He only hoped she'd be allowed a little longer than most before it did.

The sun was already drowning itself in a flush of orange and pink when Kaden stepped onto the outer bridges. He'd briefed Glon, Noreena, and Dak on the council's orders and sent Whilm and Ronus back to the Empire with word of what had transpired. The High Canopy had offered what little they could for the envoy's trek to Izier—extra provisions, sealed rations, and a single blanket woven with Resonance thread, said to hold warmth so long as the Aeon slept. Superstition or not, Kaden wasn't about to refuse it.

Frost filmed the ropes and armor in white, and the air worked at his exposed skin until it stung. Glon and Noreena were already mounted. Dak was mumbling to himself about the cold, while Commander Thalor sat on his horse in front of his two dozen soldiers like a carved figure. His eyes were fixed on the dust clouds of snow rolling through the forest ahead.

Kaden took one last look back toward Aeonia, the elderwoods' canopy alive with faint light where palace and forest had long since become one. Somewhere in there, a princess kept her faith like a candle against the dark. And further beyond the horizon ahead, a mage was probably fighting to keep herself alive.

"Ready?" Thalor called.

"As I'll ever be." Kaden urged Brogan forward. The stallion's hooves broke the crusted snow, their breath rising together into the pale air.

Behind them, Aeonia's lights faded, and beneath the snow, the Aether whispered—ancient, patient, bleeding still.

CHAPTER 40

Kareth Hollow

The world had narrowed to the sway of the sea and the heartbeat of a ship. Magic recharged in Lusa, restless but weak, gathering in quiet defiance. Recalibration was always the same—her core relearning its rhythm, her body pretending not to mind. Outside, gulls cried out and the tide whispered its endless truth: nothing stays constant.

She could almost feel the Weave listening in return… the Aether's breath beneath the surface. Lusa sat cross-legged on the floor beside the captain's desk, the chill of the boards seeping through her pants. The lantern swung with the choppy waves, light spilling and retracting in patterns over the bowl of tropical fruit collected from that dreadful island.

Three days.

Maybe four.

Once again, she wasn't counting.

Each slow pull of exhaustion, each faint whisper of magic returning to her core, marked the days better than any count. The ache of depletion had dulled, but too slowly to bring comfort.

Confinement, at least, was a small mercy. They hadn't chained her or thrown her in a hold. She'd seen the look in the captain's eyes when she woke, understood the careful way he'd told her to stay put. It had felt more like a warning than a command. Fine by her. She was too tired to argue and figured it made a decent excuse to meditate. And thankfully the darkling hadn't come once since the night she'd lost control. She closed her eyes at the resurfacing memory.

The pit.

The roots.

The suffocating pull of his will invading her mind. She'd thought she knew what it felt like to lose herself.

She'd been wrong.

The Dark Magics had whispered before… tempted, begged, seduced. Lazorious had commanded, forcing her hand toward Kaden's throat. Even then, she'd fought until her body broke. But Malvian hadn't needed to whisper, tempt, or fight his way in. He had simply *entered.*

And that was the worst kind of fear. The kind that didn't end when she woke. It haunted. Fed on itself. Nested deep inside her, spreading through her marrow like rot on wood. An infestation disguised as memory.

Even now, she could feel the echo of him… the cold, wicked hunger behind his eyes. A fascination so intimate it felt like being unmade from the inside out. He had tried to bind her in understanding, to own her through sheer will, but chose not to. And somehow, that restraint terrified her most of all.

The silver hairpin was cool beneath her fingers as she traced the delicate curve of the metal. If there were a spell to keep it from ever falling out again, she'd find it.

The hum beneath her skin was finally returning. It was only a matter of time. Waiting was a skill she had learned the hard way, even if patience had never been her virtue.

She lifted her gaze toward the small porthole above the desk. The sea beyond it was deceptively calm. Somewhere ahead lay Velkher, the island of the Dark Elves. Malvian's home. His father's domain.

Her pulse quickened. Lusa wasn't sure which frightened her more: the thought of never leaving the island alive… or seeing the darkling again before they reached it.

As if answering that fear, land crept into view through the porthole. It began as a faint gray line on the horizon and grew thicker with each breath, rising from the sea in jagged cliffs as dark as iron. Heavy fog clung to their edges.

Velkher.

Blue-violet flickers stirred in the fog along the cliffs. Ghost lights, floating like sprites. But sprites didn't glow that color. Her fingers fidgeted with the pin. Beneath that island she could almost feel the pulse of power, the ley lines thrumming through rock and soil. The rhythm felt wrong.

The ship groaned as the sails strained against a slowing wind. Voices stirred above deck. Lusa rose, legs unsteady, and crossed to the desk. She'd hoped to find her bag, her books, her sword. The wood was worn and scarred from years of use, each mark a story she would never know. Nothing of hers remained. Only a silver compass caught her eye, resting at the desk's center. Its needle spun in frantic circles, chasing something unseen. The sight pulled at her—familiar in a way she couldn't name, unsettling in the way déjà vu hits.

Lusa caught her faint reflection in the porthole glass. The heavy shadows beneath her eyes, the pale sheen of exhaustion, the streak of dried blood still at her temple. She looked like a ghost of herself, and in some ways, she was. Part of her had never climbed out of that pit.

A knock broke her reverie. The door creaked open, and Tessanee's small face appeared in the gap. "We'll be docking soon."

Lusa straightened. "How soon?"

"The prince is already on deck."

The title soured something in her gut. She hadn't heard him called that aloud before. *The prince.* The words tasted wrong in her mouth.

Her gaze flicked to the porthole where the dark outline of land edged closer. She wanted to ask what would happen once they reached shore—if she was to go with him, if she was still a prisoner or something else entirely. But Tessanee wouldn't know, and she'd be damned if she'd approach either of those men.

The girl offered a small smile, leaning through the crack of the door. Her hair barely passed her shoulders. It had been brushed recently.

"He said there are bunnies at his villa. I've never seen one before."

Naïve. Too innocent for this world. The girl's hope was a fragile thing, and Lusa couldn't bring herself to break it. She forced a small nod instead, even if her chest felt like it was about to explode. For Tessanee's sake, she hoped Malvian's promise was real.

When the door shut, Lusa pressed a hand to her chest, feeling the uneven thrum of her magic, half-healed, half-starved. She'd need every shard of it if she were to make it off this island alive.

The docks glimmered at the edge of the horizon, ghostly and black, rising from gray waters. Mist draped the cliffs ahead, their peaks jutting through the clouds like broken teeth. The closer they got, the warmer the air became. Magic shuddered beneath the waves, deep and discordant.

Velkher. The Capstone Isle. The realm between decay and renewal. The border between life and what refused to stay dead. Or so she'd read once.

The gangplank groaned. Malvian was already gone, his cloak a smear of shadow disappearing into the fog, Tessanee and his lanky servant close behind. Aleric's hand caught her elbow as she approached the railing.

"Keep your head low," he murmured. "Don't draw attention."

She ground her teeth. "Why do you care?"

"Because once Draevyn notices you," he said in a gruff whisper, "there's no undoing it."

He let her go, turning to give orders. Ropes had been traded in for clinking chains. Boots scraped over old wood as the captives moved toward the shore. Lusa followed them down the gangplank, blending into the throng.

The moment her boots met land, pain flared up her legs—magic striking against her core like a slap. The Capstone's pulse twisted through the ground, alive but broken, churning endlessly with nowhere to go.

Basalt arches rose along the docks, their hollow tunnels exhaling mist. Those tiny specks of blue-violet light hovered near, and she realized what they were. Flame moths, probably drawn to the overabundance of magic that sat in the veins of the island. Dark Elven statues lined the cliffs, frozen in triumph or torment, stone eyes glowing faintly with trapped Resonance. Every surface throbbed with violet light, as though the island itself were one vast, diseased heart.

Aleric spoke with the dock guards. They were tall and unsettling in their beauty, a common trait among Dark Elves she figured. The docks narrowed into a black road leading inland. Mist hung low, twining around their ankles. Aleric led from the front, captives trailing behind.

"Welcome to Kareth Hollow," a soldier sneered.

Lusa's gaze swept the horizon as she held back a snort. This place was anything but hollow. Apparently, the Dark Elves pretend emptiness to hide what's festering underneath. The air itself felt bloated, the ground straining with power searching for an escape.

Darkling soldiers flanked the path. Skin the earthy hue of Malvian's, luminous where the grayish sunlight caught it. Some even had eyes like molten amethyst beneath crested helms. Their armor shimmered in faint shades of violet and obsidian; metal interlaced with an organic sheen that looked grown rather than forged.

Aleric slowed at a checkpoint, speaking in low tones to the officer there. Lusa caught only fragments through the hiss of wind and surf.

"Shipment… humans… mining."

The officer's scars glowed faintly along his throat as he studied them. His gaze passed over the captives and paused on her. Lusa's pulse spiked. She was standing too straight and probably looked more aware than terrified. She quickly lowered her gaze and slid closer to a captive, easing her wrists together so her sleeve hid her unbound skin. The clink of real chains nearby hopefully masked the ruse.

The officer's expression wavered, curiosity dimming to boredom. He gestured them through.

"Remember what I said," Aleric whispered as her group passed him. There was something in his tone she couldn't understand… protectiveness?

Her jaw flexed, and she shot him a cold glare. Leaving her here carved a mark she meant to return. Deep and as fierce as her will to survive.

The trail clung to the cliffs. Dead flame moths littered the dirt, tiny husks still faintly glowing. Around the bend, a path opened, revealing a vast sinkhole carved into the island's heart.

Kareth Hollow.

Veins of violet fed into metal scaffolds that spiraled around a towering black spire at the pit's center. Further from the center, the edge of the island dropped off into the Straight of Thalara. There was a continuous, low, resonant hum that seeped into her bones.

It couldn't be the Aether's murmur. The Aether was breath without voice, endless and wild. This pulse had cadence… a mind behind its rhythm. She'd learned that long ago, the Aeon and Aether had been one, thought and energy intertwined. When the gods split them, balance demanded silence. Yet here, silence had broken. The Weave itself was whispering, and the sound was wrong—like the world remembering its own dismemberment.

Every strike of a pickaxe sent up a shower of violet sparks. The air rippled with each impact, warping like a heat mirage. Hundreds of gaunt figures worked below, their faces blank. The wind carried the scent of iron and smoke—strong enough to sting her throat. Some of the workers were human. Others…

Her stomach twisted when her gaze caught a familiar scrap of dark blue fabric. The cloak and its stitching, the sigil half-burned away. Temple-issue. Mage.

They moved like ghosts wearing skin, their eyes dull, their cores long emptied. When one fell, another dragged the body aside without a word. No cries or rebellion, only the rhythmic clash of metal on rock and the heavy, obedient silence between each strike.

No human could survive that close to raw ley energy. It burned. It consumed. It erased.

But these weren't humans anymore.

The truth wrapped its claws around her heart and squeezed. This was why. This was how. All this time, she'd carried the weight of being the last mage, thinking she'd caused it, thinking their deaths were the price of her surviving the Temple. But it hadn't been just her or the sorcerer. It hadn't been the Empire and their bounties. It was everywhere. The mages had been hunted, harvested, hollowed out from all sides and here she stood, a witness to their fall.

It was hard to breathe. Someone pushed them into motion from behind and she nearly stumbled into the man ahead of her. They weren't captives, but slaves. This wasn't mining. It was siphoning.

And Velkher was feeding.

CHAPTER 41

The Seed

Days bled together, though she wasn't sure they ever truly began. On Velkher, the sun rose somewhere she couldn't see. Obsidian peaks drank the light before it ever touched the ground, trapping the island in half-shadow—too dim for day, too stark for night. Even as heat pressed in, the world looked drained of color, stripped to its harshest edges.

Sweat stung her eyes, earth clung to her skin, and every breath felt hotter than the last. Her tongue stuck to the roof of her mouth. She couldn't remember the last time she'd tasted water. Her body ached for it, but thirst had become as constant as the heat—just another pain she had to ignore if she wanted to stay clear-minded enough to survive.

Lusa fell into the rhythm the others followed: carry, sort, obey… pretend. Her fingers were raw from hauling crystal-veined rock into iron bins; her throat scraped every time she breathed the dust. But it wasn't the labor wearing her down. It was the silence.

The workers barely spoke. When they did, their voices came out thin and distant, as if echoing from somewhere behind their own skulls. The humans were the worst, with their gray skin, blank eyes, and bodies moving without urgency or intention. Automata. It made her skin crawl, seeing people move like that—like life had been drained from them drop by drop until all that remained was obedience. A future she refused to share, no matter how starved or weak she grew.

The once-mages were no better. When she tried to question them, hoping for even a hint of who they'd once been, she got nothing but vacant stares. Their cores were gutted. She felt it in the air around them, a faint residue of magic like smoke clinging to dying embers. Sometimes the glow of the ley lines reflected in their eyes, alluding to consciousness, but there was no will left. Only obedience shaped by the Dark Elves' Resonance.

If she let herself think too long about it, she could almost imagine that emptiness eating into her, too—like the island was waiting for a moment of weakness, a single slip, before it devoured the rest of her.

If she didn't find a way off this cursed island soon, Velkher would whittle her down to that same mindless silence. She couldn't let that happen. She wouldn't.

Lusa kept her head down, but every so often the island seemed to whisper against her, curious. It should have weakened her. Broken her. That was the point of this place.

But it didn't.

The first time she noticed it was in the quarters at night, if you could call them that. She lay on cold stone inside one of the rock alcoves, eyes shut, and instead of the slow, aching drip of recovery she'd come to expect… her core renewed. A flood where there should've been a trickle. Every breath brought more energy. Every heartbeat, more strength.

It terrified her. Strength here couldn't be a gift. It had to be bait. A lure. And she didn't know what it wanted her to become.

Nothing on this island gave back. Nothing.

But the Capstone thrummed beneath them—this ancient, hungry thing—and she could feel it recognizing her. Drawing her deeper into its current. Feeding her instead of draining her.

The thought stayed with her as she watched the overseers pacing the ridges above. The Dark Elves where armored in black plates, their movements elegant in a way that didn't belong to their surroundings. One gesture from their fingers, and the entire pit froze. Another, and the workers moved in eerie unison. Power without effort. Authority without question. She hated it.

They didn't speak often, but when they did, their voices carried something older than language. The hairpin shielded her from their compulsions, but she mimicked the others to avoid attention. At least until she'd find a way out.

Escape wasn't a plan so much as a pull—something her mind reached for whenever the dark crept in. She refused to die here. But her cores still tore at her instead of working together, and she was surrounded by darklings who'd happily toss her into the Strait without breaking stride. She just needed a crack in the routine. A moment. One misstep. She wasn't picky.

An overseer struck a woman too weak to lift her bucket. The sound reverberated through the pit and vanished into the hum. No one looked up, let alone flinched.

The Dark Magics shifted beneath her skin, instinct tightening its grip. The hairpin dimmed Them, but the pressure remained, a quiet reminder of what They wanted her to do. Something shifted in the air. Something… wrong.

The hum of the ley lines dipped a full octave and workers froze mid-motion. Overseers straightened on the ridges, their heads tilting like animals catching a scent. A cold ripple skated over her skin. Instinct said keep her eyes down;

some deeper feeling said it wouldn't matter. The ground shivered under her boots. Ominous. Purposeful. Not a quake. A summons.

One overseer dropped to his knee. Then another. Within seconds, the whole ridge bowed as one. No command given. She followed their gaze.

A figure stood at the top of the sinkhole, half-swallowed by mist, cloak unnaturally still despite the heat rippling around them. He didn't announce himself. He didn't have to. The pit did it for him—violet veins brightening, bending toward him like loyal hounds. An obsidian crown of thorny vines crested his brow.

Draevyn, the King of Velkher.

He descended the ridge with the unhurried gait of someone for whom the world always made room. His retinue flanked him, steps falling in time with the island's pulse. He didn't glow or gesture. Reality simply shifted to accommodate him.

Without any warning, her Light punched beneath her ribs with the force of a blown star. The Dark Magics pulsed in her temples, cold and inexorable. And then—terrifyingly, impossibly—they locked into the same beat.

The island seemed to recoil. She felt the interior snap, the unmistakable blaze of a convergence she should never have been able to summon, let alone reveal. How? She wasn't even thinking of them or trying to use them. Was it him?

As if answering her question, his eyes instantly found her. Nothing in his expression changed except for a slight gleam in his eyes, the quiet satisfaction of a prediction fulfilled. With that one look, the ley network responded.

Power cracked through the pit. Pain speared her chest. Her knees buckled. Her cores slammed into a rhythm that belonged to neither of them.

Lusa snapped a glare his direction. He knew. But she didn't have time to process what that actually meant as a second, heavier force smashed into her, driving the air from her lungs. She flew back, skull striking stone, vision bursting white. Instinct took the reins and Light flared from her palms in a sweeping arc.

Dust exploded. Rock splintered. The slaves nearest her crumpled under her shockwave. A brief flicker of horror rose as their bodies hit the ground beside her. But the Dark Magics quickly smothered it.

Survive first. Regret later.

The elves reacted instantly. They moved toward her in perfect sync, hands carving sharp patterns. Resonance snapped around her in a trap of violet bands, locking her arms to her sides before she could react.

The Dark Magics writhed under her skin, murderous intent not entirely her own dominating her thoughts. Light swam through her, too much, her heart racing with amplified everything as it tried to find a way out. All the while, her amulet burned over her chest, fighting to contain the surge of two powers pouring into it.

Finding a way to control them had to be the answer. In their brief convergence earlier, she'd felt it. They were stronger together. She dragged in a breath, teeth clenched, and reached inward to force the currents together on her terms. If it burned her from the inside out, so be it. Better that than letting these darklings choose how she died.

Heat flared in her chest as the powers strained against her pull. Pressure mounted. Vision smeared. Her ears rang, and her body felt one breath away from boiling. She sharply twisted her wrists inward, dragging the currents into collision, and something inside her finally gave.

Light and Dark locked into the same rhythm.

Primordial. Cataclysmic. Brilliant.

Power filled her to the brim, impossible, limitless, an electric rush reaching every nerve. A smile slipped out before she could stop it. Feral exhilaration. It was intoxicating. The Dark Magics leaned into it, urging her to use everything while she still could.

With a single thought, the amulet answered her. The Resonance bands snapped away in glimmering flecks. Twin torrents burst from the Source—gold and black twisting together as they burst free. Hot and cold. Radiance and void. A single fused strike that ripped through the air with a sound like metal shearing under too much force.

An elf flew back, smashed into the ridge. Another's Resonance slipped out of pitch, and he fell. Two more were throttled out of sight, their screams swallowed by the Straight somewhere behind her.

Free of the binds, Lusa dropped to her knees. Her chest heaved. Her eyes burned. The cores inside her fell back into dissonance.

Protect. Destroy.

Hold. Break.

Gold and black bled into the edges of her vision—the spill of these two powers desperate for escape out of her in whatever way possible. She couldn't hold them. She couldn't contain it all. She needed distance. A breath. Anything.

The king stepped closer instead.

His eyes caught the two colors flickering in hers. Recognition. Dark and certain. Wind swept his long dark hair behind him; the upper half bound in a gray-streaked knot that marked him like an ancient king of shadow.

"Ah." His voice dropped, almost reverent. "The seed has been delivered right to me."

Her hands clenched, knuckles white. She didn't know what that meant, but she'd rather die fighting than kneel. She forced herself upright, every nerve screaming, and leveled her best glare while scrambling to pull her Magics back under her grip.

Draevyn smirked, tilted his head, and stepped aside, offering her up to his soldiers like an experiment. So that was it. He wanted to watch her struggle. To see what power she'd reveal.

Five elves closed in fast, moving like a single mind. One cut low. Another high. A third already shifting into the next strike. Light responded quicker and she hurled it out. The bolt shot between two elves and hit the female square in the chest. She dropped, dead or out cold. Lusa didn't care.

The others didn't slow. Their gestures blurred—quick, brutal, practiced. Resonance thickened the air until it felt like wading through tar. Gravity twisted. Sound warped. A concussive blast struck her right side.

She twisted, but not fast enough. The impact slammed her into the shattered scaffold. Pain flared across her ribs, head still throbbing from the earlier impact.

Move.

Get up.

Don't be an easy kill.

She rolled just as another strike carved a trench where her skull had been. She flung up her arm, the Dark Magics ripping free in a vicious smear of black smog. It collided with an elf's Resonance mid-air, detonating in a flash that rattled her teeth.

Light reached to shield.

Dark lunged to rend.

They weren't listening to her. She could feel herself tearing again.

The elves pressed in, sensing her struggle. The pit hummed as their Resonance built toward another coordinated blow.

Lusa forced herself to stay standing. Her magic spit sparks up her arms—unfocused, dangerous. Control wasn't working. So, she stopped trying.

A scream tore out of her as she thrust both hands forward. The power wasn't a spell anymore, but instinct, agony, and something feral fighting to be free. Gold and black erupted together in a braided, violent, unstoppable current. Blood trickled from her nose as the blast ripped across the ridge.

Elves flew.

Armor cracked.

The stone beneath them buckled and split, the Weave shuddering like something had struck its spine. A ringing haze filled the pit, humming through her teeth and bones and skull. Lusa dropped to her knees, breath tearing in and out. Her vision doubled, the world smearing at the edges. She lifted her chin anyway. She wiped the blood from her nose with the back of her hand and fixed her eyes on the figure before her.

Draevyn hadn't moved.

Not when she screamed.

Not when the blast tore the ridge apart.

He simply stood there, the violet sheen crawling along the ground toward him as if the island sought to kiss his boots. With a simple raise of his hand, the ground answered.

A force slammed into her midsection—gravity fused with pressure, driven by a will colder than magic. Her body jerked upward, breath crushed out of her chest. A twist in the air, and the current flung her back down. Her scream died on impact.

Dark sputtered.

Light winked out.

Her cheek smacked against the dirt. Grit and blood filled her mouth. Every part of her burned, magic slipping through her fingers, siphoning into the Capstone on his command.

Tethers of violet bands leapt from the hands of the elven soldiers—Resonance twisting around her again… wrists, throat, pulling her limbs in against themselves. She tried to push power into her veins, to spark something, anything, but her cores only fluttered, dim and unresponsive.

Draevyn's shadow fell across her face as he moved closer. His gaze assessed her with a kind of cool appraisal, lacking cruelty, full of certainty.

"I expected fire," he said. Soft. Almost admiring. "You do not disappoint."

She tried to lift her head.

Tried to glare.

Tried to make her body respond.

It wouldn't.

He knelt beside her, the way someone examines a weapon they've just claimed. His hand hovered just above her brow, close enough for her skin to prickle with the faint echo of his power.

"Sleep, little fracture."

His violet Resonance dissolved between her eyes—soft, suffocating, final. Malvian's bloodline had a gift for forcing sleep, apparently. And she hated that he was the last thing in her mind before the dark wrapped its fingers around her.

CHAPTER 42

The Wrath Divine

The world returned in fragments of sound. A deep hum first, reverberating through her bones. Then heat, followed by the taste of metal on her tongue. Lusa opened her eyes to violet light encompassing her.

Panic hit her in one hard wave, her heart dropping before she could rein it in. She forced a slow inhale—another—until the spiral eased. Deep breaths. Think.

On the ground far beneath her, the crystals encircling the Capstone rose from the black rock like spears. Its facets pulsed with veins of light that climbed toward her, as if reaching to feed.

Sawtooth peaks climbed toward a smoky gray sky ahead of her. Behind her, she could feel the land falling away toward the cliffs, where the Strait of Thalara churned far below—a river of mist and silver foam cleaving the continent in two. Wind funneled through the passage, tugging at the bindings and setting her body swaying.

The Capstone wasn't merely a structure. It was alive. Each flash of light shivered through her chest, feeding the violet haze around her. She forced herself to take in the terrace. The Dark Elves moving in perfect sync. Their gestures tracing sigils through the air. The hum rising in lockstep with each motion.

A ritual.

The realization settled cold in her gut. Whatever the elves were doing, she wasn't just a prisoner—she was the focal point. And beneath her, at the ritual's center, was Draevyn.

He waited unmoving at the eye of it, hands folded behind his back as if the outcome had already been written. Midnight-blue robes stirred around him as his attention fixed wholly on her. She refused to give him the satisfaction of flinching. If he expected her to fold under it, he could choke on the disappointment.

Two elves in ceremonial armor flanked his right—one silver-haired, eyes assessing her like a specimen; the other younger, watching with a hungry sort of curiosity. Royal line, she guessed. Or whatever passed for it here. And slightly behind them…

Malvian.

Silks layered beneath thin armor, bracers glowing in rhythm with the Capstone. Deep revulsion cut through every other thought. Of course he'd stand here, ready to deliver her up like an offering. After the way he'd forced his will against hers, she expected nothing less. But the sight of him among them still sent a ripple of hate down her spine. Her jaw clenched along with her fists.

That's when she noticed Aleric.

Kneeling off to the side of them, wrists locked in Resonance cuffs, a bruise darkening one side of his jaw. He wasn't the Dreadstar's captain here. He wasn't anything more than another piece on Draevyn's board.

Her throat tightened. "What are you doing?"

Draevyn smiled. The lines of his face were carved with something that might once have been compassion, hollowed now into devotion.

"Velkher is starving," he said, his tone soft enough to be mistaken for sympathy. "For centuries, we have fed it fragments. Resonance from the earth, from the fallen, from what little your kind left behind. But the Weave demands balance."

His hand rose, and the light from the Capstone spiraled up toward her. "The seed of Light and Dark has been made flesh and found its way to me."

"I'm not your offering," she hissed.

His expression shifted into awful certainty. "You misunderstand."

A flick of his fingers. The air twisted. The tatters of her tunic disintegrated into glittering dust, whisked away by the wind. In their place, threads of light and shadow spiraled up her limbs, weaving around her like ribbons spun straight from the ley. Layer after layer formed a gown of deep violet silk and smoke, ethereal yet weighted, its trailing ribbons floating as though caught between gravity and dream. The fabric glowed faintly where it touched her skin, alive with the Capstone's pulse.

Rage consumed every thought. She wasn't his puppet. She wasn't anyone's. And for one reckless heartbeat, she almost wanted to let the Dark Magics take her. If only to see these bastards pay. A terrible temptation. If only she could release the hairpin.

Draevyn watched the transformation as if conducting an orchestra. "You are not the offering," he corrected, his voice deepening, almost matching the hum beneath her.

He extended a hand toward the crystal spire. Its veins flared, reaching for her wrists.

"You are the conduit."

The circle of elves tightened their cadence. Hands shifted in synchronized cuts, each motion forming another layer of restriction around her. Their powers thickened, curling up her legs, her chest, her throat. The binds snapped tighter and the first surge tore through her.

Ice-cold Resonance knifed through her body. It drew from her, siphoned through the tethers into the Capstone below. Heat flared from her amulet, followed by a flood of darkness that burned like fire. Her scream echoed against the rocks until it was indistinguishable. Draevyn closed his eyes, face tilted slightly upward.

"Do you feel it?" he murmured. "The world returning to harmony. The Weave remembering its design."

Lusa fought to breathe. "You're killing it," she rasped. "You're killing everything."

"Sacrifice is not death. It is renewal."

Her body convulsed as another torrent of energy ripped through her. Images bled across her vision—forests dying, ley lines cracking, seas turning to glass. The Aether screamed, and the sound lived inside her, twisting, clawing, tearing.

Her twin cores fought like beasts in a cage. Light pulled upward, trying to sever the tether; Dark contracted inward, ravenous, trying to swallow it whole. They collided in her chest hard enough to steal her breath. She squeezed her eyes shut, biting down on another scream.

The Capstone's pulse quickened. It fed on her. Drank her. Every heartbeat was an unraveling. Strands of her magic pulled from her veins and funneled into the current below. Her vision flickered… color, then void, then nothing but violet haze. Her limbs numbed. Her breath stuttered into short, shallow tremors.

She was breaking.

Every nerve was flayed open. Thoughts scattered like dust in the wind. She could feel herself thinning—magic, will, identity—pulled thread by thread into the spire. The elves' chanting rose around her, eerie and hypnotic, each gesture stripping another piece of her away.

A sound tore out of her, half-sob, half-rage.

She couldn't fight this.

That cold truth slid through her, and instinct tore through the pain searching for anything—anyone—to anchor to.

And it found him.

Malvian stood at the edge of the ritual circle, mist clinging to his armor, eyes locked on her through the blaze. He looked untouched, molded from the same shadow as his father—but his fingers curled at his sides, tendons straining.

She didn't realize she was reaching for him until it happened. The Light inside her flared first, desperate and blind. The Dark followed, possessive, unwilling to be left behind. Together, they stretched through the Weave, latching onto him.

It wasn't speech. It wasn't even thought.

It was need.

A wordless *help me* that broke across the space between them.

Malvian jerked as if someone had struck him. His breath hitched; his gaze unfocused for one fractured second, like something inside him had answered before he could stop it. She didn't know how she was doing it. She didn't care.

Help me!

Her twin cores resonated against his—Light against shadow, chaos against precision, cores against Seryn—striking a harmonic so sharp the air quivered. His expression tightened; his posture locked.

Through the blur of agony, she felt that cold, fast slice of calculation he lived on. He'd never defy Draevyn. Not openly. But something in his eyes shifted… a flicker of recognition, not of her, but of the anomaly she was.

The Resonance tightened. The Capstone roared. Her body convulsed, and her scream ripped free again.

Please!

Her lips didn't move, but the word tore across the Weave itself.

Malvian's eyes widened—a flash of shock, maybe something else—and then, so subtly that no one but her would notice, he moved. A single intentional break in the rhythm.

The harmony shattered.

The ley lines shrieked.

Elves staggered, their formation collapsing. The Capstone lost control and cracked upward in a torrent of blinding light that punched a hole into the sky.

Lusa's restraints snapped away. The blast threw her back, her body vaulting through the explosion of power around her. Tears streamed. Cliffs cracked. For one suspended heartbeat she hung above the Capstone—blood, magic, sky all burning the same violet-white.

Then gravity took her and she surrendered to the illusion of freedom.

Silk and ribbon whipped around her as she plummeted. Her twin cores locked like a bone forced into place. Pain detonated through her, but she bit through it as Light and Dark finally worked together again, slowing her fall.

Her magic landed first. A fault cracked across the terrace. Grit plumed upward. Power surged through her spine as she slammed down next, the shockwave tossing elves like ragdolls and sending scaffolds groaning on their supports.

Across the Strait, fog ripped like cloth. On Aeonia's cliffs, banners glinted. An army gathered at the rim. She didn't have time to see who—they vanished from her thoughts the instant she looked back at the king.

Draevyn lifted his hand, bending a single glowing finger. "Out."

Gates yawned open across the basin. Humans and mages spilled out—slack-eyed, ash-gray, too many. Strangers and faces she knew only by the echo of shared misery.

The king sliced three sigils through the air.

Their bodies jerked as one. Puppets.

Lusa's cores bucked hard. She snapped up a palm and a thin shield of radiance flashed into existence—too late to brace, just in time to survive. Draevyn moved in answer, one smooth gesture slicing the air. Shadow braided the rim of her shield, tightening like a noose before it shattered. The impact rattled her teeth and sent her skidding backward, feet barely scraping the terrace.

He didn't fight. He conducted. Every sweep of his hands wove threads of violet light that lingered like smoke before hardening into burning sigils suspended between them.

Lusa acted faster than thought. She swept her arm in a fierce arc and Light answered, leaping from her fingertips in a clean, bright stroke. It carved across the terrace, clashing with Draevyn's sigils in a burst of molten brilliance. The shockwave thrust her further back, ribs jarring under the strain.

"Left!" a voice bellowed, raw with panic. "Izzy—your left!"

She pivoted. A Resonant Blade screamed past her cheek. She countered with instinct alone—Light flaring, Dark snapping behind it—and dropped the soldier in a heap.

Izzy.

Her mother.

A name no one used—except one person her mother had whispered about. Lusa's gaze snapped to the ritual circle.

Aleric. Still bound to his knees. Still bruised. Staring at her with wide, horrified eyes—not seeing her, but the woman he'd lost. The fury on his face split into something raw.

Her stomach dropped.

In his moment of panic, he hadn't yelled Lusa.

He'd shouted Izzy.

And the pieces slammed together so hard she nearly lost balance—wrinkled blue eyes and worn hands holding a silver compass… the memory of being thrown laughing into the air, a memory she'd half convinced herself she invented.

Aleric was her father.

The truth hit like a punch to the gut.

Fury quickly replaced her shock.

He'd known.

Or maybe he hadn't. But he'd left her and her mother alone in a world that wanted them dead.

No time to unravel what that meant.

No breath to waste on him.

She tore her gaze away, jaw locking hard enough to crack, and flung herself back into the fight. Light snapped up to shield, Dark knifed vicious slices through the air—all of it amplified with a truth she wasn't ready to face.

But the distraction had cost her.

Dozens of puppets jerked toward her in perfect, horrifying unison. Lusa's heart raced. She couldn't hurt them.

She *wouldn't.*

Dark roared for blood, eager for an excuse. Light braced, desperate to protect. Neither offered a path she could live with. And she had seconds—maybe less.

She thrust both hands out, forcing her magic into a shape she'd only managed once before in the canyons.

A wave of Light burst outward, blinding, white-hot brilliance that washed the world clean. The puppets froze mid-step, hands grasping at the air as the glare scalded their vision. It bought her inches. Only inches.

She dragged the Dark Magics up through her spine. They writhed—furious, hungry, impatient to kill. She shaped Them anyway, bending Them into a rolling shockwave that rippled across the terrace. Not deadly. Not even truly damaging. But enough.

The ground buckled beneath the oncoming horde. Bodies toppled in a cascade of stumbling limbs—human and mage alike hitting stone with dull, harmless thuds instead of screams. It wouldn't hold long. But it gave her a second to think, breathe, collect herself.

Lusa staggered back, sweat stinging her eyes, lungs fighting for breath. The Magics clamored inside her but for the first time since the ritual began, she'd done something that belonged solely to her.

She planted her feet. Lifted her chin.

"Leave them out of this," she snarled.

Draevyn answered with a flick of his wrists. Ley stirred violently beneath her, the ground convulsing as it tried to drink her empty.

An elf vaulted the pit, hands carving sigils so fast they blurred. His strike folded the air between them. Compression hit a beat later—she twisted, let it slide past, then snapped a lash of shadow at his ankle. He spun midair, crashed, rolled, rose again.

Relentless.

Flames spilled from her fingers, disrupting his harmony. She reached down—past Light, past Dark—into the narrow seam where both cores touched. She set her will there and pushed.

The elf flung a Resonant strike. She twisted, redirected it—

—and too late saw where it was headed.

It slammed into Aleric's chest.

The force hurled him against the terrace wall. His body sagged, the magical restraints flickering weakly at his wrists.

"No—" The word escaped, lost under the roar. She lurched toward him, fighting through air that pushed against her every move.

Her father's head lifted—dazed, unfocused.

And then she saw it. *Her,* in the slope of his nose. The shape of his jaw. The blue of his eyes. Recognition stabbed through her… but it didn't matter. Aleric's body slumped to the ground.

Something inside her tore wide open. The world pinholed to light and loss. The scream clawing up her chest broke free—not from her throat, but from her cores.

It detonated.

A burst of radiance erupted outward, raw and unshaped. The wave slammed across the terrace, shredding Draevyn's sigils and snapping his hold on the nearest thralls. Chains of Resonance disintegrated. Puppets collapsed again, gasping as awareness flickered back into their eyes.

Lusa staggered, breath hitching, hands shaking. The radiance dimmed, but the hollow left behind felt cavernous—grief sharpened to an edge.

Around her, freed slaves blinked, dazed, clutching their heads as if waking from a nightmare. That flicker of clarity was all she needed to see. If she could cut one thread, she could cut them all.

She just had to hold.

A flicker of motion—Malvian.

He hadn't moved to help. He didn't try to stop her. But something in him seemed to have shifted. His gaze snapped from Aleric's fallen form to Lusa, and for one split second, his expression cracked—shock, recognition, and a flicker of something that looked too close to concern.

It vanished quickly, swallowed by cold discipline.

Draevyn noticed. Displeasure flashed across the king's features like a ripple. He drifted a finger and a ring of soldiers obeyed, pivoting as one and charged her.

Lusa met Draevyn's gaze across the chaos—a silent promise sparking between them. He could command the island, but not her.

She slammed both palms to the stone.

A burst of both magics ripped outward, gold-white edged in bluish black. It lifted the charging elves and hurled them backward, shattering Draevyn's formation and stealing his hold.

Far across the Strait, battle horns blared.

She didn't look.

Couldn't.

Elven bodies slammed into the rock, armor splintering. They'd rise again. Their resilience was a kind of madness. Exhausting. Annoying.

Draevyn's eyes cooled, a matching exhaustion settling in his stare. For a beat, they simply regarded each other. Two forces worn thin, refusing to yield.

His hand twisted.

The ground split open beneath her.

The drop tore the breath from her chest. Instinct snapped to life. *No.* She would not let this cursed island swallow her. Magic surged tight around her ribs, forming armor of pure will. Her fall slowed, caught, held—twin cores flaring behind her heart like two rising suns.

Using her power as current against gravity, she lifted herself out of the chasm, inch by inch, defiance built on nothing but stubborn breath and burning magic. When she rose to meet Draevyn's gaze, the island seemed to pause.

"Very well," the King murmured, a cruel smirk appearing.

He flung both hands wide.

Violet flames erupted from the Capstone, a pillar of power that screamed up toward her. Lusa braced, crossed her arms, and met it head-on. Light and Dark fused into a golden-black barrier, the force slamming against his in a blast that shook the terrace.

The air buckled between them. A grinding struggle—her shield devouring his flame, inch by relentless inch.

For the first time, she felt it: the advantage.

It didn't last.

Two shadows stepped forward.

Draevyn's sons.

Malvian stood slightly back, watching with that unreadable stillness that always made her uncertain. But his brothers lifted their hands in unison, sigils igniting across their skin. Their Resonance shot outward in braided strands, latching onto their father's power and feeding it.

The ground vibrated.

Draevyn's flame surged.

The advantage slipped from her grasp like sand. The combined force pushed against her shield. Her amulet flared, but it was too much. A thin fissure cracked down its center. Dread crawled up her spine and her shield ruptured like glass.

Light imploded. Pressure snapped. The world went white, and the amulet cracked. The blast hurled her backward—and down. She hit the terrace hard and skidded straight onto a jagged crystal spike, one of the Capstone's protruding veins. It punched through her side before she could even scream.

A sound tore out of her anyway—half gasp, half ragged cry—cut short by shock. Heat flooded her torso. Blood slicked the silk clinging to the stone. Her breath hitched, caught between agony and disbelief.

The horizon swam, blurred. The Capstone's hum drilled into her skull, feeding, devouring. Her twin cores convulsed. The two forces continued to rip at each other with no rhythm, no mercy. Each brutal clash struck like a hammer inside her ribs. And she was pinned to the center of it.

Wind tore at her hair, dragging strands across her face. She closed her eyes, and for the first time, stopped fighting and let everything she'd been holding together press in. The pain. The noise. The endless tug-of-war between what she was and what she'd become.

Maybe this was how it ended: bled out on foreign stone, another broken mage feeding the world's balance.

Fate's inevitability.

Ley lines always crawled back to their Capstones. The Aether always reclaimed what it needed to stay whole. Why would she be different? Every breath, every strike, every spark of magic she'd ever given had been another offering to something too vast to make a difference.

Her pulse slowed, blood warming the crystal skewering her side. Her twin cores thrashed weakly against each other, refusing to align—and she didn't try to force them. Balance had never been peace. It was the price of staying alive in a world that demanded pieces of her just to keep turning.

So why was she still trying?

Why crawl toward survival when survival only gave her another fight, another wound, another breath she had to buy with pain? Every victory had led her here—bleeding, breaking, watching the world take and take and take.

She was bone-deep tired. Tired of being the balance's consequence. Of bending to a pattern that only tightened the more she struggled against it.

Maybe letting go wasn't failure.

Maybe it was the first mercy she'd ever been offered.

Maybe surrender was just… release.

When she opened her eyes, Draevyn was no longer looking at her. His gaze had shifted past her, across the strait. The expression pulled across his face wasn't triumph but recognition.

Lusa forced her head to turn.

Through heat-haze and pain, she saw the cliffs of Aeonia ignite with light. From their edge, a structure unfurled—a bridge of pure Resonance sweeping out over the mist. Each span crystallized into place from the harmonies of the Light Elves, a translucent arc stretching toward Velkher.

Her fingers scraped the dirt, curling into fists.

Kaden.

The name barely surfaced before the king flicked his fingers and sent another wave of power knifing into the crystal—and through her.

She bit back a cry and pushed against the stone, arms shaking. The crystal lodged in her side shifted with her movement. White-hot pain smothered her, stealing vision, stealing breath. She coughed, blood wetting her lips.

Draevyn's shadow slid over her.

"You burn beautifully," he said. The glow from the Capstone painted him unreal, his features lined in gentle cruelty. "But I've grown impatient."

He lifted his hand. The gesture was slow, almost reverent—a conductor calling the next note in a dirge. Pressure invaded her skull. A violation without force. A hand closing around her thoughts and squeezing until they dissolved.

Her magic lunged to rise, but the ward inside Kaden's hairpin only sparked once before going dark. Snuffed out against a power too vast, too ancient. Something colder seeped into the cracks exhaustion had left behind.

Draevyn didn't crush her mind.

He entered it.

Cold spread behind her eyes, down her spine, until pain blurred into something distant… happening to a body that didn't belong to her.

Stop.

The plea went under with her.

His will folded over hers—smooth, absolute, effortless. Nothing like Malvian's curious invasion. The king's touch was practiced. Clinical. Certain.

He found her Dark core first.

A gasp tore from her throat as he brushed it, felt Their hunger. The Magics shuddered in response. They surged toward him like starving beasts recognizing the hand that would release Them.

Her back arched as they thrashed outward and the world flashed black. The Magics didn't whisper this time. They howled.

Exultant. Starved. Free.

They wanted out.

They wanted everything.

Her Light core flared instinctively, trying to contain Them, but Draevyn's Resonance wrapped around both cores like a leash, wrenching them to face each other.

He wasn't asking for balance. He was commanding it.

Pressure built behind her temples until she thought her skull would split. Through her cries, his voice slid into her mind—warm, venomous.

"I know what you crave."

The words vibrated through her bones. The ley lines answered him, the Capstone's veins blazing brighter and faster. Behind him, the slaves began to stir again, sigils glowing on their foreheads.

"Please," she gasped.

Draevyn tilted his head, pity softening his inhuman gaze.

"Why beg me?" he asked gently. "You have only to want it."

The Capstone roared and the ground trembled, as if the island itself braced for her surrender. He reached for her and the Dark inside ripped toward him—eager, wild, ravenous.

"Drink," he whispered to Them. "Take what the vessel denied you. Feed the wound."

Her Light core strained to hold the line, a lone beam against a flood. Her muscles seized. It twisted inward, then outward in a spiral of agony.

She screamed as the power rushed her. The silver hairpin flared, overwhelmed in one brief starburst, and shattered. Fragments of metal and warding sigils spun away on the wind.

Somewhere above the haze, the sun broke through. Warmth brushed her face—soft, almost kind. Kaden would've told her to hold on, to see it as a sign. But what if he saw her now? What if he knew what she was about to become? Would he still reach for her if she crossed that line? If she turned into what she'd always feared?

Her body quivered. Breath thinned. Every heartbeat was a battle she no longer had the strength, or want, to win. She stood at the edge of herself, suspended between who she'd been and what she was turning into.

Lusa closed her eyes. Tears slid warm down her skin.

Without the pin's barrier, the breach in her mind yawned open. Draevyn's power flooded in unchecked, drowning every corner of her will. The Dark Magics savored the taste of unleashed dominion, allowing it.

Her scream cracked into a ragged sob.

The world thinned to light… to shadow… to nothing. Before the Dark Magics fully seized her under the king's command, she thought of Kaden.

His voice.

Her promise.

The one she could no longer keep.

She hoped he wouldn't see her like this—wouldn't remember her as the thing she was becoming. Only the woman she'd been.

Then the void took her.

And that woman was gone.

CHAPTER 43

Rift and Ruin

The world was burning across the Strait of Thalara.

Snow still webbed the firs behind Kaden, brittle on the boughs. Aeonia's breath hung pale in the air. Ahead, the storm was a boiling wall of wind and ozone, carrying the scent of scorched sap. Frost steamed off cloaks.

From the cliffs of Aeonia, it looked like the island itself was crawling with every kind of magic Aetherealm had known. Violet veins rippling through obsidian, towers collapsing beneath waves of gold and smog. And at the center—suspended above the Capstone, framed by ruin and storm—was Lusa.

She wasn't a dark mage anymore.

Light and shadow burst from her in alternating waves—faster, brighter, blacker. Kaden had never seen magic move like that: wild, unbound, alive enough to shake the bones of the world. Light. Dark. It wasn't harmony. It was overload. The Aeon had found a way through her and was pouring itself out all at once. The Weave quivered.

"Sweet Eldere…" Dak breathed, wind shredding his words.

They were too late.

Behind them, Commander Thalor shouted orders. Elves took their marks, jade-colored sigils stacking in tempered chords. A span of emerald light knit itself across the Strait. Resonance glass.

The bridge grew beneath their feet, each harmonic hand gesture sending out Resonance that caught and held against the gale, its brilliance mirrored in the churn of silver mist below.

Kaden couldn't look away from Lusa.

He knew fear—ambushes, evil sorcerers, the night she'd nearly died in his arms—but this was different. This was watching someone he'd sworn to protect tear herself apart while an ancient thing watched through her eyes.

"She's fighting them," Noreena said tightly. "Look. She's striking the elves."

Shards of white and sheets of black scythed through formations, knocking soldiers—and what looked like humans—into the dust. The island surged when she did, feeding on her.

"She's not—" Kaden's voice came out raw. "She's not in control."

Thalor stood at the lip of the span, silver hair whipping in the wind, both hands anchoring the harmonic line.

"Then pray she doesn't turn that power on us before we reach her."

On his command, they ran. The bridge sang underfoot, heat rippling through the light-forged panes. Below, the sea frothed where raw magic bled into it. Every step dragged them closer to the roar, but it wasn't fast enough.

He could feel her. Her pain, her rage. A brilliance that couldn't last. He'd seen her near breaking, but never with the sky itself bending around her. Lightning spidered the clouds.

The island bucked as another beam tore out of the Capstone, scattering elven ranks. The Aeon recoiled, a wounded thing. It ripped broken lines through the haze above the basin. A rift, tearing the seams of the world open.

"Bridge integrity dropping!" Thalor shouted.

Kaden barely heard him.

Lusa dropped, landing on a crystal spur. His hand lifted on instinct, useless across the distance. "Lusa!"

The wind stole his cry. He thought she lifted her head—saw them. *Just hang on a little longer, love.*

Clouds broke apart the same time violet fire rose and swallowed the view. The bridge shuddered beneath him. Heat blasted his face, searing his lungs. The world ahead was collapsing, but he kept running. All he could see was her.

He'd thought he understood power before, but this was something else. This was creation clawing its way out of her body.

And she was dying for it.

Lusa was suspended again, floating, light pouring from her like the world's veins had burst open. The sun broke through the clouds, shining down over the rift. On her.

He pushed harder, the bridge splintering beneath his boots, fine cracks webbing across the light-forged span. Every stride sent another vibration radiating outward— as if even the magic that built it couldn't bear what he carried inside him. His own Resonance, rising unbidden.

It answered her.

He hadn't felt that ancient hum under his skin in years, the part of him that wasn't human. Now it woke, fierce and desperate, responding to her like two halves of the same song. The princesses golden charm slapped against his chest.

Dak shouted somewhere behind as the bridge quaked. Glon's voice joined—orders, prayers, he couldn't tell. The cliffs ahead erupted, rock plunging into the throng. Frail figures scattered, humans screaming as black tendrils of her Magics struck them down.

She was being devoured by her own power. Those demons inside her were striking others. Killing in her name. Kaden knew this was the one thing she'd never forgive herself for… becoming the very thing she feared most.

Every blast that tore through the humans, every scream that wasn't hers, was her nightmare made real. He could almost hear her voice from that day on the shores of Anora: *If They ever win, don't let me become Them.*

And now They had.

Not much further.

His lungs burned. Wind slapped his face.

Figures moved on the ridge opposite her. A king crowned in obsidian armor stood with Resonance streaming from his hands in visible waves toward Lusa. Behind him stood three others. Two joined him, tall and regal. One remained in shadow, simply watching. Their threads of violet light wove together, pressing against her. Her body was forced back, now hovering over the open expanse of foam and teeth of Thalara below.

"No!" His hand brushed the hilt at his side—but what good was steel against the apocalypse?

Instinct sent a flinch through him as the rift in the sky suddenly widened. Light and Dark collided in a cataclysm of motion just below it, radiance and shadow devouring each other, birthing something raw and blinding between them. Kaden shielded his eyes through the glare to keep his eyes on her: floating still, struggling, arms thrown wide, every muscle straining against their pull.

She screamed—a sound so forceful it bordered divine. The vibration rattled through him, its pitch leaving a painful ringing in its wake. The cliff face cracked, raining rock into elves and humans alike.

"Lusa!" he shouted.

His throat tore with the words. He ran faster, body breaking past its limits as his dormant power woke. She wasn't too far. He could reach her.

"Lusa!"

Her screams cut off mid-breath. The brilliance of the glassy sphere surrounding her stilled. Magic curved over its iridescence, reflecting every color of the chasm. Slowly, she turned toward him. Had she heard him? Hope drove him faster. Almost there.

He couldn't see her face through the glare, only the faint tilt of her chin, the recognition in the way her body eased. Her hair, once black as ink, drifted in pale waves—color leeched until it was all white. Whether it was the Aeon or her demons, something had drained his Lusa of even that.

Kaden reached for her, boots pounding over rock. The light around her swelled. Pressure built, rising until it throbbed inside his head. His ears popped. Blood ran warm from them and his nose.

The rift ripped wider. Her amulet flared with two lights, one white, one black, blinding, holding, fighting. A bolt of pure violet lanced up from the Capstone. Another struck down from the rift, bluish-white lightning meeting it midair. They collided at her heart.

"No!"

Her cry was the sound of worlds breaking. Kaden skidded to the cliff's edge, reaching for her ankle—

The light detonated outward, a tidal wave of force slamming into him like a collapsing sky. He was airborne before he realized it, flung backward across the rocks. The impact knocked the breath from his lungs, left his vision white and ringing, the world spinning. When the glare finally broke, Kaden pushed himself up on spasming muscles. Everyone lay flattened to the earth—

—and Lusa was gone.

Golden and violet motes scattered on the wind, swirling upward, downward, weightless, impossible. He scrambled forward through his physical pain, on hands and knees, to the edge where he'd almost reached her.

The amulet hung suspended in the air, enveloped by the glittering motes. A golden flame moth fluttered towards it in that beat of silence before the amulet plummeted to the silver waters of Thalara.

Kaden couldn't move.

Sound rushed back all at once—the wind, the screaming, the shattering of stone—but it all felt far away. He stayed frozen, chest heaving, eyes locked on the empty air she'd, seconds ago, filled.

His hands dug into the rock, rough edges biting skin, breaking nails. He didn't feel it. Didn't feel anything except the hole widening in his chest.

"No," he rasped, voice strangled.

His hand lifted like he could catch the remnants of her, but his fingers closed on air. The motes slipped through him, warm for a second before fading.

A scream ripped out of him, more animal than human. He screamed until his throat burned, until the storm drowned him out, until there was nothing left.

She was gone. Gone in a way that defied sense. Like she'd been erased.

Something in him broke then—not the kind that healed, but the kind that split a man down the middle and left him hollow. His fingers dug into the ground, blood and dirt blurring together. He couldn't breathe. Couldn't think. The world had fallen silent with her.

Through the haze, a glint caught his eye as sunlight blinked off a shard half-buried in the sand. A fragment of silver and marcasite bent and broken. He didn't reach for it. He only stared.

The ward. The damned hairpin ward.

He'd built it to protect her mind—to keep Them out. He could still see her face when he gave it to her, the quiet way she'd said his name. He'd sworn it would hold. And now all he could think was that it hadn't been enough.

He hadn't been enough. Not when it mattered.

Kaden pressed his forehead to the earth; jaw locked against the tremor in his chest. Behind him, the bridge whined in the wind, voices continued shouting—he didn't care.

All he wanted was to hear her again, see her again, hold her in his arms.

His dormant elven power that had breached a place long unused reached for her still. It flared behind his ribs, desperate, wild—the song of a heart that refused to accept what his eyes had seen.

The ground trembled softly with it. Magic rippled through the earth, uncontrolled, answering his grief with a small force.

"Kaden!" someone shouted from somewhere.

He didn't care.

The pain came out of him like a roar, shaking apart what little still held. He slammed a fist into the ground. Once. Twice. Again. Bones cracked, skin split, and the earth answered like the world groaning in sympathy.

He lifted his head, vision blurred by tears and dust. Across the shattered cliffs, the last of her light faded into the horizon, sparks of gold twisting away into violet haze. He reached for them.

"Come back," he whispered, broken.

The wind stole even that.

He fell forward, hands trembling, and stayed there kneeling at the cliff's edge while the storm faded and the ashes of the woman he loved vanished into the air.

And it seemed, in that breath between rift and ruin, even the Weave went still.

EPILOGUE

What the Realms Say

They say a tale lives many lives, changing with every tongue that gives it breath. Sit long enough in any teahouse from Aeonia's dense forest cliffs to the desert markets of Asban, and you'll hear someone claim they know what befell Velkher. Some murmur it over cooling tea; others recite it as if hoping the walls themselves are listening.

But the beginning never alters:

The last mage went to an island and did not return.

Some insist she tore open the rift in the sky in wrath, that her power fed on the helpless until even the heavens refused to look upon her. Others argue she was born half-monster, that the shadows she carried finally rose to claim their due. And a bolder few mutter that she meant to unmake the ley lines themselves—retribution for the Temple that died in flame.

Comforting fictions, all of them.

Velkher's version spreads the fastest. Their king—somber, grieving, reverent in the right measure—speaks of how the "Last Mage" unraveled under her own strength. How she fractured the Capstone. How he and his sons barely escaped her ferocity. How the drained once-mages and hollow-eyed humans were the result of her fall, not his design. How Velkher stands shoulder to shoulder with the rest of Aetherealm in the long rebuilding.

Well-crafted sorrow from a kingdom that still carries the scent of ruin.

The truth they buried lies deep beneath that island's ash. Who will speak against a ruler who claims tragedy? The taken cannot answer. The dead drained of their cores leave no testimony. And those pulled from the mines remember only fragments—pain, sigils, the sense of being someone else's instrument.

Convenient forgetfulness for an inconvenient truth.

Even when the Light Elves reached the island—late, weary, unready—they saw only what Draevyn allowed. A shattered spire. A basin in ruin. A young woman ablaze with power no mortal body could contain. Exactly the vision that served his tale. Even Aeonia and Izier, certain of their wisdom, returned home believing the mage had gone mad.

Yet there remain a handful who speak of another possibility. That nothing on Velkher was accident. Or madness. Or pure result of a fallen mage. They share their questions in quiet halls and shuttered rooms, passing doubts between them like contraband.

They possess no evidence.

Their voices hold no sway.

Still, their mutterings persist, carried on the breath of a realm still unsettled.

Aetherealm has not healed since that day.

Ley lines falter. Fields struggle to renew. Storms rise early, heavy with omen. Aeonia and Izier maintain peace with uneasy hands. And Velkher bows low, claiming humility, claiming damage, claiming weakness—while every wise soul wonders what strength it hides behind its lowered head.

And all across the land, those attuned to magic, however faintly, feel it:

Something remains.

Something watches.

Something endures beneath the surface of things.

"Balance returned," the official accounts insist.

But those who stood on Velkher's stone that day know better. Balance never rights itself for free. Someone always pays.

And though every proclamation repeats that her body was never found because there was nothing left to claim, there are still many who do not accept it. They whisper by candlelight. They pause when the wind shifts. They claim the Last Mage walks somewhere still.

The Shore

Where the Strait of Thalara meets the open sea, the waters braid silver paths across the stones. Most days, the tide carries nothing more than kelp and driftwood.

But on this one—

A lone figure moves along the pebbled stretch, boots murmuring against the Aeonian shore. A solitary shape against the sinking sun, cloak drawn close against the seas wind. Something gleams beneath the retreating wave.

They halt.

The tide slips back, leaving a sliver of metal half-buried in sand and foam. A fractured, silver pendant of fused stone, golden light barely aglow intertwined with a dark crystal heart.

The amulet she wore on the day the rift opened.

The figure slowly kneels and lifts it from the shallows. For a time, they remain there, bent toward the surf, holding the relic between both palms.

A breath.

A whisper.

A voice scarcely rising above the tide:

"…There you are."

The amulet warms.

Not bright—only enough to show life.

Weathered fingers sweep the grit from the fractured crystal.

"Patience never suited you," they murmur, slipping the amulet into their pocket with a careful pat. They look far above the waves, as the sun lowers and the gulls wheel through gold and ash.

Even the sea cannot keep what was born of the Weave.

www.ingramcontent.com/pod-product-compliance
Lightning Source LLC
Chambersburg PA
CBHW021841010726
47493CB00005B/1498

* 9 7 9 8 9 9 3 4 5 1 3 2 9 *